A TASTE OF DARKNESS

AMY McCAW
AND
MARIA KUZNIAR
KAT DUNN
KAT ELLIS
RACHEL FATUROTI
KATHRYN FOXFIELD
DAWN KURTAGICH
AMY McCULLOCH
CYNTHIA MURPHY
MELINDA SALISBURY
LOUIE STOWELL
ROSIE TALBOT
MARY WATSON

A TASTE OF DARKNESS

■ SCHOLASTIC

Published in the UK by Scholastic, 2023
1 London Bridge, London, SE1 9BG
Scholastic Ireland, 89E Lagan Road, Dublin Industrial Estate,
Glasnevin, Dublin, D11 HP5F

Anthology © Amy McCaw and Maria Kuzniar, 2023
"The Visiting Grey" © Kat Ellis, 2023; "The Beast and the Beast"
© Rachel Faturoti, 2023; "Come Find Me" © Kathryn Foxfield, 2023; "And the
Waters Crept In" © Dawn Kurtagich, 2023; "The Wolf and the Witch" © Maria
Kuzniar, 2023; "The House With Teeth" © Amy McCaw, 2023; "Something Wicked"
© Kat Dunn, 2023; "'Til Death Do Us Part" © Cynthia Murphy, 2023; "Saint Clover"
© Melinda Salisbury, 2023; "The Party" © Louie Stowell, 2023;
"How to Disappear" © Rosie Talbot, 2023; "The Chiming Hour" ©
Tiger Tales Ltd, 2023; "The Midnight Kiss" © Mary Watson, 2023

ISBN 978 0702 32917 3

A CIP catalogue record for this book
is available from the British Library.

Printed and bound in Great Britain by
Clays Ltd, Elcograf S.p.A
Paper made from wood grown in sustainable forests
and other controlled sources.

1 3 5 7 9 10 8 6 4 2

www.scholastic.co.uk

CONTENTS

HOW TO DISAPPEAR

ROSIE TALBOT

1

Frost came to the village last night. Finch Walker-Tate's arse is going numb on the plastic folding chair. He's sitting behind his mother's pottery booth at the annual harvest festival put on by Gore Heritage Society. With the sun gone, the frost creeps back in, glistening the green and numbing Finch's fingers.

Always after the first frost.

"We need some hot chocolate to warm up." His mum, sallow-skinned and puffy-eyed, digs through the unused cashbox with clay-stained fingernails.

Finch checks his messages again, disappointed.

Behind the stalls, the generator hums: a choked rumble powering the candy floss cart, food trucks and the too-strong lights that stretch out across the table of his mother's booth. The shadows of the slender pots and arranged vases disappear into the dusk in long streaks. His own shadow lurks among them, like something inhuman stalking between trees.

The thought makes him feel sick.

Finch scans the crowd for Theo. From here, he has a good view of the little festival – couples sharing hot oily chips from small paper baskets, kids having a go on some of the naff games, dogs pissing up people's legs. Finch knows they have nothing to celebrate. Jessup's farm on the south side of Gore just had the worst harvest in a decade. Finch overheard the landlord at the Chalk and Cheese pub talking to old Mrs Heal about her marrows, ruined by blight, and how five of Farmer Benson's ewes sickened and died overnight.

Always when the crops fail.

Where is he?

Three hours ago, Theo West helped his uncle move hay bales to make more seating around the crappy stage that's really just wooden pallets and a mouldering carpet. Two hours and five minutes ago, he was over by the strong man game, handing a scrawny kid the mallet. Then, he was near the candy floss cart chatting to Rory Griggs and Jane Heal, who used to be called "Plain Jane" until she dyed her hair green, pierced her nose and started learning corsetry. When Theo saw Finch watching, he'd shot him a wink.

2

As long as he's here, he's safe. But it's been twenty-six minutes since then and Finch is on edge.

"Here, love." His mum presses a tenner into his hand. "Get what you like. I fancy a white choc with oat milk, oh, and see if they have those little waffle things."

He hesitates. They can't really afford a treat. The stall costs enough as it is. Finch tried to dissuade his mum from booking it. As much as she needs to pretend otherwise, he knows no one from the village will buy anything that comes from the hands of Clarice Walker-Tate, not after her husband took those teenagers into the woods and one of them never came back.

All they found was a glove. There's no concrete evidence linking anything to Finch's dad, no murder weapon, not even a body, but the village condemned him anyway. Maybe he could have stayed in Gore, but he didn't. Finch wishes he and Mum could move away too, but on an artist's income there's nowhere for them to go. Although the roof leaks, the electrics are shot and it's bloody cold, even in summer, their cottage is a home that's paid for.

So, the locals won't buy any pottery. But maybe someone who's driven over from the surrounding villages is looking for a very early Christmas gift. A woman in a navy gilet comes down the row. His mum sits up straighter, slipping on a smile. The oversized bag on the woman's shoulder sweeps the corner of the stall, catching a slender vase and toppling it over the edge.

Cursing, Finch ducks around the side to scoop the piece

off the grass. There's been plenty of footfall along this side of the green, softening the turf to mud. The ceramic isn't broken, just dirty. He wipes it clean with a bunched-up sleeve and sets it right.

"It's fine."

Mum nods, tight-lipped, as she wraps her old fleece around herself. The woman in the gilet didn't even look back.

Finch crushes the money into his pocket. "White chocolate?"

"Please, love."

Standing behind a bickering family, he joins the café queue and checks his phone again. Theo still hasn't texted him back. Above the roofs, the moon is a sliver amongst a scattering of stars, muted yellow by the lights of the festival.

Always on a waning night.

Three for three.

Shit. It's happening now.

Abandoning the queue, Finch curses himself for not putting it together sooner. He doesn't know why he's so sure they want Theo, only that like his brother before him, Theo is beautiful, popular and talented – exactly what they hunger for. All the village kids are dissuaded from going into Liksplit, but *they're* tricksters. In his dad's stories, there's always a lure – something irresistible that calls to each victim.

The village green isn't big. In four minutes, Finch has circled it twice. Theo isn't here, but with her bright hair

4

and brighter laugh, Jane is easy enough to find. Her lips are flossed, pink sugar sticking to gloss.

"Hey." Finch tries to sound casual. The one time she spontaneously spoke to him was to tell him he was beautiful in the way ravens are – sharp cheekbones, plum lips and dark messy hair. Since then, she's pretended he doesn't exist. "Have you ... seen Theo?"

Licking sugar from her thumb, she tilts her head quizzically. "Why?"

"Jane ... please."

"I don't know where he is right now, probably with his secret boyfriend or something." Digging in her shoulder bag, she pulls out a compact hand sanitizer. "Look, I'm meeting him and Rory up at Liksplit in fifteen. I can pass on whatever message you want."

An ice-cold wave crashes through Finch. "The woods? Theo can't go into the woods tonight."

"You're kidding, right?" She leans in. "You of all people must know what today is. He wants answers; we're going to get some."

Turning his back on Jane, Finch walks away from the festival, his mother and their booth. Gore is just three roads meeting at the pub, a tiled, timber-framed building with a small car park. Everyone squeezes their Land Rovers along the verge, making the already narrow street almost impassable for traffic. Because of the festival, the cars go all the way up to the last house. After that, the village drops off to fields and scrubby orchards.

Using his phone as a torch, Finch turns off the main road and on to the gently sloping track towards home. The breeze stirs, billowing the stink of rotten apples into his path. He slows, casting the torch over the nearby orchard. Its trees are wizened and twisted, centuries old and hung with rot. A whisper stirs through the branches – tongues tasting the sweat on the back of his neck and bone clawing against his scalp.

Switching off his light, Finch runs through the dark.

Up ahead, a beacon spills over pocked earth and tangled grasses. Two boys, exactly where Finch thought he'd find them. One of them bends down, head swaying, and the beam of light – from his head torch – becomes a glowing ray into his open backpack. An Ordnance Survey map is spread on the gravel track beside a worn cricket bat.

Rory is a farmer's youngest son but is training to be a mechanic. He thinks he's funny when he's actually just cruel. He and Theo have been inseparable since the cradle. Seeing Finch's light, he whacks the second boy on the leg. "There he is."

"Got my text then?" Theo smells of wintergreen and something sour. He's made of parts that don't make sense to Finch. A soft mouth that always looks on the edge of speaking. A too-delicate nose that turns up at the end. His brother's eyes – green flecked grey – and a strong jaw darkened by stubble, which makes him look much older than his seventeen years.

Finch remembers what Eli's eyes looked like when the life bled right out of them and can't help a shudder.

"N–no?" He checks his phone. Only two bars of signal and no data.

"No matter, you're here anyway. Will you be our guide?"

The question swells between them. Theo's lips press and flutter, knowing an explanation isn't needed. Finch feels himself running out of silence.

Gesturing to the dark line of trees up the slope, he says, "We're not going in there. Just come back to the festival."

"Oh nah, nah, mate." Rory starts to laugh. He heaves the cricket bat over his shoulder. "Tonight we're going monster hunting."

2

There are old stories told about Liksplit, local tales whispered by grandparents with gnarled hands, paper-thin skin and long memories: a wife went to pick Liksplit blackberries and gave birth to a fae babe, dogs chase hares into the trees and come back with rotting wounds, later attacking their owners and having to be shot. And then there are the boys.

Every eight years, Gore loses a son.

Some, like Eli West, were seen going into Liksplit. They were with friends or maybe a trusted adult. Then they vanished. Others are thought to have taken the bus to Brighton or London, changed skins and started a new life. They never call home again.

No one really knows what happens.

Except Finch.

He's seen what waits in the woods. Hidden behind a tree, he watched, shaking and afraid, as Eli died. For a reckless second, he wonders if he could tell Theo the truth; he might forgive him and they can … what? Live happily ever after? No, boys like him don't get endings like that, but he'll protect Theo from the same fate.

No one wants to believe the warnings. The villagers have convinced themselves it's nonsense and folklore, that it can't *possibly* be true. And so their boys keep vanishing.

"You know the woods better than anyone," says Theo, his voice like honey. "Please, Finch. I want to see where they found Eli's glove. Take us there. We can look around for something the police might have missed."

It's freezing out, but Finch is sweating under his hoodie and jacket. "Let's go tomorrow morning. We're more likely to find something in daylight."

"You know that's not true." Theo steps closer. Finch glances at Rory, wary and worried, but Theo doesn't seem to care if his best friend suspects. "If they're going to show themselves, it'll be tonight. We could take photos, film them, whatever it takes to prove it's got nothing to do with your dad." He raises his brow, the hopeful lilt in

8

words saying something more: *Then we can go public and we won't have to hide.*

The one time Finch tried to bring up Liksplit and what happened there, Theo changed the subject — *I don't want that between us.* Because of Eli. Because of Finch's dad. Of course, Theo doesn't believe the accusations. Why would he have anything to do with Finch if he did? But this is the first time he's hinted that he might believe in *them.*

Rory doesn't believe. He probably thinks this is Theo's way of coping with his brother's disappearance. Stomping around the woods all night is better than sitting at home doing nothing.

Theo is hurting so badly he doesn't realize how much more he's got to lose.

But I can't refuse him anything.

Finch pretends to study the map. The clearing where Eli's blood-smeared glove was found is too far in, at the heart of the old wood. In the dark, he might be able to lead them to a second, similar clearing closer to the edge. There, escape, if they need a quick one, would mean crashing through a shallow bank of stingers and briars to the back garden of Finch's cottage, rather than crossing the entire wood.

Follow Dad's rules: Keep moving. Don't stray from the path. Don't follow any strange lights or sounds. Don't speak to anyone you meet. Don't eat anything they give you.

In and out within the hour. Hopefully they'll see nothing, but if they do, at least it will exonerate his dad. Maybe, after this, he'll come home.

"Fine, I'll take you. Do you have any iron?"

Theo looks wary. "Like?"

"Nails, a hammer, those old horseshoes, even some cutlery?"

The boys shake their heads.

"We're not going without it. Follow me."

Finch lives further up the track. Just before his dad abandoned them for good, he installed iron bars on all the windows, including on the pottery studio. It's really just a converted woodshed around the back of the cottage and smells of dank earth and cold water. The overhead light sparks and fails, so Finch has to search in the dark for what he needs, careful not to upset the rows of finished ceramics waiting for their glazes.

The torch is stashed behind the potter's wheel. It goes in the pocket of the spare fleece hung on the back of the door for particularly cold days. The most important item is buried under the workbench, just centimetres down and wrapped in a plastic bag. It only takes a couple of minutes to unearth it, shaking off the dirt. Even after all this time, it's free of rust. The metal gleams as if new and the polished handle is smooth in his palm.

One day, they'll come for one of your friends, maybe even for you. On that day, you come back and dig this up. If they touch iron, it burns. One strike and they'll go down.

Handle as long as his forearm, the hammer isn't too heavy. The iron head has a blunt flat on one side and a chiselled wedge on the other.

10

"Hey, did you—" Theo rounds the door, his phone light settling on Finch. When he sees the hammer, his smile falters. "What's that?"

"Iron and ash." Finch stuffs it head first into the free pocket of his fleece. The wooden handle knocks against his elbow.

"That's going to fall out if you wear it like that. Here, try this." Lifting it by the handle, Theo sets the hammer on the workbench, then pulls Finch to him and slowly unbuckles his belt.

Is the eye contact strictly necessary? It makes Finch's skin prickle and his throat thicken. Rory is *just* on the other side of the door. Theo's wearing a lazy half smile, like he knows exactly what he's doing.

"Theo—"

"I hate hiding." His whisper chases over Finch's skin, swallowing his breath as their lips meet. He tastes of salt and caramel apple. Being this close to him makes Finch's belly ache. Too soon, Theo pulls back wearing his sly smile and a promise. "By tomorrow, there'll be no more secrets."

Loosening the setting by two, Theo buckles Finch's belt again, then sticks the hammer through the new slack on his hip between the leather and the waistband. His fingers linger on Finch's waist. "There, much more secure."

The hinges on the old door creak and Finch springs away.

"What do we need iron for?" Rory asks from the doorway.

Finch clears his throat. "Just a precaution. You're the one who said there'd be monsters."

With a shrug, Rory spins his bat over his shoulder. "Lead on then."

They make sure to leave the cottage's porch light on.

3

The treeline comes right up to the end of his garden, but Finch takes them back down the track to a broad path used by the woodland management to care for the land. The signage is lopsided and rotting, but it's an official footpath.

Rory looks down the hill to the glittering lights of Gore. "Are we waiting for Jane?"

"She's probably not coming now." Theo claps him around the shoulders. "Next time, invite her to the cinema like a normal bloke."

A few metres into the trees, the dull hum of the busy road beyond Gore fades and the signal and wifi on their phones drop out. Finch feels pinched and swallowed, but he doesn't panic. This happens every time he enters the woods.

He doesn't need the map, but he pretends to be reading it anyway. Used by joggers, the path they turn on to is winding. Cleavers and burdock speckle their trousers with burrs. After what he saw, the urge to tease out the secrets of this place is always a steady pulse against his throat. There are patterns here: the birdsong, the leaf fall, the creak of the trees.

At a crossroads of trails, Finch points left, sticking to the new wood. "This way."

Rory squints into the dark. "Are you sure?"

"Positive."

They follow. Finch often looks behind them.

The path is a track used by animals and they have to move single file. Is that music? It sounds distant and unreal. Finch pauses to listen and Theo, just behind him on the path, staggers into him. Their bodies are tantalizingly close for a moment – chest to back, hip to the small of his back, hand to shoulder sliding down to catch on his elbow and stop them both falling. The only thing Finch can hear is their breathing.

They find the first pile of bones stacked carefully at the base of a young pine, mostly deer and some fox. The second pile is two metres away into the trees, posed on a mossy tree stump. Badger, probably. A few paces further along, the trail narrows and divides. The third bone pile is in the centre of the path, right at the junction – fragments of deer antler, squirrel skulls and a long bone Finch hopes is from a large dog and not a person.

Theo takes photos, asking them to angle their flashlights so that the light glints off the bones. They're polished, like they've been licked clean.

"It's some seriously messed up art installation." Rory

kicks a bone pile off the stump, sending the antlers clattering.

"Don't," says Theo, a warning in his voice.

Rory looks uneasy but he still manages a sneer. "Classic folk horror. Well done, Finch, very impressive."

"He didn't do this." Theo moves on to photograph the second stack.

Finch scans the trees. He's seen much worse in Liksplit than piles of bones: human teeth embedded in gnarled wood, a skinned squirrel caught in clawed branches, the rapping of sticks as the sun sets, shadows moving through the trees. But this is the young wood. There should be nothing like that here.

Go back. Get out.

Except the wood is shaped like a bow, twisting back on itself to cup the fields and Finch's small cottage home. The fastest way out is through.

"We should keep moving," he says.

Stepping over the third pile of bones, they take the left path, sticking close to the edge of the wood. It doesn't take long to reach the clearing Finch is aiming for. It's sizable, an open swathe amongst the dense pine. The waning moon glowers down at them, ghostly behind thin cloud. A fog is coming in, reflecting their torchlight. That's unusual, but tonight is no normal night.

"They found Eli's glove here somewhere." Finch gestures, then checks the time. He frowns. Two hours have gone by. But they've been walking for forty-five minutes at most.

"Let's spread out," says Theo. "Work left to right. Photograph anything you find before you pick it up."

"Mate." Rory is looking around, unimpressed. "This isn't it."

"Yeah, it is," says Finch.

Rory paces around the clearing. "I'm telling you, he's messing with us. Remember the photos? There was this tree in the background, big, old, with a branch ripped off so that it looks like it's screaming, and under Eli's glove there were deciduous leaves on the ground, not—" Digging fingers into the thick carpet of pine needles, he scoops them up and lets them fall.

They have the crime scene photos? Finch didn't know. For a half breath, he's hurt that Theo didn't share them with him, but he understands why he wouldn't, and also how Rory got them. Sarah's mum was the detective in charge of Eli's disappearance. Rory and Sarah dated all last year.

Theo rounds on Finch. "Is that true?"

"I … no, I honestly thought this was the place…"

"Bullshit," spits Rory.

Cracking in the trees.

Finch raises his hand. "You hear that?"

"Stop trying to scare us into leaving." Rory's not bothering to whisper. "It's just the wind."

Theo turns to face the sound. It's coming closer. "There is no wind."

He's right. The fog hangs, unmoving. The trees are

static. A tumbling echo sends the boys skittering, spinning on the spot as they search for the source. Is something dropping stones from the canopy? Rocks against bark, clatter and spin. Suddenly, there's something more sinister about these straight, unyielding trees than the twisting, mossy mass of an ancient wood.

Finch steps closer to Theo. Rory's back is to them, the light beam from his head torch frantic as he tries to catch every shadow. Theo just stands there, numb, his torch shining in one steady direction. His breathing picks up. Finch thinks he can hear his boyfriend's pulse as a thrumming in his bones, but of course that's impossible.

Silver fur and gleaming antlers.

"Is that a stag?" whispers Theo.

The boys turn towards it, closing their circle. Theo stumbles forward, like he's being drawn in on a string. Beneath the sharp, sweet musk of pine, the air stirs with the stink of rotting flesh.

"Theo, don't get close," Finch whispers. Sweat on his neck.

The antlered shape lopes forward. Its gait is slow and faltering at first, then faster. Stags don't move like that. Finch catches a familiar flash of sinew stretched over bone, gnarled claws, a long jaw riddled with too many teeth.

They're here.

And where there's one, there's more.

Grabbing the collar of Theo's jacket, he drags him backwards, shouting, "Run!"

4

Branches whip faces and bite at ragged hands as the boys crash through the trees, driven by the heat of panic, fear snapping at their heels. The gaps between the pines tighten, dead wood sticking out, like spines to catch prey. There is no path. Underfoot is treacherous, but Finch brought them in this direction because it's the quickest way out. He's level with Theo, Rory panting behind them.

Beyond that *they* follow, their grunts and calls like laughter mixing with the strange beating crackle of stick on stick and stone on stone.

Warm light spills up ahead, a growing glow through the trees. The cottage. They're so close. It's gone ten. Mum will be home by now, pissed that he left her to pack up their stall alone. She never even got her hot chocolate. If he dies tonight, she'll have no one.

A thin branch sears his cheek, narrowly missing his eye. Blood on his fingertips. The pines give way to oak, birch and scrubby hawthorns. The brambles are thick but they'll have to push through. A yelp and a curse as Rory drops. Theo skids to a stop, scrabbling on loose leaves, shouting his name.

Finch turns and slips too. The bank is a short, shallow dip and he slides down it, cracking his elbow on something hard. No time to nurse the pain; the first of them are here. Clawing the hammer from his belt, he rises and swings as a dark, bony shape lunges from the fog.

A scream splits the night. Something smacks his wrist aside – Theo's hand – slipping up to graze against the iron head of the hammer.

The creature ducks under Finch's arm and starts to swear. Green hair cropped to her shoulders, a mustard-yellow coat—

"Oh my God, *Jane*?" gasps Finch.

"What the hell?" she shouts, trembling.

There's nothing surrounding them but fog, bracken, brambles and trees. No panting beasts, no sinew and bone or eerie music.

From the ditch, Rory starts a tight and halting laugh. No one joins him. "You scared the shit out of us."

Jane sniffs. "Yeah, well, Finch almost brained me with a bloody hammer, so…"

Clutching his throbbing elbow, Finch struggles for calm. He was centimetres from hitting her. If Theo hadn't stopped him, he'd have smashed in her skull.

Death is better than what they'll do, son.

Eli's wide eyes. Blistering skin. White bone. Blood on his jacket.

Theo can't know the truth; he wouldn't understand.

"You're bleeding." Theo tilts Finch's chin up, snapping him back to the present. Finch winces, meets his eyes, then lowers them. The pad of Theo's thumb rests on his jaw. Too close, they'll give themselves away, but Finch doesn't care. He wants to hold Theo, sliding cold hands beneath his layers to feel his reassuring breaths and heartbeat against his palm. He wants to tell him how sorry he is. Reluctantly, he steps back.

Theo drops his hand and Finch notices a red welt on his palm and wrist. "God, did I do that?"

Theo balls his fist. "The hammer caught me. Rory, did you bring that first-aid kit?"

"Yeah, but I'm using it first; this *stings*." Rory turns his leg, revealing a nasty gash along his shin. Jane is already digging through his backpack.

"How did you find us?" Finch asks her, when he should be saying sorry.

"I've been right behind you, shouting for you to wait for me this *whole* time."

"We didn't hear you," says Rory, wincing as she dabs at his cut with antiseptic.

"I saw your torches just as I got to the woods. You went without me even though I shouted. If you didn't want me here—"

"Honestly, we thought you weren't coming any more, and then we just didn't hear you calling us." Rory puts a hand on hers. "Promise."

"The trees," mutters Finch. "They swallow the sound."

He looks for the cottage lights. They should be just beyond the briars and bracken. He knows he saw inky skies and a warm glow. Now there's nothing but older oaks, birch and hazel. The pungency of pine has broken for the peaty smell of wet earth and decaying leaves. Red berries underfoot. Yew? He hit his elbow on a mossy fragment of old medieval headstone caught amongst the roots. They litter the woodland floor, sticking up like jagged teeth.

"Is this the old plague church?" asks Jane. "That doesn't make sense. You took the left off the main track and followed the treeline north-east."

"North-east?" snaps Rory, hauling himself up. "They found Eli's glove to the west."

Don't leave the path. Never follow the lights.

Tricksters by nature and Finch has been played. Somehow, they're miles from the cottage, right on the other side of the woods. In Liksplit. The heart of the old forest.

Right where they want us.

His phone says it's midnight – time is moving too fast. He has to get Theo out of here. Where did he put the map? He starts to pat himself down, feeling a guttural ache in his chest. *Don't panic.* But the map is gone. Did he drop it while they were running? Finch sways, dizzy.

Theo lays a steadying hand on his back. "Are you OK?"

"We can't stay; we have to keep moving. They're coming."

"What's coming?" asks Rory.

"You saw the stag?"

"Yeah?"

"It wasn't a stag and you know it." Finch looks into Theo's eyes. "They want *you*, Theo, the same way they wanted Eli."

"What are you talking about?" demands Jane.

"Old things. Older than Gore, older than these woods, as old as the earth and always hungry."

"Are you serious? Shit like that doesn't exist; they're just stories," says Rory. "I brought you out here to catch a human monster, not to hunt after some stupid folklore."

This was all Rory's idea. A terrible thought dawns on Finch. They're best friends, as close as brothers. Theo would follow Rory anywhere.

"It's you," Finch whispers. "You're the lure." Then he says it again, louder, spitting it at Rory as Theo holds him back.

"I don't know what that means!" Rory yells.

Theo puts a hand on each of their chests, keeping them apart. "Stop it, both of you."

"He needs to explain why he took us to the wrong clearing on purpose." Rory leans over his best friend's shoulder to glower at Finch. "And don't bother denying it. It's bloody obvious you're hiding something. We all know what your dad did to Eli, everybody knows."

"The police never found a body," says Theo.

"Which is why we're *here*, mate. You agreed that we should look for evidence ourselves. You insisted on *him* coming along because he knows the woods better than anyone, fair enough. But then he led us away from where the evidence is. He's protecting his dad."

Theo calmly takes Finch's hand, lacing their fingers together. "He'll do the right thing. I trust him."

Theo's the only person in the ditch not wearing a look

of shock. Instead, he has a small secretive smile tucked into the curve of his lips and a defiant blaze in his eyes.

"*Him*?" says Jane. "He's your mystery boyfriend?"

Finch moves closer to Theo, their combined hands a "fuck you" to all the moments they missed because they had to hide – eating together at lunch with knees touching under the table, taking the bus back from school holding hands, hanging out with friends as a couple, kissing without worrying that someone might see. All things they can now have, if they survive the night.

"Yeah. Me," Finch says, emboldened.

Rory sets his jaw. A pulse beats in his neck. "So that's it, you trust the son of the bloke who killed your brother and left him to rot in the woods, over me, your oldest friend?"

"I love him." Theo says the words fast and hard, like they can't be questioned, sending Finch's blood thundering in elation. They've whispered it in stolen time, bunking off on the same day to hide in the hay bales. Here it is spoken loudly, for witnesses.

Theo looks like he's going to cry. "And I'm not choosing him over you. You're both important to me, Rory."

"Do you hear that?" asks Jane. She's wandered closer to the trees, head cocked and hand raised for silence. "It's … like … music?"

"They've found us," Finch whispers, knowing that the terrible things never truly lost them – they've only been waiting.

A seething insectile mass bubbles from the space

22

between trees. Bone piles walking like puppets, antlers atop distended jaws, cracking open to dart and suck. With a bellow, Rory strikes at the nearest skull. His cricket bat splinters. What were only trees are now creatures with too many eyes and fingers. Sapling slender, fur slick. A tail root lashes up as the earth rumbles and twines.

Rory screams without his tongue. The bellow comes from his belly, panic beyond panic.

Somehow, Finch makes his body move down as Rory's is lifted up into the canopy. Finch grasps in the leaf litter, not able to tear his eyes away from the splayed arms, sweatpants shorn and bloody and the tang of urine. Rory pissed himself, the last act of a short life.

Grasping the polished handle, Finch hacks with the hammer, calling Jane and Theo, pulling him back from grinding teeth and nipping jaws.

Rory is gone, but the sounds don't stop. Jane is crying, smearing the blood speckling her face like gory freckles. Theo whispers something, gently rocking as he grasps Finch's free arm. Finch holds the hammer high, the flat of it bloody.

There is nowhere else to go other than back towards the ruined church. After almost seven hundred years of abandonment there isn't much left of it, but the east entrance still exists, an archway and three quarter walls with no roof.

Together, the three throw themselves across the threshold and raise arms against an onslaught that never comes.

23

Silence. The woods are still in the frantic beams of their torches.

"Hallowed ground," gasps Jane. Finch hears the hope in her voice.

5

He'd forgotten how cold he was before they started running and screaming and dying, but now the frost creeps back. Finch is shaking and he can't stop. Theo puts arms around him, tucking his head into his neck as they both breathe each other's scent, marvelling at still being alive. When Theo pulls back, thumb on Finch's lower lip, his face is cast with bruise-dark shadows.

"I … I thought they were after *you*," says Finch. "I was so sure, I never thought Rory was the one they wanted. I'm sorry."

Theo kisses Finch softly and says nothing. He's shaking, probably in shock.

"We're going to die." Jane's voice is high and tight. She wipes at puffy eyes.

Finch puts an arm out, expecting her to pull away – they've never been friends – but instead she leans into him. The three of them shuffle closer, their huddle blocking out the world.

"You won't die," he promises. "It's over."

"How do you know?"

24

"They only ever take one, and never a girl."

She still cries for Rory. Finch does too, even though he didn't know him well and didn't like what part of him he knew. How did he get it so wrong? Yes, Rory was handsome enough, good at sports like Theo and just as popular. The guilt of his mistake aches alongside the guilt of his relief that Theo is safe.

Coming into the woods was Rory's idea. If he wasn't luring Theo, what brought him here?

They unfold slowly, Theo peeling off first and helping Jane up, then Finch. One of the torches is dead, its casing smashed open against the door arch. Jane uses her phone light instead, but her battery is low.

After the Black Death did its worst, stone was stolen from the church to rebuild Gore further down the valley. Time has worked on the rest, the woodland clawing it into disorder. Around them are ragged walls grown over with ivy and moss. Spiny hawthorn has grown into the holes, muffling the wood beyond. Trees press close enough to form a kind of roof.

"We know where we are," says Jane. "If you find the old church on the map we can hike out from here."

"I lost the map," Finch admits, rubbing his aching elbow. "I know the way back to the main footpath from here, but in the dark everything looks different. I don't want to risk getting us lost." He checks his phone. Still no signal. "I think we should wait for morning. Five hours till dawn."

Jane seems unsure, but Theo agrees with Finch. "I'm not going anywhere until the sun is up."

"Fine, then let's find somewhere we can rest," says Jane. "Preferably a corner so those fuckers can't sneak up on us."

Finch tucks the iron hammer back into his belt. "The hunt is over; they're not coming back."

"There's something over there." Theo points to the single young oak growing from the damp leaf litter inside the church. At its base another cluster of bones is stacked on a bed of sticks and moss. It almost looks like a shrine.

Jane's phone light catches it. "You were saying?"

Finch approaches slowly, crisp leaves rustling underfoot. "They leave these all over the woods."

At first, he thinks it's another stack of animal bones, but there's no antler, horn, small squirrel bones, or canine jaws.

A single skull sits on top.

Human.

There's a circular depression the size of a two-pence coin in its forehead. The bones are clean. The curved break and the spider-fine cracks stand out against the pale as dark lines. Ink maybe, or some kind of dye to mark the mottled pit. Finch dares to get closer. Parts of the skull around the depression are textured. A surface burn penetrated as deep as bone.

Crouching, Theo places a finger at the edge of the circular wound, running it down over the eye socket, to the cheekbone. His hand reaches beneath the pile of bones and sticks to point out a folded coat, stiff with old blood. Brown tweed, green lining, yellow cord collar.

"Eli." Theo's voice twists with grief.

Jane's hands fly to her mouth. "Oh God, they took him too."

"No, they didn't," whispers Finch.

He doesn't realize his dad's iron hammer is in his hand until he's hovering the blunt end above the circular fracture. A perfect fit. *"You're better off dead than what they do to you."* That's why his dad did what he did, in the end.

Finch shouldn't have gone into the woods that evening, but he was eight and he didn't want to miss out. Especially after his dad promised he'd teach him everything about being a woodsman, but never did. Mum was on the phone to a London friend. The door was unlocked and Finch figured he could keep up and keep hidden.

He saw everything: the piles of bones. The cracking of sticks. Antlered beasts separating Eli from the others. The way Eli opened his arms for them, as if he was embracing his fate. Chest pressed to a mossy trunk, Finch watched as his dad lifted the hammer high and struck. Eli went to his knees and the whole woods shuddered. Blood ran into his jacket. Someone was screaming.

Finch!

The creatures gathered like a wall with eyes in their mouths and ribs made of twigs. He remembers Dad's arms carrying him, the tang of iron and the way the air smelled fresher when they broke the treeline, sweating and fearful. They went down into the frosted grass in the back garden, breath steaming. The creatures didn't leave the trees.

That night, Finch helped his dad bury the iron hammer in the dirt under the workshop and promised to keep all he'd seen a secret. While the village bayed at the door and searched Liksplit for clues, his dad finally taught him what he could of the old ways.

They take a boy every eight years. Before tonight, the cycle has never been broken. They'll want revenge for that. Beware the lure, Finch, and follow the rules.

Dad put iron bars over the cottage windows, and then he left.

Jane backs away from Finch. "He really did do it?"

"It was a mercy," Finch whispers.

"A mercy? Your dad bashed Eli's head in with a hammer!"

"You saw what happened to Rory. That would have been Eli's fate too. They were surrounded."

Theo picks up his brother's skull, handling it like a relic. "You knew."

His face is impossible to read, but Finch feels the pain of his loss. He deserves hatred. Before he can tell Theo how sorry he is, a distant voice calls Rory's name, then Jane's.

"Ted?" Jane gasps, recognizing her uncle's voice. She runs to the little window in the ruined wall to peer through the bushes and saplings.

Another shout. Twigs snap. People moving through the woods. Torch lights. A dog barks. Are they real or is this another trick?

Jane sprints for the entrance, crying. "We're here, we're here."

It's over.

Theo yells in surprise. His brother's skull tumbles from his grip, cracking open. Roots grasp his ankles, twisting up around his legs to pull him down. Arms reach for help. Theo is dragged, thrashing, across the dirt towards a gap in the walls. Finch throws himself forward, narrowly missing his outstretched fingers. The hawthorn parts and the yawning darkness beyond swallows the boy Finch loves.

"You can't have him." Finch struggles to his feet, winded and aching.

As if hearing his challenge, the spines on the hawthorn lengthen, branches swelling to burst and ooze as roots shear the packed earth, twisting into a barrier. He hacks with the hammer. Where he strikes, yellow sap oozes and the wood blisters like flesh. The stink of carrion rises. The roots loosen, shying back from the iron and leaving Finch just enough room to push after Theo. Thorns tear his clothes as he topples into warmth.

6

It feels like summer but it stinks like a grave. The air is muggy and heavy in his chest. Filaments drift round him like ash. They might be pretty if he wasn't so horrified. The tunnel is circular and cramped, like a distorted, woody intestine. Are they underground?

A muffled cry up ahead.

"Theo?" Finch calls, gripping the hammer and stumbling on, desperate and weary. It should be over. They have what they need, so why also take Theo?

Because this time, they need two.

Finch groans. Hating himself for not putting it together sooner. In murdering Eli eight years ago, his father stole their chosen sacrifice, forcing them to go hungry that cycle. Now they need to make up for the loss.

They'd targeted Theo from the beginning and he'd let his guard down because Finch had told him it was over.

The walls are sticky. There is a beating in them, like a heart. The same sickening music that has followed them since they entered the woods echoes in Finch's ears as the tunnel opens gradually, widening into a cavern shaped by the tangled roots of trees above.

He tastes blood. Did he bite his tongue?

A sound like scurrying echoes through the dark. He drops his torch and accidentally kicks it, sending it spinning. Light flashes around the cavern until it comes to rest, illuminating a vast central structure. The twisted root system is wrapped around the sunken remains of old timber-framed buildings, crushed wattle and daub walls fragmenting plaster on to the earthen floor. The original village of Gore, abandoned because of the plague, has now been claimed back by the trees.

A whimper escapes Finch as he inches forward, not wanting to believe what he sees. Corpses. They hang like husks, bodies half turned to wood and growing into the trees. There is one with mushrooms sprouting from the sockets of its desiccated skull. Beside it slumps the remains of a skinny man with thin white hair and lined skin.

Picking up his torch, Finch shines the beam along the dead. He's afraid to breathe. Each lungful tastes like death. More faces, all sunken and wizened. Scraps of clothing are gripped in woody knots – a plaid shirt and jeans. One body still wears a rotting pair of breeches.

Boys have been going missing every eight years in Gore for a *very* long time. But these husks are not boys, they're old men.

They aged here, a whole human lifetime sucked out of them in eight years.

Around him is the slow drip of water and the sound of his own ragged breathing. There's fresh blood running between some of the roots, like someone has been newly absorbed.

No, no, please not Theo. Please. I promised to save you.

It's Rory, his skin laced with dark filaments, chest and shoulders plunged through with spines. A wax-pale sapling grows up from bulbous lips, seeking the sun far above. Movement. Rory's face shudders, wide eyes rolling to fix on Finch with a desperate stare. A groaning plea bubbles around the young tree rooted within him.

Finch's stomach buckles. Acid in his throat as he lowers the torch, arm over mouth to stop the rising bile. Rory is still alive, fed by the woods and feeding it in turn.

He has to get him out, but even if he had an axe, the roots are too thick and there is so little of Rory left to save.

Better off dead.

Finch raises the iron hammer.

"Don't, he's where he's needed."

Gasping, he spins.

Theo is unbound and unhurt save for a red blister along the side of his hand. *When he stopped me from braining Jane, he touched the iron hammer.* Finch thought it was just a graze from the motion, but it looks like a burn.

"No," he whispers, heart breaking.

Theo's gaze peels Finch apart, shedding layers right to his heart. Like a saint, he wears his truth like a halo the sticky dark of old blood. It fogs the air around his head, moving like a mist with his breath. The glamour of him is breaking and Finch doesn't know how he ever thought that too-beautiful face, those eyes, were human.

"You're the lure."

"Like my brother before me."

The truth is a blow so hard that Finch staggers. His agonized groan echoes through the hollow. He sees the past more clearly – Eli's open arms as the creatures swarmed amongst the trees and the blistering scars on his skull from the blow of an iron hammer. Finch's dad didn't kill Eli to save him from being dragged here; he killed him to stop him taking a victim that night.

Who was the target? One of the friends who'd gone with Eli into the trees with him, or the little boy he'd told about a fun midnight trip into Liksplit? Eli knew Finch would follow. He made the adventure sound irresistible.

In the hollow under the woods, the creatures of the

mound stir and tremble. Creeping from the darkness, they hoot with mouths in their foreheads, rictus grins filled with too many teeth as they gather behind Theo, the most terrible of them all.

Stolen glances, the smell of hay, cotton sheets and sunlight, trailing kisses across his shoulder, apples, cinnamon and the taste of autumn in the air.

"I trusted you," Finch whispers through his tears. "I loved you. I came here to *save* you." Clay slips under his trainers, but something has him by the waist, winding under the back of his jumper and shirt, sliding up his spine. "You said you loved me too. You *liar!*"

"Didn't your dad tell you?" Theo's reply is eerily calm and measured. "My kind cannot lie."

The look he gives Finch is one of such adoration it engulfs him completely. *Is it possible to drown without liquid?* Before, Theo was always slightly out of reach. Now, he is laid bare and Finch sees the truth of his love – pungent and burning – and so easy to mistake for hunger.

He can't lie.

He loves me.

Sharp pain blooms at Finch's neck and along his waist. Blood begins to flow as the roots start their work. He squirms, wrestling against too-strong tethers.

"Let me go." It comes out as a sob.

"I can't." Theo gestures to the empty tangle of roots and briars beside Rory as if he is an estate agent showing a client a nice ensuite. "This is where you belong."

Long bone fingers break from the roots to pull Finch back, settling him beside Rory in his living coffin. He won't die for a long time. They will have years together.

No, he hasn't accepted this.

If I don't come home, Mum will have no one.

Eli's skull, broken with a single blow.

One strike, and they'll go down.

The torch is gone, cut from his hand by the tightening briars, but he still has the hammer. The head of it is slick with pus and sap. It seems to hum up his arm, hungry for blood. Finch tastes bile and desperation. His right hand is still free but it won't be for long.

Theo isn't quite close enough to reach. Not yet.

"You're right, I … I do love you, Theo." Finch chokes the words out as waxy stems slither over his shoulder, curling towards his elbow. "I belong here with you."

His vision starts to blur, but he can sense how close Theo is. Even now, something in Finch burns at the thought of hurting him. The roots tighten on his skin. Only seconds until he's completely immobilized.

"Kiss me. Please."

Theo's smile splits his face. He steps forward. With the last of his strength, Finch raises the hammer.

Every eight years, Gore loses a son.

THE HOUSE WITH TEETH

AMY McCAW

The house was whispering. It had a tendency to do that. Violet preferred it slightly to the slow expand and retract that simulated breath. And it was so much better than that chewing thing it did. When you lived in Vivus Manor, it was better not to ask questions. As long as the house behaved tonight. She turned up the stereo, blasting "Girls Just Want to Have Fun". Maybe some Cyndi Lauper would get it to chill the hell out.

Violet spun around her room as she sang along, the pale pink walls and curtains blurring with movie posters. Her mother had insisted on the sickly pink, hoping to smooth Violet's sharp edges. In response, Violet had plastered her interests all over it. It was the 1980s, not the 1880s. A girl could decorate for herself. She had a thing for love stories and happy endings, contrary to what most people would believe, so her walls were covered with posters of the latest John Hughes movies like *The Breakfast Club* and *Pretty in Pink*.

"Alone" by Heart replaced Cyndi, and Violet returned to her make-up, applying thick black mascara until her eyelashes looked like spindly spiders' legs. That was appropriate since the extra four legs of her spider Halloween costume fanned out on either side of her, with a full-length black leotard and leg warmers. She'd already secured her auburn curls with a black scrunchie on top of her head. Her little sister, Tina, would've loved to have done her hair, plaiting and twisting and taming the curls with surprising skill for a thirteen-year-old. But her parents had made certain that Tina was far away tonight.

That was everything done up here, so she turned off the music and locked her door. Who knew what unthinkable things could happen in bedrooms at a high-school party? Especially in this house.

She stepped on to the landing and looked down the mahogany staircase that opened out into the entrance hall. With any luck, the Halloween decorations, food and beer combo would keep the party guests on her side. Her mum had pinned a garland along the wall, its black plastic thorns and fragile white ghosts dangling down. They drifted back and forth, but try telling the house there shouldn't be a breeze inside.

She walked down the stairs, imagining the panelled walls and sour-faced ancestors' portraits as her peers would see them. There were skull and bat motifs carved into every surface as if they'd always been there. The house probably thought it was adding to the Halloween ambiance, if *thinking* was the word for whatever the hell it did. Violet was glad she'd never had friends around before to notice the difference. She was a core member of the popular crowd but had always preferred to keep them at arm's length.

Violet ran her finger around the new skull frame on the nearest painting. The tiny heads were the size of newborn babies. How lovely. Her finger came away coated in dust. The house could change its décor at a moment's notice, but learning to clean? Forget about it. Her parents had tried hiring cleaners and groundskeepers, but they tended to up and leave without a word. Easy to understand why.

Her sequined stiletto boots clacked on the polished floor as she crossed the entrance hall to the dining room. The kegs were still set up in the corner where she'd left them, so that was a promising start. Her parents treated her like the adult that she'd be in a few days. They'd bought the drinks on her assurance that things wouldn't get out of hand. Surely they knew she couldn't keep that promise in a house like this.

The long table was laid out with plates of snacks covered in clingfilm: cubes of cheese and pineapple on sticks, cocktail sausages and pizza rolls. One end of the table was taken up by rows of brightly coloured drinks with names like "Witches' Brew" and "Pure Poison".

Everything was perfect. Most importantly, her parents

were out for the night, dragging a reluctant Tina with them. Her mum and dad had insisted that Violet needed to do this on her own tonight.

Her guests should be along any minute. She strode back up the stairs, ready to make her entrance.

Jake had picked the *Top Gun* flying suit and sunglasses because he'd thought it would be an easy costume, but he was already regretting it. Why had he gone for Tom Cruise, with all of his swagger and hair gel? It was completely out of character. The whole night was out of character, if he was being honest. He technically wasn't even invited. He'd tagged along with the crowd, and no one had called him out so far. But Violet Vivus hadn't handed him a glossy black invitation, looking right into him with those strange grey eyes.

He'd only moved to the school a few months before, following his mum's job at a brand-new law firm, and he doubted Violet even knew his name. But maybe he could change that tonight.

"Dude! I should've gone as Goose to your Maverick." Dom hooked an arm around Jake's neck and half-dragged him towards the gates of Vivus Manor. Jake and Dom had only become friends the past couple of weeks, discussing everything from Ted Bundy to Ralph Macchio. For the first time in his life, Jake had been folded into a fun, rowdy group of friends – a mixture of newspaper and theatre kids. He hadn't figured out how he felt about abandoning his lone wolf status, but his mum was thrilled. It was just the two of them, and she'd almost cried with happiness when he'd told her he was going to a party.

Dom had gone for a Danny Zuko look, rolling his hair into a gelled quiff and donning a leather jacket over black jeans and a white T-shirt.

Bella Lake tottered alongside them in heels. She was the smartest girl in their class and often considered the hottest, though not his type. He preferred his girls on the brooding and mysterious side, like a certain party host. Bella already looked like Whitney Houston in the "I Wanna Dance with Somebody" video, with her mass of tight curls lightened to a sun-kissed gold. She'd decided to embrace it. Jake knew nothing about fashion, but even he could see that the body-hugging lilac dress and vibrant make-up looked amazing against Bella's brown skin.

The three of them were at the front of the group when they reached the gates. Dom plucked a piece of paper from the ornately spiralled iron. He was Bella's match in every way, and Jake knew some girls in their year would trample their friends if it meant getting close to Dom – he of the angular cheekbones and long eyelashes. Their words, not Jake's. Dom would've ruled the school if he hadn't channelled his ruthless ambition in other directions.

Dom read the note in a clear, confident voice: "Proceed to the back entrance. Follow the path between the graves, and then the fun can begin." He paused for effect, holding up the card. "Looks like it's written in blood."

A severe spiked fence ran in either direction, cutting off the Vivus family from the world. As Jake's group set off walking, trees with heavy canopies made the darkness complete. If Jake twisted his ankle and got separated from the others, he didn't like his chances. These felt like the kind of woods where predatory eyes gleamed in the darkness, waiting for fallen meat to pick from the bone.

Dom had had the presence of mind to bring a torch, so he led the way. He wrote for the school newspaper and had aspirations of crime journalism, so he lived for creepy occasions like this. Bella and Jake got to walk on either side of his pool of light. Everyone else was squealing and laughing behind them. Between the fear and excitement, Jake was running on a high.

The back gates were open, revealing a sprawling graveyard and the house standing sentry beyond it. Vivus Manor had spires that carved the darkening sky into pointed shards. What kind of family would choose to live there?

Jake's imagination had always ventured to some disturbing places, so he kept his eyes on the house instead of fixating on the slabs that marked the bodies beneath him.

"Look!" Dom sounded way too gleeful for someone staring at a tombstone.

"Vivienne Vivus," Bella read, peering down at the grave just off the path. "Must be one of Violet's ancestors. She died when she was seventeen."

Jake was the same age and couldn't fathom the concept

of being snuffed out of existence. He hadn't done enough living for all of this to end.

"Yeah, that's a good omen. Let's get to the party," Dom joked.

They carried on walking. Vivus Manor inched closer, and Jake got the strangest sensation that it was slowly advancing towards them instead of the other way around.

A shadow skittered between the stones: too small and quick to be human. Dom flashed the light over it, provoking a wet, guttural hiss.

"Let's walk faster," Bella said, grabbing Dom's free hand.

A hulking figure lurched in front of them, roaring. Adrenaline shot through Jake, and he took off from the path. Exercise was not his friend, and immediately his lungs ached.

Jake was about to turn around to see what was happening when something grabbed his ankle. He went down hard, only spotting the ... *thing* by chance. Sour bile spilled into his mouth as he watched the severed hand skittering back towards its grave. His eyes were adjusting to the darkness, and he made out bones showing through leathery flesh and a ragged end where the hand had been severed. Then it was gone, with only a small mound of churned earth as evidence that it had appeared at all.

Jake's heart raced as he pushed himself back to his feet and staggered towards his friends. He hadn't gone far, and he heard raised voices and laughter. He wondered if they'd seen him hit the dirt.

"For real?" Dom was saying to Chris as Jake rejoined the group. "You almost gave me a heart attack, dude!"

Chris was dressed in a convincing Freddie Krueger costume, the red-and-green striped jumper straining across his broad shoulders. He was wearing a glove with thin knives attached to each finger and a mask that flexed with his face as he laughed. That sound gave him away – the joyful braying that made everyone laugh with him. "Sorry, mate…" he gasped. "I had to do it … her dad paid me. These guys are really going all out. I was meant to chase you through the graveyard, but I think I got you good enough."

"Are you all right?" Bella asked, frowning down at Jake's clothes.

No one else seemed to have noticed Jake's absence, but you couldn't get anything past Bella. Jake did his best to brush off the mud, his ankle stinging as the adrenaline faded. "I'm fine."

Dom swung the torch round, bathing Jake in light that made his eyes throb. "You sure, dude?"

"I just did something to my ankle," Jake said, already rationalizing what had happened. Violet Vivus and her loaded dad must have put an animatronic hand in the graveyard and used Chris to steer him to it. He'd seen *Labyrinth* – they could do all kinds of things with clever mechanics and enough money. That was the only explanation that made sense.

Jake took the opportunity of Dom's light to check the

damage. There was a cut on his leg with something stuck in it. He pinched it between two fingers and dropped the object like he'd been burned. It was a crusty, shrivelled fingernail.

Violet wished she felt regal as she descended the staircase to greet the first cluster of guests. The doorbell chimed again before she reached her position halfway down. More people flooded in, and she wondered if her parents knew how fast parties could get out of control these days. Her mother had held her party in the sixties, and who knew what happened then? She couldn't see Courtney and the others yet, and that suited her. She'd prefer to get this done without their heckling.

"Welcome, everyone!" she called, spreading her arms to show the spider legs in all their glory. Even if she felt awkward as hell, she looked good. She'd only have to roll out this speech for the first batch of guests, and the rest would pick it up from whispers. "My house is your house. The DJ will be starting soon, and there's plenty of food and drinks in the dining room." God, she felt ridiculous. Couldn't they have figured it out themselves? The word 'drinks' earned her raucous cheers and a round of applause, so maybe not.

"If you choose to party the night away, go right ahead. But for the bold among you, I have a challenge. When the clock strikes ten, the first clue will appear on these stairs. That's when the game begins. You can play any time from then, but the longer you delay, the less chance you have of winning."

"What's the game?" Of course that was Dom – so much for no heckling. Dom had a beautiful face but was stuck so far up his own arse it was amazing he hadn't turned inside out.

Violet cut him down with her most vicious glare. "A treasure hunt, oh impatient one. And before you ask what the prize is – that's the fun of the hunt."

She clicked her fingers, a cheesy but effective touch that told the DJ she was ready. The gongs and percussion of "Walk like an Egyptian" by The Bangles blasted through the hallway, and the crowd threw their arms up and screamed.

That was one task done. Now to the obligation of wearing her smile mask and pretending to have a good time. Had anyone in history ever enjoyed their own party?

With her gaze still vaguely turned in Dom's direction, she noticed a boy with him. She wasn't sure if he'd come from school or was one of the strangers who normally found their way into a big blowout. He was dressed as Tom Cruise but much better looking – more like Christian Slater in *Heathers*, with his lean build and wry expression. He had more personality in the arch of his eyebrows than most people in this room had in their whole bodies. Then the crowd shifted, and she lost sight of him.

The doorbell chimed again and more partygoers poured in. Violet didn't know half of this group. She already foresaw the huge mess she'd have to clear up. Still, her parents were right. Her eighteenth birthday was a big deal and couldn't go unmarked.

She was about to join the swell of bodies when Maverick found her. Out of necessity, she usually kept her distance from people, and the immediacy of attraction caught her off guard.

Violet had paused at the bottom of the stairs, alone for once. Jake went for it, holding her gaze even though it sent heat surging to various parts of his body. He shouldered his way through the crowd, only realizing he had no plan and definitely no game when he landed in front of her.

She raised an eyebrow at him. "Tom Cruise is an interesting choice."

"I didn't put that much thought into it," Jake confessed, failing to keep his cool in her proximity. She was even more beautiful from this close, her grey eyes cool and fathomless and her full lips painted with a purple gloss.

Violet's laugh was as brittle as it was enticing, like glittering fragments of broken glass. "Thanks for the effort. So, what brings you to my party, *Maverick*?"

"I…" Shit. She knew he wasn't invited – of course she did.

"Relax," she said, her eyes shining. "I didn't choose to have this party anyway."

"I know how that feels," Jake said. "Walk This Way" by Aerosmith was playing and people were dancing themselves into a frenzy, but he and Violet had found a quiet moment of connection.

Those glossy lips parted, and Violet stepped towards him. For the first time, Jake wasn't sorry they'd moved here. He inched towards her too, anticipation kindling heat that radiated through him.

"There you are!" Courtney sprang up between them, her blonde hair big and crimped and long chains swinging around her neck. She threw an arm around Violet, not acknowledging Jake's existence in any way.

He noticed the tightness of Violet's body even if Courtney didn't. Just before her friend dragged her away, he caught an apologetic smile from the mysterious host.

Spotting Dom and Bella in the corner, Jake dragged himself over to them, the tingles from his encounter with Violet fading. Before, she'd seemed as unattainable as a movie star, but now he was utterly captivated. She was unapologetically herself, her wit and intelligence sharp enough to cut. She'd certainly left a mark on him, and he wanted more.

Bella and Dom were chatting earnestly about entering the treasure hunt, and it was obvious they'd decided that they were going to win.

Jake half listened as the bass boomed in his chest, and he quietly sang along to "Don't Stop Believin'". The hallway was packed, but every once in a while he caught sight of auburn hair or a spider costume.

"So, you're into Violet Vivus?" Bella asked, saying her full name like most people did.

46

"What makes you think that?" Jake asked, sipping a too-sweet drink that Dom had handed over. The room was getting hot, and Jake peeled down the *Top Gun* overalls. He tied the sleeves around his waist, glad he'd put a T-shirt on underneath.

"I don't even know where to start," Bella said, gesturing up and down at him with her almost empty bottle, "but I'll give you some advice. There's something … off about her. Just be careful."

"You've got nothing to worry about," Jake said. What were the chances of someone like Violet reciprocating his crush anyway?

Bella's attention drifted to Chris, who was thrashing around on the makeshift dance floor with the Freddy Krueger blades whirling around him. Jake would bet everything he had that Chris or someone else would get jabbed with the knife gloves before the night was out.

"My mum would agree with Bells," Dom said. She rolled her eyes at the nickname, pretending she hated it. "When I told Mum there was a party here, she started crying and made me promise not to go. So if she asks, we were studying at your place for a big maths test."

"Is this story going somewhere?" Bella asked, swinging her bottle between her finger and thumb and leaning against the wall. She couldn't have looked less interested, but Dom had Jake's full attention.

"Patience," Dom said. "My mum wouldn't talk about it, but Dad filled me in later. Apparently, there was this big party here in the sixties, and my mum convinced my uncle to go. He was sort of a loner – like you used to be." Dom nudged a shoulder into Jake. "She was hoping he'd make some friends, but instead he got way too drunk and there was some kind of accident. He died here."

"Fun story," Bella said. "You really know how to get into the party mood."

"Sorry, man," Jake said. He liked Bella, but tact wasn't her strong suit.

"Thanks," Dom said, his smile sad. "It sucks, but it happened before I was born. So, let's talk strategy," he continued, swiftly changing the subject. "We grab the clue first and stay focused, yeah?" Dom scanned the room as if he was weighing up the competition, though Jake guessed he was also trying to shake off what he'd just told them. He was probably also fascinated by Vivus Manor like everyone else. Dom's life revolved around hunting for the next story for the school paper, and this house probably had plenty of those. Jake suddenly felt oddly protective of Violet and her secrets.

The three of them sat in the corner, watching the minute hand creep around the grandfather clock. There was something off about that clock. It was too human-like, with its hulking shape eerily similar to a body and cogs like owlish eyes. The clock face was watching them too, counting down their lives one second at a time.

"It's ten! It's ten!" Bella leaped to her feet, abandoning her drink on the table.

She and Dom marched across the room towards the staircase, leaving Jake picking his way through the dancers behind them. Jake was beginning to think that being sociable was overrated. Watching *The Twilight Zone* in his pyjamas was looking better by the minute. If it wasn't for the treasure hunt, he might have made his exit. But Violet had finally spoken to him, and the thought of creeping around her house stirred his curiosity.

Dom and Bella hadn't needed to be quite so single-minded. As they pushed through the thrashing crowd, who were shout-singing to "Livin' on a Prayer", he saw no one else beelining for the first clue. Some girls were pointing that way as they untangled themselves from a pile of beanbags, but they showed none of his friends' urgency.

A string of dolls was looped between the wooden struts of the banister. Dom and Bella were already scrutinizing each doll and moving up the staircase.

Jake grabbed one that they'd already dismissed. It was a rag doll, likely handmade based on the uneven stitching. A string threaded through the throat connected it to the others. That was creepy enough, but the face made it worse. The eyes were glossy black beads with red felt tears dripping from them. The mouth was a wide grimace packed full of spiky teeth that looked all too real. He dropped the doll, leaving it where it dangled.

"Got it!" Bella held up a doll victoriously, the string trailing. Its stomach had jagged black stitching across it with a slip of paper sticking out, as if it had been torn open and sewn back up with the prize inside. Jake pressed a hand against his own midriff.

Bella yanked the note out, tearing the stitching, and opened it to read. "The library. Choose the one among you who most fears confinement. Send them in alone."

"Well shit," Dom said. "That'd be me then."

He was grinning defiantly, but fear showed through. Ordinarily, Jake would give Violet the benefit of the doubt, but he had to wonder what her problem was in leaving that clue.

"That's my boy," Bella said, tucking the clue back into the doll as a group of girls approached. "Any ideas where the library is?"

"No," Jake said. "I think Violet just gave us a licence to snoop." Excitement quivered through him, snarled with a barbed thread of guilt. He scanned the room for Violet, but she'd vanished with Courtney.

"Come on!" Bella said, dragging Dom upstairs as the girls examined the dolls.

Every room was more ridiculously lavish than the last. There was a study with mahogany walls and a blood-coloured carpet that swallowed your feet, a bedroom with a four-poster bed and walls that seemed to be covered in gold silk and the most intimidating corridor Jake had ever walked down.

It was tall, narrow and panelled in black wood, but that wasn't the disturbing part. The portraits were looking at them. And not in that "eyes following you across the room" way. As Jake progressed, he couldn't tear his gaze from them. The portraits were otherwise unremarkable: stern, probably long-dead people painted in oil, the colours dreary. But there were holes cut into each portrait and glossy, very real eyes blinking and staring intently at the passing teens.

"Are the portraits...?" Jake couldn't bring himself to finish. Saying it meant accepting that disembodied eyes were watching them and a dead hand had crawled out of the grave.

"Remote-controlled eyeballs," Dom said. "They might even be cameras. The Vivus family has way too much money."

Jake wasn't sure which option he preferred – being watched by a malevolent relative or a frightening, not quite alive thing that Jake couldn't even name.

Behind the fifth door, they found the library. It seemed disproportionately large for the size of the house: the high ceilings and walls stretching on and on, all lined with leather books in a variety of muted shades. The books were on two levels, and there was one of those ladders on wheels.

Jake had an urge to climb it and ride around the room, letting off some steam. Bella and Dom seemed more intent on the mystery, scouring the room impatiently. They looked under the brown leather armchairs and pulled out books. Bella tilted her head to look up the chimney. Jake would prefer not to put his head inside any part of this house.

She had drawn his attention to the fireplace. A lion was carved on each side, their mouths open to display long, curved teeth.

Jake had always had an insatiable desire to *know* things. He'd burned his fingertips because he'd had to know how hot a pan was, and he'd wobbled on the edge of cliffs because he had to look down into the churning sea.

He itched to touch one of those teeth, mesmerized as he held his hand over it. He only resisted for seconds before running a finger across one of the points.

Blood welled up on his fingertip, and he'd left a smear on the pristine white tooth of the lion. He freed one of the sleeves tied around his waist and was about to wipe away the evidence when it faded subtly.

As he watched, the blood seeped into the stone. It didn't trickle down it or into some crevice. The stone soaked the blood up, crimson erased by white.

"Well?" Dom asked, forcing Jake to set aside what had happened. This house was getting inside his head – who knew what he'd seen? Perhaps that sugary drink had been stronger than he'd thought. He sucked his throbbing finger, the blood coppery on his tongue. "How do we find the next clue?" Dom went on.

They all noticed the cupboard at the same time. Jake was unsure why he hadn't homed in on it before. It was out of place in this room of cosiness and learning. Everything in this house was expensive and elegant, but the cupboard was a roughly crafted eyesore.

Wood of the palest cream had been hacked into the shape of a large open mouth. Even though the craftsmanship was questionable, the shape of the lips, swollen tonsils and lolling tongue made it clear.

Jake moved towards it, hand reaching for the handle that he suspected was meant to be shaped like an oversized tooth. His fear was a quiet thing, still buried deep. Desire to reveal the cupboard's secrets was much stronger.

When he drew nearer, he realized it was only slightly shorter and wider than him. He pulled on the handle, but the door was stuck. He pulled harder, the need to see inside it growing. Jake was getting hot and flustered, pulling over and over again as the others joined him. "I can't open it," he said, breathless.

"The clue said to go into the library alone," Dom said, swallowing. If Jake didn't know better, he'd say his bold friend was afraid. "Maybe you two should wait outside?"

Jake followed Bella out of the library. As they waited in the hallway, Jake couldn't hear any party noise. No voices, music … nothing. Alone with Bella, the absence of Dom left a hole that slowly filled with unease.

"Well, this isn't as fun as I thought it was going to be," she said. "And the other teams are going to catch up at any minute."

"I can't hear them yet," Jake said. "Dom will be done soon." Bella's waning enthusiasm wasn't a good sign. Jake wanted to carry on. There was something about this house, and this girl, that he couldn't let go of.

Dom's yell cut through the thick door. Jake grabbed the door handle and pushed, but the door resisted. He pushed again, at the same time that Dom let out an anguished scream that cut off abruptly.

"What the hell?" Bella nudged Jake out of the way, her motions quick and panicked.

Jake rammed his shoulder against the door. It gave easily, and he stumbled into the library. Dom was gone. Bella looked under the claw-footed sofas and checked behind the curtains, calling Dom's name with an edge that quickly shifted from annoyed to nervous.

In Jake's mind, there was only one place he could be. He went across to the cupboard like he'd approach a tiger, knees flexed and ready to bail. The cupboard was almost his height before, and now it'd shrunk to below his shoulder. The enormous mouth was crumpled and cracked. Even worse, the gaping lips had closed in a wicked grin, as if it had bitten down and was satisfied.

The silence was so unnerving that Jake was almost relieved when he heard a quiet sob. That was much better than never hearing Dom's voice again.

Jake grabbed the tooth handle, and it bit into the meat of his palm much harder than he was gripping it. Still, he hung on and pulled, finally wrenching it open.

Dom was curled into a ball inside the cupboard, knees up and tears pouring down his face. His whole body was shaking with sobs. The bowed walls and ceiling were pressing in towards him. Dom looked up, relief breaking through the anguish. "Is it over?" he asked, his voice quiet and trembling.

"What happened?" Jake asked.

Bella flew across the room as Dom clambered out of the cupboard. She wrapped him in a tight hug. "Easy," he gasped.

"What happened?" Jake asked again, gentler this time. Dom's face was tear-stained and a graze ran along his cheekbone. The quiff of his hair was flat, and Jake's imagination filled in how easily his skull could've got the same treatment. Would bone crumple under the pressure of wood?

"The note asked for someone who fears confinement, right?" Dom asked, brushing off his dusty clothes and keeping his tone light. The grazes on his knuckles and puffy skin around his eyes said otherwise. "I opened the cupboard and a note inside told me to get in and close the door, so I did."

The cupboard that wouldn't open for Jake … and had almost crushed his friend inside it. Jake had no trace of claustrophobia, but he saw the horror in what Dom had suffered. A door closing, cutting out the light. That dizzy sensation of breathing in your own air. The wood cracking and reshaping, closing in on him. Could that last part seriously be real?

"Let's go," Bella said. "I never knew what to make of Violet, and it turns out she's an asshat. We don't need this."

"Hell no," Dom said. "I'm not letting her beat me.

We're going to finish this thing, find the treasure and I'm going to shred her in the next edition of the paper. Maybe I'll even sell my first real story off the back of this."

On one level, Jake agreed with Bella. He'd kept the severed hand incident from the graveyard in that disturbing little box where nightmares cut their teeth. But now he'd let it out, disembodied hands could easily live in the same world where wardrobes slowly squeezed the life out of you … and statues tasted your blood. The wrongness of all of this was an ache inside him, but even worse was the thought of walking away and not figuring it out. "I'm with Dom."

"Of course you are." Bella sighed. She folded her arms as if she was angry at them but retained a twinkle of good humour. "What now?"

Jake approached the cupboard with much more trepidation this time. Think pleasant thoughts – don't upset the temperamental furniture.

A white card sat on the pale wood at the bottom of the cupboard. Jake reached for it, very conscious of the length of his arm passing inside the cool space. Then he snatched the card up and backed off.

Jake turned the card over. "It's another clue." He cleared his throat, preparing himself to read it aloud. "The study. Choose the one who fears things that crawl. Send them in alone."

He heard the chatter of the next group outside the room

and forced himself to follow his friends. Only a vague awareness clung to him as Bella warned them, which they ignored with a laugh.

Jake was too frightened to concentrate. This clue was for him.

Violet had promised herself that she'd try to enjoy her party and let the ridiculous treasure hunt play out. She listened to Courtney and the gang chattering, a smile fixed on her face, but her attention wasn't with them. It was with Maverick — the boy she'd found so intriguing that she'd neglected to ask his name.

She needed a breather, and snooping on the treasure hunters while they snooped in her house only seemed fair. It was kind of disappointing that only a few groups had taken up the challenge, and one had dropped out already. Still, it wasn't like she'd put in much effort. The house had done everything — even resetting each part of the hunt between groups. Technically, they only needed one group for the night to be a success.

The house folded a fresh nook into the wall for her, and she slipped inside to watch Maverick and Bella from down the corridor. Bella was tapping her foot impatiently, but it was Maverick that drew her in.

He was good-looking, with floppy black hair that probably never behaved, and intelligent, dark brown eyes that popped against olive skin. But it was more than that — a certain giving-no-craps quality. She doubted he was drifting through life like she was, letting his parents make every little decision.

Dom screamed right on cue, and the other two bolted into the library after him. The plan appeared to be working, and Violet felt a confusing cocktail of guilt, anxiety and pleasure. She wasn't sure if the emotions were for herself or the intrepid treasure hunters. Either way, it'd all be over soon. She found herself thinking about Tina – her little freckled face looking up at Violet with adoration. Tina knew there was something amiss with their family, but would she idolize her big sister so much when she was told the whole story?

Violet pictured them massaging Dom's bruised ego, all the while leaving her stuff covered in their memory. It'd be hard enough to forget tonight without imagining them touching her books or sinking into the ridiculously comfy leather chairs her father had imported from Texas.

Dom's fine-featured face was blotchy, and the tight smile seemed forced. She hadn't expected to enjoy this part, but it gave her a mean satisfaction. Dom always had to be the best – strutting around and writing stories that stripped people's lives bare. He wasn't so high and mighty now.

Unlike Dom, Maverick didn't look ready for a fresh pair of underwear. He looked afraid – she would've been concerned if he hadn't. But he exhibited more than a little curiosity too.

The house had given this corridor a castle-like aspect, with stone walls and slits for windows where someone could fire an arrow if the mood struck them. The Maverick boy's eyes were wide as he took it all in, and Violet's desire for him stirred, settling low in her stomach.

The boy glanced back, and Violet lurched behind the corner, heart pounding. Had he seen her? That wasn't part of the plan.

Someone was watching them. Jake felt the prickle of it when they left the library. This part of the house was the coolest yet. The old stone reminded him of the stories about Robin Hood and King Arthur that he'd always loved. The blending of magic with the everyday from those tales was like being in this house.

Jake had stuffed the note into his pocket. The card dug into him, reminding him of the threat it contained. He'd heard the arguments: bugs are so small; they're more afraid of you than you are of them... He knew those things were true, and yet the back of his neck was already beaded with sweat. Already he thought about Dom's confinement and projected that out to all of the crawling, flying and slithering things that could be waiting.

"You don't have to do this, dude," Dom said. On the face of it, he'd recovered quickly from his ordeal. "I have enough for a story. Violet Vivus is screwing with us, and we don't have to play into it."

That sounded reasonable, and yet Jake was already walking back towards the study. Facing his phobia loomed large over him, a horrifying but maybe ultimately satisfying concept. Whatever Violet had lined up would be nothing like a spider on a towel or an ant on his plate. For all he knew, the exposure might snap him right out of it.

There were also questions he had to answer. Why would Violet do this to her party guests? How could she guess what they feared or which guests would happen across those clues? Jake had to know – it was that simple. He couldn't reconcile the kind of person that would torment others with the wry, interesting girl he'd met earlier.

"I'll be fine," he said eventually.

"If you're sure…" Bella said. "Let's hurry up. I must be next."

Jake couldn't imagine what would frighten Bella. Her quick comebacks usually made her the source of fear.

The three of them retraced their steps, heading back into the hallway full of portraits with eyeballs. Jake kept his gaze locked on the hardwood floor so he wouldn't have to see those blinking, living eyes with too much sentience behind them.

Dom and Bella stood back, silently watching as he gripped the door handle of the study. He paused, wondering if there was another reason he was so willing to plunge into his own nightmare. Was he pathetic enough to go in there simply because Violet Vivus had set it up? He hesitated long enough to notice that the handle had been crafted to look like a spine – miniature vertebrae cast in silver and stacked one on top of the other.

He wrenched the door open and entered the study. It was unchanged: a stuffy room for stuffy people who worked too hard. There was one small window, wooden panelling on the walls and a carpet the colour of clotting blood.

A bookshelf crammed with legal texts, a large desk and two chairs were the only furniture. A computer and neat stacks of paper covered the desk. Dom couldn't see any creepy crawlies or clues.

When he walked to the far side of the desk in front of the window, he noticed a card on the chair. It was unusual for a desk chair – a red velvet armchair with a high back instead of the usual bland office furniture. It had highly polished wooden arms and legs.

The card read "Sit on me". That was way too much like *The Human Chair* for his liking – a story about a person who hid inside a chair to get closer to the object of his affection. Dick move. That probably wasn't what he should be obsessing about, but it distracted him long enough to sit in the damn chair.

The velvety, cushioned fabric moulded to him the moment he sank down. Fleeting comfort settled around him before the impossible happened.

The smooth wooden arms of the chair shifted under his hands. Before he could snatch them away, the wood flowed over them and clamped him in place.

With that, his bravado was snuffed out. This wasn't the way to conquer his fear or impress Violet Vivus. What had he been thinking?

He tugged against the wooden binds, but they were unrelenting. The wood had formed a perfect glove around his hands, tight enough to pinch the flesh and grind his bones together. Pulling sent hot pain lancing through his hands, so he soon quit.

Dom had only been gone a couple of minutes for the cupboard ordeal. They might have been the worst minutes of his life for all Jake knew, but it was just time. He could get through it.

Then he felt spindly legs graze his neck. Panic hit him all at once, his heart pounding so fast that he felt dizzy. He wrenched at his hands again, thrashing his head around in the hopes that the thing would fall. He felt tearing skin and stinging wetness around his wrists so he stopped, closing his eyes and letting his other senses take over.

He could do this. Eyes closed, mouth definitely closed. Get through it, and get the hell out of this house. Violet Vivus could keep her secrets and mystery. He was done with her.

Something walked across his face. Long legs and a light touch. A spider? It started at his jaw and crept towards his mouth. He pressed his lips together as hard as he could, taking shallow breaths through his nose.

Adrenaline made every sense brutally sharp as he felt those legs, one after another, slow and deliberate. One grazed his lip, and he let out a muffled scream, his hands burning when he unconsciously pulled on them.

The creature continued its progress up his cheek. His

heart kicked up to an unbearable intensity when it lingered around his nose before advancing again.

It settled on his eyelid. Tears pooled in his lashes and trickled down his cheeks. His skin was achingly sensitive. Even his ears seemed to pick up the creature's scratching, tickling steps as it moved again. This time, towards his ear.

Terror pinned him in place. He wanted to shake the thing off, but what if it bit him? What if it got frightened and found somewhere warm to hide? Like his nostril or ear canal.

A shudder went through his whole body as he felt a long leg skim inside his ear. Sucking hopelessness washed through him. He wasn't sure how much more he could take, and then … it was gone.

His hands came free with a creak of bending wood, and he scrabbled frantically over his face. Eyes open, the light seemed too bright. He probed his ear with his fingers and ran his hands all over his face, but he was safe. The creature was gone. Like Dom, he'd been left alive and mostly unscathed.

Giddy relief rushed through him, so pure and joyful that it was almost worth what he'd suffered. Almost, but not entirely. Dom and Bella were right – it was time to go. He was ready to tell them that as he burst out of the study, but the two of them weren't waiting for him. Violet Vivus was.

"Enjoying the party?" she asked.

He'd never felt such potent anger. She knew what she'd done to him, and she was grinning about it. "Sure. If facing my worst nightmare is your idea of fun. What's going on here? And where the hell are my friends?"

Her hard expression faltered, and Jake was definitely a hopeless case because he felt for her. He saw something genuine in her huge grey eyes. Regret, or indecision maybe. "I don't know where your friends are," she said, a little spiky. "And you don't have to stay if this isn't your thing."

Jake usually rose to a challenge, but he wasn't taking her bait. He stepped towards Violet, annoyed with himself that he still felt her pull. She stood her ground, hands on her hips and shoulders back. Jesus, she was something else. Sure, she was beautiful, but it was her steely strength that he found so compelling. This girl would never back down.

"Come on, Violet. Tell me what's going on."

What was she thinking? A hot guy put her on the spot, and she was ready to let generations of secrets come spilling out.

She'd had doubts when her parents told and retold the stories over the years, even more so with her eighteenth birthday days away. But this was her first concrete desire to betray them. What would the house do?

She and the boy were facing each other, the atmosphere between them charged with all the potential of attraction. If she went for it, what would happen?

He made the move for her, edging closer with undisguised wanting on his face. She responded in kind, the need for him unravelling through her body. Violet moved to meet him, and that was when the house acted.

The floor became liquid beneath their feet, the wood swirling and sucking like quicksand. The boy was already submerged to his knees. He scrabbled at the solid floor around the hole, but he couldn't get purchase.

Death was Violet's deepest fear, and she loathed the house all the more for turning it on her. The idea of not existing was horrifying, and yet here she was, being absorbed into the house. God, what would it do to Tina if the house took her?

Viscous wood gave way to stone as she sank down to her waist, a slippery sensation twining around her legs. The liquid passed her chest, and the horrible thought occurred to her that wood made fluid could also solidify. Would she breathe it in and feel it harden in her lungs?

She'd soon find out. The wood swelled and undulated around her throat, pressing on her windpipe. Then in the space of a moment, it was past her face.

Long prongs of wood wrapped around her and gently deposited her on the ground. Jake was already in front of her, and his reaction was another point in his favour. Most people would be terrified, but he looked angry too.

Violet felt enough terror for both of them. She hadn't technically broken the house's rules, so she had no idea what it was doing. Her mum had never said anything about this. It occurred to her that perhaps the house had made its choice, but why take her too?

Violet had never been in this part of the basement. Who knew if it'd even existed before tonight? The walls were stone, slick with moss and slime. A mouldy smell permeated the air and clung to the back of Violet's throat. There were cells along one wall with metal bars separating them. Another stench surfaced – the rotten meat odour of decaying flesh. Was that a warning about what might happen to her if she didn't comply?

"What happened?" Jake asked, fear making his voice uneven as he peered into a cell. "Whose bones are they?"

"I have no idea." Her answer was true for both questions.

"Did the same thing happen to Dom and Bella?"

"No," she said, fairly certain it was true. The house could have frightened them away or moved them, but it only needed one.

"You get that we just got sucked down through the floor, right? Are you doing this?"

There was that disgust she'd dreaded.

"Not me. It's the house."

He laughed, but then his eyebrows pulled together and his smile slipped. "You're not joking."

She shook her head. "Every eldest child in our family is lumbered with our … tradition … I guess you could call it. Once a generation, the house takes a sacrifice. It's up to the older sibling to make sure that happens, or they'll be taken themselves when they turn eighteen. The house was supposed to take someone I didn't know... Either who wouldn't be missed or whose disappearance could be

66

explained away with money in the right hands and clever stories." She'd known that it would be her burden for as long as she could remember, but her little sister might not escape cleanly. If she had a child before Violet, they would be cursed to continue the legacy.

Jake's eyes narrowed, his hatred showing. This was what she'd been afraid of. "And you get to decide that?"

"It's how it's always been done. The story gets passed down, and we play our part. I get it – nobody should have to die here. But what was I meant to do?" she asked, certain she'd lost any sympathy he might have shown her.

"I don't know," he said. "But this can't be the only way."

It was impossible. Every part of his logic told him this was an elaborate prank. But he knew that wasn't the case – he'd felt an insect crawling over his face while the chair pinned him down. He'd passed through a solid floor. There was only one explanation. In some dark, impossible way, the house was alive. And it wanted him.

Jake started checking for exits and patting down his pockets for anything he could use. He wasn't willing to die so Violet and her messed-up family could keep doing this for generations to come.

Violet just looked at him, her grey eyes as deep and treacherous as a storm-torn ocean. He tried again. "It has to end – you know that."

"It will," Violet said simply, so cold that he felt truly afraid.

The nearest wall rippled and bulged grotesquely, swelling and retracting as he watched. A figure slowly materialized, its shape almost human. The outline pressed against the wall, and then a boy about Jake's age emerged.

He was slight and his skin was a mottled grey like the walls. Glossy black hair that rippled like stirred oil fell to his collar. His eyes were marbles of solid wood, but Jake could tell they saw everything. "What a pity," the boy said in a quiet, ageless voice. "You had such potential, Violet."

Jake watched her reaction, assessing the flicker of surprise. Had Violet never seen the boy before?

Violet lifted her chin, showing some defiance. "You were supposed to choose someone I don't know – you broke the rules."

"Did I? What's the boy's name?" The creature's smile looked perfectly human, and yet Jake's body hummed with the chilling evil behind it. "Tell me that, and I'll release him … choose a nameless sacrifice as befits our agreement."

Violet glanced at Jake, and he almost laughed through the potent frustration and disappointment. He was going to die because she didn't even know his name.

"You don't know," the creature said, "so the boy will die. That's how it's always come to pass. You brought me subjects to scare, but their fear is not sustaining enough. Do you want to join those ancestors of yours who failed to fulfil their end of the bargain? There are plenty of spaces in the graveyard."

How many people knew with certainty the moment

before they were going to die? Jake felt eerily calm as the boy melted into the wall, his features elongating and body flattening until he was absorbed back into the house. Then the wall slowly opened, a huge black hole forming.

It was endless. To all intents and purposes, it was death.

Jake and Violet stood in front of the hole together. Jake was startled to find her hand in his, her grip menacingly tight. She pulled him forward and he stumbled, trying to wrench his hand free. He wouldn't go without a fight.

The concrete under his feet trembled, a rippling wave of the ground as the house urged him closer. He could almost taste the gaping darkness, the sour chill of it seeping under his skin even before it claimed him. Between the house and Violet, he was dead already.

He twisted and fought against Violet's grasp as she looked up at him, her expression inscrutable.

Then Violet released his hand and stepped into the black hole without him.

COME FIND ME

KATHRYN FOXFIELD

Imagine an antique doll. A hand-painted porcelain face with sky-blue eyes, long eyelashes and rouged cheeks. Real human hair, chocolate brown and curled into flyaway ringlets. A pretty, frilly dress – all scratchy lace and starched bows. She has bubblegum lips, and clackity wooden joints that rattle like a bag of bones when she's shaken.

Now imagine that doll tossed into an abandoned well, deep in the woods, while her ten-year-old owner screams and screams. Her china face shattering against the bricks. Her dress collecting filth and cobwebs on the way down. Her limbs tangling. With more of a plop than a splash, she is swallowed up by the dirty water and she's gone.

But don't worry. The girl who owned the doll had it coming, and the girl who threw her into the well didn't actually mean to do it. Or maybe she did. She doesn't remember any more; neither of them do. After all, one girl is now dead and one has no memory. The doll waits, and she waits.

I've not been home in eight years, and the first thing I have to do is help Grandmother collect a dead bird from the long, straight road that runs past the woods. The crows are holding a funeral when we arrive, and twenty or more birds have settled in the spindly branches of a lime tree. They announce the death of their comrade in shrill voices. As we approach, a wintry gust sweeps through the dead crow's feathers, as if urging it to take flight. Maybe the wind knows what Grandmother has planned and finds it as revolting as I do.

"Crows are difficult to stuff," Grandmother grumbles, glaring at me as she speaks. "Tiny, brittle bones."

She unceremoniously lifts the dead crow by its wing and places it in a large Tupperware box. My grandmother is a strange woman. Even if the house was burning down, she'd still insist on dousing herself in hairspray and applying a thick layer of frosted rose lipstick before stepping outside. God forbid anyone see her looking less than a "lady".

Tucking the box under one arm, she squelches down the muddy verge in her welly boots. She's wearing a boxy floral dress in this shiny polyester fabric and a string of pearls, but she has thrown an ugly green shooting jacket on top because it's winter and she feels the cold more keenly than most. I remember these little details about her not in my head but in the pit of my stomach, and in the little hairs on the back of my neck.

"Will you *please* get a move on, Avery? This bird needs skinning before it starts to decay," she says.

I'm still standing on the road, not willing to sacrifice my Converse to the oozing filth of the countryside. Like the crows, I'm in black head-to-toe. Mourning clothes. It's been two days since my life as I knew it ended and I was forced to come back here, to this hell-forsaken place. Am I being a melodramatic teenage cliché? I think maybe I am.

A truck passes by and its horn startles the crows into a sudden chorus of caw-caws. For a moment, I'm back at Everstone Academy, kneeling on the polished wooden floor as I slam my fist into Annabelle Harper's bloodied face, again and again. The tightening circle of students around us screech and flap, in their stiff black blazers and shiny shoes.

Ten minutes earlier, Annabelle had played a cruel joke on me by locking the door of the English room stationery cupboard while I was inside. I don't remember those ten minutes. I don't fully remember flying at her after the teacher let me out. I do remember wanting to smash her perfectly made-up porcelain face into a million pieces.

Don't ask me why. I don't know the answer.

"Oi!" Grandmother snaps her fingers at me and I jerk back to the now. Dazed, I stumble and the bank vanishes beneath my feet. The thick mud makes an indecent fart noise as I land, oozing itself between my fingers and thighs, even glooping inside my shoes.

"For pity's sake." Grandmother turns her Tupperware box away so that I won't splash her crow. "What did you do that for?"

"I slipped," I gasp. "It wasn't deliberate."

"Wasn't it? It usually is." She doesn't help me get back up.

By the time we reach the house, the mud on my jeans has started to stiffen. But at least it gives me an excuse to shed my shoes and clothes at the front door and run up to the room I slept in as a child. I'm not sure I could bear to witness the crow's butchery. Grandmother's taxidermy horrifies me. Her big, draughty house is full of it, gathering dust on every surface. There are badgers, foxes, deer and all manner of birds – even a couple of squirrels that she's posed as if they're boxing.

When I arrived here yesterday, she confiscated my phone. "Your generation spends too much time staring at screens," she told me. "It will do you good to live in the real world for a while." So here I am, living in the *real world*, surrounded by my grandmother's collection of death. No, it doesn't make sense to me, either.

When I was ten, I hit my head on a tree root and was in a coma for twenty-eight days. When I woke up, everything had changed, but I couldn't remember enough of the before to understand how. All I knew was I no longer fitted in my own life, like broken china glued together with the cracks forever on show.

Sometimes I dream about the accident. I'm always

running from someone, through beech trees that grow so close together I can barely squeeze through the gaps. The woods stretch away from me in every direction; a repeating image that goes on and on. I can never remember who I'm running from, just that I can't let them catch me.

Then someone calls my name and I glance over my shoulder. A trip. A crack. Nothing.

Every time I wake gasping from the dream, I briefly think I'm back in the hospital surrounded by noise and bright lights and people who ask me all these questions I can't answer. "Who were you with?" "What did they do to you?" "Where did they take her?" It always takes a few minutes before the ghosts of the nightmare fade and I finally remember that eight years have passed.

Eight years, but the Avery who lived in the before remains a stranger to me, as does my grandmother. It was her suggestion that I move straight from the hospital to Everstone Academy. And she was the one who encouraged me to stay at school over the holidays rather than return to this house. To protect me from the "bad memories" that I can't actually recall. I think she's the one who needs protecting. Being around me – the new me – reminds her of what she lost.

A thick layer of dust has settled over my childhood bedroom. That's the only way I know it's not changed since I was last here. It feels wrong that I lived in this house for six years between the ages of four and ten, yet nothing in this room feels familiar to me. I run my fingers over every surface, hoping something might trigger a memory, but all I get for my troubles is a runny nose and itchy eyes.

There are old toys on a high shelf. I stand on tiptoes to reach them; only when I try to pull down a tatty stuffed bear, I dislodge a doll hidden out of sight in the corner. She falls in a rush of frilly petticoats and smacks into a chest of drawers with an awful crunch. She lands facedown at my feet with her tangled brown hair splayed out.

I pick the doll up by the edge of her dress and let her rotate to face me. A battered porcelain face comes into view. There's a nasty crack running across one of her cheeks, giving her a Joker-style smile. When I give her a little shake, her wooden joints make a clacking sound and brown water trickles from her broken mouth.

"Urgh." I reflexively toss the doll away and wipe the foul water off my fingers.

The doll's not mine. I can feel this in my bones. She shouldn't be here. She doesn't belong.

Snatching her up, I run downstairs, my bare feet slapping on the wooden floors. I don't dare look at the doll, hanging from my hand, although I can hear her rattling and rustling and sloshing. I take her outside through the kitchen door and shove her into the black bin, before slamming down the lid.

"She's gone. She's gone," I say to myself. I close my eyes and breath in and out, in and out. Count to ten.

When I return inside, the kitchen is no longer empty. There's an awkwardly tall boy placing two paper bags of produce on the kitchen table. He glances up at the sound of the door closing and startles, dropping one of the bags on the floor. Fruit escapes in every direction.

"You shouldn't be here," he gasps.

"I live here," I say.

His jaw tightens and he crouches to collect scattered apples from under the table. "You left. I didn't think you'd ever come back."

I stoop down to his level and help him retrieve the spilled shopping. Close up, there are dark circles under his eyes that make me wonder when he last slept. "Do we know each other?" I ask.

His bloodshot eyes flick to my head, where my short hair covers the scar from my accident. "I'm James. My mum's the cleaner here and I work at the grocer's in town. I deliver your grandmother's shopping."

"That didn't answer my question." I laugh, but it comes out as a crow-like squawk.

"No. It didn't." He abruptly stands and clunks his head on the underside of the table. He marches out of the room, and I hear the front door open.

I catch up with him as he's leaving. "Wait. James. Can we talk?"

"No. That wouldn't be a good idea," he says, slamming the door behind him.

Grandmother has laid out an outfit on my bed. The pleated satin skirt and matching tunic top make me look like a child playing dress-up in her grandmother's clothes.

Swamped by the skirt, I search my room for a brooch or a safety pin to stop it from sliding down. When I can't find one, I try the room opposite to mine.

I discover another child's bedroom, this one unlike my own in that it has been kept meticulously dusted despite clearly being abandoned for many years. There's an old-fashioned dress lying on the bed, and a gold pendant nestled in its skirts. A little bird with a diamond eye. I loop it over my head and run my fingers over the bird's sweeping wings.

A tapping, scraping noise makes me turn abruptly. There's a huge walnut wardrobe looming in the corner of the room. It feels like it's sucked all the light and warmth from around it, so that it stands in cold shadows. The double doors are decorated with hand-carved designs. Little woodland creatures and leaves. Nothing unusual. So why are my palms slick with sweat, and my teeth chattering?

Part of me wants to open the doors and look inside. Prove to myself that there's nothing to be afraid of. I can't do it, though. I'm too cowardly. Besides, I'm already late for dinner.

"Manners are the only things that matter in this world." Grandmother is waiting in the poorly lit dining room, in front of an untouched bowl of soup.

"Sorry. My skirt keeps falling down," I say, trying to force a laugh. "I think it's a bit big."

"No. It fits you perfectly. Sit."

There's some kind of thick soup waiting for me halfway down the long table. It's a dark, reddish-brown colour, like cooked blood. When I stir it, the skin on top breaks and releases a gamey, metallic smell that turns my stomach. Like the dead crow split open on the road.

"Stop playing with your food. I shouldn't have to still be telling you this at your age." She tilts her chin down so that she's glaring at me with the whites of her eyes visible under her irises. It makes her look terrifying, which perhaps is the whole point.

I take a spoonful of the soup and try to swallow it before the taste hits. Only, right then, I see the smirk on Grandmother's lips and I *know* what she's done. I picture the crow's bitter, stringy meat filling my mouth and it won't go down.

Something catches at the back of my throat, and I start to retch, over and over. I cough and I cough, my eyes watering, my chest burning. I can't breathe; I can't think. I rise from my chair and am only vaguely aware that it tips over backwards with a noisy clatter.

"Stop that immediately," Grandmother orders, but I can't stop.

I think I'm going to choke to death. Then, finally, a violent heave dislodges the obstruction and I scrape a long, matted clump of brown hair from my mouth. It smells as bad as the dirty water that filled the doll's mouth and looks like something a cat would sick up. I try to flick it away, but it's stuck to my fingers.

"What is that?" Grandmother spits.

She marches over to me and I offer up the lump of hair to her. Doll's hair, I think. She ignores my hand like there's nothing there and snatches the bird pendant. I'd forgotten it was still hanging around my neck.

She pulls on it so hard the chain digs painfully into my skin. "This isn't yours. How dare you steal this."

"I was just looking at it," I say, still coughing. "I'm sorry."

"You nasty little thief. This was hers, not yours. It will never be yours." Grandmother tries to pull the necklace over my head, but it gets snagged. Her knobbly fingers dig into my scalp and tear at my hair.

"Stop, you're hurting me," I cry, but she doesn't stop. She yanks and she rips, and eventually the chain snaps.

She clasps the pendant to her heart. "It's your fault," she says, her voice a terrible wail. "It's all your fault that she's gone."

That night, I dream of the woods. Like always, I'm running and I can't let them catch me. There's a voice calling my name and I look back, only for my foot to snag on a tangle of roots. I lose my balance. I fall. Everything ends.

In my post-nightmare haze, I can't remember where I am. I struggle to focus on the bedroom; my eyes can only see trees. The whole world is tilting beneath me, and I grope at the bedsheets, hoping to steady myself. Only my fingers fall on something smooth and cold, tucked up beside me.

In my panic, I tumble out of the bed. The doll falls out with me. She's filthier than ever, stained with waste from the bin and smelling like something dead. Her awful, cracked smile seems to laugh at me.

"What do you want?" I sob. "Why are you here?"

Is she here, though, or is it my nightmares bleeding into the real world? Reality flickers and one moment I'm in the bedroom that's not mine, the next I'm back in the woods. I squeeze my eyes closed so hard my muscles purr. When I open them again, the doll is still lying next to me.

The same rage I felt when Annabelle locked me in that cupboard takes hold. I snatch up the doll by the hair and race downstairs. I burst into Grandmother's workshop, where yesterday's fire still burns low in the hearth. The rest of the house may be cold and soulless, but this room is always as hot as hell.

It smells like coal in here, and old meat. On the table, there are metal trays laid out with scalpels for slicing through skin, meat and bone. Tweezers for the tough little tendons that hold everything together. Hooks for removing the brains and wire brushes for scrubbing away lumps of bright yellow fat that cling to the delicate hides.

The glow of the fire brings Grandmother's taxidermy back to life and the monstrous creatures prowl across the walls and ceilings. I stumble through the room, but accidentally knock over a jar of glass eyes. They scatter across the floor, noisily pinging off the crowded furniture and cupboards. Dozens of severed animal heads, posed and mounted, judge me from the walls.

I throw the doll into the grate. Her porcelain head clunks against the metal and her nose chips away to leave a gaping hole through which I can see tangled-up leaves, hair and mud. Water trickles out of her cracked face. The fire hisses and the glow fades.

"No, no, no," I sob.

I toss in more coal from the copper bucket and, grabbing the poker, try to jab the fire back to life. Thick smoke rises from the damp doll, but she doesn't catch. I need something I can use to get the fire going again. There's a cut-glass decanter on the sideboard, half full with Grandmother's favourite brandy. I slosh it on to the coal and, finally, flames whoosh upwards.

The doll's petticoats burn first, then her hair, with an awful popping, crackling noise. But even as the paint on her face bubbles, she continues to grin at me like she's the one who's won.

"Leave me alone," I gasp. "Just leave me alone!"

I run back to my room. I shove a chest of drawers against the door in case the doll tries to return. It doesn't, though, and when I sleep, there are no more dreams.

Morning brings with it bright winter sunlight that scours away my fear. But I know it will return and I need to be ready. I think of James, with his tired eyes and clenched fists. He knew the old Avery. I have no memories of my own, so his will have to be enough.

I put on my coat, black like the crows, and I tiptoe out of my room. My plan is to escape through the front door before Grandmother can catch me, only the other girl's bedroom door is standing slightly ajar and I can't help but take a look inside. Angling myself away from the wardrobe, I approach a shoebox Grandmother's left open on the bed.

The box is full of photos and mementos. There's a lock of brown hair tied up with a yellow ribbon, some dried flowers, and a silver pill pot that, when I open it, contains tiny human teeth. Quickly closing the pot, I turn my attention to the photos. They are all of a brown-haired little girl with downturned lips and pale cheeks.

In all the photos, she wears a variation of the same prissy party dress that lies on the bed, with frills around the neck and sleeves. She is almost always clutching the doll that haunts me, undamaged with perfectly rosy cheeks and a cold smile. I know I should recognize the girl, but the memories hide just out of reach. So I take one of the photos and I sneak out of the house.

The path into town runs through the woods. My feet remember the way even if I don't, and I weave through the bare trees, with their twisted branches that remind me of a child's scribbles. The ground is carpeted in wet, brown leaves broken apart by bright splashes of green moss and ivy.

I pause at a half-collapsed tree stump and run my fingers over the age lines. There's a memory hiding here. I can feel it even if I can't see it. Somehow, I know that if I turn off the path and follow the animal tracks between the tangled brambles, I will eventually emerge in a hidden clearing. There's a well there, covered over with a metal hatch and obscured by nettles.

A sudden lurch in my chest makes me snatch my hand away. Breaking into a jog, I don't stop until I reach the town. I identify the greengrocer's by the racks of fruit displayed outside. I can see James through the window, dressed in jeans and a brown apron. He's smiling and it makes him look younger, but the second he spots me at the door, his expression hardens.

"What are you doing here?" he asks, standing in the doorway so I can't enter.

"I need to talk to you."

"No. You need to leave. Go back to wherever you've been for the past eight years."

I hold up the photo of the miserable-looking girl with her doll. "Who is she?"

He closes his eyes and shakes his head. "You really don't remember anything, do you?" He crosses the quiet road and sags on to a public bench.

I sit next to him. "She lived in my house, but I don't even know her name."

"Lydia. She was your cousin. Her mother died when she was born, so your grandmother raised her. You came here when you were six, after your mother moved abroad." He smiles wryly. "People round here say that your

83

grandmother's cursed because everyone leaves her. Both her daughters, then you and Lydia. Only, you came back."

"What happened to Lydia?"

His jaws tightens and I don't think he's going to answer. "She disappeared," he finally says. "Someone took her."

"Took her?"

"A truck driver passing through town was eventually arrested, but he refused to tell anyone what he did with her." He looks up at me with the saddest expression. "The only other person who might have known what happened hit her head and forgot everything."

"Me." Was that what I was running from in the woods that day? The man who hurt Lydia?

Everything starts to make sense. I trace the line of my scar beneath my hair, wondering what I saw, and if I could have saved her. "This is why my grandmother hates me now."

James laughs abruptly; cruelly and with no joy. "Now?"

I return to Lydia's bedroom as soon as I get home. I run my fingers across her belongings, and her books, and her toys. I test her name out on my tongue. We grew up like sisters. There must be something here which, like the lines on that tree stump in the woods, etched itself into me and persists.

I turn to the wardrobe, standing cold and imposing. The sight of it makes my insides squirm. My body remembers something even if I don't. Today, I am less of a coward than I was yesterday. I turn the key in the lock and the doors swing open. There are a few coats inside, nothing else. No memories leap out at me, only a musty smell.

Suddenly, I'm pushed from behind with enough force that I fall into the wardrobe. My face smacks the wooden backboard and I skin my elbows on the frame. The doors slam into me, painfully closing on my ankle. I yank my foot in with me and another slam steals away the light. The lock clicks.

I turn in the tight space and slap my palms on the door. "This isn't funny. Let me out."

There's no sound from outside. Whoever it was who locked me in here hasn't moved, otherwise I would have heard their footsteps on the creaky floorboards.

"Who's there?" I say, my voice shaky.

In the dark, I run my hands over the walls of the wardrobe, testing the wood to see if I can force my way out. Not a chance; it's too strong and well-made. I try to feel for the lock and instead I find several deep grooves scraped into the wood of the door. Almost like scratch marks.

I panic and pound on the doors. "Let me out," I scream. "I can't breathe, let me out!"

"It's dark in here," a sing-song voice says, and I freeze.

There's something in here with me and it smells like soot, mud and rot. I don't dare breathe. The thing in here isn't breathing, either.

"No one's coming to find you," the voice says, now just millimetres from my ear.

I throw my full weight at the doors. I slam my body against the wood, and I hammer with my fists until the skin on my knuckles sloughs away. Part of me thinks if I make enough noise, I won't hear the thing that's whispering to me in the dark.

Suddenly, bright light spills inside the wardrobe and I fly out. I land on the floor, gasping and sobbing. Grandmother towers over me, hands on her hips.

"What do you think you're doing?" she says, so quietly I can barely hear her.

I can't string a sentence together to answer her, so I just point at the wardrobe. She pulls both doors wide and peers inside. There's nothing there. No doll hiding in the darkness, nothing.

She slams the doors closed and locks them. "I told you to stay out of this room."

"I just wanted to know more about Lydia."

"Don't you dare speak her name," she cries.

"But she was my cousin and I can't even remember her. I just want to remember her!"

"You want to know about Lydia?" she says, crouching down beside me and resting her papery hand against my cheek. It's almost tender, but the look in her eyes is not. "Lydia was a hundred times the person you will *ever* be, and if I could choose to have you swap places then I would in a heartbeat."

She leaves me voiceless on the floor with tears running down my face. I remember now. Grandmother never wanted me, only Lydia.

Something unlocks in my mind and, that night, I dream that I'm playing hide and seek. I crouch inside the wardrobe in Lydia's room, biting my thumb as feet creak on the floorboards outside. Lydia's already found James, so they're both looking for me. They're sure to find me, any second now...

"I'm bored," Lydia says. "Let's go and play in the woods."

"We have to find Avery first," James says.

"Or we could just leave her. She's such a baby. I genuinely think there's something wrong with her."

"You sound just like your grandmother when you say things like that," James says.

"Maybe my grandmother's right."

There's a long pause while I hold my breath and no one moves. "Maybe," James finally says.

Lydia whispers something and then she laughs. I hear the key turn in the lock. I pound on the door, panic making my teeth chatter. "Hey, let me out! Lydia. James?"

"I'll let her out in a minute," Lydia says, her voice leaving the room.

Only she doesn't. I scream for help, and I throw my weight against the panels. I dig my fingernails into the smooth wood, trying to prise open the doors. Splinters force themselves into my soft, sensitive nail beds. My legs are hot and wet, and the small space stinks of piss.

As my knees sag and I sink to the bottom of the

wardrobe, the dream dissolves around me. I jerk awake and find myself sitting in a puddle of urine on the floor of Lydia's room. In front of me, one of the wardrobe's doors stands open. The doll is nestled in the darkest corner. Her face is a latticework of cracks and holes, her clothes are burnt and tattered, one of her arms is missing.

I scream. Not in fear, but fury and frustration. I drag the doll out of the wardrobe by her leg, her head bouncing against the wood. I need to get rid of her, for good this time. I burst outside through the kitchen, into the eerie blue of the dawn. The trees are painted ink black against the sky.

I run towards the woods. I'll throw her down the well, then I'll cover it over and forget about her. But when I reach the treeline, I stop. The woods are dark, and my feet are bare. An animal screams somewhere out of sight and I back away. Instead, I carry the doll to Grandmother's vegetable patch and throw her on the lumpy mud.

There's a gardening fork dug into the ground. I fight it free and slam it down on the doll, again and again. The porcelain smashes into shards and powder, and still I keep bringing the fork down on her. One of the prongs catches in her dress and I accidentally fling her into the air. She falls, her limbs clattering and her dress fanning out around her. The image briefly ignites something in my memories but, at this point, I have no idea what is real and what I've imagined.

The ground is frozen solid and I can't dig a proper hole.

I scrape at the soil and stamp what's left of the doll into the shallow trench, then cover her over with clods of earth and rocks. I jump on the grave to flatten the mound, but a rock painfully cuts into the sole of my foot and I fall, my ankle turning over.

I curl up into the fetal position on the soggy grass, clutching my ankle. "What do you want from me?" I sob. "I don't know what you want."

"Everything you took from me," a voice replies.

"Wake up. Avery." I blink my eyes open to find James gently shaking my shoulder. I'm a block of ice on the lawn.

"I must have sleepwalked out here." I let him help me sit up. My feet are muddy and streaked with dried blood. One of my ankles throbs with pain.

"Come on." He leaves Grandmother's shopping on the lawn and scoops me up like a baby, carrying me back to the house. He sits me on the table and cleans up my feet but avoids looking me in the eye.

"I'm sorry," he finally says.

"For what part?" I say.

His mouth lifts in a brief half-smile that dimples one cheek. "All of it. I just thought you'd got away, so when I saw you here..." His fingers still on my skin. "What happened?"

"I got into a fight," I admit. "A girl at school locked me in a cupboard and I just lost it. Bad memories, I guess."

"Oh." His cheeks flush with shame. "Hide and seek. I

89

shouldn't have let Lydia do that. I shouldn't have let her do a lot of things, but I was always scared of her."

I think maybe I was too.

James goes over to the sink. He runs the water but doesn't wash his hands. He just stands there. "When we were little, we used to joke about running away together. I don't suppose you remember that."

"I don't remember anything that actually matters."

I see the corner of his mouth twitch into an almost-smile. "We'd talk about hitch-hiking along the road out of town. Finding a truck driver who'd take us as far away from here as we could get." He turns off the tap and faces me. "I have some money saved up, so we could still do it."

I laugh, not because it's funny or anything. I'm just surprised. His hopeful expression falls away.

"Yeah, it's a ridiculous idea. Forget it."

"No, I didn't mean it like that." I hop off the table, wincing at how much my feet sting and my ankle screams. I take his hands in mine. They feel bigger than they're meant to, like my fingers remember his knitting through mine as kids. "I just think maybe I've done enough running."

"Sometimes running takes you somewhere better."

I smile at him. "And sometimes you trip over a tree root, then you have to live with a traumatic brain injury."

We both laugh at this, even though it also isn't funny. Being here with him, though. That part's nice. He feels more like home than this house ever will. Or ever has.

A slamming door and footsteps pull us apart.

Grandmother walks into the kitchen and slaps a dead rabbit on to the table. Its eyes are open and there's blood around its mouth. "What's going on?" she says, looking between us.

"Nothing, Mrs Rose." James flexes the fingers that briefly held mine, then he rushes outside. "I'll fetch your shopping."

Lips pursed, Grandmother watches him hurry across the lawn to where the paper bags still lie at the edge of the woods. Then she turns back to me. "Stay away from him," she says. "I won't have you throwing yourself at boys while you live under this roof."

I want to scream at her, and I want to keep screaming until she hears me. But I don't. Instead, I nod. "Yes, Grandmother," I say quietly.

She sniffs. "You'll help me stuff the rabbit." It's not a question.

"Rabbits are easy to skin," Grandmother says. "The pelt should come off in one go."

I shudder as she tugs at the skin and pulls it away from the musculature with a horrible ripping noise. The sight of the rabbit's shiny pink flesh turns my stomach. The heat, the smell and all the gore make me light-headed, and I stumble into the table. A sack of the sawdust Grandmother uses to stuff her subjects tips over, spilling on to the floor.

"There's something wrong with you, Avery. You have always been such a baby," she says.

The thing with *final straws* is that they don't have to be big and dramatic, or even all that terrible. Most of the time, they're something that would go unnoticed by most people and if you ever try to explain what your breaking point was, it will sound so insignificant and petty. But it's the combined weight that matters, and the realization that nothing is ever going to change.

"I can't do this," I say, more to myself than her. I stand up straighter. Speak louder. "I can't do this!"

"You're more than welcome to leave," she says, slicing a lump of flesh away from the rabbit's skeleton. "I'll even give you fifty pence for the bus fair."

She's not listening to me. I sweep a tray of surgical instruments off the table. My grandmother startles at the noise and her blade slips. It slices into her own finger, and she cries out in pain. "You stupid girl!" she shouts. "Get out. Now."

"No. Not until you tell me why you hate me so much. You've always hated me, and I don't know what I did wrong."

She composes herself and stands up primly, cradling her injured finger as blood runs down her wrist. "If you have to ask, you'll never know."

I'm not letting her shut me down. When she goes to walk away, I shove her hard from behind and she thumps into the table with a cry that sounds every bit the old lady she is.

"You loved Lydia but never me. Why couldn't you love me?"

Clutching her belly where she hit the table, she turns to face me. "What's there to love?" she says viciously, and right then I know she doesn't care about me, never has and never will. Nothing is ever going to change, unless I make it change.

I'm caught between now and then, split into two people who are existing in two different timelines. I know that the sweltering hot taxidermy workshop is real, and the woods are all in my mind. And yet I can smell the musty stench of decaying leaves; I can feel the wind whipping through my hair. It's a nightmare, only I'm awake.

This time, I'm not running. I'm facing Lydia across the old well while the trees rustle around us like gossiping onlookers. I'm holding her doll over the mouth of the shaft and all I am thinking about is how much I want to hurt Lydia. She has *everything* and she's still a monster to me.

"You wouldn't dare," she says. "You're too much of a coward."

"Maybe I've just had enough," I say. "You left me in that wardrobe for eight hours!"

"That was funny. James thought it was hilarious."

She must notice the flicker that crosses my face, because she sticks out her bottom lip at me. "Ah, did you actually believe he wants to run away with you? He doesn't like you, Avery. Nobody likes you."

"That's not true," I say quietly.

"Isn't it? Because your mum left you, and Grandmother can't stand you, and James only feels sorry for you." She smiles sweetly at me. "If I was you, I'd throw myself down the well and do everyone a favour."

All the fight goes out of me. The hand holding the doll falls limp and her porcelain arm slips from my grasp.

"No, don't!" Lydia cries, lunging at me.

We struggle, and she screams, and the doll falls. On the way down, her china face shatters against the bricks and her limbs tangle. With a quiet plop, she sinks into the dirty water. I stare down the well, but she's gone. I didn't mean to drop her. I only wanted Lydia to know what it feels like to have someone you love stolen away, like she stole all of Grandmother so there was nothing left for me.

I run and I don't look back. I have to get away from Lydia, and away from the terrible mistake I just made. But then I hear a voice calling my name and I trip. I crack my head open like an egg and while I lie there, in a dreamless sleep, I don't see what happens to Lydia. Maybe she tried to beat me home and rushed out in front of a passing truck. Or maybe the driver found her sobbing by the road and snatched her away. After the police tracked him down, he refused to tell anyone what happened to her.

"You all know I did it so why don't you tell me where she is?" he said. Not long after that, he was dead and Lydia was gone forever.

In the same way I dangled Lydia's doll over the well, I now offer up Grandmother's taxidermy to the fire. I drop creature after creature into the flames and it feels good. A pheasant, a squirrel, a fox. They burn fiercely with hissing, popping sounds.

I grab the crow – the one we picked up off the road – and throw him in as well. Only, there's not enough room in the grate. With one wing ablaze, he falls on to the carpet. Grandmother tries to stamp out the flames, but they spread hungrily. From carpet to the spilled sawdust, to the long velvet curtains. Once again, I've gone too far.

I run from the room and from Grandmother's awful screams. Because this is what I do. But maybe it's time to stop running from the secret that torments me. Maybe it's time to face the truth. My legs carry me out of the house and through the woods. I turn off the path at the tree stump, tearing through the thorns until I find myself where everything started, or ended, depending on your perspective.

Overgrown brambles and nettles completely obscure the old, forgotten well. I claw them aside and I don't even feel the scratches and stings. I yank on the rusty metal handle until the hatch lifts. The water at the bottom is a black mirror. It hides the truth and reflects nothing back.

There's a collapsing wall nearby, and I heave over one of the larger rocks. I shove it into the well. It is time to break the mirror and see what lies beneath. My fractured memories tell me that I dropped Lydia's doll down the shaft. I can remember her smashing against the walls, twisting as she fell, skirts flapping around her limbs.

I'm not sure my memories can be trusted, though.

The rock splashes into the shallow water at the bottom of the well. Briefly, it displaces the water and churns up all the mud and leaves and filth. A flash of white floats to the surface, only it's not a doll's porcelain face but a human skull. Lydia's skull.

I can remember now. Struggling with her over the doll. Lydia: falling, smashing, sinking. Me: fleeing, running, tripping. It was Lydia who fell, not her doll. I killed her.

I kneel next to the well and I don't know what to do. Maybe Lydia was right and I should throw myself in. Do everyone a favour. I lean out, staring down at the blackness below. That's not what I want, though.

A sudden shove sends me toppling forward, and I know it's the doll, with her stench of rot, ash and secrets that refuse to stay buried. I fall, but then I don't. A yank pulls me back from the edge. I lose my balance and land heavily on top of James, with his arm wrapped tightly around my stomach. "Avery, no," he pants breathlessly. "Please."

"It was the doll," I say, but I know how ridiculous that sounds. "Lydia's doll."

James releases me and staggers upright. He approaches the doll, lying next to the mouth of the well, somehow no longer battered and burnt but as perfect as she was eight years ago. I can see the truth now. How my memories have been trying to force themselves to the surface, making me imagine hair in my mouth and whispers in the wardrobe.

"I always hated that awful thing." James kicks it into the well and it rattles like a bag of bones all the way down. "Now it's where it belongs. With Lydia."

"You knew?" I say.

He sits next to me. "I followed you both here that day. And after Lydia fell, I promised myself I'd make sure no one blamed you for what happened. So I covered over the well and I hid the doll on a shelf in your house. I even told the police that I'd seen a truck driver hanging around suspiciously." He shakes his head. "I didn't know they'd find some guy to pin everything on."

"But I … why?"

"I thought we could run away. Together. Only, when I chased after you and called your name…" He closes his eyes.

"I tripped and fell, and you had to carry the secret all by yourself."

"It was OK. Because I thought you'd escaped."

Through the trees, I can hear the sound of sirens approaching. The smell of smoke drifts towards us on the breeze. I know that I have to run, but maybe this time I'll find a way to not just run away from my past, but towards a better future. One which I'll make for myself, as far away from here as I can get.

"Come with me," I say to James, holding out my hand.

This time when I run, I won't be alone, and I won't trip.

THE WOLF AND THE WITCH

MARIA KUZNIAR

Anka lived in a little cottage buried deep in an ancient forest. Her village was engaged in a battle that the forest was winning. Trees nestled around the few shops and establishments, pressing against walls, their roots warping the paths into fat snakes. Wild mushrooms grew next to front doors, berries could be picked from the brambles bursting across windows and the air was thick and loamy. When it was summer, the villagers' world was ceilinged by a lush canopy, a patchwork of leaves and chinks of sky. But in darker months, the cold bit fiercely and their world was one of shadows.

On the day our story begins, Anka was running home with a loaf of fresh bread. Either side of the twisting path was a carpet of emerald moss. She longed to sink her feet into it, but her grandmother's warning rang through her head: *never veer from the path, lest you be snapped up by a roaming wolf. Or worse.* Anka ducked under an overhanging oak branch by habit, slowing when the cottage she shared with her grandmother came into view. Built by her grandfather, a man she'd never met, it was a single storey, formed of large planks and whitewashed. Painted blue and violet crocuses clambered up between windows and danced over the scalloped trim beneath the thatched roof. The shutters on the windows were thick oak with iron bolts.

"You're late," Babcia, her grandmother, announced when Anka entered the cottage, her blue eyes fixed on the cake that she was dusting with sugar. It was a light sponge with a dark, syrupy centre that Anka couldn't help thinking looked like blood. A plum cake. "The moon will rise soon. A hunter's moon." She cast a furtive glance out of the nearest window. "And nothing good comes of a full moon in these parts."

"It's not even sunset yet," Anka protested, taking off her red woollen cape and sitting at the table. She rested her cheek on a hand and looked at Babcia. Babcia's face was an older mirror of Anka's: sharp cheekbones, small chins and pert noses marked them as grandmother and granddaughter, only where Babcia's eyebrows and hair had greyed, Anka's were strong and thick, her oaken waves carrying wild streaks of auburn and sunflower.

Babcia creaked to her feet and slammed the cottage door shut. "You know the rules, Anka." Drawing out a thick plank of wood, she slotted it over the door, reinforcing it.

Then she bolted it. Sturdy iron bolts clanked into place, anchoring the door to the surrounding walls and down into the floor. Next, Babcia methodically went through the little cottage, opening the windows to bolt the shutters closed before locking the windows shut. She pulled the curtains closed to ensure not a scrap of light could twinkle through. Dangerous things prowled beneath the hunter's moon and each time one rose, the moon full and fat and red, Babcia turned their cottage into a fortress.

Anka did not dare grumble aloud, though she wondered if she would ever be allowed to leave their village. Babcia believed that it had everything they could ever need. Anka wanted more. There was an entire world out there: oceans and rivers and cities she had never seen in all her sixteen years. Some nights she felt a stirring deep within her, a hunger that scared her. Those were the nights when temptation, a slippery creature of half-promises and flawed logic, visited her. When her fingers twitched to silently unbolt the window and steal out. Anka sighed to herself and got up to tend the huge stove that lumbered across an entire wall of the cottage, heating water for tea. Babcia's back was bent over the chest between the two bedroom doors. She pulled out a bag of salt, scattering handfuls in protective lines across the doors and windows. Anka could hear her muttering as she worked her way through the cottage, entreating the domowik, their house spirit, to protect them.

The forest was an ancient place and in deep pockets

forgotten creatures and demons were rumoured to lurk. Things that walked the darkness, feasted on flesh or drank blood. Things too dangerous to even think the name of, because thinking their name was tantamount to summoning the demon itself. Deadliest of all was Baba Jaga. The soul-devouring witch who ate raw bones and decorated her hut with human teeth. Some called her a goddess, others a demon, yet the truth was, nobody was certain what she was. Only that she had been there for all of time, before the first stone had been laid in the village, before the ancient forest had rooted itself around her. Anka's fear took wing at the thought of that being walking into their village. She shook it away. Baba Jaga was nothing more than a story, told by the superstitious elderly who still practised the Old Ways. The winter was harsh and the forest was hungry, human and beast alike, that was all. They had learned to guard themselves against its tooth and claw.

A thud summoned Anka back to the present. Babcia had set a crossbow down on the table, along with the thin iron bolts she shot from it, and eased herself into a chair. Anka poured two cups of tea and sliced the plum cake. She ate hers while she watched Babcia use her sharpening stone to file down the points until they were wickedly sharp and could slice through bone with ease. "You're being more cautious than usual." Anka laid down her fork and frowned. "Did something happen in the village today?"

The stone grated against the iron like nails down a door. It set Anka's teeth on edge.

"I have a peculiar feeling about tonight," Babcia muttered, eyeing the bolted door. "Be on your wits."

That night, the forest fell silent. Anka lay awake in her bed, crawling with anticipation after Babcia's words. Not the scurry of a dormouse nor the chatter of a squirrel could be heard. Even the trees were still. The rustle of their leaves had ceased – the forest was holding its breath. When at last sleep dragged Anka under, she dreamed of swollen moons staring milkily down at her, of nails that grew into claws and teeth that glinted like daggers.

She awoke with a start. Something was crawling over her hand. She lurched out of bed only to discover it was not her blankets she had been lying on but moss. She was outside. And, forging a path along her hand, up her arm, towards where she had been sleeping with her mouth open, were maggots. Anka screeched and batted them off. Their pale, soft bodies burst against her fingers and she gagged. She closed her eyes and took several deep, fortifying breaths to steady herself. But this morning, the forest was not scented with dew and earth and the green of living things. It smelled rotten. Her eyes flew open. She was standing in a mossy pocket between two great oaks. And surrounding her were chickens. They had been ravaged by some wild beast: terrible claw marks dragged across their bodies; the moss was soaked in their blood; feathers drifted down like ash after a fire. Maggots feasted on their remains.

Anka ran home.

The cottage door was still bolted. Anka pounded on it. "Babcia? Babcia!" she called until she heard the clank of the bolts. She stumbled into the cottage. Babcia looked at Anka's torn nightdress, the tangle of her hair, the chicken blood and dead maggots streaked down her arms. "Fill the tub," she ordered. "Wash yourself at once before the villagers see."

"But I don't understand," Anka half-sobbed.

Babcia's face softened. "You must have walked in your sleep. Opened your window shutters and climbed out." She crossed the cottage with a stooped back. Long winter nights set in her joints and stiffened them until she creaked and cracked like an old oak. When she reached Anka, she pressed a hand against her cheek. "Go and soak the dirt away and I shall fry you up a plate of pierogi."

Anka pulled the old cast iron tub from out behind the cottage. She filled it with water direct from the well, too desperate to scrub the blood away to wait for heated water from the stove. Its bracing cold nipped at her skin and she shivered as she quickly washed herself clean. It was only after she had drained the tub that she noticed that the shutters on her bedroom window had changed. A secret fear that she did not know how to voice whispered at her as she ran a hand over the shutters. These were paler, less weather-worn, and rougher round the edges.

A sharp pain bit her hand. A splinter. Anka gritted her teeth and pulled it out, sucking at the blood that welled in its wake as she stared and stared at her shutters. Her new shutters. Babcia must have risen at the first hint of dawn to replace the old ones. Hard work for an elderly woman. But why? And why had she not whispered a word of this to Anka?

She re-entered the cottage, the silence thick as old bark. Filled with dead-rot from all the things they did not say to each other.

Later that day, Anka dressed in her red woollen cape, slipped her basket over her arm and trod the path to the village square. The little cheese shop leaned crookedly between two wych elms. Two lanterns hung outside, their light buttery splashes on the green stones. A bell rang when she pushed the door open, joining the queue. A few moments passed before she realized that nobody was purchasing cheese.

"Janusz said that he saw the beast with his own two eyes," a woman Babcia's age was telling the others.

Anka suppressed a shudder and listened more closely.

"A wolf, greater in size than a bear. With claws that could rip a man in two."

"We are fortunate it only feasted on Bogdan's chickens. But I fear that cannot sustain its appetite for long."

The cheese seller nodded gravely. "It is the hunter's moon." Her gaze rested on Anka. "Buy what you will, Anka, and hurry home. This is no time to venture out of doors. We are all at the forest's mercy tonight."

Anka bought a few goats' cheeses and set off back across

the square, noticing clusters of people here and there exchanging whispered news. The chill of fear was settling down over their village like a shroud.

Twigs snapped beneath her feet as she walked home, the route engraved in her memory. Over the stepping stones. Duck beneath the low-hanging oak branch. Walk across the carpet of springy moss that had grown over the path, fading back into the forest as if something beneath the soil was sucking it down. A little family of wild mushrooms had sprouted up overnight and Anka wandered over to them, her thoughts clouded with creamy mushroom soup and uszka – small pierogi stuffed with wild mushrooms made in the ear shape they were named for. Their stems were fat and white and as she picked them, she couldn't help thinking back to the maggots bursting under her fingers. Her stomach rose. She swallowed it down, folding the cloth back over the basket and standing. It wasn't until leaves crunched beneath someone else's foot that Anka realized she had left the path.

"Who's there?" she called out, swivelling round to search for anything moving between the trees.

A sudden wind shook their branches, the forest coming alive in a thousand whispers. Anka stretched out her foot, stepping nearer the path. A stick snapped and she froze, the leaves whispering louder still. A cold finger of fear stroked Anka's spine. Panic set in and she leaped for the path, running the remainder of the way home, her basket regurgitating mushrooms as she ran.

When she approached the cottage door, she slowed. She didn't want to admit that the forest had spooked her, nor that she had been so foolish as to wander off the path. It was this slowing, this pausing to breathe, that allowed her to hear voices creeping out from within. The door had not been closed properly. Anka was on the precipice, about to push it open, when she registered that the hushed conversation was not an exchange of village gossip but an argument, disguised within an old friendship.

"You have no proof of any of this," Babcia was saying, her voice sharp enough to pierce skin.

"I know the wolf walks among us, wearing a human skin," Babcia's oldest friend, Walentyna, said. "You know as well as I do the signs and the stolen chickens will not be the last of its prey. There are two more nights of the hunter's moon to come yet." She paused. "I noticed the new shutters on Anka's window. How long until the rest of the village turns its attention to her?"

Anka choked back a gasp. Footsteps sounded on the other side of the door and she stepped back, retreating down the path until the trees closed around her and she was swallowed by forest once more. Pressing a trembling hand to her mouth, she leaned back against a trunk until her legs steadied. Sometimes all it takes is one word, one sentence, to bring a mountain of truths down. To start an avalanche. That windswept afternoon, a secret spilled out into the forest, behind a door that ought to have been closed but wasn't quite. A sliver of wood. That's what came to make the difference between Anka knowing and not knowing.

That evening, as darkness thickened within the forest, Anka studied Babcia's face while she was occupied with dishing out gołąbki, stuffed cabbage leaves in a thick tomato sauce. "I heard what Walentyna said," she whispered.

Only the stiffening of Babcia's spine as she bent over the oven indicated she had heard. She shuffled over and placed a plate in front of Anka. The tomato sauce looked like chicken blood and for a moment, she was back there. Waking covered in their blood. Tainted with the rotten smell of death.

Babcia's chair screeched against the flagstone floor. She sat, closed her eyes. "There are many stories from my past that I have not yet shared with you. Ones which beat with a dark heart of their own."

The blood. The maggots. The new shutters. Anka clenched her fork harder. "If it concerns me then you owe me the story."

"I know," Babcia whispered. "But I am not yet ready."

"Babcia—"

"No, Anka. This is my decision – and my right."

"Fine. But you must tell me why Walentyna thinks that I had something to do with killing the chickens." The words left Anka's lips in a rush.

Babcia's expression turned to stone. "She doesn't."

"I heard you," Anka reminded her babcia.

"Eavesdroppers are destined to only learn partial truths,

107

never the entirety of the matter. Let that be a lesson to you." Babcia lifted her fork and pierced one of her cabbage rolls. The meat burst into the blood-red sauce and Anka's stomach roiled. She would never learn the truth now.

That night, sleep was a trickster. Each time she neared that slippery verge, it eluded her. How could she submit to sleep when she might be capable of untold horrors? And then she heard it. Metal clinking against metal. Not the sharpening of Babcia's crossbow bolts but something *else*.

She stole out of bed and crept from her room, taking care not to make a single sound. It was coming from Babcia's bedroom. She pressed her eye to the chink of light between the door and door frame, and there, in the glow of a single lantern, sat Babcia, slowly pulling thick iron chains out of the bottom of her wardrobe.

Anka stifled a gasp and crept back into her own bedroom. Pressing the door closed, her heart beating harder and harder until she grew dizzy, she returned to her bed. Was Babcia waiting for her to fall asleep so that she might chain her to her bed? Surely not, surely her imagination was just poisoned with old stories and older superstitions. *Chicken blood. Maggots. New shutters.* Anka squeezed her eyes tightly shut as if this would stop the conjured images.

The next time she opened them, the sky was bruised with sunrise and Anka was lying in the forest once more. A girl lying on blood-soaked ground. She screamed. Her scream soared above the treetops on wings of fear and pain.

Though her nightdress was torn, the blood did not belong to her. She was not the sole person lying in the forest, though the other stared up at the trees through milky, unseeing eyes.

"What have I done?" Anka whispered, biting down on one of her knuckles as she pulled her knees towards herself. As if she could retreat from the terror pounding inside her own skull.

Somewhere in the forest, a stick snapped like a spine.

Anka stumbled to her feet. She could not be seen with the body; the other villagers would hunt her down for such a crime. Her heart thudding like a hunter's drum, she fled. Running through the trees, faster and faster, sharp stones and twigs cutting into her bare feet, the forest hungering for a taste of her blood. There sounded another crack, closer this time, and she slowed. Yet before she could carve a new path, the nearby undergrowth rustled and a figure stepped clear.

"Anka."

"Babcia," Anka half-sobbed in relief. She went to her grandmother, needing to be gathered up in her arms. But Babcia was staring at her bloodied, torn nightgown. Her weather-worn face was a rictus of horror.

Anka swallowed her tears. "I–I did not—"

"I know." Babcia closed her eyes for a beat too long. Panic swelled up Anka's throat and she turned and retched into the undergrowth. Babcia must have closed the distance between them, for Anka felt her hands smoothing her hair from her face while she emptied the contents of her stomach. When nothing more was left, she slumped to the carpet of moss. They were far from the path now, though she supposed that did not matter. A life had already been lost. *No*, Anka amended, *a life has been taken – by me.*

"Where is the body?" Babcia asked.

Anka pointed.

Babcia sighed and passed Anka a small bundle she had been carrying – her red woollen cloak. "Cover yourself as best you can and wait for me." She trudged away.

Anka could not have followed her anyway. She rested back against an oak, her thoughts swollen with fear. The villagers had a name for the beast that lived within her. A skin-walker. When the hunter's moon rose in the sky, she would slip into the skin of a wolf and hunt through the forest. The sole cure for a skin-walker was death.

A gloom of a day followed the sunrise. Thin, ragged clouds were all that could be spied between the gaps in the canopy. They looked like mangy fur. Babcia's slow, shuffling walk echoed between the trees before she appeared.

Anka stared up at her miserably. "What did you do with the body?"

"It is better you do not know."

Anka dragged a hand through the earth at her feet. "You knew this could happen. This is what you've been hiding from me."

Babcia hesitated. "Yes."

"How did you find me?" Anka asked.

"I heard your scream. I recognized the pain in it. It guided me to you. Come, Anka, we must return now. Before we are found."

Though it was day, the forest was dark as dusk. The cottage flickered with candlelight as Anka sat before the fire, watching her torn nightgown blacken and burn. Hiding the blood that had stained it. Stained her with murder. Her fingers trembled around her mug of tea. Babcia had sweetened the black tea with berry jam, yet it tasted bitter on her tongue. Or perhaps that was the tang guilt carried.

Babcia eased into her rocking chair. It creaked like branches in the wind and Anka jumped. "I am sorry that I did not prepare you better for this. I had hoped that perhaps you would never need to know."

"I need to know now." Anka forced her spine to straighten, her chin to lift. "Tell me everything."

And in the oldest traditions of their land, within their tiny crooked cottage, within an ancient forest that had witnessed myths stalk through its trees, Anka heard her babcia's tale by firelight. When all was said and done, she stared at her grandmother, her tea placed down on the floor, long forgotten. "I don't understand," she said slowly.

"My dear child." Babcia leaned forward and held Anka's hands in her gnarled ones. "I am cursed to be a skin-walker. Now that I am old, it does not happen as often as it once

111

did. I had thought it had disappeared. Yet this month, something strange and unsettling has taken root in the forest, in me. I can feel the wolf in my bones, hungering for the hunt."

A fresh horror was dawning on Anka. She glanced down at her grandmother's hands. Was it the flicker of firelight or were her nails dark as claws? She shivered, resisting the urge to pull her hands free. "You killed those chickens. And that … that man." A hard lump formed in Anka's throat. It felt like a piece of gristle. She tried to swallow around it but could not. "But you replaced my shutters? If it was you then how did I find myself in the forest?"

Babcia bowed her head. "I pulled you from your window." She let Anka's hands slip free. "Something within me must have recognized you before it was too late. Smelled that we were kin and turned its hunger elsewhere." Babcia's sigh was thready. "I failed at keeping you safe, away from all of this. When you were younger, your father took you away when I felt the change coming. Your mother carried the curse of the skin-walker and though he did not, his love for her could have outshone the moon."

Anka knew this. It had left her father a shadow of a man when her mother perished of an illness when she was too young to remember. Her father had finally followed some years later, an infection setting in after he had caught himself on his woodcutter's axe. The forest was unforgiving like that. "Had mother been ill or was it this … this curse that took her away from us?" Anka whispered.

The fire crackled, sending shadows skittering around the cottage as Babcia admitted, "It was the curse."

Anka stared into the fire, her eyes burning.

"She was often sick, and the change requires strength. After a time, her body could not bear it any longer and she faded away before my eyes," Babcia continued as Anka angrily swiped her sleeve at her eyes. "Not long after she died, I went to find Baba Jaga."

Anka jolted. "Did you find her?"

Babcia's face was illuminated by the fire, the lines that crept around her eyes digging in deeper. "I did."

"She's real? Her hut is really there?" Anka sat forward, her shawl slipping over her shoulders.

Babcia tutted. "Of course. Haven't I taught you anything? All of the Old Ways are real. You've seen the crumbs left by the domowik. Felt the spirits watching you in the forest even if you haven't glimpsed them for yourself. And Baba Jaga is the realest of them all." She rocked back, the runners of her chair grating against the wooden floor as she spoke on. "Her hut lies west of the lake. Far enough that you wouldn't stumble upon it by chance. Not so far that you couldn't discover it for yourself if you had reason to seek her out."

"What was she like?" Anka asked, the story creeping into her imagination, distracting her from the stench of burning flesh the fireplace seemed to be emitting now.

Babcia's eyes were unfocused as she stared into the past, that murky clump of memories and regret. "A dark and terrible beauty. With teeth that would drag your mind free of your body if you gave her the chance." She looked at Anka, her tone turning urgent. "If you ever find yourself in her presence, do not let your guard down. Conduct your business in careful words and half blinks and when you're free of her hut, run. Run until your legs cannot carry you any further and your lungs are afire."

Anka nodded. "They say she's a witch."

"*Nie.*" Babcia shook her head. "We call her a witch as we have no other word for her. But she's something more. Something greater and more powerful than we mortals might understand. I had heard stories that she could reverse the curse on our family, rip it from our blood and bones and send it cowering into the darkest shadows of the forest."

Hope flared within Anka. Small and fragile, but there nonetheless. "Can she?"

"I have never known the old stories to lie. Yet I am ashamed to admit I could not ask her. I saw her only from a distance and my legs turned to water. Despite the wolf that lurked within me, I did not have enough courage that day. Nor any days since." Babcia shuddered.

"The curse on our family," Anka slowly repeated. Realization was sinking in, ice travelling along her veins.

"I am sorry, Anka. You too carry the curse in your blood."

"No," Anka whispered.

Their cottage door slammed open. A dark figure stood on the threshold.

Anka leaped to her feet, her heart thudding like a branch tapping on the roof.

The figure stepped forward, into the pool of candlelight. Walentyna. The forest was dark at her back, the day shrouded. Walentyna's eyes flitted warily between Babcia's and Anka's.

"She knows all," Babcia said wearily.

Walentyna nodded. "The villagers have noticed one of our own went missing in the night. Under the hunter's moon. They are talking of keeping us all beneath one roof tonight. To learn which of us walks in the skin of the wolf."

Anka inhaled sharply. "But that would mean—"

Walentyna nodded once more, heavy with sadness. "You must leave before sunset."

Babcia pushed herself up to standing, and that slow movement tore at Anka's heart. "No!" she cried out. "My babcia cannot leave her cottage, where would she go?" Her grandmother was too old for such a journey, and the pity in Walentyna's face showed that she too knew Babcia would not survive this.

"Nor will I have my granddaughter where it isn't safe," Babcia fretted, closing a hand around Anka's. A flicker of anger rippled through her eyes. "We must think of a plan."

But the thought of Babcia struggling through the forest with no warmth, no good food, no clean clothes, ripped something inside Anka free. "I will seek help."

Walentyna looked puzzled. But realization was settling on to Babcia. "No."

"Yes," Anka said with fierce determination. "You told me that the old stories say that Baba Jaga can remove this curse, that those stories never lie. If anyone is powerful enough to do this, it would be her. I will go to her and ask her to take this curse, this death sentence, away from us. Before tonight."

"You will never find her." Babcia's hand tightened around Anka's.

"You said her hut was west of the lake," Anka said. Her determination was blazing hotter than the fire now. "I have heard those same stories, that you can tell where she lives because no bird will sing near her, and the trees will all point away from her hut."

"She will devour you alive," Babcia whispered.

Anka wrapped her cloak tighter around herself. "I have the blood of the wolf in me; I'm not afraid of her." She pulled her hand from Babcia's and marched out into the forest.

Somewhere in the distance, a storm was swelling. Anka felt it in her bones. The air was damper, mossier, and the ancient trees seemed to crackle with anticipation. She ventured deeper into the forest. It grew ever-darker, the smell pungent with decomposing leaves and wet bark. Anka was used to the depth of dark in the forest – layers of cloud and leaves often left them living by candlelight as if it were the midnight hour – yet this darkness set her nerves crawling with anxiety. It was different, thicker. As if

Anka had crept into a shadow. Or death itself. She gritted her teeth, thought of Babcia's dwindling hours back in the cottage, and walked faster.

Some hours later, she reached the lake. It was eerily still. She bent to drink from it, ice-cold water trickling down her throat too fast and making her cough. It echoed out across the water. She turned west and continued walking. It was scarcely a hundred steps later when Anka first became aware of the silence around her. The chirp and hum of the forest had fallen away. No nests perched among branches, no animal tracks pressed into the moist earth, not a bird nor deer could be glimpsed. Even the trees leaned in an odd configuration, their trunks arching away from the hint of a clearing. *This was it.* Anka had one chance to plead for Babcia, her grandmother's life a fragile beating thing in the palm of her hand. This gave her the strength to walk into the clearing.

Then she saw it.

It was something from an Old Tale conjured into being. The crooked house clambered up towards the sky, ramshackle boards nailed together in contortions that shouldn't have held. Slightly raised off the ground too. Anka squinted at the mess of thistles, weeds and thorns knotted around the base of the hut. She could just make out the shape of scaly talons folded beneath the wood. Her feet stilled with shock. Chicken legs, that's what the Old Tales claimed rooted Baba Jaga's hut to the earth. Chicken legs that could pick up the crooked wooden house and run through the forest. No wonder Baba Jaga always captured her prey in those stories; nothing could run faster than magic. It stank of magic too. An odd and twisting scent that intoxicated Anka. Lured her feet into moving closer. Until she reached the little gate at the end of a path that led to the door.

Only then did the wooden door open. Its hinges screamed. And Baba Jaga stepped outside and sniffed the air. She slowly turned towards Anka.

Anka's insides curled with terror.

Long midnight hair poured down to her feet, her lips a deep, true red, that might have been painted in blood. She wore a gown that echoed the shades of the forest: verdant greens in leaf-shaped snatches of material pieced the bodice together, darkening around her waist to the colour of moss after a storm, falling into fluttering skirts of chestnut and oak. Rings of blackened thorns crept up her pale skin, winding around her arms and ankles. She was a nightmare made flesh. Though it was her eyes that sent Anka's thoughts crawling with fear. They were missing. And where they had once been, the empty sockets were sewn up, thick black stitching that Baba Jaga was pointing in Anka's direction. Her lips suddenly carved a smile across her face. It made her stitches gape and Anka faltered.

"I wondered when you would be paying me a visit," Baba Jaga said.

Anka was still at the little gate. Its wood was faded, the fencing around the hut peeling with age. Years of neglect and forest living chipping away at it. Baba Jaga's eye sockets lingered on Anka. After a long pause, she turned away, leaving Anka feeling strange. Bereft of her attention.

"Do come in," Baba Jaga called, her voice a sweet melody trickling down the white path between her gate and the front door she had disappeared back into.

Anka followed it.

She tripped along the path, the jagged pieces of white stone forging an uneven pavement. She made the mistake of glancing down. She was walking on skulls. Hacked into smaller pieces to form a yellowing mosaic, here and there a jawbone or eye socket stared back at her. Anka's vision warped with fear. Before she could convince herself otherwise, she flew down the rest of the bone path, her feet skimming along it, unwilling to stand upon the skulls of Baba Jaga's fallen prey.

Inside, the witch's hut was narrow. It vaulted up high above a central room, a huge fire pit in the middle. Bunches of herbs twisted with little bones and raven feathers were strung along the two gloomy windows. At the back, the hut led off into what looked like a warren of darker cave-like rooms.

"How do you know who I am?" Anka stood on the threshold, Baba Jaga the far side of the fire pit. It spat and crackled between them, a smoking barrier that lent Anka a shred of confidence to speak her thoughts.

"I smelled the wolf. It has rooted within you." Baba Jaga waved her fingers, her elongated nails clacking against each

other. "It slinks through your veins, stronger than blood."
Once more she lifted her face to Anka's, the stitching
through her sockets stark against her face.

Anka struggled to breathe. "Can … can you see me?"

"I see all. My eyes merely clouded my true sight. Since
I carved them out, I see things much clearer." She pointed
to a battered rack of shelves between the windows. A jar of
milky fluid held two eyeballs, their mottled flesh floating in
the liquid, pupils following Anka as she pressed a hand to
her mouth, catching the scream that pulled at her insides.

Baba Jaga stepped forward, her dress rippling in the
heat of the fire. "Speak. Ask of me what you will," she
commanded.

"I want my babcia to be safe at home."

"You are creatures of the forest, not greatly unlike
myself. This is your home."

Anka shook her head. "I need something to strip the
curse from my family's bloodline. I know you have magic;
it can't be a hard task for someone as powerful as you."

"No."

Anka stared at her. "No?"

"You belong in the forest." Baba Jaga watched her
through the flames. "Foolish girl, wishing to undo that
which makes you special." She threw a pinch of something
from a fogged jar into the fire. The flames shot higher,
darkening until they were black as night. Tiny figures
danced through the burning scene – no, not dancing, Anka
realized, they were running. Fleeing the great wolf that

tracked them. Crying out for help. Anka recoiled. Was this a vision of the future? Her future, one in which she became more beast than girl?

Baba Jaga pointed a long fingernail at Anka. "This is the truth of you. The wolf has always crept inside you, biding its time. I can separate you no more than I could strip a lake of its water."

Anka pressed trembling fingers against her eyelids. Time was trickling away, fast and faster, and soon the sun would set and the villagers' test would commence. "Please. There must be something you can do so we can stay in our village. Some magic that would suppress it so no one needs to know about it. And … so we don't hurt anyone." Panic reared its head within her once more. "I don't want to be a monster."

Baba Jaga slowly tilted her head to one side. Her eyes in the jar turned with her movements, watching her from behind. "Why are you so certain that you are a monster?"

Scraps of blood-soaked memories. Waking in the forest covered in maggots. The man her grandmother had ripped apart with her teeth. Anka shook her head in desperation.

"This is all the help I can offer." Baba Jaga tossed a small vial through the smoking fire. Anka caught it as it exited the other side. "With this, you can shed your skin under any moon or sun. Become the wolf." The stiches on her eye sockets tightened as she widened her eyes with delight. "I will enjoy watching you devour the villagers that you once lived among."

"Thank you," Anka said by rote, tucking the vial

into her cape. Despair threatened to overwhelm her; she couldn't think of the monster lurking within her, the one which Baba Jaga seemed determined to unleash; she needed to think of a different plan to save Babcia, but time was already her enemy. She cut a path to the door. She had risked her life entering this being's hut and if Baba Jaga was not going to help her then she needed to leave. But the hut was crooked and filled with things sharp as teeth. Anka felt only a pinch as she caught her shin on a jagged shelf-edge. She paused, glancing down. Blood welled.

And Baba Jaga's nostrils flared.

Her rational words had disguised the discord within the witch. But nothing stays hidden for long. It curled out of her like smoke. Anka backed towards the door as Baba Jaga began singing, her melodious voice dropping in timbre, the words scraping out harshly. "Truths are twisted in your head, mustn't let you join the dead."

Anka backed away another silent step. Just two steps to the door now. If she didn't breathe, perhaps the witch would not hear her, would forget there was a girl standing in her hut.

"Oh, how your blood whispers to me," Baba Jaga said suddenly.

Anka hurried back another step. The door swung shut behind her with a thud that shook the floorboards. Anka glanced to the side – the witch's eyeballs were following every move she made.

"I must not eat the wolf," Baba Jaga sang. "Must not eat

the wolf that will wreak carnage on the forest. Must not carve out those pretty, pretty blue eyes." The witch wore her hunger plain on her face and Anka shivered; the hunger was a stronger beast than the witch's willpower and all trace of her schemes and rationale were lost now. *She will devour you alive*, Babcia had warned. Anka's conversation with Baba Jaga had dulled her fear that the witch would carve her apart, made her more afraid of that which lurked inside Anka. But then she had cut herself, her blood summoning the witch's true nature. Anka ran to prise up one of the windows, but it was nailed shut. Little lines of teeth crusted the edges. They bit into her hands when she pulled at it.

And closer and closer Baba Jaga stole, arguing with herself. "Must not scoop out her marrow and suck her bones clean."

Running to the second window, Anka found it a twin to the first. Tendrils of panic slipped down the back of her neck. The fire smoked up in a thick column that filled the hut with suffocating heat, turning the entire round hut into one large cauldron. She had to escape.

"Must not lick her salty blood from my fingernails."

Anka risked a glance back. Baba Jaga's face was carved open into a terrible, wide smile. Too wide, like a snake that had unhinged its jaw to gobble down its prey. The witch's teeth were on display, each one ending in a wickedly sharp point, teeth for piercing flesh and biting into bone.

Anka ran.

Charging through the black smoke choking the hut,

past the witch herself, Anka ducked her head and dove into the cave-like rooms winding out the back. Hunched over, she scrabbled through the low rooms. They had been built straight on to the clearing; there was no wooden flooring here, just more jagged bone and loamy earth. Jars of murky substances were stuffed into the corners along with stacks of bones, strings of flesh rotting on them, and ravens with their feathers plucked. Anka gagged at the stench. She searched for a door or window but there was none. She would have to break her way out.

A scrabbling sounded at the entrance. Anka froze as Baba Jaga lowered her face in to stare after her. Anka held her breath as Baba Jaga slowly turned her head from side to side. Listening. Then she sniffed. Her head swivelled to fix Anka in her sightless gaze. Anka kicked at the wooden wall. The planks held fast. Kicking again and again, desperate to break free, she watched Baba Jaga crawl towards her. The witch's face was contorted with hunger, saliva dripping from her sharpened teeth, her long twisting fingernails stretching closer and closer to Anka's hand.

"Such soft skin, little wolf. Soft enough to wear," she purred.

With a loud splintering, Anka's foot broke through the wood. And became stuck there. Ramming her other foot at the wood holding on to her, keeping her entrapped in the witch's lair, Baba Jaga's words registered in the part of her brain that wasn't screaming in fear. She turned to stare at the witch's dress. Her skirt was a patchwork of human skin, joined by the same thick black stitching that had sewn her empty eyelids back together. Moaning in horror, her legs shaking, Anka kicked harder and harder, even as Baba Jaga gripped her wrist and began to pull, dragging Anka's torso towards her.

"Just one … little taste…"

The wood bent and cracked, a plank snapping free.

Baba Jaga stiffened as if the sound had roused her lucidity. Her breath was sour on Anka's face as she let out a single growl. "Run."

Anka reached through the wood, clutching handfuls of undergrowth that stung and pierced her with thorns, and pulled herself through the small opening. The wood scraped painfully against her, but she could taste the fresh air; she was almost free now…

Baba Jaga rocked inside the hut, groaning. "Her blood calls to me. Just a little taste; no harm can come of one little taste."

Tugging herself out from the back of the hut, Anka fled.

She raced home against the setting sun. The sky bled in between the branches and leaves above as the forest succumbed to a pitch-black night. With nothing to light her way, Anka stumbled and fell until she reached her village. She reached her cottage just as two men were leading Babcia away in chains. Her bent figure was dwarfed by the men, her shuffling walk slower than usual as the thick iron gnawed into her ankles, her wrists. Anka's heart splintered at the sight. "No," she whispered to herself, then louder. "No!"

As she made to run after her grandmother, a pair of arms caught her. "She has confessed," Walentyna told her, holding her back. "Her sacrifice has ensured your safety. They do not know your bloodline is cursed; they believe her lie, that she was once bitten as a child."

Anka sank to the forest floor. "But they'll kill her for this."

Walentyna's nod was grim. Her mouth downturned with sadness. She let Anka go. "Yes. But you were all she cared about."

In a sudden spark of defiance, Anka leaped to her feet and raced down the path towards the village, following Babcia and the men that had put her in chains. Walentyna called after her, but the wind stole her voice. Her heart beating fiercely, Anka soon caught sight of Babcia once more: she was in the cobbled village square where a gossiping crowd had gathered – their once-friends and neighbours. Anka hid behind an oak, sheltering in the infringing forest as she watched on. She couldn't hear the words being spoken, but she saw the horror worn on the villagers' faces, saw the fear in Babcia's eyes as she searched the treeline, saw the whispers that rippled through the square like a winter breeze. And she saw the lantern light glint off the woodcutter's axe as he stepped forward, his blade raised.

"Stop!" Anka ran out from behind the trees. "You cannot kill her."

"Anka, this is no place for you," Piotr, one of the men and a leader of their small village council, spoke. "Leave at once."

Babcia raised her head and met her eyes. She nodded. "He is right. I do not wish for you to witness this." Her grey hair, usually so neat and tidy in its bun, was straggled and windswept. She looked old and vulnerable and Anka's fingers curled into fists. She did not leave.

"Very well," Piotr replied, his patience fraying. He gestured to the woodcutter. The other man forced Babcia to her knees.

"No!" Anka rushed towards her grandmother. The villagers moved away from her, their faces carved with fear. Fear of her, she realized. A hairbreadth away from reaching her babcia, something heavy slung over Anka, catching her in place. She whirled around in confusion. Chains. Before she could muddle through her thoughts, she was dragged to her grandmother's side.

Anka suddenly wished she could become a wolf. Big and powerful enough to break through iron with her jaws. And there was a vial in her cape which would allow her to do just that. The councillor who had caught Anka in chains had taken pity on her and they were loose. Leaving enough space for one hand to wriggle into her cape pocket and liberate the vial.

"Anka," Babcia murmured at her side. "What are you doing, child?"

"I'm going to save you," Anka said fiercely.

"If you spare my granddaughter, I shall not fight," Babcia told the gathering. "I shall go easily knowing that my light, my joy will live on." Her voice cracked.

But Piotr only laughed. High and reedy, it sent anger coursing through Anka's veins. "You are in chains," he hissed at Babcia. "And I shall not be making you any promises now that your reign of terror has ended." He stepped back, signalling the woodcutter to take his place.

The woodcutter stepped into position. Anka could not tear her gaze from his axe. The metal was dull. "You have one final chance to stop this," she declared, glaring at the villagers she had once considered friends and family. Her fingers trembled around the vial, clenched in one hand.

But nobody moved. Save Babcia, who was telling Anka that she loved her. And the woodcutter, who had raised his axe above her head.

Anka drank the entire vial.

Her blood began to bubble like the witch's cauldron. And then one by one, her bones cracked and broke, snapping in new directions as she screamed. Her chains shattered. Gasping for air, she stretched out a hand to the woodcutter, grabbing his axe. A hand that suddenly reached, coated with fur and ending in claws long and sharp as daggers. The woodcutter relinquished his axe at once, falling back with Piotr as they both stared and stared at her.

Anka fell forward, landing on four large paws. She growled her anger at the villagers, who were screaming and fleeing the square as she sniffed the air, scenting her prey. Wasn't she here for a reason? She could no longer remember. Something sliced into a soft part of her, and she yelped, turning to see the man that seemed to be the source of her anger. *Piotr*, she suddenly remembered, snarling at the bloodied dagger he held. Anka pounced, her paws landing on his shoulders and knocking him to the ground. She bit down. At first, curious for a taste, then, a deep, gnawing hunger overtook her and she forgot her own name as she feasted.

A cruel laugh sounded.

Anka glanced up. Baba Jaga stood where the trees met the square. Holding her eyes in their jar and watching. Watching... Anka looked down. Horror seized her, a white-blind panic that swept over everything. *No*, she tried to scream out, but her mouth was no longer a mouth but a muzzle, wet with blood.

Baba Jaga's voice came to Anka as if she were standing right next to her. "Do not fight it, young wolf. This is your nature; blood is your birthright and the forest your home."

Anka tried to shake her head, to argue against the witch, but she could not. She was trapped in a body which she did not know.

"Look up," Baba Jaga said.

Above, the hunter's moon gleamed in the sky, red as blood. Anka stared at it. It called to her, singing a tale of hunger and hunting that coiled around the young wolf's bones as the witch smiled her terrible smile. Anka lifted her head and howled at the moon. A second howl echoed at her side, and she whipped around, fixing her sight on another wolf with greying fur.

"Now go and hunt, my wolves," Baba Jaga whispered, flicking her long fingernails at the dark line of trees. "Bring me something bloody and gruesome to chew on."

The two wolves ran into the forest. It was alive with a thousand heartbeats, with the creak and rustle of trees, with the creep of things that once would have filled the young wolf with horror if she could remember who she was. They ran and howled and hunted, snapping up all that dared to leave the safety of the path, for that is the law of the forest.

And the forest belonged to them now.

SAINT CLOVER

MELINDA SALISBURY

One of the altar servers winks at me across the church during the incensing of my grandmother's casket. Cherubically blonde, he doesn't look much older than me, though he must be because it's Monday, a school day for everyone not attending funerals.

He winks again during the Eucharistic Prayer.

If he's still an altar server at his age it means he either seriously loves God, or he loves *someone* who loves God and wants to make them happy. But clearly he doesn't love this person, or God, enough to keep from winking at grieving girls in a church. I don't know what to do. How do you deal with flirting over your dead grandma's coffin?

I get a third wink while we sing "Holy, Holy, Holy".

But then he lifts his hand to his right eye, removing something and wiping it discreetly on his alb, and I realize he wasn't winking at me at all. A violent blush erupts across my cheeks and I lower my head like I'm deep in prayer to hide it. I don't think it says good things about me that I'm spending the funeral of my last formerly-living grandparent wondering whether an altar boy is coming on to me. He's not even cute.

To my left, my mother is rubbing circles on my father's back, making static crackle along the polyester of his cheap suit. He's not crying, none of us are; we weren't close to my grandma, and from the emptiness in the church, it seems no one was. Besides us, there are only two older women stood together halfway down the left side, and a young guy alone at the back. I've never seen any of them before, and he's the only one who looks truly sad; white-knuckled grip on the back of the pew in front of him, eyes black holes in a blood-drained face. He *is* kind of cute, or at least he might be if he didn't look so haunted.

Then it's time for communion and I'm surprised when my dad stands and shuffles out of the pew, my mother following. I am not in a state of grace, so I stay kneeling as the two women also join the queue for the Host. I wonder if the sad boy is still here, graceless like me, and I subtly turn to look as I put the Bible back in the rack of the pew in front of me.

A prayer pamphlet slips out from between the thin pages and falls to the floor, distracting me. When I pick it up, intending to put it back, I flip it over to see which saint it is.

St Clover.

I've never heard of her.

My parents didn't have me baptized, send me to a Catholic school or have me confirmed, three of the many reasons they and my grandma weren't on the best of terms, but I know a lot of the saints anyway, because five years ago I decided that I was going to be a nun.

Obviously, I didn't really want to be a nun; I was twelve and overnight my body had become a stranger, betraying me constantly in weird, embarrassing ways and I hated it, especially the attention that came with it. So, it seemed like the best thing to do was marry Jesus and put all of the awkwardness and uncertainty firmly behind me.

My mom and dad couldn't stop laughing as they told me *no* and that *I'd thank them for it later*, but that only made me love the saints even more. My favourite, St Lucy, who plucked out her own eyes because a man said he admired them; St Agatha, whose breasts were torn off with tongs when she refused to renounce her devotion to God and get married; St Brigid, who begged God to make her ugly so men would leave her alone. It felt like it was only a matter of time before an angel of the Lord appeared and told me what to do to get out of this mess, and I couldn't wait.

Instead of an angel I got two cups of cheap vodka and orange soda at Isabella Maxwell's fourteenth birthday party, followed by my first kiss with her brother, and I forgot the saints when he asked me to be his girlfriend.

We dated for two months before he dumped me for a high school freshman who'd let him put his hand inside her shirt. I like to think my relationship with Jesus might have lasted a little longer and he definitely would have been less horny.

My parents file back into the pew for the final prayers and I stand, shoving the pamphlet for St Clover into my pocket. When I remember to glance towards the back of the church, the semi-cute boy is already gone.

Graciously you chose St Clover as patroness of the hungry, and of flowers, and so I beseech thee, Lady of the Blossom, to hear me now at the time of my need. St Clover, grant me flowers, sate my appetites and fill my stomach with the gifts of the bounteous earth. St Clover, I pray thee come and deliver me from my hunger.

I examine the novena to St Clover on the way home from the cemetery. There's something about it that seems off but I can't put my finger on it. Trying to puzzle it out, I turn it over and peer at the picture of the girl on the front. Her hair is long and dark blonde, her glassy blue eyes cast upward to heaven. In one hand she holds a rose and in the other a peony, both pink, blousy in full bloom. She's wearing white – a gown that looks like a regular T-shirt to me, and it makes her seem modern, more like the Marto kid saints than my former beloved saints. She's also vaguely familiar and I try to place why.

I open the pamphlet.

I blink, surprised, because it's really short; two-thirds of the page is taken up by a beautiful illustration of a silver platter heaped with roses and peonies. It says St Clover died of *a consumptive illness*, aged seventeen, and was buried under a mountain of flowers. It doesn't mention when or where she lived, what she did to become canonized, or even when her feast day is. I pull my phone out of my pocket and open the browser, ignoring the messages.

"I hope you're not making plans for tonight," my mother says from the driver's seat, eyes flicking between me in the rearview mirror and the empty road ahead. "I know we didn't see her much, but she was still your grandmother and we owe her respect. Family time."

"She can go out if she wants," my dad replies, ever-mild and conflict-averse. "I don't mind."

He cried at the graveside when we threw dirt on to the polished surface of the coffin. No one else from the church came to the burial, not even the sad boy.

"I'm not making plans. I was looking something up."

My mother's eyes move back to me, drop to the pamphlet in my other hand, then back to the road.

"What's that?"

"Just some pamphlet I found at the church. St Clover. Do you know who she is?"

"Tell me you're not starting with all that again," my mother says as she turns on to our street.

"No, I'm not *starting with all that again*. I just want to know who St Clover is. If you don't know, I can search for her."

"Do not take that tone with me, Cicely, today of all days."

By the time we pull on to our drive we're in a full-blown argument about my attitude *today of all days* and neither of us notices my dad get out of the car and let himself into the house until we hear the front door slam behind him.

I'm grounded, and my mother has taken my phone and laptop until tomorrow so I can't look St Clover up. Instead, I lie on my bed and read the pamphlet again, the single sentence about how she died, and the novena.

In the top of my wardrobe is a box full of my old saints' pamphlets – I was too superstitious to throw them out – and I get it down, tipping it on to my bed and collecting them up. I arrange them around the one of St Clover, novena-side up, and I spot instantly what struck me as so strange when I first read it.

St Clover's pamphlet doesn't mention God, Jesus or even Mary. The prayer for intercession is only to St Clover.

I scan the others; Father, Son, Holy Spirit, Mary, Mother of God, all of them mention at least one of the Trinity, or the Virgin, but not St Clover's.

There's a knock at my bedroom door and, anticipating my mother, I scoop the pamphlets up and place them back in the box, leaving only St Clover's out.

"Come in."

To my relief, it's my dad.

"I came to find out if the prisoner would like some gruel? Or chicken Alfredo, as it's also known."

"Do I have to come down for it, or can I eat in my cell?"

He gives a wry smile. "I think we can arrange to bring it to you in solitary. What are you doing?" He nods at the box.

"Just checking something."

"Is that what you had in the car? Can I see?" He points at St Clover's pamphlet, and I hand it to him.

"It's weird, right?" I say. "No feast day, no mention of God, or why she's even a saint."

He turns it over, mouths the opening, and frowns. "She could be one of the newer ones? Maybe the church is trying to appeal to the younger generations. I'm surprised there isn't a QR code on there, scan her into an app and collect her like a Pokémon."

I laugh. "I would have loved that, can you imagine? Mom would have gone ballistic. Ballistic-er."

He shakes his head, not rising to the bait. "I'll bring your pasta up. Want garlic bread?"

"How is that even a question?" I ask. Then, when he reaches the door: "Hey, Dad? I'm sorry about Grandma. And for fighting with Mom earlier. I didn't mean to make today worse for you."

"Thanks, Cissy." He crosses the room and rubs the top of my head. "It's OK."

When he's gone, I pick up the pamphlet and I read the novena aloud.

"Graciously you chose St Clover as patroness of the hungry, and of flowers, and so I beseech thee, Lady of the Blossom, to hear me now at the time of my need. St Clover, grant me flowers, sate my appetites and fill my stomach with the gifts of the bounteous earth. St Clover, I pray thee come and deliver me from my hunger."

There is no amen, so I don't add one.

Almost as soon as I'm done, my dad knocks again with a tray loaded with chicken Alfredo, garlic bread, and half a sleeve of cookies, and I smile.

"Prayer granted," I say, scooping a forkful into my mouth and burning my tongue.

"What?" my dad asks, but my mouth is full of pasta. "Well, I'll leave you to it. Bring the dishes down?"

I nod, already refilling my fork.

I eat it all, hungrier than I'd thought. Thirty minutes later I sneak downstairs and find the other half of the cookies, a family-sized bag of chips, and three apples, and I devour all that too.

Without my phone alarm I wake up late the next morning and have to rush to get ready for school, skipping breakfast so I can print my homework. By the time my mom drops me off, my stomach is cramping with hunger.

She drives away without saying goodbye because we're still not speaking to each other, and I race into school. I left a muesli bar in my locker last Friday and now I shove it into my mouth, barely getting the paper off before my teeth are tearing at it. I have never in my whole life been this hungry before; I feel as if I'm seconds away from going full Meat-O-Vision and imagining my classmates as walking, talking burgers and hot dogs.

I hear a disgusted sound to my right and find Isabella Maxwell, whom I have not been friends with since her brother dumped me back in eighth grade, watching me with a curled lip.

"What is wrong with you?"

Instead of answering, I open my mouth wide, showing her the mash of oats and raisins on my tongue before I swallow it down and take another bite.

"Get help," she says, then slams her locker door.

It bounces back open as she walks away, but I don't call after her. Instead, I look around and, when I realize the hall is empty, I peer inside.

Our whole school career, Isabella and her brother have brought brown bag lunches to school because their mother thinks cafeteria food is trash and some part of me, the hungering part, has remembered this. I watch my hand, moving as if it doesn't belong to me, reach in and take out her lunch, shoving it under my sweater before I close both of our lockers. Then I head to the bathrooms, hide in a stall and consume tuna fish on wheat, a little bag of seedless black grapes, an apple, and a carton of strawberry milk, ignoring the bell when it rings. It takes everything I have not to eat the paper the sandwich was wrapped in too.

I don't feel at all guilty for what I've done. In fact, I wish I could do it again. I'm still hungry.

At lunch I buy two cheeseburgers, some fries, a salad bowl, another tuna sandwich, a brownie and three cartons of chocolate milk. The lunch lady gives me the eye, but she says nothing as she rings it up.

I eat one of the burgers at the cutlery station, still chewing the last of it as I carry the tray to where my friends wait at our usual table.

"So you're not dead, then?" Zoe, my best friend, looks up from her BLT. There is mayonnaise at the corner of her mouth.

"Dude, not cool," Addison, sat beside her picking at a Caesar salad, stage-whispers.

"I wasn't talking about the funeral, I was talking about not answering my messages," Zoe says.

"Hello? Cissy? You OK?"

I can't stop staring at the mayonnaise.

"What?" Zoe says.

I manage to stop my finger just before it becomes obvious that I'm planning to scoop it right off her face myself, instead tapping the edge of my lips.

"Oh. Thanks." Zoe's tongue darts out to lick the mayonnaise away. "So? Why didn't you reply?"

When I swallow, my mouth is thick with saliva and I pierce one of the cartons of milk and drain it before I can talk.

"Sorry." I sit down and shove a handful of fries into my mouth, then another, trying to keep my hands occupied. "I got into it with my mom yesterday and she took my phone."

"Jesus, are you training for an all-you-can-eat contest?" Addison asks as I lift the second cheeseburger to my lips.

"Just hungry," I say.

Across the hall, Isabella Maxwell is in the lunch queue. When she spots me across the room she scowls, and I pick up my tuna sandwich, biting into it to hide my smile.

At lunch the next day I get the same again, only I add an extra cheeseburger and a BLT to see if that will help me get through afternoon classes without going wild with hunger.

"Do we need to stage an intervention?" Zoe asks, staring aghast at my plate.

I nod through a mouthful of fries, then roll my eyes.

"Hollow legs, my mom calls it when my brother eats like that," Addison says.

Addison is delicately nibbling a slice of pizza. Why didn't I get pizza too?

"Your brother is a running back," Zoe says. "He has to eat, like, nine thousand calories a day to stay in shape."

"It's not that many."

I leave them bickering and head back to the line with a cheeseburger in hand to buy the last slice of pizza.

"Hollow legs," I manage to say to Zoe and Addison,

both watching me with wide eyes as I cram it into my mouth when I get back.

When I get home that afternoon my parents are still at work, so there is no one to stop me ordering two large pizzas with the works – I've been craving it since the meagre slice I had at lunch. I eat it all, hunched over like a hawk mantling my prey, and when both pies are gone, I lick the grease from the boxes before I take them out to the trash and bury them under a bunch of stuff.

My dad pulls into the driveway just as I'm wondering if it's too late to order another.

"What's for dinner?" I ask when he enters the kitchen. "I'm starving."

St Clover, I pray thee come and deliver me from my hunger.

I spot it right before I hand my English homework to Ms Doherty the next morning, written at the end of the second paragraph.

"Can I take this?" she asks, as I pull my hand back.

"One second. I just need to check something."

I ignore her protest and turn away, scanning the rest of it.

My heart is thundering in my chest. I wrote the essay Sunday night, the day before the funeral, before I'd even heard of St Clover, and I haven't opened it since except to print it out.

"Cicely, are you handing that in or not?" Ms Doherty asks.

"I am, I just … there's this extra line. I don't know

142

where it came from. Some kind of technical glitch, I guess? Can I cross it out or will that affect my grade?"

Ms Doherty gestures for the paper and I hand it over, gripping it tightly until the last.

"What's it from?" she asks, spotting it immediately.

"I don't know," I lie.

She hums thoughtfully. "I guess we can cross it out, it's only one line. By the way, did you get the notes you missed from Monday?"

But she's lost me because I've spotted a packet of strawberry licorice in her half-open desk drawer and my fingers are already snaking out towards it. I've been starving since lunchtime ended, sucking on the sleeve of my sweater in class to try to keep my stomach from rumbling, but now, in the face of actual food, I lose control.

"Can I?" I ask, hardly waiting for Ms Doherty's shocked nod before I take a fistful of licorice, more than I leave behind.

She closes the drawer deliberately, staring at me.

"Well, you'd better get to your next class," she says finally, as I suck my fingers clean.

In maths, I find the prayer scrawled angrily over every page, obscuring my work, and have to pretend I've forgotten my book. The same in AP biology, and in government, and not just in my notebooks, but the textbooks too: every single page has St Clover's novena adorning it violently.

I consider eating the pages to solve both of my current

problems and barely manage to stop myself. In the end, I have to sit on my hands and I play the grief card, pretending I've forgotten my books, and get away with it.

Later that night, I pile mac and cheese on to my plate, spooning it from a dish meant to feed eight, ignoring the way my parents look at each other as I go back for seconds, thirds, fourths. I shovel it into my mouth, filling my fork as soon as it's emptied like I'm on a production line.

"That was supposed to feed us tomorrow too," my mom says.

"Sorry. Is there dessert?" I ask, as I scrape the last bit out of the dish.

"Aren't you full?" my dad asks.

I'm not. I'm really not.

Four days after my grandmother's funeral I wake up and find myself stuck to my sheets. I peel them away in the dark, ignoring my stinging limbs, my attention already on what I'm going to have for breakfast.

It's as I climb out of bed that I smell the blood and I flip the light on and stare at the sheets, at the thing printed across them in crimson.

.regnuh ym morf em reviled dna emoc eeht yarp I ,revolC tS

For a moment only the word "reviled" makes sense, but then my brain, prompted by the weird capitals at the end, makes sense of it. I gaze down at my skin to see it written there, right way around, across my arms and my legs and my stomach. When I look in the small mirror on the vanity, I see it on my back too, etched wherever I could reach. The only place I haven't defiled is my face.

My fingernails are rusted when I examine them and in the back of my mind I know I should be horrified, screaming for my father, terrified that I somehow contorted and scratched St Clover's words *into my skin* and slept through it all, but all I am, all I *feel*, is hungry. All I can focus on is filling the cavern in my belly. I look at the crusted blood on my hands and think about jelly donuts, pancakes, chicken and waffles.

I dress in long sleeves and jeans, then I strip the bed and take the sheets to the laundry room. On the way I put a frozen lasagna in the microwave and take a handful of cereal from the box on the side. Back in my room I eat the lasagna between putting fresh sheets on the bed, scraping the container with my finger.

"Did you put laundry on?" My mom enters my room without knocking and I spin to hide the lasagna tray behind me.

"I got my period in the night," I lie. "I changed the sheets."

She sniffs the air. "Have you been eating up here?"

I shake my head. "Nope. I was just coming down for breakfast."

"I'm surprised you can eat at all after last night's banquet."

"Guess I'm in a growth spurt," I say. "Do we have eggs? I'm thinking scrambled eggs and waffles, with bacon. And syrup. Do we have sausage links?"

"Cicely, it's a school day."

"It's Friday. Practically the weekend already. And we're up early enough. I'll even do the washing-up."

My mom throws her hands in the air. "All right. I guess I should be grateful that you're not trying to diet yourself into nothing."

I laugh, too loud and too long.

The following morning I wake up early, creeping down to the kitchen before it's light, and make two rounds of toast, then two more, and two again, eating them dry and butter-less, until the entire loaf is gone. I find bagels in the freezer and toast those too, nibbling at a still-frozen one when the toasting takes too long. It's not enough. By the time my mom comes in to make coffee, I have water boiling for pasta while I microwave a burrito.

"All right, enough now. Do you want to explain yourself?" she asks, hands on her hips.

"I told you, must be a growth spurt."

"I'm talking about the mirror."

I can't wait any more. I take the burrito from the microwave before it beeps.

"What mirror?" I manage to ask before I start eating.

"The bathroom mirror. The writing on it."

I shake my head, not wasting my mouth on speaking. The burrito is still cold in the middle, but I don't care.

"Come on. Who else could it have been? And my best lipstick too. I thought we were friends again."

I pour penne into the water, the entire bag.

"Wait, are you making pasta? Cicely, it's six in the morning."

"It's for lunch," I say, heading towards the door. "I'm meal prepping."

"Where are you going?"

"To see what I'm supposed to have done to the mirror."

I finish the burrito on the stairs and immediately my stomach cramps, wanting more.

St Clover, I pray thee come and deliver me from my hunger.

It's written in my mother's lipstick across the mirror.

I don't remember writing it. Like the words in my schoolbooks and on my body, I don't remember doing it.

Suddenly I am gripped by searing panic because something is very, very wrong with me. I'm doing things I can't recall; I can't stop eating, can't stop stuffing myself; I'm hurting myself and I don't know why or how to make it stop.

Without warning my stomach gurgles loudly, then spasms, and I cry out, bracing myself against the door as waves of pain crash through the centre of my body.

"Cicely?" I hear my mom's tread on the stairs and my dad coming out of their room.

The pain comes again and my mouth floods with thin, metallic-tasting saliva and I know what's coming. I barely make it to the sink before everything inside me rises and I open my mouth.

I vomit flowers.

Peonies and roses pour from my lips, filling the sink, cascading on to the floor.

"What the hell?" my dad says.

I turn to him, petals still spilling out of me.

I'm sent back to bed.

My dad is in the hall on the phone to the doctor while my mom sits with me, feeding me sips of water. But I can't even keep that down and now the room stinks of flowers. Every time it happens my mom rolls her eyes as if I'm doing it to be dramatic, which is cold, even for her.

My dad comes in. "We have to take her to the emergency room."

"Ben, is that really necessary?" my mom asks.

Though I'm surprised by how she's acting, how *absent* she is about it all, I do agree with her.

The hunger that has consumed me since the funeral is finally gone and the writing has disappeared from my skin, as if it never was. I bet if I checked my books, I'd find them normal again too. If it wasn't for the vomiting flowers, I'd say I was completely fine. That it was over.

"It's probably just a twenty-four-hour thing," my mom adds.

"And if it isn't?" My dad is bewildered, on the verge of tears, staring at us in turn. "What if we only have a short window to get treatment?"

I shrug.

My mom stands. "I'm just saying let's give it another

hour or two? Please? If it wears off by itself, we're going to spend a tonne of money for nothing and I doubt our insurance covers this."

That's the magic phrase.

"Fine," my dad says, shaking his head. "We'll wait until after lunch. But if it happens again, we're going, no argument."

"Get some rest." My mom gestures my dad to leave with her, and he leans down, kissing my forehead.

"Yell if you need anything," he whispers, and I nod.

As soon as they're gone I take a sip of water, then retch, bringing up a waterfall of peonies. My dad has been taking them from me, flushing them away, so these are the first ones I've touched. They're silken and delicate, tearing like tissue paper when I pull at them. It's the dryness that I find strangest; they shouldn't be dry, but they are.

St Clover's pamphlet is on my bedside table, mercifully overlooked by my mother, and I pick it up, staring at the cover.

Part of the "L" in her name has rubbed away, around a quarter of the way down, so now it looks more like an "i", St Ciover. I open it up and stare at the picture, of the platter of roses and peonies.

Buried under a mountain of flowers.

I take another drink and bring up a shower of tiny rosebuds.

I don't think it's a doctor I need.

*

149

Just after lunchtime my parents drive me to the emergency room, where the triage nurse is on the verge of kicking us out until I drink the cup of water on her desk and spew flowers on to her computer. After that I'm sent straight to an examination room, where I repeat my party trick for another nurse, who doesn't even bother filing paperwork, bringing a doctor directly to me.

He clearly thinks I'm faking, but orders blood tests, an X-ray and an ultrasound. When they show there is not a single thing inside my stomach, the doctor asks me to take a sip of water. I immediately regurgitate a bouquet into my lap and this time he looks at me with real fear in his eyes.

"This isn't possible," he says.

Captain Obvious.

"You must be able to do something," my dad says. "For God's sake, this is the best hospital in the state."

The doctor lets out a long breath, shaking his head in confusion. "We're still waiting on the bloodwork. In the meantime, we'll admit her for observation and put her on fluids. I'll also reach out to some colleagues, specialists in gastroenterology, and see if they've treated something similar."

And so I am admitted to the hospital, given a private room and an IV. But no sooner has the nurse inserted the cannula into my hand and the saline has started to flow than the flowers flow too, from my lips to the bed, then the floor.

The nurse, who is wearing a tiny silver crucifix, falls

to her knees and makes the sign of the cross, staring up at me, and I get the impression the doctor is a hair away from doing it too, only stopping himself at the last second, remembering what and where he is.

My dad starts to cry and I sit in my self-made bed of roses, until the doctor has the presence of mind to take the needle from my arm and put a stop to it. Then everyone leaves to talk about me. No one touches the flowers.

They keep me in overnight, my dad staying with me, crumpled in a chair by the bed. A nurse comes in to record my vitals every hour, so neither of us gets any rest. I finally fall into a kind of sleep after my dad tells me he's going to find coffee and when I wake, seconds or minutes or hours later, feeling eyes on me, I expect it to be him.

But it's the boy from the church who is standing by the door, wearing a black jumper and a haunted expression as he stares at me.

As soon as he realizes I'm awake, he bolts from the room, and by the time I reach the corridor, dragging the IV behind me, he's gone.

"Did you see that boy?" I ask a passing orderly. "Blonde, slim, black jumper?"

He looks at me curiously, then shakes his head, and I go back into my room.

I think the boy is something to do with this – in fact, I *know* it. I know it in the same way I know this is all happening because of St Clover. It's the same feeling that makes you

151

wake in the middle of the night because something is wrong, or tells you to cross the street because you know, without even needing to look, that you're being followed. There is a knowing that is formed in the blood and the guts and the bones of you, and this is that kind of knowing. The boy and St Clover are tied together and unravelling them might be my only hope.

I'm unceremoniously discharged from the hospital that night. The nurse with the crucifix comes in and tells us we can go, and when my dad asks why, and what's going to happen, she says breezily that I'm fine, the doctor said so. He asks about the flowers and she says "What flowers?" before leaving us.

Baffled, I get changed back into my clothes, my dad signs the forms, and we go.

"We'll find somewhere else," he mutters as he bundles me into the car. My mom is in the passenger seat, on her phone, and she stares at me as I put my seatbelt on.

"What are you doing?" she asks, her voice rising.

"We're taking her home," my dad tells her as he gets in.

My mom frowns, then nods slowly. "Home. OK."

On the way back we drive past a man on a street corner holding a sign that says *Hell is already here*, and I have an idea.

"The church," I say. "The one Grandma's service was in. I want to go there."

It is worrying that they don't argue, glancing at each

other in silent communion. Then my dad swings the car around and we drive across town towards St Mary Star of the Sea.

I undo my seatbelt before he's stopped the car.

"I want to go in alone," I say as I open the door and climb out.

I don't give them time to disagree, striding up the steps of the church and through the thick wooden doors.

The boy is in the same pew he sat in at the funeral, and he looks at me, wild-eyed.

"Don't run," I say, before he can bolt again. "I just want to talk."

I approach him slowly, sliding down the pew and sitting a few feet away.

"You were at my grandmother's funeral," I say. "And the hospital."

He nods.

"How did you know I was there?"

"I followed you home after the funeral. I saw you pick up the leaflet. I've been watching you." He speaks softly, reverently.

"Creepy, but OK. Do you know what's happening to me?"

He nods again.

"What's your name?" I ask him.

"Rafael."

"Rafael," I repeat. Like the archangel. "Who was St Clover?"

"Clover," he says, his expression pained. "Clover is my sister."

That surprises me. "Your sister is a saint?"

He shakes his head. "No. Not before…"

I wait.

He swallows, his throat bobbing, and when he continues his voice is hoarse, as if he's been crying. Or screaming.

"We were at our cousin's wedding here, and she found this leaflet thing in a Bible. She thought the girl on the front was cute. Then she read the prayer on the back, said it was weird, but put it in her purse anyway. The next day, she started eating everything, and I mean *everything*; getting up in the night to make food, eating it still frozen, even eating raw meat—"

I shudder, grateful to have escaped that fate.

"And then, a few days later, she drank a glass of milk and started puking up flowers."

"Then what happened?"

He is silent for a long moment before he replies. "She disappeared. I don't know what happened to her."

All the air rushes from my body, my blood thickening like molasses.

My voice sounds far away when I say, "Is that what's going to happen to me?"

Rafael shrugs. "I don't know."

We're both silent for a long moment.

"How long did it take?" I ask finally.

"Nine days."

Of course. You say a novena aloud for nine days and then the saint will answer your prayer. I read it the night of the funeral, right before my dad brought my dinner up and the hunger began. I count the days back. Seven.

Shit.

Then I remember something else. "Wait. You said she thought the girl on the front was cute. It wasn't St Clover – your Clover?"

Rafael shakes his head. "When she took the booklet, she wasn't on the front. It was a red-headed girl. St Coleen."

A chill ripples down my spine.

"So you're saying the pamphlet *became* St Clover after she vanished?"

He closes his eyes in confirmation.

"Did you bring it here? Is that why you were at my grandma's funeral?"

"No." He is vehement, his eyes burning into me. "I wanted to talk to the priest, to find out if he knew anything. But he thought it was a prank. He won't see me now."

"What about the internet?" I ask. "There must be someone out there. Some forum, or something on the dark web."

"We looked." Rafael is miserable, desperate. "There was nothing. Nowhere."

For a moment we both fall silent.

"So … that's it," I say. "In two days I'm going to turn into some kind of haunted pamphlet and if some other person finds me and is ridiculous enough to read the novena out loud, the curse, or whatever it is, will pass to them. And it'll just keep going and going. Why isn't this in the news? Why isn't it being reported? It doesn't make any sense. I saw doctors. There are notes on my medical records. What?" I ask Rafael, whose expression has become grimmer. "What now?"

"Everyone forgets."

"What do you mean, 'everyone forgets'?"

"Our parents don't remember Clover. None of her friends remember her. Our teachers. Her ex-girlfriend. Her boss at the bookstore. I think the only reason I haven't forgotten her yet is that we're twins… How do you forget the other half of yourself? But every day that passes, I lose her a bit more." He gives a bitter laugh. "You know, I couldn't remember her name until you said it just now."

"But all of her things. Her bedroom? Photos of her? Do they just disappear?" My voice is razor-edged with panic as I think of the nurse who'd been so dismissive when she'd discharged me, as if she'd forgotten getting to her knees before me. "Rafael, please."

A tear makes a shining path down his face. "They can't see them. Our parents are calling her room the guest room. When I said 'what about my sister', they laughed and told me it was too late for them to think about having a second child. They don't remember her at all – their own daughter." A sob escapes him, echoing in the cavernous church. "And I think someday soon, I won't either. Or you."

I think of how distant my mom has been in the last day, how surprised she looked when I got in the car. Almost as if she didn't know me.

My fate throws its arms wide before me.

But I will not step into them willingly.

"There has to be something," I say. "There has to be."

I leave Rafael weeping in the church and return to the parking lot to find my parents' car is gone. I figure they've just found somewhere else to park, so I pull out my phone and call my dad.

"Where are you?" I ask when he picks up.

"Who is this?"

A cold sweat breaks over my body. "Cicely. Your daughter."

"Oh." He pauses. "Right. Well, we're at home. Where are you?"

The hairs on the back of my neck stand up. "I'm still at the church."

"Why are you at the church? You know what, doesn't matter. Dinner's almost ready, hurry back."

I choke out a goodbye and then stare at my phone.

It's really started.

I fake a stomachache so I don't have to eat with them. They startled when I let myself in, both of their gazes blank and wary, like they couldn't place me, before it came to them: *Cicely, our daughter.*

In my room I open my laptop and search for everything

I can find about chain letters and curses, reading page after page of creepy pastas, conspiracy theories, film plots, but nothing that's real. I stay up all night, wishing for coffee but not wanting to deal with the roses, exhausting every avenue I can think of. When I finally fall asleep as the sun rises, I'm no closer to an answer.

I sleep through most of the penultimate day of my life. No one gets me up for school, and Zoe and Addison don't text to find out where I am. When I make my way downstairs, no one is home, though both of them should have finished work by now and neither of them have messaged me to say they'll be late.

When I shower, water gets in my mouth, and even though I don't swallow, I still have to spit out petals.

I push down the fear, my gorge rising, tasting of roses; it's not over yet. It can't be. I have one idea that might work. The priest wouldn't listen to Rafael, but I can *show* him it's not a prank. There might be one thing he can do to break the curse.

Once I'm dressed, I walk across town to St Mary's.

"I need to see the priest," I tell a nun who is dusting the confessional boxes.

I expect her to argue, to tell me that I can't just demand to see him, but she looks me up and down, tells me to take a seat, and then disappears through a door to the side. A few moments later the priest comes out, dressed in an ordinary black shirt and trousers. If it wasn't for the white collar, you might not even know he was a priest.

"How can I help you, my child?" he asks. "You're not part of this congregation."

"No. My dad was, and my grandma. You did her funeral a week ago. Cicely Armitage. That's my gran. Was my gran. And me too. I was named for her."

"Ah, Cicely. She was one of the first to welcome me when I joined the parish. I'll miss her a lot. How can I help you?" He sits down next to me, keeping a respectful distance.

"I think I need to take Holy Communion, urgently. I've committed no mortal sins and I haven't eaten or drunk anything recently." Not since Saturday morning, in fact.

"Are you baptized into the Catholic faith?" he asks, but I can tell from the tone he knows the answer; I bet my gran told him.

I consider lying but decide it won't help.

"No, but I really need it. It's a matter of life and death."

It's the only thing I can think of. That if I take the Host into me, it might burn the curse out, countering St Clover's fake holy with something real. Like how a crucifix can keep a vampire back.

The priest shakes his head. "Cicely, you must know I can't give you Communion unless you're a Catholic. What I can do is give you a blessing—"

"I don't need a blessing!" I shout, the words echoing back to me as he flinches. "A blessing won't help. Please, you don't understand, this time tomorrow you won't even remember me – no one will – and I'll be gone. I'm going to disappear."

The priest's face darkens and he stands. "Oh, I know what this is. Your friend was here, playing the same game, talking about flowers and saints."

"It's not a game. It happened to his sister, and now it's happening to me. Look, I can show you—" I get up, moving towards the font, planning to just drip a little water into my mouth, but he blocks me, looming over me, face puce with barely contained fury.

"Young lady, I know your family is grieving, so I'm loath to tell them what a wicked trick you and that boy are playing, but if you don't leave my church now and stop this nonsense, I will speak to your parents about this. And the authorities too."

When I leave the church, chased out by the furious priest, I know it's over. That tomorrow I will find out what happens when you become a saint.

Because I have nowhere else to go, I go home for the last time. The front door is locked and I have to ring the bell.

When my dad answers, there is a second where I can see he doesn't recognize me.

"Oh, Cicely," he says finally, but he's still slow to let me in, as if he's not totally sure he does know me.

I flee to my room before he can decide I'm a stranger.

On the last day of my life, I feel strangely calm. I get up and put my things in order. I change the sheets on my bed, dust and vacuum the room. Even though I know they'll never read them, I write goodbye letters to my parents, and to Zoe and Addison. Then I write a detailed account, starting with finding the pamphlet and then day by day what happened to me, and post it online. I doubt anyone will ever read it, but I had to do something.

By the time I finish, St Clover is almost gone from the pamphlet, her blonde hair now almost the same brown as mine, her eyes darker too. She's filled out a little, and instead of the white T-shirt she wore nine days ago, now she has on the same kind of rose-coloured shirt I put on this morning. It matches the flowers she holds perfectly. The "v" and the "r" in her names are the only parts still not fully changed, but even as I watch, I see the "v" turning clockwise and the corner softening, the "r" rotating the opposite way and growing a tail.

I wait in eerie, saint-like serenity on my bed, until I hear my dad come home from work, then I creep down the stairs. I don't speak to him, I don't let him know I'm there, I just watch as he goes to the fridge, takes out the milk and drinks from the carton, something he'd never dare do if my mom was home. When he goes through to the lounge I sneak into the kitchen and out of the back door, where I hide at the side of the house until my mom's car pulls into the drive. She looks tired as she gets out, but then her face lights up and my dad appears with a mug of coffee in his hands for her. When they go into the house together, I leave.

I spend the early evening walking, not knowing where I'm going, pulled along by something tugging in my stomach, another hunger or instinct, following my feet until I reach the woods on the outskirts of our part of town. I know what I have to do now. I walk into them for an hour and then, in a grove of sycamores, I find a spot and begin to dig a grave with my hands. It gets dark, and the moon rises, high and bright and yellow as butter, lighting my way.

When the grave is deep enough, I climb inside, arranging my hair around me.

Then I eat the first mouthful of dirt.

It isn't long before the grave reeks of peonies, but still I keep putting earth in my mouth, pushing the petals aside to reach it and swallowing as much as I can. The world above me turns pink as I transform mud into roses, and finally, I become Holy.

Graciously you chose St Cicely as patroness of the hungry, and of flowers, and so I beseech thee, Lady of the Blossom, to hear me now at the time of my need. St Cicely, grant me flowers, sate my appetites and fill my stomach with the gifts of the bounteous earth. St Cicely, I pray thee come and deliver me from my hunger.

THE VISITING GREY

KAT ELLIS

1

Gemma's nails dug into the front passenger seat of her mum's car as they hurtled down the lane towards the Bowen family's cottage. She'd only been there once before when they'd basically grilled her about her babysitting credentials. Gemma's mum had driven her then too. Even though it hadn't been pouring with rain that day, the car had still skidded into the overgrown hedges lining the lane, leaving a web of scratches all over the Fiat's paintwork. The steep, mud-slicked lane certainly hadn't improved in the last week. But then neither had Gemma's mum's driving.

For the millionth time since they'd moved from Manchester to Glyn Newyn – a tiny village skulking deep in the heart of Wales – Gemma asked herself what the hell her parents had been thinking. Or her dad, mostly. He was the one who'd grown up in rural Wales (not Glyn Newyn, but somewhere just as grim-sounding) and he'd been filling her mum's head with rose-tinted ideas about them buying a place with enough land to grow their own veg and spending their free time hiking through the hills or whatever. In the three months since the move, Gemma's parents hadn't even mowed the lawn, let alone planted a veg garden. And their brand-new hiking boots still had the stickers on. Now they were firmly in December's clutches and facing months of ice, frost, snow and even more snow.

Gemma hated it here. *Hated* it. She'd left all her friends, and all the cool things she used to like doing, back in Manchester. There'd be no more trips to Immersive Gamebox in the Arndale Centre. No catching the latest films at the Printworks or wandering the Christmas markets that would be spread throughout the city centre at this time of year. She had none of that in Glyn Newyn. For the first time in her sixteen years, Gemma felt … lonely.

Gaming was the only thing keeping her sane, at least until school started up again after Christmas. Except she'd already burned through her collection of games, and her parents refused to buy her the new Xbox game she *needed* for the sake of her mental well-being unless she – *shudder* – earned it. So here she was, on her way to babysit for a nine-year-old weirdo in the middle of nowhere.

The first time she'd seen the cottage, Gemma had thought it looked like something from a dark fairy tale: all ivy-strangled stone walls and crooked chimney pots, with poky little windows peeping out here and there. It was almost invisible to her now, though; the wet, wintry night had crawled down into the valley, swallowing it like some dark leviathan.

Gemma opened the car door before her mum had even come to a complete stop. With no streetlights, it was impossible to see much of the cottage beyond the glow of the lantern hanging above the front door.

"Hey! Wait a sec, will you?"

Gemma leaned her head back inside the car. "What is it? I'm already late, Mum."

"One minute won't make a difference. Listen, James's dad said he could give you a lift home when they get back later, but if there's a problem, just give me a ring and I'll come and get you. OK?"

"Got it. Thanks."

"And you've got your phone on you?"

Gemma blinked slowly. *Obviously* she had her phone. "I'll see you later, Mum. *Loveyoubye!*"

She swung the car door closed and hurried across the yard to the cottage, skipping over the deepening puddles. There was no doorbell at the front door, only an old-fashioned knocker. She rapped it three times, then once more for the hell of it.

Gemma turned to wave to her mum, but the car taillights were already snaking their way back up the lane. A faint haze surrounded the twin red, glowing points, making it seem as though some demonic creature was watching her, its glare searing the rain to mist.

Mist? Oh, that's just perfect.

The Bowens would probably decide the weather was too bad to risk going out and leaving their precious little James behind. No babysitting meant she'd have wasted most of her Friday evening and be no closer to getting her new game.

"Gemma."

Had someone just said her name? The sound had been barely more than a whisper above the thrumming downpour, but it sent a shiver down her spine like the scratch of a damp fingertip. It seemed to have come from the shadows at the edge of the yard. Gemma peered into the darkness. Something moved there – a faint twist of grey on black, but she couldn't tell who, or what, it was.

"Hello? Mrs Bowen?" she called, but there was no answer. No movement now, either.

Probably just the wind.

Although there didn't actually seem to be a breeze at all this evening. If anything, the air was unnaturally still.

Gemma gasped at the sound of the door opening behind her.

"Ah, Gemma, there you are!" Mr Bowen greeted her, his loud voice and cheerful Welsh accent breaking whatever eerie spell had momentarily sunk its claws into her. "Come in out of this rain, won't you?"

Gemma cast one final glance at where the movement had been, but the darkness held its secrets from her. Stifling a shiver, she pulled her coat tighter around her and stepped across the threshold into the cottage.

This place is so creepy, she thought. Then she painted on her most responsible babysitter smile as the door closed with a creak behind her.

2

"You remember James, don't you?" Mrs Bowen said, not looking up from where she was digging through her handbag.

"Yeah, of course. Hi, James," Gemma offered with a wave. James was a sallow-looking boy, with dull brown hair and eyes the colour of a stagnant pond. She usually got along fine with young kids, but last time she was here she'd called him "Jamie" by mistake, and he'd hissed at her like a feral cat.

James stared at Gemma in silence while his parents continued rushing around, making their final preparations to leave. Gemma raised her eyebrows at him, like *can you believe how much fuss they're making about one poxy night out?* James just kept staring. She'd never known a child who could look so serious while wearing a onesie.

"Right, I think we've got everything. Help yourself to drinks and snacks, and James usually listens to an audiobook to get to sleep, so you won't need to read to him or anything like that."

"No problem," Gemma said as she ushered the Bowens towards the front door. They were almost – *almost* – outside when Mrs Bowen caught hold of Gemma's wrist. The woman's face twisted into a peculiar frown.

"I know you're a sensible girl, Gemma," she said, voice low, like she was about to share some awful secret. "But … don't be upset by anything James says, will you? He can be a little peculiar at times, but he's a good boy, really. He just gets a little fixated on things, you know?"

"Yeah, of course." Gemma nodded in what she hoped was a reassuring way. She'd already figured out that James was a bit on the strange side but was surprised his mum felt it strongly enough to warn her about it. She went to free her arm from Mrs Bowen's grip, but the woman didn't let go.

"I probably shouldn't say this, but we only get the chance to go out for our anniversary, and I just worry… You see, last year the babysitter couldn't even last one evening. Promise me," Mrs Bowen said, her voice practically a hiss. "Promise you won't leave him on his own."

"What? God, no, of course not! I'd *never* do that." Seriously, the last sitter couldn't even hack one night with the kid before bailing? That was so not her.

It's not like I've got anywhere more important to be on a Friday night, anyway.

It had taken Gemma a while to accept that she was, in fact, stuck in Glyn Newyn for the foreseeable future, and by that time all her new classmates had decided she was too stuck-up to bother with.

I'll make more of an effort after the holidays, she thought. *New year, new me and all that.*

Making friends with the local teens had to be a better prospect than spending her weekends hanging out with James, at least.

"Good." Mrs Bowen released her grip on Gemma's arm as she turned her gaze on James, still hovering in the kitchen doorway. "And you'll be on your best behaviour tonight, won't you? Go straight to bed without any fuss, just like we talked about. And stay in your room, yes?"

James nodded silently.

"Good," Mrs Bowen said, smiling now as she turned back to Gemma. "There'll be an extra tenner for you if everything goes well, OK? And call me if you're worried about anything."

With that, Mrs Bowen finally allowed her husband to steer her out through the front door, leaving Gemma alone with James.

"Fancy playing a game or something?" Gemma asked.

He stared at her.

"Don't suppose you've got an Xbox, have you?"

Silence.

It was going to be a *long* night.

It turned out James didn't have any kind of games console, so they were stuck with a pack of yellowed playing cards Gemma had found at the back of a drawer. She'd explained how to play rummy, and even though he hadn't appeared particularly interested while she went through the rules, James seemed to have a perfectly good handle on how to play.

"Do you know what tonight is?" he said.

Gemma glanced up from her cards. It was the first time James had spoken since his parents left. She'd almost forgotten what his voice sounded like, with the same mid-Walian accent all the locals had, only with a faint lisp.

"It's your mum and dad's wedding anniversary, isn't it?"

James shrugged, laying down a card. "Do you know what else today is?"

It almost sounded like James was gearing up to tell a joke or something. Gemma felt highly sceptical, but played along anyway. "No, what is today?"

"It's midwinter night."

"Oh … cool," Gemma said, trying to sound enthused. "That means it's the shortest day, right?"

"And the longest night. Do you know what happens on the longest night?"

"What happens?"

"Mari Lwyd comes knocking."

OK, if this really was a joke, the kid needed to work on his delivery.

"Who's Mari Lwyd?" Gemma asked dubiously. The name sounded Welsh, but she hadn't met anyone named Mari in the village. "Is she someone local?"

Gemma flinched as the lights flickered overhead, then flared back to full brightness.

"The Mari Lwyd isn't a person," James answered matter-of-factly. "It's the grey mare. A trapped spirit." He frowned, looking very much like his mother had just before she left with her whispered warning to Gemma. "It comes in midwinter, calling door to door, and it seems to like ours in particular – maybe because we're all alone out here at the far end of the valley. The Mari Lwyd is searching for souls to drag down to the underworld to try and bargain for its own soul back."

Gemma bit the inside of her cheek so she wouldn't snigger. This kid was ridiculous, and he looked so serious with it. "Is this a story you learned at school?"

James ignored her question. "If the Mari Lwyd doesn't claim at least one new soul each midwinter, it can't get back to the underworld. But it can choose who it takes and if you're kind, it leaves your soul alone."

Souls? The underworld?

This seemed like kind of a scary story for a kid James's age to be learning at school, but maybe it was just some local folklore he'd picked up. Either way, it sparked a glimmer of interest in Gemma.

"What does Mari Lwyd look like?"

"It's a monster made of leathery skin and brittle bones," James said. Gemma narrowed her eyes, wondering if this was the beginning of some horrible nursery rhyme she'd never heard. "Its body is shrouded in a thin grey veil, a horse's skull its mask. Be sure to feed its hunger before the beast can ask." James glanced pointedly at Gemma. "That's

171

the only way to keep the Mari Lwyd from taking you – invite it in and offer it food."

With that, he looked away and carefully laid a card on top of the pile between them.

"Okaaaay."

"You know when the Mari Lwyd is coming because you hear its song." James's voice had dropped to a murmur, and Gemma had to strain to make out his words. "Then it knocks on the door, and if you don't answer, it finds another way in. And when it gets inside, it eats your soul."

Gemma narrowed her eyes teasingly. "Are you trying to scare me with some creepy ghost story? Is that what this is?"

James blinked at her. "Why would I do that?"

"I think maybe you like to play jokes on poor, unsuspecting babysitters. Well, I'm not falling for it, mate. Nice try, though." She grinned so James wouldn't think she was telling him off. The last thing she wanted to deal with was a cranky kid for the rest of the night.

James's gaze snapped to the clock on the mantelpiece. "It's nearly time for bed. I should go and brush my teeth."

Gemma stared after him as he disappeared into the hallway. What kind of kid *volunteered* to clean his teeth and go to bed?

Feeling more weirded out by this turn of events than by the Mari Lwyd stuff he'd tried to sell her on, Gemma listened for his footsteps climbing the stairs. Instead, she heard what sounded like someone fiddling with the front door. She hurried out into the hallway. Sure enough, James was there, pulling back the deadbolt.

"What are you doing?" Gemma demanded.

He flinched, then turned around with a deliberately vague expression on his face. "Just checking the door before bed."

"I locked it after your parents left," Gemma said, then stepped past James to re-bolt the door. When she checked, she saw all the other locks had also been undone.

"Don't do that," James said sharply. "The Mari Lwyd won't like it."

"The Mari Lwyd can jog on, then," Gemma said.

"No, you don't understand; it's dangerous!"

"It's more dangerous to leave it unlocked, I promise," Gemma insisted.

"It's not! You have to listen to me, Gemma. Last year—"

"OK, fine," she said, sensing a meltdown looming. She pulled the bolt back again and held up her hands in a placating gesture. "See? It's unlocked. Danger averted."

James stared at her again, frowning deeply.

"Go on upstairs and start your audiobook. I'll be up in a bit to check on you."

"And you won't lock the door again?" he asked, features still tight with what looked almost like worry.

"Nope. Go on." She shooed him upstairs, waiting until he shuffled into the bathroom before quietly re-locking the door and returning to the living room. Gemma collapsed on to the couch with a massive sigh, then started scrolling through her socials, checking what all her old friends in Manchester were up to. She couldn't seem to focus, though. Shoving back to her feet, she went and checked the front door locks again, half expecting to find a horse's skull staring in at her through the frosted window next to it.

Ugh. Why am I letting this kid get inside my head?

Mrs Bowen really hadn't been exaggerating about James being peculiar. Not even a bit.

3

Gemma stood at the rear patio door, looking out over the garden. The darkness had intensified since she'd arrived, the shadows no longer separate but a deep grey mass looming beyond the windowpane. She imagined it might almost have its own distinct feel were she to run her fingers through it. Like velvet, perhaps. Or maybe it would feel like some unearthly fingers brushing back against her own. Gemma pulled the heavy curtains closed as a shiver ran through her.

"Gemma."

She paused halfway back to the couch. Gemma had almost forgotten about the voice whispering her name when she arrived at the cottage, but the faint sound repeated itself now, as insubstantial as a breath and just as effective at raising the hairs at the nape of her neck.

"James?" she said, not loud enough for her voice to

carry upstairs, if that was where he was. He'd hear it if he was hiding somewhere nearby, though. "It's not time for messing around now. Go to bed and I'll be up in a bit to check on you."

But it wasn't James's voice that answered. From the patio door, Gemma heard a distinct *scriiitch* – as though a long fingernail was being dragged against the glass. She flung open the curtains again, throat tight as she braced herself to come face to face with someone outside – *probably the grinning face of a devious nine-year-old*, Gemma tried to convince herself – but what she found instead was … nothing. There was nobody standing beyond the patio doors. She craned to see if someone might've ducked down out of sight, but anyone hiding from her had done a good job of it.

"James?" she called, unable to hide the slight tremor in her voice. "Are you outside?"

Her breath misted the glass. Gemma wiped it away with her sleeve, and as it cleared, she found a face peering back at her, pale and hollow-eyed. Gemma yelped as she scrambled back, instinct taking over before her brain caught up to the fact that the face in the window had been her own.

"Just a reflection, you knob," she breathed, leaning heavily against the arm of the couch as she tried to slow her racing pulse. And that scratching sound was probably just a tree branch or something scraping against the window in the wind.

Except there is no wind tonight.

"I told you not to lock the front door."

This time, Gemma screamed as she whirled to face the open hallway door. James stood there, blinking up at her like she'd lost her mind.

"God, James! Don't *do* that!" Gemma snapped, nerves overriding her usual patience. "Get back up to bed *now*. And you're not having your audiobook on after messing with me like that. And I'm pretty sure your mum and dad would be angry if I told them you snuck outside when you're supposed to be in bed."

She meant it very much as a threat, but James only squinted at her in confusion.

"I haven't been outside, Gemma. I just heard you call my name and came down to see what you wanted."

"I didn't…" But Gemma trailed off as she realized she *had* called James's name a minute ago. Still, he was probably just saying that. Because she'd heard *someone* whisper her name, and then tapping on the window, and they were the only two people here.

Then she noticed James's feet – bare and clean. If he'd been creeping around in the dark outside the cottage, they would be filthy. Gemma barged past him to check the hallway for discarded shoes, but there were none.

It really hadn't been James out there. But if it wasn't him … who was it?

Someone who knows my name. Who knew I'd be here tonight.

Only four people fit that description, and they were James's parents and her own – none of whom would prank her like this.

"James, go back up to bed," Gemma said, trying to steady her voice. There was no way she could let James know how jittery she felt. "Go to sleep, OK?"

Gemma was already pulling out her phone as his footsteps creaked back upstairs. She dialled the number Mrs Bowen had given her. It only rang three times, but by then Gemma was already starting to feel like a fool.

Why was she letting a few strange noises get to her? It was probably just a bird or a tree branch or something tapping on the window. And maybe the Bowens had a wind chime or something that made a sound like her name. OK, maybe that was a stretch, but there was probably some non-serial-killery reason she'd heard her name being whispered.

"Hello?"

"Oh, hi, Mrs Bowen. I'm sorry to interrupt your anniversary dinner, but I think there's someone outside… I mean, I think there might be? I'm sure I heard someone say my name and tap on the window. Do you have any idea who it could be? Should I call the police?"

"Hello? Gemma? Are you there?"

Gemma pulled the phone away from her ear and frowned at it. "Mrs Bowen? Can you hear me?"

"Hello? Gemma? Is everything—"

The sound of Mrs Bowen's anxious voice cut out at the exact moment the lights in the cottage died, plunging Gemma into darkness.

4

Her breath came in sharp gasps, the sound too loud in the sudden dimness. The dying embers of the coal fire gave Gemma barely enough light to see her surroundings, but she was grateful for what little light it did offer. Shadows flickered and stretched up the walls. Gemma's eyes darted to follow them, expecting at any moment that one might unpeel itself from the plaster and lunge at her.

I've been watching too many horror movies, Gemma told herself. *It's a power cut, that's all. Maybe even just a tripped switch in the fuse box.*

That was something she could check on, at least. Something grounded and normal, that didn't involve flinching away from draughty windows and creaking floorboards. After a few minutes of searching, Gemma found the fuse box in the alcove under the stairs.

With the lights on, she hadn't thought anything of the little nook, but in the dark, it somehow yawned deeper than it had before, as though the shadows were feeding it, making it swell. Gemma used the torch on her phone to light her way into the alcove, but she still jumped when something brushed her neck. She yelped, swatting it away. But it was just the sleeve of James's raincoat hanging on its hook. Taking a deep breath to chase away her nerves, Gemma checked the switches were all in the correct positions.

That's when a strange sound reached her. It seemed to be coming from outside: high-pitched, almost keening. It

sang out an eerie melody Gemma had never heard before –
a song of emptiness and hunger, and the yawning chasm
of time. She felt it coursing through her flesh, her bones,
the sound an icy blade. And while there was something
hauntingly beautiful about it, Gemma wished more than
anything that she could just make it *stop*.

Stifling a whimper, she crouched in the alcove, tucking
herself in tight next to the small table the house phone
rested on.

The house phone!

She snatched it up and dialled her mum, having to
try three times before her trembling fingers hit the right
numbers. Still the howling song echoed around the cottage,
as though it was filling the entire valley. The plaintive wail
was why it took Gemma a long moment to realize there
was no dialling tone coming from the phone. She hung up
and tried again, but the same thing happened. The phone
was cut off. *She* was cut off. Alone in this creepy house,
with God only knew what moaning outside.

"Gemma?"

She jumped, whacking her elbow on the telephone
table.

"James!" Gemma had almost forgotten the boy she was
supposed to be looking after. "What are you doing out
of bed?"

"I heard the Mari Lwyd singing," James whispered,
peering down through the banister at her as she crawled out
from her hiding place. "You didn't lock the door, did you?"

"I…" A lie was on the tip of her tongue, but she bit it back. "Look, it's not safe to leave the doors unlocked at night."

James's eyes widened until Gemma could see the whites all the way around his irises. "Unlock it, now!"

"No way, I told you—"

"Unlock it before the Mari Lwyd knocks! If the door is locked when it knocks, you'll make it angry."

Everything in Gemma's head told her this was the opposite of common sense, the opposite of the right thing to do. And since when had she listened to the advice of strange nine-year-olds? Hadn't James's own mother said not to listen to him?

"Gemma, *please*."

Still, she hesitated. And that was when the knocking started. Three loud raps, more like a hammer strike than simple knocking.

"Oh no… It's too late." James's voice cracked on the words.

Fear spiking through her, Gemma bared her teeth. "Back to your room, *now*!"

James hurried away. Gemma didn't know if it was her sharpness or the sound of that knocking that had sent him scurrying, but either way, she was relieved not to have his wide-eyed accusations prodding at her.

The singing, if it could really be called that, had stopped at the same time the knocking ended. Perhaps the silence should've unnerved Gemma even more, but it instead made her doubt herself.

What was so scary about someone knocking on the door, anyway? It was only about half nine, so not exactly the middle of the night. Maybe the Bowens had asked a neighbour to check in on her or something.

Without telling me?

There was no peephole in the Bowens' front door, only a frosted pane to one side of it. The outside lantern glowed through the glass.

Wait … the outside light's working, but none of the inside ones?

She decided it must simply be something to do with faulty wiring in the old cottage. Yes, that was probably to blame. Faulty wires, and a fox or something making that hellish noise out there.

A fox hadn't knocked on the door, though.

Gemma pressed her face up against the frosted window, watching for any movement outside. Something – probably a moth – swooped past the glass in front of her eyeball and she yelped, then laughed at herself for being so jumpy.

Could the wind have set the knocker clanging like that? Or maybe it hadn't even been the knocker, but some other sound – loud, but far away. Hunters shooting in the woods, or—

A dark figure loomed from the night, blocking the glow of the lantern. Gemma reared back, gulping as she tried to swallow past a knot of terror. Her heels snagged on something and she sprawled backwards, landing on the stairs.

The knocking started again.

BANG! BANG! BANG!

Gemma threw a glance upstairs, but James's bedroom door was firmly shut.

What should I do? I can't call anyone. Can't go anywhere. What if whatever's outside gets bored with knocking and breaks in?

Not *"whatever"*, she chided herself. Who*ever*. Because there was no way James's wild story about some supernatural creature that liked to eat souls whenever it felt a bit snackish was true.

... Right?

This had to be some Welsh trick-or-treat type of thing, didn't it? Maybe if she treated it like that, whoever was at the door would go away.

Making her way carefully so as not to trip on any more furniture, Gemma stumbled to the kitchen and tried to remember where Mrs Bowen had said the snacks were kept. She found the cupboard and grabbed the first thing that came to hand – a close inspection showed it to be a Mars bar.

The pounding knock came again, startling Gemma enough that she dropped the chocolate.

Let's see if this shuts you up.

Gemma snatched it up and made her way back to the front door. She couldn't exactly open the door with some creep outside, though. So Gemma pulled open the letter box and posted the chocolate out into the night.

"There you go! Now piss off and leave me alone!" She

waited, half-expecting to hear children giggling outside, or even more knocking … but there was nothing. "OK?"

Still, there was no answer.

OK, then.

She backed away from the door slowly, as though it might blast open. It didn't. Breathing a sigh of relief, Gemma was about to turn and head up the stairs to check on James when the letter box opened and closed with a *snap*. She froze, then noticed the Mars bar lying on the welcome mat. Lying there, rejected.

"What…"

Snap. Snap, snap, snap!

The letter box opened and slammed shut, faster and faster, the sound like machine gun fire. Gemma's heart seized in her chest. Because as she stared at that blinking rectangle, she glimpsed a long, white skull peering back at her, its eye sockets empty but for a dark blaze.

A dark blaze that was focused entirely on *her.*

5

Gemma shrieked, flying up the stairs. James's room was right at the top, and she went to fling the door open only to find it locked.

"James! Let me in!"

"*No.*"

His voice was muffled by the door, but there was no

mistaking his frightened tone. "*You're* the one who didn't listen and made the Mari Lwyd mad. *You* locked it out. Now you have to deal with the consequences."

"What consequences?" Gemma practically screeched.

"It wants a soul, and it's not eating mine."

"James, stop saying that! Let me in, OK?"

There was no answer this time. Gemma rattled the knob, but it was still locked. She hammered on the door.

"James! You little…"

Gemma sagged back against the wall. A little turd he might be, but she couldn't exactly hide behind a nine-year-old, could she? It was better if he did stay locked in there, at least until she'd got rid of that thing outside.

Just as she thought about the person – creature? – out there, Gemma realized the letter box had stopped making its awful racket. Could they have got bored and left?

Sure, because I'm dead lucky like that.

Like a cat, she edged her way silently downstairs again, keeping close to the wall so she'd be all but invisible if anyone peered in through the frosted window by the door. The outside light was still on, though, and Gemma couldn't see any sign of someone lurking out there wearing that horrific horse-skull mask.

Who the hell wears a horse's skull as a mask, anyway?

Not someone you wanted to open the door to, that was certain. Or leave the door unlocked for… Wait, had James only unbolted the front door? Or could the little creep have left any other doors or windows unlocked as an invitation to whatever was out there? Cursing him silently, Gemma hurried to check.

The back door in the kitchen was locked. Windows, then? And there was the patio door… No, that was fine too.

Why is it so quiet?

Her skin prickled as she turned to face the room. And froze.

There, in front of the fire, stood the Mari Lwyd. Its massive frame was shrouded in layers of grey, gauzy material, but it was its face – or rather, its mask – that Gemma couldn't tear her gaze from. The deep, hollow eye sockets locked on to her, pinning her like a butterfly under glass. There was a smell to it, too, she thought, like wet leaves left to decompose. It was rot and age and decay, and Gemma wanted to scrub its scent from inside her nostrils.

In the flickering red glow of the embers winking out in the grate, that long, bony skull nodded faintly.

Gemma.

She heard her name, but it was as though it had been whispered inside her mind.

Come.

"No," she answered it aloud, voice cracking with terror. She backed up until she felt the fabric of the curtains covering the patio door, searching with her hands for the key to open it. The Mari Lwyd made no move towards her, only watched from inside those fathomless eye sockets. Slowly, from the depths of its shroud, a bony hand emerged. It was yellowed and ancient-looking, like it had only recently been dug up after centuries in the soil. The creature reached for her, its skeletal fingers outstretched.

"No!" Gemma cried again and fumbled for the door handle. She had to get away from this thing – get out, *now*.

But no matter how she tried, the key wouldn't turn in the lock. The handle wouldn't move. She was trapped.

Unless I can get past it and out the front door...

Gemma was aware, in some vague corner of her mind, that that would mean leaving little James behind with this monster. But right now, she was too terrified to care about that. And why should she care, anyway? James had locked her out of his room, hadn't he? She just needed to escape.

With a desperate scream, Gemma threw her shoulder at the patio door.

It didn't budge.

She slithered down to the floor, chest heaving as tears rolled down her face. The Mari Lwyd watched on, unmoved.

"What?" she sobbed. "WHAT DO YOU WANT?"

It stared at her a moment longer – long enough for Gemma to regret to her very core that she had asked that question. Because she didn't want to know what it wanted with her. Didn't want to know *at all*.

The Mari Lwyd opened its arms, and the shroud billowed apart. Eyes wide like the snared animal she was, Gemma waited for its hideous true form to be revealed. But underneath the veil was only a void. Empty, hollow hunger.

"What—"

The monster's horse-skull mask yawned open, letting loose a wail so piercing Gemma had to cover her ears. And then she felt it tugging at her – like the sound itself was pulling her towards the creature. It was as though some unnatural gravity well hid beneath the shroud. She skidded across the stone floor, hearing the patio doors flying open behind her, the dying fire in the hearth snuffing out as she passed, extinguished by the howling gale happening inside the Bowens' living room. Gemma tried to scream, but her lungs could no longer find any air to draw in. Gemma clawed at the floor, rolling to try to free herself, but she still kept inching closer and closer to the Mari Lwyd. Her fingernails snapped painfully, but she still couldn't utter a sound, only leaving red smears across the stone floor behind her.

Something lashed her ankle, tightening like a shackle. She looked down in time to see the creature's cold, bony fingers fastened there. And that touch was pulling at her too … draining something from deep down inside her. It hurt at first, stealing all the warmth left in her, all the *life*, as though she were bleeding out. But Gemma knew she wasn't, that what it was draining from her was worse than that – more *vital* than that.

"And when it gets inside, it eats your soul."

NO!

But no matter how she struggled, she couldn't break free from the monster's grip. Its shroud closed in around her, sealing her in, consuming her, until everything beyond the veil ceased to exist.

6

Gemma stirred, her mind a fog. She'd been asleep, right? But she was moving now. In a car? No, it wasn't that kind of movement. More like she was being carried… And there was something over her face.

She brushed her hand to remove what she assumed was a mass of her own hair – or tried to. Her fingers met with something hard and smooth.

Definitely not my face.

It came back to her then – her harrowing encounter with the Mari Lwyd. Her certainty it was about to kill her, eat her soul as James had said.

Thank God I got away. I must have…

Gemma opened her eyes, and the awful truth settled in her gut like a mass of glass shards. She was outside the cottage, being carried away from the glow of the lantern above the front door. And she was looking out through two round eye sockets that weren't her own. The Mari Lwyd had taken her – had *consumed her.* And now it was dragging her away into the night.

No…

Just then a car pulled into the yard, and for a moment Gemma thought it must be her mum, but the car was wrong. The Bowens tumbled out of it, leaving the car doors swinging open in their rush to get to the house.

"James! JAMES!"

Mrs Bowen disappeared inside while Mr Bowen paused in the doorway, dragging a hand through his hair as he peered out into the mist surrounding the cottage.

Help me!

Gemma tried to cry out to him, to plead with him to notice that she was being dragged away, but she was already past the reach of the lantern. Slowly, silently, she passed through the trees surrounding the cottage. She couldn't stop it. Couldn't move. Couldn't make a sound.

Help me, somebody!

"James, did it work? Did it take her?" Mrs Bowen's frantic voice came from inside the house.

"It got her!" James wailed. "I know you told me not to, but I had to try to warn her. She didn't listen, though, and it got her! Just like the last babysitter…"

"It's OK, love," his mother replied. "Better her than one of us, eh?"

Oh my God, they planned this! Gemma realized.

Whatever else the Bowens said was lost as Gemma was hauled deeper into the trees. Grass gave way to moss-covered rocks, then dirt, then…

The creature paused, and for a brief, flickering moment, Gemma hoped it had changed its mind.

Yes! Yes, please let me go!

But the Mari Lwyd instead began moving again. Down

189

this time. Through her terror, Gemma felt confused – how could it be moving *down* when the valley rose up on all sides? But as the darkness solidified around her and she smelled the cold, damp stink of earth, the true horror sank in. James's words again echoed through Gemma's mind.

"It comes in midwinter … searching for souls to drag down to the underworld..."

Oh God.

Oh, please God, no!

That's where it was taking her. The ground opened up and sucked her into its embrace, as deep and terrifying as eternity.

I should have made sure it took James instead, was Gemma's last thought before dirt and soil cascaded over her in a cloying, dreadful shroud, separating her forever from the only world she had known.

She belonged now to the Mari Lwyd.

AND THE WATERS CREPT IN

DAWN KURTAGICH

The Urgency followed me from Ireland.

It hung from my neck and draped down my back like a crepuscular cloak, always there, always tugging. It stepped in my footprints as I boarded the ferry in Dublin, tripped me up when I docked in Mostyn, and rode beside me on the long coach journey to my new situation. It had been with me since I was born, a constant, terrible companion – telling me, always, that time was running out.

My arrival at Gwydir Castle was accompanied by the mournful cry of peacocks and the silent pressure of the Urgency, dusk spreading a hazy orange gaze over plum-coloured roof tiles. A knot garden in the small courtyard leading to the Tudor house was still in bloom, despite it being late in September, while an ancient wisteria draped the mullioned windows and doors with purple filigree. It was like something out of one of the fairy stories Daideó told me over an evening.

Yes, I thought. *This'll do nicely.*

I had walked the mile or so from Llanrwst where the carriage had dropped me, the erstwhile driver pointing a tired finger vaguely in the direction of green rolling hills, traipsing through blue, mist-curled fields and barely discernible muddy roads, all while clutching my bag of meagre belongings in frozen, rigid fingers.

Time's short, my Urgency breathed with every beat of my heart. *Time's short*. The same refrain for as long as I could remember. But this was an opportunity. The only one I had received since Daideó passed. Without it, I'd have had to seek employment in one of the factories further south.

It was later than I'd hoped to arrive, but smoke still rose from several of the chimneys, and I was, after all, expected. The housekeeper, one Miss Bess Griffiths, had written to accept my application the week prior. As night crept in, leaching the air of warmth and colour, I took a breath, lifted the knocker and let it fall twice.

The door groaned open and an aging face both agitated and resigned peered out.

"What hour do you call this?"

"A good day to you, missus. I am Aine Byrne calling for work. I have a letter here."

I reached into my pocket, dodging the rabid claws of the Urgency, and pulled it free. The old woman did not take it.

Instead, her lip curled with distain. "And I suppose the Irish don't know how to keep time?"

I flushed with shocked indignance and bit my lip.

She considered me. "Well. Aren't you the poppet?" Her words were curdled as sour milk.

"Oh … I – thank you, madam."

"It's Bess, if you please, an' nothing more."

Bess stepped back for me to enter, and what little light there was disappeared the moment the door closed behind us. The strike of a Lucifer, the match catching, a puff of phosphorous sulphur and then the paltry glow of candlelight splashing over lime-washed walls.

"You will wake before dawn," Bess said, walking briskly through the first hall, the orange glow from her candle warping grotesquely over curved walls into terrible shapes as we moved. Her voice bounced along and echoed back, giving the impression of space where there was, in fact, very little. She turned into a passage before climbing a set of uneven stone steps. I followed at a trot, trying to keep track of the rambling corridors. "Sir Wynn breakfasts in his rooms, but those requirements are variable." She paused to glare back at me. "I will see to him. Light the fires first – you can get the materials from the wood store outside. Gareth will show you later. The groundsman," she clarified, moving swiftly down another narrow corridor and entering the first door on the right. It led to a small, boxy room laid in grey and blue. I followed Bess in and waited.

"Here you are then," she said stiffly.

I glanced up, at first not understanding. Was I to begin cleaning now?

"Rest. Tomorrow the work begins."

The Urgency had sunk into a chair beside one of two narrow windows, apparently appeased.

A ludicrous notion was forming in my mind. Surely this could not be … mine?

"This is yours now," Bess confirmed, again with that odd, thorny tone. Her voice was like nettles prickling at the throat.

"I am very grateful," I stammered, placing my bag on the uneven floor, "for this opportunity. I'm honoured to be working under your guidance—"

Bess snorted. "The master'll not hear your obsequious platitudes on this side of the house, and they're wasted on me. You arrived too late for the kitchen, but I'll see that some bread is brought up." She looked me up and down. "Wake before dawn, seek Gareth in the grounds, and light all the fires. After that, go to the kitchen for the laundry and assist Cook. We'll see how well your pretty words do then."

Perhaps Bess had been forced to hire an aid, I thought. Perhaps this pretty room had once been hers and she resented being replaced, resented getting older and needing the assistance. Perhaps she feared her position being usurped, of being tossed into the world, alone. I myself had realized that I must make myself vital to some proper family before I grew old in order to prevent just such a fate. But only having to seek employment at sixteen, and to find it as a junior maid in such a grand house, *and* to receive my own bedroom? Fate had been kind.

"May I air out the bedclothes?" I asked, daring a little frankness. The room, though pretty, reeked of old mildew caught in heavy tapestry, and I very much doubted it had been tended to.

Bess walked briskly out, but at the door, glanced back, her gaze cold as the Shannon. "We live on a floodplain. You can light a fire in the grate, if it pleases you, but you best be getting used to the damp. It won't be going anywhere."

And nor will I, her expression seemed to say.

She placed the candle on the table and turned to leave, closing the door behind her, and I listened to the clop of her shoes as she marched away, apparently so familiar with the house that she needed no light to guide her steps.

The Urgency licked its lips.

After putting my belongings in the small armoire in the corner and changing into my least threadbare of two nightgowns, I crept across the frigid floor and timidly pulled back the heavy covers on the bed. A puff of mildew assaulted my nose and after coughing the putrid mould from my lungs, I determined to air everything out during the day the moment I got a chance.

In the meantime, I would light that fire Bess said I could have. I hurried to the grate, toes protesting the icy flagstones, expecting to find a tinderbox and brimstone. I was pleased to discover, however, that Gwydir appeared to keep strikable matches everywhere. I reached forward to rearrange the wood, only to find that it was damp and soft, fleshy like mushrooms. Clearly this room had not been seen to in some time.

The cold was seeping in from every corner, much like the shadows, so I abandoned the fire and hurried to bed.

The heavy blankets were clammy as I slid beneath them; even the downy mattress was moist and cold. I shuddered with distaste as I covered myself over, hoping that there were no vermin burrowing in the lumpy bedclothes.

I must be grateful, I chided myself, *for an opportunity such as this*. A roof over my head, employment with regular salary, and a room of my very own – not a cloister bed in some draughty kitchen or attic, forgotten with the spiders. And if I did not have a friend in the whole wide world, beside that of my Urgency – well, what of it? Plenty of women had less, and my cheeks burned with shame when, despite it all, I began to cry.

I lay, stiff and cold and miserable – and saw a puddle of water on the sill, glinting in the moonlight.

The bread never came.

Bess was no warmer in the morning.

I found her in the kitchen, after a labyrinthine walk through desolate, twisting corridors. The kitchen, at least, was warmer, without the smell of mildew detectable in the air.

"You'll have to be more punctual than this," Bess snapped when I entered. "The peacocks rise earlier."

"Pardon me, ma'am – Bess. I got lost."

"The house isn't as big as all that," the housekeeper muttered, giving an old woman I took to be Cook a look that made me flush with shame.

Cook looked me up and down with rheumy eyes, licking her thin, cracked lips as she offered me a bowl of pottage, still warm from the fire. When I took it, she sucked in her thin cheeks, paper over bone, and scowled.

It had been a rough night, full of uncanny dreams of blue-tinged windows, and a waterlogged voice calling to me through rainfall. A cool caress upon my cheek and an ancient name whispered in my ear. When, before dawn, I woke with a film of icy sweat over my body, I attempted once again to light the sodden wood in the grate to no avail, and then spent a good few hours shivering in bed, examining the strangely shaped wall behind me. Unlike the rest of the walls in the room, it was knobbly in one section, like scarred flesh, the stones laid haphazardly before being set hurriedly with lime mortar. The incongruity was bothersome.

"Cook doesn't speak," Bess said, sweeping up the ashes from the inglenook.

I had little experience in grand houses, but I had never heard of a housekeeper who stooped so low as to sweep the hearth! That was for the junior maid – for me, surely. It seemed that the hierarchy in this household was utterly fluid.

Like water.

"The fires, girl," Bess snapped into the fireplace. "The wood is in the store by the solar tower gate in the courtyard."

She waved a hand that I took to be a dismissal. I had hardly touched my food but was no longer hungry anyway.

The Urgency followed me into the grounds, appearing from behind a curve in the wall. It scratched its nails along the stone, but was, for the first time in memory, silent. It watched me with a cocked head and did not speak. I found this, if possible, more unnerving than the constant whispers of *time's short*. I ignored it and sought out the wood store, dodging sleepy peacocks along the way.

When the wood was chopped and the fires lit, the grates swept and the floors washed, when the laundry was hung and the shutters opened, the dusthole cleaned and the shoes shined, the hankies made up and the coffee ground, the breakfast got up and the butter collected from the milk shop – and a dozen other scullion duties seen to – night had once again fallen.

When Cook served lamb cawl before the kitchen hearth, I was blackened with soot and had a fair few bruises on my knees and knuckles, my hands red and raw.

Bess scooped up the last of her stew with a piece of malt bread, and a slow, nasty smile crawled over her face. She ate the bread and handed her bowl to Cook wordlessly.

"Well," she said, hugging her stomach comfortably as she leaned back on the bench. "Someone survived her first day in the nethers."

I swallowed meat and potato. "Nethers?"

"'S'what we call life here, work here."

I said nothing.

"Indeed," Bess said, sharing an amused glance with Cook. "You've done well. All mucked up to show it."

Cook did not smile, but something in the old woman's face unsettled me. I examined my hands. My once-pink nail beds were thick with grime, black as the flue.

"It is a beautiful house," I said tactfully. "And the work is not as challenging as I had thought."

"Well, we must rectify that. Master in't paying for lazy girls."

I scolded myself and my big mouth. The work was exhausting, and I thought I could hardly be expected to take on more.

"We'll see how long it takes," Bess said cruelly. She sucked on her teeth. "No doubt you'll scarper."

A long silence fell, punctuated by the puff of Cook's burps now and again and an occasional pop from the grate.

"Did you ever hear tell of the creature what lives in these parts?" Bess said casually.

I had grown sleepy with the warmth. "Beg pardon?"

Bess leaned forward, her eyes glinting with a strange cunning. "They call it the *Afanc*."

"I've not heard of it."

"A demon, some say. A water demon. Lives in the lakes and floodplains round these parts." Bess leaned back again, waiting for my reaction, watching me closely.

"What does it look like?" It was a small challenge. *Tell me of your water demon*, I thought. *Tell me what you have seen, so I may know your ignorance.* My Urgency was dancing in the inglenook, making merry with the flames. It had not spoken a word to me all day. I frowned at it. Did it seem … diminished? Or no. Perhaps it was just a trick of the light.

"Some say," Bess said in a low, dramatic voice, "it resembles a beaver-crocodile monstrosity. Some say a short man…"

I relaxed. It hardly sounded alarming.

"But no one tha's seen the Afanc has lived, so who can say? Maybe it is like nothing anyone could describe. But the Afanc devours those who enter its waters, to consume the body, and to capture the soul. I believe," she added solemnly, "that the Afanc comes to take the souls of sinners. Work of the devil, if you ask me."

Cook nodded sagely and I again swallowed my smile. We had all kinds of fae fancies in Ireland, and I was oddly comforted by their appearance here in this new land. It was, perhaps, not too dissimilar from my home. There was a kind of warmth in that.

Bess spat into the fire and it hissed back at her. "They say it takes a particular fancy to that bedroom you lay your head in."

Now we had come to it. The reason for the tale.

I decided to indulge her. "My room?"

"Oh, aye. So watch you keep good with God."

I nodded, biting my cheek to keep from laughing. She meant to scare me; it was clear.

"Get gone," she snapped, waving a dismissive hand in my direction. Perhaps she had sensed my amusement.

"Take a candle," she added, removing one from the hearth box and lighting it in the fire. And then she leaned in and whispered, "We don't like you, famine rat. You will never be one of us. And I shall do my utmost to drive you gone."

She let wax dribble, sharp as a sting, on to my hand before handing the candle over.

I took it and turned away, tears pricking my eyes.

The shadows pillowed my steps like a faithful dog all the way to my room.

I broke the thin layer of ice in the wash basin and scrubbed what I could of the grime from my skin, and then I collapsed on to my bed, shivering. Through my tears, the Urgency watched me curse myself for forgetting to replace the wood in the grate so that I could have a fire. After a moment, it blinked and then melted into the wall, leaving me utterly alone.

My tears added to the dampness of my pillow.

"I miss you, Daideó," I whispered, longing for him to hear me.

Someone else answered.

It was a waterlogged voice, deep as an abyss – bottomless and strangely hollow. Familiar, like something out of a dream.

"Aine," it whispered, rippling like a current through the room.

Outside, the rain began in earnest, fat gobbets hitting the window like pebbles.

I wiped my eyes and sat up, looking around for the Urgency.

The whisper came again, an inlet into the room. "Aine."

"I am she," I called tentatively, feeling the coldness in the room deepen. The rain continued, and a small leak in the seal of the windowpane let in drops of water that ran to the sill.

The water seemed to have infected everything.

"Why do you weep?" It was a man's voice, of that I was certain.

The darkness deepened in the corner by the hearth and I stared hard, trying to make shapes where there were none.

A pause, and then, "I am utterly alone," I admitted, for if I was going mad, I had nothing to lose.

"I know loneliness," the voice said, deep as black water. "I am one who piles grief upon grief."

"Y'are not real," I whimpered, even as I understood the weight of the words profoundly.

"Not alone," the voice assured me, "now I am here."

I blinked and more tears fell, and the heaviness in the room subsided and the voice spoke no more.

By the time I was safely ensconced beneath the covers, I could almost ignore the strange rising smell of mould in the room and the way the mocking shadows bunched in the corners, as though holding secret congress over my tattered skirts and rough, soot-mired hands.

As the rain beat down, a maelstrom to accompany my grief, a potable voice whispered, *"I am here."*

A week later, Sir Wynn's son, Henri, found me in the garden doing the laundry one chilly afternoon. I was barefoot, letting my toes dip into the icy waters of the lake as I scrubbed the sheets on the washboard. He was a pink-faced boy, tall for his thirteen years, with ears that were overlong for his head and beady, tenacious eyes that saw all. I had noticed him watching me yesterday when I served breakfast but took it for nothing more than idle curiosity. Quick as a nipper, he grabbed for my skirts, cackling raucously, and when I yanked them from his grubby hands, his pink cheeks glowered rudely red.

"You have to do what I say, mucky filth!" he screamed. "Now give me your skirt so I may rip it from seam to seam, and bite off those pale toes!"

When I did naught but stare, he grabbed my swollen hand and rubbed his thumb roughly across the palm. Something ugly glinted in his eyes.

It was a mercy that, in that moment, Bess and another of the younger servants, Gwenan, rounded the corner, stopping in surprise when they saw us. Henri dropped my hand and sauntered away, his cheeks still burning an angry red.

"Well," Bess said slowly, a particular cunning to her

voice that could wilt glass. "Someone has designs above her station."

I flapped my mouth, aghast at the suggestion. "Please, no! I would never!"

Gwenan glanced between us and said nothing.

"He likes the poppets, he does," Bess said, taking my hand just as Henri did. "Most 'specially the ones all rosy and rustic, grubby from their labours. I expect you think he will fall under your spell, drape you with fine jewels and make you his Lady. No doubt you daydream of his declaring that he would, all told, crush a million cochineals to see fine carmine silk against your milky flesh, aye?"

I tugged my hand away for the second time today, and Gwenan opened her mouth as if to say something – then seemed to think better of it and lowered her gaze.

I clenched my teeth and spoke through them. "Please, stop."

"You may daydream all you like, pet. As I said, I don't doubt you'll be off away 'fore the fortnight has passed." Bess glanced at the timid Gwenan and back at me. "Gwenan here survives because she does her chores and minds herself to herself. You … you put your nose into pies in't yours!"

I turned away and plucked a linen from the soapy water, intending to continue my work. "I have never done any such thing—"

Bess slapped it from my hands and stepped up to me, her large bosom in my face, teeth bared. "You remind me of a boy who came to work here some forty years back. Poppet he was, just like you. Young Demain, his name was. Lazy lad. Ideas above his station. Master came to rely on him, trust him … but he ran away, didn't he? Abandoned Sir Wynn in his hour of need with a handful of Sir's coins along with him. Well, I won't let you do the same. So, play at being sweethearts with young Henri, go on. I'll be poisoning his left ear against you just as you whisper your sugared nothings into his right." She glances at my bare feet, which I had been dipping into the water as I washed. "And if you sin, so much more delight for the Afanc, which will surely come for you."

"I have no designs on that, that" – I paused, trying to hold the word in, but it stumbled past my lips, unstoppable as a torrent – *"brat!"*

Gwenan gave a little gasp, but Bess just laughed. It was an ugly sound.

"Cook will have a laugh at the temper on you, little lass." Her smile fell. "Get back to work a'fore I dismiss you and send you scampering. They keep lists of undesirables round these parts – for miles you'll not find another position if I deploy your name upon it. Put on your shoes, scullion maid, and know your place."

With that, she turned and sauntered back towards the house, Gwenan following behind with sympathetic glances in my direction, leaving me shaking with fury and fear. The Urgency picked blades of grass and flicked them away like so much fluff, and I realized that it has faded – like the phantom lines of erased chalk on the charity school chalkboard.

The room was frigid cold.

The damp was in everything.

And though I replaced the wood in the grate each day, lighting a fire in the evenings and falling asleep to a merry blaze, what char remained was spongy as mushrooms every morning, waterlogged once again. The mildew reek was as pungent as ever — and more — so that even when outside doing laundry, my nostrils were stuffed with it.

Freshly cut grass reeked of mould.

Morning bread tasted of blight.

There was a mustiness to life that I could not shake.

The Urgency, slowly erasing itself a little at a time, finally vanished the previous afternoon as I emptied the sop buckets. It stood a little apart from me, opened its mouth as if to say something I never heard, and then was gone — a winter ray of sunlight blotting it out entirely.

I had not seen it since.

My dreams were waterlogged with rot, frigid with cold, but that warm, deep voice continued to call out to me. I woke in the early hours, just past midnight, and answered.

"Are you there?" I asked, not sure which would be worse: to hear the voice or not.

"Aine."

I sat up and hugged the covers closer, despite their clammy dampness. "Show yourself."

He dripped from the walls, seeping through like so much floodwater, materializing into a man. Tall. Dark of hair and strange of complexion like the bottom of a murky lake, unseen, unfelt. Two gnarled horns much like the antlers of a proud male deer grew from his head, tinged green with lake weed, and a cloak the colour of a midnight river waterfalled down his back to pool on the floor.

I blinked, frozen with shock, half expecting him to vanish. "Who are you?"

"I am Arawn, King of the Underworld."

I began to shiver, my breath coming in thick white plumes. "This is not real."

Arawn stepped closer, his foot quaking the floorboards, and puddles of water trailed behind. "Mine is a kingdom beneath the water, and it is very much real. *I* am very much real."

"You were in my dream… I heard you calling in my sleep."

He watched me with bottomless eyes. "I heard you singing."

"I don't sing," I protested weakly, staring at his horns, which brushed the ceiling.

"At the lake's edge, doing laundry. You dipped your toes into the water and sang a sad song."

I vaguely remembered now. I had been thinking of my daideó and feeling the loss of him. The hole his absence had left in the world. *'Sé mo laoch mo ghile mear…*

I swallowed. "In Ireland … there's tell of the Tuatha

dé Danann. Folk of the goddess Danu." I stared into his uncanny face, my breath catching in my throat. "Powerful beings, kings and queens of the Otherworld. My daideó always believed … in the *Sidhe*. Fairies. Powerful fae who interact with our world."

I waited for him to scowl at me. To laugh and deride me. To tell me I was a child with a girl's fantasy in her mind and naught else.

Instead, a small smile crept on to his lips, barely there. "Is that what you think me? A fairy?"

"A god," I clarified.

"I am no god. And you will find no gods or goddesses in Cymru. The *Tylwyth Teg* are the closest," he added. A glint in his eye. "Fairies."

"You're a fairy, then?"

"I am King of *Annwvn*, nothing more and nothing less."

"But you command the water," I said, gesturing to the puddle at his feet. "It follows you."

"The water is where the kingdom of *Annwvn* lies."

"And you came because you heard my singing?"

"There is … something." His eyes moved over my features. "Something about you. It intrigues me. Calls me. Maybe you have some goddess blood in you, ringing out into the Underworld."

Despite myself, I enjoyed the idea of this. That I was, in some small way, blood of the Tuath Dé. That I was more than a poor, famine-fleeing girl, more than a ridiculed servant. An outsider.

"I *am* named for the goddess Áine," I told him carefully. "Goddess of the summer. In one story my daideó told often, she was said to live at the bottom of a lake..."

He seemed amused by this, and I noticed a dimple in his left cheek when he caught himself in a half-smile. "Your daideó?"

"My grandfather." My voice caught and I swallowed, blinking fast. "He died."

"You miss him."

"Yes. He was all I had."

The Fae King – Arawn – glanced out of the window at the blackened grounds. "I know what it feels like to lose someone. To lose the only people you have." His voice darkened. "To be alone."

There was a strange kinship between me and this creature – this man. He was utterly otherworldly with his antlers draped in lake weed, his cloak pooling like shadows at his feet, his black, midnight eyes...

He was enchanting.

"The people here are merciless," I muttered, pulling the covers higher over my shoulders. "They don't know what it is to have nothing."

"No," Arawn agreed. "They seem ... casually callous."

"You've been watching them?"

"I've been watching their treatment of you. You don't belong on your knees, Aine, goddess of summer."

I flushed with pleasure. "I am a servant ... now."

"Would your daideó be pleased to see you brought so low?"

"No. He never could have foreseen the need for me to flee Eire. He could never have foreseen the famine. His death. My situation." I was unable to stop the tears. "He would be brokenhearted."

"You should not be sweeping the grates of those inferior to you."

"I am inferior to them."

"No."

"I am nothing of significance."

He considered me, and then turned away, walking slowly to the wall he had seeped from. "Not yet."

And with no parting goodbye, he melted into the wall and was gone.

I dreamed of waterlogged plaster, of dripping lime, mildewed sheets and mouldy curtains. I danced in twisting riverweed and gloried in the frigid waters flooding in around me. I laughed as I drowned.

I daydreamed through most of my chores over the next few days. My mind was full of all the stories that Daideó told me growing up. As I hung the sheets in the grounds to dry, I daydreamed of Clíodhna, queen of the banshees, and how she fell in love with Ciabhan, a human man, and left her perfect isle to be with him. When cleaning out the dusthole, I daydreamed of Oisín, a mortal who fell in love with Niamh of Tír na nÓg and left his life to be with her. As I knelt in the kitchen larder, I thought of Fionn and Sadhbh, of Diarmuid and Gráinne... Endless examples of two people divided by mortality and race, joined together by love. All of these stories kept me going through the long day, bearing the bruises on my knees and the rawness of my fingers. But one tale in particular stayed with me.

Hades and Persephone.

I always preferred the version where she ran away of her own volition to be at Hades' side. It's the version I dwelled on as I swept the kitchen grate.

I didn't hear Bess. So when she gripped my arm and scalded me on the scorching iron kettle she held, I screamed and scampered back, clutching at my hand.

"You aren't paid to stand daydreaming, *Poppet*."

I gritted my teeth against the impulse to strike her.

"I won't tolerate a laze-about in this house. It's enough you bringing the blight here to us without earning for free." Her eyes betrayed a deep hatred I hadn't suspected before now. "Get to it or have your wages docked."

Behind her, Arawn rose from the flagstones like a silent waterfall, his eyes blazing. He reached for her with hand crooked into a claw, his teeth bared in fury. For a moment I almost let him do it. Whatever it was he could do. But then sense returned, and I shook my head at him. He hesitated, seeming to fight with himself, and then dropped in a pool of water that splashed her skirts. She yelped and spun, finding nothing but wet flagstones before her. Stunned, she looked up at the ceiling.

"Damned rain," she muttered, walking off in a hurry.

Later that day I stole a pale soapstone from the lake and pocketed it before anyone noticed. I pilfered a knife from the kitchen and in moments of calm, when Bess was nowhere near, I sat and I carved. My hand smarted, but I ignored it. The carving was a slow, meditative activity, one I used to do often back home. When I came to Wales, I had to leave behind my collection. This would be the first of many, I vowed, and kept scratching away at the stone, until twenty-one lines – twenty horizontal and one vertical – had been cut in.

For supper, Cook gave me a rotten potato with my cawl, cackling when I discovered it. I ate it all, secretly delighting in the mould in my mouth. It made me think of Arawn. The horrified look on Cook's face was a bonus. I smiled through the meal, knowing that Arawn would be waiting for me in my room, delighting in the knowledge that I had a secret friend. It gave me comfort and courage.

"Why did you stop me?"

Arawn was in the darkest corner of the room, his eyes glinting like a cat's as I entered.

"I thought you would kill her," I admitted. "And I couldn't have that on my conscience."

"I would have. That she would dare lay a finger on you. It boils my blood."

I was oddly charmed. "Thank you."

"Here, let me see the damage."

I walked towards him, the uncanny feeling of approaching a crouching tiger, and held out my hand. It was red and inflamed, blisters forming along the edges.

He lay his frigid hand upon mine and the pain diminished, cooling into a bearable ache. I shivered, only partly from the cold.

"She keeps trying to scare me," I told him tentatively. "She told me a tale of a water beast that devours sinners. An Afanc or some such. Said it favours this room. She attributes the water to that creature, when all along it was you…"

I marvelled at him, taking in every peculiar inch.

"I would grind that beast of a woman into dust," he said through gritted teeth.

A startled laugh escaped me. "I think that's extreme."

"Don't let that old crow colour your view of Wales," he said gently. "She and Cook have been hideous their whole lives through."

"How long have you been watching them?"

"A long time. Gwydir is precious to me."

I wondered how long he had been watching me.

"I made you something," I said, digging in the pocket of my skirts for the soapstone. "Here."

He took it from me and frowned down at it. "Steatite? And this symbol … what is it?"

"It's called Ogham. Ancient writing from my country.

213

These marks," I said, running my fingers over the lines, close to his, "they mean water."

His hand closed around the stone, my fingers with them. His eyes met mine, and he seemed almost sad. "Thank you."

It was strangely easy to love this immortal man. Perhaps he was my Urgency made real. Our midnight conversations were why I began to lag with my chores, fatigued and clumsy, until Bess threatened to let me go and Sir Wynn scolded me for bungling his morning plate. Often, during our late-night conversations, I fell asleep mid-sentence, waking hours later in the early hours to find him sitting in my chair, turning the Ogham stone over and over in his hands, a peculiar expression of pain on his face.

There was an odd sense of unshackling from the world, as though Arawn was drawing me closer to his realm and farther away from my own. This, I delighted in. One evening, in the fifth week of our friendship, I told him about my Urgency.

"It was a kind of shadow-figure," I explained. "It followed me for as long as I can remember, always whispering that time was running out. It was like ... an hourglass, reminding me that the grains of sand of my life were almost done."

He nodded, his horns swaying. "I know very well the feeling that time is short."

I laughed. "You do? Is it not incongruous with immortality?"

He smiled and leaned towards me. I didn't pull away. "I like your laughter," he whispered, his mouth close to mine, breath like the Wybernant.

When his lips pressed against my own, I was not shocked by the cold or the mildewed taste. Both had become somehow beloved. Necessary.

Urgent.

"Perhaps," he whispered into my lips, "love banished your Urgency." He kissed me again, deeply, desperately. "Perhaps it left so you can begin your new, rightful life."

I blinked up at his, my breath caught in my throat. "Arawn…"

"Be with me," he said, clutching my hands in his own. "I'm alone, Aine. Alone in *Annwvn*. I seek my queen. Be her. Be mine."

There was less than a moment's thought. Less than the span of a blink. Less than the pulse of my heart.

"All right."

He startled, pulling back to look at my face, eyes searching. "Are you saying yes?"

I giggled, Persephone to his Hades. "Yes."

He closed his eyes, releasing a shuddering breath. I laughed, overcome with giddy joy at the pure relief I saw on his face. He loved me, I thought. He wanted me *this* badly.

In the second heartbeat, I realized something was wrong.

He stepped away from me, his eyes bleeding of colour, the black draining away to reveal a startling blue.

"I'm sorry," he whispered, and melted away like ice.

And then the room began to change.

It darkened.

And the waters began.

At first, a monotone sound – *dink, dink, dink* – of water hitting a sharp surface.

The water dripped from some hidden crack in the ceiling on to my bed curtains; it seeped in between the gaps in the windowpanes; it leached up, some impossible way, from the flagstones at random intervals – like a bleeding wound continually picked at. The walls were sweating coldly too, the lime wash clammy as a corpse.

My bed now stood in a pool of dark, brackish water. A sinister Claude glass.

I'm losing my sanity, I thought, even as the Urgency's voice pricked in my head: *Time's up. Time's up. Time's up.* Not gone, after all. Merely absorbed.

And then the chimney began to leak.

I had not thought I could be more frightened, but the insistent *tap, tap, tap*, which was *certainly* coming from the chimney, was enough to make my heart stutter to the same rhythm.

"Arawn?" I called, my voice warbling feebly.

There was no reply.

Slowly, silently, unable to resist the urge that told me to *look*, I collected the chamberstick and candle from the bedside table and knelt by the hearth, placing it down.

I carefully moved aside the fire screen and took out the sodden wood from the grate, scraping it away in spongy handfuls. Then, inhaling a steadying breath and once more picking up the chamberstick, I removed the iron grate and crawled into the fireplace.

And looked up.

The meagre light in my hand, which draped itself along the flue, was enough to reveal the horror above. Some six feet up sat an illimitable ceiling of inky black waters, only revealed by the flecks of orange candlelight glinting on the surface. I blinked, trying to make sense of this hideous reversal of the world. It was as though I was somehow floating in the air looking down at the surface of a deep, impenetrable lake. Or down the long, yawning neck of a well.

And deep in the depths of the watery ceiling, a pair of incandescent, terrible eyes stared back at me.

I watched, frozen in silent, rigid terror, as a webbed claw slid from the liquid murk and slammed – nails biting – into the chimney stones, and dragged itself from the water. Its mouth was slimy – plump and wide, like that of a lusty woman – but when the lips parted they revealed an arsenal of pikes' teeth, needle-sharp. Its movements were both jerky and lithe, and when it hauled itself closer, silver scales and lethal dorsal spines glinting, I dropped the candle, which snuffed out and extinguished the light. I could still hear it above, the squelch and scrabble of piscine flesh and nails on slate. Coming closer.

I scrabbled out of the chimney, but my nightdress caught on the poker stand and I fell bodily to the flagstones, splashing in water that was ever-rising. Still, the urge to get away was desperately strong, and I dragged myself forward, my nails bending past the quick – anything to get *away*.

A full-bellied wolf moon hung low in the sky, spilling silver light over the flagstones and coming to rest at the base of the chimney.

The creature – the *Afanc*, I realized with sudden horror – heaved itself out of the grate, one giant claw at a time, fins and dorsal spikes erupting from surprisingly human skin. There the similarity to my species ended. Two predatory eyes that seemed lit from within punctuated its ichthyic face, and where it walked, slimy algae-infected water followed.

By the time it reached me, the waters were gushing down the chimney, beckoning it home.

When it grabbed my ankle and crushed the bone, I knew it was over. Even so, as it dragged me back towards the grate, I screamed and begged and pleaded for it to have mercy. When it defied gravity and climbed the innards of the chimney, I had that same disembodied and peculiar sense that I was being dragged into the depths of a pitiless well, and I could no longer tell up from down.

I scrabbled at the stones, tearing my nails and fingers in my attempt to prevent the inevitable.

The water, like the cold grip of an unwanted lover, of Arawn himself, slid over my flesh until, with horrifying finality, it slipped over my head and I was pulled up, up, up, and down,

down,

down

to a watery grave.

It is dark.

But no longer frigid cold. There is air in his lungs. Sensation in his flesh. Solidity to his form. He opens his mouth and exhales a hot breath, testing his voice, tasting his tongue.

"I…"

He is alive.

Really, truly *alive*.

A laugh escapes, bubbling in dry air.

He did it! He is free. But … where? Why is he confined? Why is it so dark? A fetid chill is rising, seeping warmth from fragile mortal flesh.

A voice undulates through a space nearby, rippling through his skin.

"You tricked me."

A chink of moonlight, a sliver in the dark. He presses his eye to the opening and sees her materialize in the bedroom beyond, splendour and terror personified. Aine… Her skin is tinged the green-grey of winter lake water, her hair thick

219

and knotted like midnight riverweed. Two proud algae-draped horns grow from her head to scratch at the ceiling, and a black cloak, dotted with spots of mould, waterfalls down her back to pool at her feet like so much shadow.

She is magnificent.

As he was.

"I'm sorry," he says, his voice breaking. "I had no choice. I had to find someone to take my place."

"Hades and Persephone," she says, smiling to herself. "I thought that was our story." She turns burning black eyes on him and he cowers as much as the confined space allows. "But you were a genie in a bottle."

"I had to break free," he says desperately, begging for her to understand. "I was trapped in that place – cold, bitter cold. And alone. Alone for so long, trapped by that creature…"

"The Afanc," she says, nodding. "My murderer. My jailer."

His voice is wheedling, a thin, mewling thing. "You don't know what it's like."

"I do now."

He tries to raise his arm, to reach out for her, but he can't move. Cold stone presses in on him. In his hand, carved soapstone, the ridges of her Ogham letter beneath his fingers. *Water.*

"What is this? Why can't I move?"

"You won your life back," she tells him. "Just as you wanted. Just as you bartered. Your flesh was revived upon your bones, and life returned you to where those bones lay. Buried behind the walls of this room."

A gelid, carrion realization chokes him. He has seen the crooked, irregular wall in her room many times. Thought nothing of it. Now, he wants to shriek at the dawning horror. He was *buried* here. Hidden away … maybe by young Bess. Maybe by Sir Wynn. Decades ago, when he first came to Gwydir as a hall boy. When he was Demain Goss, sixteen and eager. When a beautiful man with horns called Arawn seduced him into taking his place.

"No," he wails. "No!"

"Was it worth it?" she asks, stepping up to the wall and pressing a watery hand to it. Caressing it like flesh. "You trapped me in order to free yourself." Her laugh is a maelstrom. "Now you'll rot and die behind this wall."

He jerks and sobs. The wall is unmoved. "No! Please! Please, help me! Aine!"

"*Arawn*," she corrects him. "My name is Arawn. Queen of the Underworld. Queen of *Annwvn*. Where you put me."

Desperation claws at his throat. "Aine, please! Release me! Help me! I'll find someone to free you, someone to take your place, I promise! I love you! I was tricked! Please, I promise I'll help free you! We can be together!"

"I will be better than you," she vows, and he knows that she *is* better than him. She will make a majestic queen, ruling over the dead with honour, not tricking the lost and the vulnerable into taking her place. But then she speaks again, her voice as cold as he has ever heard it. As cold as dead water. "I will break myself from this prison, and I will live free and whole." So. She will do as he has done after all. They always do. "But first," she adds, her voice so chilly that he shivers, "I will feed the water that rots your flesh. I will watch you moulder and turn to mushrooms."

He shrieks,

And he pleads,

And he rages,

And he begs.

She smiles, but there is no joy.

She is a prisoner queen, and she lifts her chin high.

She smiles, and the waters creep in.

THE PARTY

LOUIE STOWELL

This time it was going to be different. New school, new me. I would be painting on a pristine life canvas, like snow without footprints or dog piss.

I played with my ring as I got ready, like some kind of jumpy Gollum.

I'm going to do better this time. I'm going to find people who are good for me. I'm not going to wreck everything over some toxic girl.

My mother looked up from her computer when I came down for breakfast.

"You're wearing that?" A perfect eyebrow raise. "It's not very flattering."

Thanks, Mum. I've only spent the last week planning what to wear, carefully selecting items to project exactly the right kind of impression.

This outfit was meant to say, "Hey, teachers, I'm

non-threatening and diligent" while also saying, "Hey, hundred or so girls who are about to be my year group who've never met me before, I am incredibly cool in an understated, not-trying-too-hard manner."

And now all the near-religious faith I had imbued these clothes with had flipped into self-conscious self-loathing. My jeans felt too tight, my T-shirt too baggy, my overshirt wrong and ugly in some secret, third way I couldn't even imagine but my mother had managed to intuit in a glance.

My mum has SKILLS. A true assassin of confidence.

My dad had already gone to work, which I was glad of. He never actually defended me when she attacked like this. He just looked a bit sad about it all, so I had to feel guilty about making him feel awkward while also getting busy hating myself.

Mum works from home, which meant she is always there, ready to strike.

I sat down and poured some cereal. She was too wrapped up in a news story on her laptop about a recent murder to comment on how much I took, or how whole milk is a type of moral failing. So I suppose I should take that as a small victory. Thank you, whoever got murdered, for the distraction, I guess.

When I was ready to go, she gave me a few "encouraging" words. "Please, darling, make the most of this opportunity. You were very lucky to get into this school. While you might have been above average at Finchley, you can't expect to find it easy at St Mark's. It would be such a shame if you didn't make the most of this unique chance."

That is, don't shame me, my child of shame. My failchild.

Luckily, we'd agreed I would take the tube on my own, so I had time to calm down before I stepped inside the not-at-all-terrifying wrought-iron gates of my new school. Compared to fifteen minutes of psychic torture with my mother, forty-five minutes slammed in a stranger's armpit was like a spa break.

The dark red brick building looked like a Victorian prison. But the sort of prison where you had to be a multimillionaire supermodel convict to deserve to go there. I held back before going through the gates, watching girls swish through them, long hair flowing, like a flood of beauty and flowers.

OK, there were also some hardcore weirdos, just to break up the flow of models. That was reassuring at least. One of them was carrying a teddy bear. The other one had a bag with graffiti drawn on it in sparkly gel pen. In Latin.

So in I went.

The entrance hall was vast, and the floor was covered with marble squares. I was used to fancy buildings – my parents were always dragging me to fundraisers, and my old school was not exactly a concrete box. But this school was next level.

It was cool inside, which was a relief. I was still a bit

sweaty from the tube. I took a deep breath and got ready for my minty-fresh new start.

But when I saw her, I knew everything was already ruined. Nothing ruins a do-over like your ex turning up.

She was looking at me across the marble hallway. Her eyes roamed up and down me, and I couldn't tell if she was judging my outfit or picturing me naked. Those cold, blue, beautiful eyes. They still gave me shivers. I had to remind myself why we broke up. Even while resisting a strong urge to run my fingers through her tousled blonde hair.

She's bad for you. She's bad for EVERYONE. Everything she touches turns to shit.

But that was a bad thought to have. Because now I was thinking about her touching me.

This is bad. This is very bad.

I couldn't decide whether to ignore her or bite the bullet right away and say a polite but frosty hello. But, like always, she made the choice for me.

"Hi," she said, sidling up to me in that graceful way she has. Moving without seeming to disturb the air. Without effort. "There you are again."

"Here I am," I said. "Why are YOU here?"

Her smile spread like poison through a glass of water. "I knew you were applying here but I wasn't sure if you'd get in."

Ouch.

"But I'm glad you did," she added. She never left it at an insult. There was always the honey afterwards.

Oh good. That old feeling's back. Sick but excited. Full of hate and the other thing.

I'm not proud of it, but my first instinct was to kiss her. Or rather, to let her kiss me. But I wasn't going there again. *That way* lies pain. Let's board up the route to that way and never mention it again.

But then again … perhaps it would be different this time? Maybe she had changed since before the summer?

Or *maybe* it was a good thing a teacher interrupted before I argued my way into making excuses for her again and mentally constructed a world in which I save her, rather than the usual she-drags-me-down-with-her.

"Lily Campbell? Jess Morgan? Welcome!" The teacher beamed at us, and as she smiled, I recognized her. It was the deputy head who interviewed me. I won her over with my cunning dropping of the most pretentious literary references I could think of. She smiled just like that when I mentioned Sartre's *Huis Clos*. I even did the French accent when I said it. Although I didn't say the main reason I'd read it in the first place was because Jess said it had lesbians in it.

I was guessing Jess didn't even have to try to wow the teacher in her interview. She was scarily, effortlessly clever and had a kind of charm that worked just as well on adults as it did on me.

She was still looking at me. I could feel it. But I kept my eyes firmly on the teacher and slapped a polite, well-behaved smile on my face.

"I'll take you to your class. I'm Ms Isaacs," she reminded me, glancing down at my hand. "You'll be pleased to learn that the seventh form has a more relaxed jewellery policy than the lower forms."

Of course I knew that. I'm the sort of person who actually reads the pamphlets schools send you, from cover to cover. I have to know everything, just in case someone catches me out.

I already knew where all the classrooms were, where the fencing salle was (yes, it's THAT sort of school), who to talk to if I needed counselling for my inevitable eating disorder, and the professions of all the key alumnae (they basically run the world). I even memorized all the faces of the girls in the brochure.

I'd already done all the reading on the holiday reading list they sent, even though the school stressed they didn't expect me to, as I might not have had such a broad curriculum at my old school. (I think the powers that be at St Mark's Girls' School see all state schools as basically feral animal pits where you spend more time on knife crime than studying. Even though my last school had a catchment area where a a shoebox-sized house would set you back upwards of a million pounds and the main crime problem was a group of the dads going to prison for stock market fraud.)

Jess, on the other hand, probably hadn't done any of the reading over summer. She didn't need to. She could bluff her way through any situation, any exam, any lesson.

It was like witchcraft, watching her bluff. I sometimes wondered if she had hypnotic powers, conning teachers into believing she'd done all the homework. Jess was a person who wouldn't know effort if it bit her on her absolutely deliciously perfect bottom.

(Yes, I'm over her, why do you ask, stop perceiving me.)

All of which is why I was so shocked when Jess first showed an interest in me back at my last school. When I met her, I knew from the very first moment our eyes met across a crowded party that, while I was the sort of person to get up in my head about that being a cliché – and start to spiral about whether or not I should approach her – she just strode over, thoughtless, and proceeded to ruin my life.

Every school has its hierarchy. Jess wasn't just the queen. She was off the charts. Maybe she was God? Or at least one of his angels. (One of the dirty, troubled fallen ones that get a new gig running hell while wearing immaculate white suits that really bring out the red in their pointed horns.) I actually asked her at one point why she was interested in me.

"Because you're real," she said. "Warm. Present. You're not putting on an act."

And then we'd started kissing and other stuff so I never did fully get to the bottom of why the coolest girl in the school was still slumming it with someone who only avoided bullying by some kind of miracle.

Maybe I'm just incredibly good at sex? Maybe my aura

says SEXCELLENT? Though my mouth often ruins it by using words like "sexcellent".

We were in the classroom now. I scanned the faces. None of the brochure girls. Maybe they were long gone by now. Ms Isaacs introduced us to everyone.

The girls all looked very interested. This was my chance at a first impression. Jess was not going to ruin this. I wasn't going to try too hard. I was going to let things happen naturally. But I wasn't going to mouse my way through this either. I was going to assert myself. I was going to…

"Shall we sit over there?" suggested Jess, looking at the chairs no doubt intended for us. She didn't need to take charge here. But with that, she was the alpha.

So much for breaking old patterns.

But a girl on the other side of me leaned over. Short, spiky dark hair, dark eyes, very intense looking. She was tall and curvy to the point that you could legitimately use the word "statuesque" without sounding pretentious. It was just accurate. They should build statues of her. Her cheekbones alone deserved some serious marble.

"Hi, new girl," she whispered, as the teacher fussed at the front of the classroom. "Here." She slid a piece of card on to my desk.

It was an honest-to-God gold-outlined invitation, in the sort of curly writing that Lady Weatherton-Smythe or whoever uses in period dramas to invite you to the ball if you're a plucky Jane Austen heroine with only a small fortune but you make up for that in polite sarcasm and excellent hats.

On the Austen theme, it really was an invite to a *literal* ball this Saturday.

You are cordially invited to a ball at
Hill House, Merton Lane, NW3 4AW
from 8 p.m. on Saturday.

Dress: black tie

Carriages at 2 a.m.

Sophia Neville-Rolfe

I looked up at the girl – Sophia, presumably – with incredulity. She shrugged. "All welcome. My parents are away. Again. I'm practically an orphan at this point."

She was having a ball at her *house*? At my last school, I was one of the rich kids because my parents owned a house with a garden in north London. I knew this school would be different, but I thought it would be "has a house with a swimming pool" different.

Not a house with a *ballroom*.

I glanced over at Jess. She didn't have an invite. But, shameless as ever, she leaned over. "We'd *love* to come," she said.

"Everyone's invited," replied Sophia, and I enjoyed Jess's slightly disappointed expression.

"So I shouldn't feel special?" I asked, though looking more at Jess than Sophia.

"That depends," said Sophia. She gave me an appraising look. "Are you special?"

This was a chance. New school. No preconceptions. She didn't have any idea that I was the underdog.

"Darling, I'm the chosen one," I said.

I think Jess genuinely flinched.

Yesss! Flinch away. I'm not just your plus one here.

Sophia laughed. "Funny. You're funny. Or maybe an enormous, shameless dork. Either way, I'm not bored. I'm very often bored."

But then the beginning of the lesson stopped any further conversation.

I was so out of my depth that I checked out mentally about halfway through the period. I didn't mean to. My mind just couldn't cling on to all the unfamiliar terms and kept slipping off the maths like it was made of greasy rocks. I started doodling on my jotter and looking around the class, trying to imagine who everyone was. There was a row of extra-glossy girls who I knew without being told were going to be out of my league and not worth trying to make friends with.

Then there was a cluster of girls ignoring the maths teacher and talking amongst themselves. At first I thought I'd identified the "bad influences" in the class, who my mum warned me to stay away from this time. But as I listened in, I realised they were talking about mathematical formulae that were even more advanced than the already Einstein-level content the teacher was giving us. There seemed to be a tacit agreement that their chatting was allowed. Then I saw a group of girls slumped further down in their chairs, exchanging whispers and glances. OK, those *had* to be the bad influences. So obviously I planned my weddings to every single one of them in my mind before giving myself a mental slap. Finally, I noticed a line of wholesome-looking girls near the front quietly paying attention. I wasn't in any way interested in them or drawn to them. So they'd probably be good for me.

With great effort, I did not look at Jess. I muttered my mantra.

> *"We must not look at goblin men,*
> *We must not buy their fruits:*
> *Who knows upon what soil they fed*
> *Their hungry thirsty roots?"*

Yes, my mantra is Christina Rossetti. What part of me reading Jean-Paul Sartre for fun made you think I wasn't a bit of a pretentious wanker?

I find it comforting. I usually apply it to not replying to terrible men in my DMs, but it came in handy when ignoring all my terrible relationship instincts too. Or it would if I actually obeyed it.

I glanced at Sophia beside me instead of Jess. That was progress, right? She caught me looking and smiled, then scribbled a note.

So, fair warning. This place is scary as fuck. They're all terrifying. But don't worry. You just have to be equally terrifying, then they won't smell the fear. I keep the fear at bay by inviting them to parties. It confuses them.

I don't know why, but I found that comforting. Maybe knowing she was scared too, and she'd been here a while. And she'd clearly got up the courage to have a party and invite everyone – there were invites on various tables in front of even the glossiest, most intimidating girls – so she must have found her comfort zone eventually. Or learned to live in a place of heartbreaking terror.

Either way, I wasn't alone.

At lunch, I got a tray full of pizza and salad, but it turns out that was a no-no. Looking around the lunch hall, most of the girls were pushing salads around their plates. *Well, I don't care*, I lied to myself, taking a pudding too. While I am scared of getting kicked out, I'm not scared of a little peer pressure. In fact, peer pressure is something I am planning to avoid here because of last time.

(Well, Jess-pressure.)

There was a moment of pure panic that I'd have to sit down at a table without an invite, but Sophia, my saviour, waved me over to where she was sitting. I was relieved to see she had a plate of actual food too.

"Welcome. So, what brings you to St Mark's Asylum for Very Troubled Girls?" she asked.

I laughed. "Does everyone call it that?"

"Well, Coops and I do. So anyone who's anyone, really." Sophia spotted another girl from the slouching group and summoned her over with a wave of her hand. The girl she called Coops flopped over and sat down in a jumble of long legs and even longer hair.

"Hello, new girl!" said Coops. She gave me a salute. "Welcome to hell."

"Everyone really loves it here then?" I asked sarcastically.

"Dearly," said Sophia. "Like a terminal patient loves cancer."

"Like a murder victim loves poison," chimed in Coops.

"So happy to be here," I groaned. But I was at least a tiny bit happy. Finding people who appreciated the fine art of sarcastic despair was rare.

That was when Jess sat down with her tray full of nothing but water and coffee and things went downhill. Coops and Sophia were mesmerized by her and ignored me.

Or that was how it felt, anyway. Occasionally, Jess deigned to bring me into the conversation, in a way that made it seem like she was giving out a great favour to a lowly peasant. And then throwing said peasant under the social bus shortly after.

"Did you know that this little bad girl was expelled from her last school?" she purred in that jungle cat low murmur she reserved for the most salacious secrets.

Sophia and Coops clustered closer, glancing slightly at me, ready to suck up the delicious gossip. I couldn't believe she was telling this story. Except I could. It wasn't as though I could deny everything. I'd lied for so long, going back on what I'd said would make me seem unhinged.

I wanted to tell them it was all Jess's fault. But getting a reputation for being a grass on day one didn't seem like the best fresh start. So I let her tell the whole story, just as we'd told it to the teachers and our parents. The dare. The can of hairspray. The match. The ever so slight explosion and … you know, the part of the school that burned down.

"OMG, you never said you were a pyro," said Sophia.

"I'm not," I said. "It was just a dare that went a bit … far."

In truth, I don't know exactly what happened. Just that I was standing outside waiting for Jess while it happened, and definitely not playing with matches. All I know is that I covered for her because she'd begged me to, looking up from under her eyelashes, and I agreed because I am pathetic.

But whatever the truth, Sophia looked actively disappointed at Jess's story. "That level of chaos is just an average Tuesday at St Mark's. You'll have to up your game if you want to keep up."

Now it was Jess's turn to look disappointed. She'd hoped to shock them. But they were delighted.

Point to me.

"No one ever gets expelled here," said Coops. "Someone's daddy's always ready with a very persuasive new library whenever anyone steps out of line. The only thing that might get you politely asked to leave is an actual murder.

Even then, I think it would be borderline if your family funded a new wing of the building to hide the body under."

"Sounds like you'll fit right in," said Jess to me. A whisper in my ear. "Though I'm guessing even your daddy's nothing compared with the ones here."

Jess was always needling me about being posh. She'd never invited me back to her house because she claimed it was a hovel compared to mine, and I'd judge her. But for all I knew she lived in a palace and was fucking with my head. It was her favourite hobby after all.

"Nice ring," said Sophia, changing the subject like a hero and taking my hand to examine it more closely.

"My grandma's," I said. Her fingers were soft and cool and soon I was blushing.

She held out her hand and showed an antique ring with a ruby in it. "Same! Well, not same grandma, unless I'm going to find out something very surprising today, but this was my grandma's too."

"Heirloom club," said Jess. For a moment she genuinely looked vulnerable. Maybe she wasn't bullshitting, and all her working-class-hero shit was real?

That said, if it was so true, what was she doing here at posh school? I thought perhaps now was the safe moment to ask, surrounded by other people, where nothing could get out of hand.

"How come you moved schools? You weren't excluded," I asked her, as though I was just a normal former classmate asking my other former classmate a normal question.

"What can I say? I missed you," she said.

Did she really change schools JUST to fuck with my head? Just to prove to me that she was as good as me? I mean, on some level it was flattering.

(On a bad level that I should never visit.)

"OK, that and the fact that my mum thought I wasn't being pushed hard enough at the old place," Jess added, apparently feeling honest for once.

"So you guys knew each other well?" asked Coops.

"Only in the Biblical sense." Jess grinned.

Coops and Sophia exchanged knowing glances. "Ahhh, I was wondering where all the really dark energy was coming from," said Sophia. "Well, in this house, we like to name the elephant in the room."

"We name him Gerald," chimed in Coops.

"Or in this case, awkward ex energy," said Sophia.

Jess actually laughed at that. "OK, you've got me." She gestured towards me. "She broke my heart. Never got over it."

"Never? It was two months ago," I said. "And you got me expelled with your … dare."

"Then let's call it even," she said. Her smile was charming. Everything came rushing back from before it was broken. Maybe … maybe it would be different this time.

(Why do I hate myself?)

"So I'm reading the vibe," said Sophia, putting her hand to her forehead as if about to do a psychic reading … then she pointed at me. "You're 'I can save her' and you…" She pointed at Jess. "You're 'I can make her worse'."

Jess threw back her head and laughed so loud the whole dining hall looked up from their lack of lunch. When she stopped, she said, "I like you, Sophia. You're trouble."

"Takes one to know one." Sophia smiled.

Oh God. They were flirting.

Which I was fine with. Because I was going nowhere near Jess ever again in that way.

On the plus side, everyone here was clearly as queer as balls.

I told myself it was great if Sophia and Jess got together. Sophia would save me from myself. Yup.

The rest of the week, I watched Sophia and Jess flirt with each other and tried to bury myself in work I didn't understand. The result was that I just felt jealous AND lost. Brilliant work, Lily; your finest work, I think.

When Sophia invited us over to get changed before the party, I knew I was welcoming a world of pain into my heart. And did it anyway because … who knows? Who knows why I do anything? If you find out, tell me. Living in my brain is like living in some kind of black hole of whirling chaos.

(I'm cheerful. I swear to you that I'm a very cheerful person if you meet me. Exterior Lily is a delight. It's just the interior version that chants "Death! Death! All is death and pain!")

Watching Sophia and Jess play fight as they shared make-up and swapped outfits in Sophia's palatial bedroom was the kind of torture that I'm pretty sure they've outlawed at the UN.

Coops glanced at me as she pulled on her black trousers. "You OK?"

"I'm wonderful," I said. "Perfect. Blissful, even."

"I find it helps if you imagine them dead," she offered. "Like, dead by something really banal. Like ... fell over a shoe or run over by a milk float."

"Thanks," I said. "I'll go with choking on a well-worn sock."

"Good choice."

The party was empty of guests at first. Of guests, I mention specifically, because it *did* have a live band, a bunch of waiters carrying trays of champagne and snacks, a bubbling chocolate fountain, and several live flamingos.

Still, in spite of all that, I felt nervous for Sophia. I can't have parties because I live in crushing fear of no one turning up. Or the wrong people turning up and making it a shit party. But Sophia didn't seem to care. She nodded to the band to start playing and started dancing in the empty ballroom. Her slinky floor-length velvet dress was HOT. She was much more graceful dancing than I thought she'd be from just seeing her at school. She swayed her hips and lifted her muscular arms above her head, and I couldn't look away.

"Might I have this dance?" asked Jess, bowing. She was immaculate in a black-tie suit. Her bow tie was one of those pre-tied ones, but she made it work.

Sophia laughed and took her by the hand.

I decided it was probably a very good time to go and find something very strong to drink. Coops came with me. And, thankfully, people started to arrive soon enough that I had an excuse to go and answer the door instead of returning to the ballroom to find them probably having sex on the dance floor or something.

I hadn't learned anyone's names yet, but first to arrive was one of the "allowed to talk in maths" girls. She looked nervous and a little bit surprised to be there. Sure, I knew Sophia had invited everyone, but I didn't think that kind of everyone would dare turn up.

(Have I mentioned I am also a bitch?)

"Is this Sophia's house?" Maths Girl asked when I answered the door.

"Might as well be," said Coops, leaning over my shoulder. "Her parents are literally never here. Come on in!"

"Drinks are over here." I gestured to the drinks cabinet that apparently Sophia's parents gave her free rein with. I quickly decided that the best way to deal with heartbreak was getting everyone messily drunk as fast as possible like some kind of stylish yet tragic and mysterious party host. If I couldn't be happy, I could be Gatsby.

And I could, of course, be drunk myself. I mixed a

cocktail. I'd never done that before, unless you count vodka and Coke. I didn't really know what would go together, but I took a punt, and I think I did pretty well for an amateur. It was so strong I nearly died from my throat being on fire after a single sip, but that was the point, wasn't it? It burned down my throat and spread me full of fire. I still had thoughts, though, so clearly I needed a few more. In the meantime, I grabbed a glass of champagne from a passing tray.

More and more people arrived. In trotted the glossy, shiny girls from class. I hadn't learned to tell them apart yet. They were a broad brushstroke of generic beauty and expensive perfume.

The whole class eventually turned up, plus a few people from other years too. And boys, obviously.

Now, boys are fine, although I couldn't eat a whole one. But they do scrub up well. A 6/10 boy put into black tie is suddenly at least an 8. They were mostly from the other nearby boys' school, not the one attached to ours. Coops informed me that the boys from ours were all absolutely hideous and surgically attached to their briefcases and calculators.

"Boys are currency at St Mark's. Sophia seems to know every boy in a four-hundred-mile radius – I don't know where she finds them – and that means everyone comes to her parties. Even people she never talks to."

"Having a house that's basically a stately home can't hurt too?" I pointed out.

"I mean, I wouldn't kick her house out of bed for farting, true," said Coops. She took a pull on her beer, then held it up. "Cheers! Here's to blacking out and forgetting the pain of life as quickly as possible."

But unfortunately, I didn't black out quickly enough. Before I could drink myself into sweet, sweet oblivion, I saw Jess with her tongue in Sophia's mouth.

So I did the rational thing and went over to dance with them to show how much I didn't care. After quickly realizing they didn't even notice me, the drinking sped up. I kissed someone. I couldn't tell you who. Several someones, in fact, unless the first girl quickly grew stubble in between kisses.

I woke up on the floor, regretting all my choices. Not just last night's. My mind spooled through every bad choice I'd ever made, dredging up ones I'd even forgotten.

I felt like pure, unadulterated shit. Like I'd literally been drained of all that was good in the world and had my blood replaced with poison.

Not to be dramatic, but I thought I might be dying. Also I was going to kill Coops, as she kept mixing me cocktails while just drinking beer herself.

Flashes came back from the night. Each one brought a wave of cringe that was sort of how I imagined being stabbed in the intestines must feel. Each one a roiling, excruciating, painful surprise.

Yelling at Sophia for moving in on Jess.

Yelling at Jess for Jessing.

Yelling at Coops because she tried to pull me off Sophia.

Letting someone give me a hickey.

Seeing Jess kiss ANOTHER girl. One of the shiny girls from my class. Then move back to Sophia.

Skinny dipping in the pool. FREEZING my tits off before I could get back into my dress.

Puking on a boy I'd just been kissing. OK, that was a bit funny.

Crying in a corner because Sophia and Jess had gone up to Sophia's bedroom.

Stumbling over the body of a girl covered in blood…

Suddenly I was very awake. What the FUCK?

The flash of what I'd seen came again. The face familiar, but I couldn't place the name. One of the shiny girls. The one Jess had been kissing.

Drizzles of blood sliding down her neck like piped icing gone runny and wrong.

I staggered to my feet. Various girls and boys were sleeping on the floor of the ballroom in nests made of coats and sofa cushions, with the odd duvet stolen from a bed upstairs. I scanned the floor for her. Nowhere.

Where did I fall over her? Was I dreaming?

Then a scream came that woke every single sleeping person on that floor. People started to run in the direction of the scream. It was outside, by the swimming pool.

"Miranda!" came a yell.

"Call the police!" came another.

"No, don't," said someone else. "My parents can't find out I was here."

Miranda — the body, the girl from my class — lay by the pool. There wasn't much blood, except on her neck. "There should be more blood," I found myself murmuring.

"Did she drown?"

"Did she hit her head?"

My eyes were drawn to the wounds on her neck. A flash came of Jess kissing her last night. No. Not kissing.

Her mouth was on her neck, not her lips, like some kind of vampire.

WAIT!

I couldn't be thinking this. This was not a thing that could happen. This was not a thing that was real. I was very hungover. I was in a very strange place emotionally. Movies are fictional. There were many, many rational explanations that were not that. I just could not think of a single one in that particular moment.

But ... I'd seen Jess in the sunlight.

Except I didn't know why I thought I knew how vampires worked, because I'd seen some films and they didn't all agree about the sun thing anyway, even if films *were* a reliable source of scientifically accurate knowledge of vampires. All I knew was that vampires drank blood and Miranda was looking very, very bloodless.

I couldn't believe how many times my brain was saying the word "vampires". Jess was very obviously not a vampire. Miranda must have died for normal reasons and this hangover had broken my mind.

Then again, Jess always said I let my anxiety run away with me.

But I shouldn't listen to what Jess said. Because she was clearly a vampire.

I started laughing. Coops came over and asked me what was going on. I pointed to the body in the garden.

"What are you laughing at?" she asked.

"I think I'm hysterical."

"I think I might be getting that way too," said Coops. "Have you seen Sophia? Jess?"

I shook my head. Not since last night.

"Ah," said Coops. "That wasn't tactful, was it? I find tact hard."

"It's OK. I think tact went out of the window when we woke up to find a dead body at the party," I said. The hysterical laughter was coming back.

The police were never called. No one wanted to deal with that. So everyone just left. Until, an hour later, Jess and Sophia emerged from Sophia's bedroom to the bomb site of the house. I took them to the body.

"Shit," said Jess. "Shit."

"Shit," agreed Sophia. "My parents are… Is there a way to stop my parents finding out? I mean, they're neglectful fucks, but I think they might start the discipline firing pistol if they find out someone died on my watch."

246

"You're worried about … not being able to have more parties?" I said, incredulous.

Sophia flashed an apologetic smile. "Did I mention that I'm a bit of a bitch sometimes?"

No, but kissing Jess in front of me said that for you, I thought.

"It's OK," said Jess. "We can just move the body and then call the police anonymously."

Exactly what a murderous vampire *would* do.

The sun hit her pale skin. Very much not burning and crumbling to dust.

Unless vampires *can* go out in the day?

Sophia pursed her lips. "Look, none of you should have to deal with this. My party, my problem. I'm going to call the police. You all leave so you don't have to get involved."

I was going to volunteer to stay, nobly. But the others left without more than a nod. And I'm not a hero when it comes down to it.

At school on Monday, there were whispers all around the class about what might have happened. Whether Sophia's parents had come home. Whether she was in jail right now.

But then she walked into the classroom. With Miranda at her side. Looking one hundred per cent not dead.

The whole class gasped, and the two girls collapsed laughing. "We got you!" spluttered Miranda.

Sophia looked over at me, Jess and Coops and shrugged apologetically. "What can I say? I'm a messy bitch who loves drama."

"That … was all a fakeout?" said Coops, looking hurt, not so much that she had been forced to go through the trauma, but more that she wasn't in on the joke.

"Mum's in film," said Miranda, putting an arm around Sophia. "I have a LOT of stage make-up around. Looking like a dead body was easy."

"I didn't even know you two were friends?" said Coops.

"I have many secrets," said Sophia. At that, her glance strayed over to Jess.

I felt even sicker than with my hangover the day before.

Actually, my hangover was no better. Two days later, it was worse if anything. I felt like my skin was on fire, and my guts were churning. Very unfair. I only drank … OK, everything in the house. But still. Two days later!

On the plus side, the pain in my head was distracting. Slightly. I only slightly obsessively watched every movement of Sophia and Jess. Every little look. Every little arm touch.

It could have been worse. I might have said something. But I felt too much like I was dying. So that was a mild win.

In the evening, my mum said I looked pale. "You didn't take drugs at that party, did you?" she asked. "I can't have you throwing away this opportunity."

I shook my head. "No drugs."

Just heartbreak and despair and an entire liquor cabinet down my gullet.

I went up to my room after dinner. My stomach was queasy. My skin was burning up.

Great. I was sick.

Actually … that *was* great. Not going into school tomorrow and seeing Jess and Sophia all over each other sounded like a gift.

Except, when I woke up, the temperature was gone, and I felt fine. Just a bit tired. So off to school I went.

Jess came over to me at break when Sophia was in the loo. "I'm sorry about the other night," she said. She sounded sincere. "I got carried away. One drink and I'm anybody's."

I shrugged. "You did nothing wrong," I said, very much hoping I projected a complete absence of caring what she did with her tongue. "We're cool."

She cocked her head on one side. "We don't feel cool."

"You feel what you like," I said, and walked away like someone who definitely didn't care.

I pretended to care about French and chemistry and art, and whenever Jess or Sophia looked like they might speak to me, I suddenly found something Coops was saying hilarious, or I needed the toilet, or a drink, or I had some very plausible reason not to pay attention to them, like inspecting some important dirt under my nails.

Though I did notice they weren't touchy-feely any more. Maybe it was a one-night thing? Maybe I was panicking about nothing?

I mean, I wasn't panicking. I was cool. So very cool I might as well be dead.

At the end of school, Jess touched my arm to say

goodbye and recoiled slightly. "Fuck, you're cold. Should you be in school?"

"I'm fine." I didn't feel cold.

On the way to the tube, Sophia caught up and made me stop and sit with her on a park bench. "I fucked up. I'm sorry. But aren't you going to talk to me about what happened?"

"What *did* happen?" I snapped.

"We kissed, Lily," she said.

"Yes, I know you did. You don't have to rub it in."

"Not just me and Jess. You and me!" She blinked at me, incredulous. "Were you really that drunk?"

I froze. "What?"

She laughed. "Oh God, you really don't remember! I thought you were avoiding me about it on purpose."

"I'm avoiding you because you kissed Jess," I said.

"I only did that to make you jealous!" said Sophia. "And I think she only kissed me to do the same."

Maybe I was beginning to remember what happened. The edges of a recollection. Lips. My fingers in Sophia's spiky hair. Her pulling me closer, surprisingly strong but oh so soft. Her brown eyes gazing deeply into mine. Then her lips on my neck.

And her teeth. And my blood. The pulse in my neck growing fainter. Until I heard a sickening crunch. She'd bitten her own wrist. Then I'd tasted blood.

A vampire's blood. I'd been bitten by a fucking vampire, and she'd made me drink her blood. Admittedly a sexy vampire with an incredible house. But wasn't that all vampires? Sexy, with an impressive real-estate portfolio.

I looked up at the vampire. Yes. The *vampire*. The beautiful, cheekbones-like-razors vampire. I should've known she was a vampire purely based on those. Except, until just now, that would have been an absurd thing to think.

She was perfectly still, waiting for me to say something. Could she read my mind? Had she realized that I knew what she was?

If you're reading my mind right now, FUCK YOU! I thought, petulantly. What I said was, "What did you do to me?" Then I edged away from her on the bench, as though that provided any kind of safety. "What happened with Miranda?"

"I don't usually eat at home when I have company, but I got carried away." Sophia sighed. "Don't worry, though. She really is fine."

"Fine?" I asked. What definition of fine was she working with here?

"Yes, admittedly, I killed her. But I also changed her," said Sophia, weirdly proud. I suppose she had basically done a God and brought someone back from the dead. "I'm not planning on making her my immortal bride, though, so there's no need to be jealous. Miranda's mean enough to make her own way. Probably after eating her family, mind you, knowing her."

"How are you outside?" I found myself saying.

Somehow responding to the horrifying things she'd just said felt outside my social range. I looked up at the strong summer afternoon sun.

"Myths are myths." She laughed. "Reality's reality." She leaned forward. "But I can show you all the secrets, in time, if you like."

"I thought it was Jess," I murmured. "I thought she was the…" I waved my hand instead of finishing. Saying the v-word out loud was too much.

"Just because she's a bad girl, doesn't mean she's the living dead," said Sophia.

I found the strangest questions bubbling up. When I should've been screaming and running, I started asking practical questions. Like I was asking about her getting a new cat or learning a language.

"How long have you been a vampire?" I asked.

"A year," said Sophia. She pouted. "You didn't think I was some creepy hundred-and-fifty-year-old, did you? The one who turned me was a bit of a creep. When I met him, I thought he was just an eighteen-year-old into retro music. But it turns out Roy Orbison was new when he was human. Next question."

I don't know why I asked what I asked next. "Do your parents know?"

That made Sophia explode with laughter. "Parents? Oh, they're dead. I soon realized they were going to be very inconvenient. They've always been very absent, but I needed them to be a hundred per cent absent forever if I was going to live life the way I wanted. Or … well, 'live' might be the wrong word." She flashed me a smile. The sharp canines I'd never noticed because you don't exactly go round inspecting people's teeth like you do with horses, do you?

It only just then occurred to me to be very, very afraid. There was no one around in the park. It was getting dark – apparently night and day had no effect on vampires, but the darkness affected whether someone would see her feasting on my blood and come and rescue me from certain death. A rush of blood pumped through me. I felt tingly and strange. Was I having a stroke? A panic attack? Turning into a vampire?

"How I feel right now … did you do something to me?" I asked. "Did you…?"

"Turn you? No. Or rather … not yet. I drained you nearly to the edge and then fed you enough to get you up and about again for a little while. But now, you have a choice. I wanted you to have a choice."

I realized I was almost disappointed. I wanted her to say she'd turned me. That I was a guileless victim. That nothing I did was my fault any more because I was a monster. I also wanted to kiss her, because look at her. *Focus, Lily.*

She held out her wrist, which I realized was bleeding. A sluggish dribble of blood rather than an arterial pump. "Drink," she said. "Or not. I can make you forget if you choose not to. But I'd much prefer if you'd join me."

"Why me? Why not Miranda? Or Jess? Aren't vampires meant to be, you know, cool?"

"See, it's exactly that kind of self-awareness that I like in you. Anyone who considers themselves cool is going to get tedious very quickly. You're the first person I've found interesting enough to consider spending eternity with."

"Eternity?" I said.

She laughed. "I think it's a nice spin on the 'second date is a moving van' cliche. Second date is eternity. But I'm not being serious. There's no obligation to stay with me, immortal beloved. But we could have so *much* fun."

I thought about it. Detaching from all the human mess of things. Not caring about Jess, or anyone. Just enjoying the feeling of thirst and killing. Next time my mum called me fat? I could drink her blood.

I felt this unsettling hunger well up in me at the thought. The blood. Sophia's blood. I could smell it. I shouldn't be able to smell it. A spicy metallic warmth. I wanted to take her wrist in my mouth and drink.

Then I did. I took her wrist between my fingers and my lips were about to close and my teeth about to bite down when there was a *thump* and a rush of air and I was holding nothing.

And Jess was standing there, holding a sharp wooden stick, and Sophia wasn't anywhere. Dust everywhere.

"What the fuck?"

"Are you OK?" asked Jess. She put the stick down and sat beside me. Where Sophia had been moments before.

"What the fuck?" I said again because it was still true.

Jess tapped the stake. "So … there might be some things I didn't tell you. Who I am. Why I started the fire that got you expelled. Why I followed you to this school."

"For her?" I whispered. "To kill her?"

"To protect you," she said. "I knew she was here. I'd been hunting her for a while. I couldn't risk her hurting you. So I got close to her to kill her. I nearly did at the party, but you kept interrupting."

"I thought you were … you know."

Jess grinned. "Oh, we were. I'm not a saint."

"Didn't you spend the night together?" I asked, narrowing my eyes.

"No, some drunk boy fell asleep in her room so I had to sleep there to make sure Sophia didn't turn him into a midnight snack." She held up her hands. "It was all above board."

"If you say so." I closed my eyes. Shit shit shit. Discovering my stunning, sexy fucking ex was Buffy the fucking Vampire Slayer was not going to help me get over her. I opened my eyes to see her looking right at me. "So you're a … vampire slayer?"

"I usually go with the term assassin. It sounds hot and fewer trademark issues." She put her hand on my arm. "You're less cold. That's good. And it'll pass."

"What will? Being cold?" I was confused. And I was panicking internally.

"Her blood, it'll leave you," said Jess. "You just might feel shitty for a few days."

"This is not the fresh start I was hoping for," I said, staring down at the pile of dust that was Sophia. Well, less a pile. More a scattering. Hardly anything left.

I felt Jess slip her hand into mine. "I'm guessing this is all a bit of a shock?"

"You think?" I said, with a very unappealing bark-laugh. I sounded like an angry seal with a bad cold. Sexy.

But Jess squeezed my hand. "Look. I know I'm a bit of a dick. But I like you. And I don't want you to get eaten."

Well, wasn't *that* just peak romance?

"I'm touched," I said. I looked up at her. "Though my first thought when Miranda … you know … was that you were the vampire."

"I do have a certain creature-of-the-night charm." Jess grinned. "It's the hypnotically blue eyes, isn't it?"

"You're so full of yourself."

"I *am* a vampire assassin," Jess pointed out.

"How are we having this conversation?" I murmured. I felt pretty wild, I won't lie. My mind felt like it was a million miles above my body. Then something brought me crashing down to earth again. The crack of a twig. A light footstep. Hands around my throat. A whisper in my ear.

"You forgot about me, didn't you?" said Miranda. She had one vice-like freezing hand around my neck and the other around Jess's throat.

You know how you always think that you'd be good in a fight, somehow? At least, I always did. I used to walk home alone at night imagining someone jumping me, and me throwing them off with the small amount of judo I learned aged ten. I always imagined instinct would kick in and I'd be able to fight for my life like an action movie hero.

I mean, instinct *did* kick in. Unfortunately, no magical co-ordination and muscle strength kicked in to go with it. My hand flailed around on the bench. My fingers bumped the wood and the stake fell to the ground. For a moment I found myself more disappointed that I hadn't magically levelled up than terrified that I was about to die.

(Help, my priorities, they are very sick.)

Then Miranda screamed. She was covered in water and started to steam. Jess bent down, grabbed the stake in one sweep, and stabbed Miranda in the chest. God, she was a sexy vampire assassin.

Miranda disappeared into dust like Sophia had.

I stared. My mouth fell ungracefully open. I chose that moment to completely lose my shit. This was too much. Just too much. I fell to my knees and started hyperventilating.

Jess held out a flask. "Vodka," she said. "I think you need it."

I took a swig and felt the hot liquid coat – and then probably strip – my throat.

"Is that what you poured on her?" I asked when I'd gathered myself.

Jess nodded.

"Vampires are allergic to alcohol? That's definitely not in any of the movies," I said, flumping down on the bench before my legs gave way.

"They are … when the alcohol is mixed with holy water." Jess smiled. "That one? Not a myth."

We sat in silence for a moment.

"Are there more?" I asked at last.

"In the world? Yes. In our school? No."

Silence again.

"Look," said Jess, "I know I've not been as nice to you as you deserve. I spend a lot of time doing … dark things. Spending time around monsters, I forget how to human sometimes. I push people away. I…"

"Get them expelled?" I suggested.

"Not my finest moment, blaming you for the fire," said Jess, not meeting my eyes. "But I couldn't have people asking questions about why I was at school that night, starting fires myself."

"Why *were* you starting fires?" I asked, leaning forward. "A little light arson as a treat, when you're not killing the evil dead?"

"The fire was the only quick way I could think of to take out a group of vampires who cornered me in that disused garage by the side of the school."

(So, fire kills vampires. I filed that one away for later. Because this is the sort of information that is useful to my life now, apparently.)

"So," I said. "What now?"

"Maybe we could start over? A blank slate? Now you know the truth about me."

"Truth? You've barely told me *anything*. I need the *whole* story immediately. How? Why? When? What the fuck? Etc etc."

"So what I'm getting is that you're not saying *no* to the blank slate."

"We'll see," I said.

"That, I can work with," said Jess. She gave me that disarming grin.

Am I a fool for giving her a chance? Look. I'm only human. And, in her defence, so is she.

THE CHIMING HOUR

AMY McCULLOCH

I wake, but I know something's wrong. I'm too awake, like an elastic band that's been snapped – not the gentle, dreamy, easy morning wakening that happens when your body rises naturally.

Something has startled me – a noise? A flash?

I wait for my eyes to adjust to the darkness, shifting so I'm sitting up against the wooden headboard.

I see Clara in the bed opposite me, the lumpy form of her beneath the duvet. Her breathing is steady, but that's when I realize what's bothering me. I can see her breath, streaming out. Our curtains are fluttering; one of our windows is open. Who would do that? It's freezing outside.

Reluctantly I swing my legs out from under the ratty duvet. I let out a hiss as my feet touch the floor. It feels like it's made of ice, not wooden planks.

I cross the room as fast as possible and shut the window, flecks of paint peeling off the ancient wood.

All is quiet outside, dark. And no wonder. The pale white face of the clock in the far corner of our room reads just gone three a.m. It's one of those old-fashioned grandfather clocks, with a pendulum that swings. At first the sound kept me up, but now it's faded into the background. Like the rest of the weird quirks of this house.

Maybe that's what woke me. The chime as the clock struck three a.m.

Now I'm up, I might as well check on the kids.

That's the whole reason I'm here. Working as a camp grunt (OK, fine, counsellor) over October half-term, supervising children their parents can't handle for a week. Although there's something in it for me too, I suppose. It's an art camp, run by the once-famous artist Genevieve Pendell, who's displayed in galleries and museums all around the world. A nice letter of recommendation from her, and I could end up at my preferred art college, so I suck it up.

There are all sorts of classes here, in painting, pottery, crafts – all kinds of activities that generally mean my arms are a permanent kaleidoscope of paint splatter and dried clay and leave me smelling vaguely like chemicals despite showering twice a day. At least I get to do what I love. Photography. And when I need some time out, I can escape to the darkroom and pretend to be processing for a while.

Besides, I need the money. If I want to get out of here

next year and head to art school in London. Rather than being stuck in deepest, darkest Somerset.

I sneak out of the room, careful not to wake Clara. She wouldn't appreciate it if I started disturbing her sleep. She reminds me of me when I first started doing this job: eager, keen, extra chirpy. Give it a couple of stints and she'll get worn down and cynical just like me.

I pad down the wooden hallway, wishing I'd put on my slippers or slept in my socks. At first I was obsessed with this old house: the creaky floorboards, the wooden panelling running up the walls, the threadbare rugs on the floors, the old kitchen with its huge brick oven. But my favourite part of the house is the Long Gallery – a hallway hung floor to ceiling with paintings and portraits. They date back to the sixteenth century, all these long-dead people, their personalities and deeds and talents long forgotten, but their likenesses preserved forever in oil and on canvas. They watch us as we take over for the week, their eyes following us down the hallway. No matter what angle you look at them from, they always appear to be watching.

And it's not only old paintings hung up there. The Long Gallery is an exhibition of artwork, curated by Ms Pendell herself. To be up on the walls is the aim of all the kids who come through the art camp. There are plinths to display sculptures, places to show off bespoke macramé and knitted objects, and of course, my speciality – photography. It's a clash of styles and tastes and talents, but somehow it works.

Everyone wants to get their art displayed. Every so often, Ms Pendell will be so impressed by someone's work that she'll call it out. Make room for it in the gallery. It's like a prize – something for us to work towards.

But in the middle of the night, when I'm all alone, the Long Gallery can only be described in one way: creepy AF, and I rush through as fast as I can.

The whole house changes mood when it's dark and quiet. Like it's observing everyone who passes through its doors. Like it's breathing. And it must have seen some things. The history of the building dates back to the Tudor age – there's a crest on the wall that we tell the parents means Henry VIII visited sometime. I wonder which one of his wives (or mistresses) he brought here. There's a bloody history too – Catholic priests ripped from their hiding places, bitter family feuds, and then children brought here during the Second World War. Layer upon layer of history so deep I suspect there are as many secrets holding this place together as there are bricks. History is told by the victors, isn't that the saying? I wonder how much has been lost, fallen between the cracks, buried, plastered over and forgotten.

I relax when I reach the first bedroom, opening the door a fraction, and I can tell by the sound of steady breathing that all the children are fast asleep.

It's not the same in the second room. As I approach, the silence is so loud it's almost deafening. I open the door and walk to the first bed – empty. I roll my eyes. I know what that means.

I find them gathered in the third room. One of them – the ringleader: Jack, I think his name is – has a torch under his chin, shining up beneath his eyes. He's a show-off, a total extrovert. His artistic talent is the ability to spin a lot of BS. Still, he's entertaining. He seems to be coming to the end of his story, so I linger in the doorway.

"That was the last time that anyone ever laid eyes on that little girl. And if you listen carefully, during the chiming hour, you can still hear her screaming for help…"

"What happened to her?" asks one of the other boys, almost breathless.

"They don't know. No one ever saw her again. And that's why this place is so creepy. Her ghost still haunts the hallways – especially…"

"The Long Gallery," says another kid, rapt, terrified.

"But if we all hold hands and chant together, we might be able to call her down here."

A ripple of fear spreads round the room, and I know if this goes on much longer, we're going to have a whole load of overly tired, cranky children to look after in the morning.

I push the door open and it bangs against the oak-panelled wall. "OK, you lot, back to bed. Don't you know what time it is?"

I can't help but laugh as they jump, seeing me in the doorway. But I quickly turn serious. If Ms Pendell had come down and realized they were all still awake, there would be hell to pay. There's a wild scramble as they head for their beds.

"What's going on?"

I spin around and see Clara standing behind me, rubbing her eyes.

"Jack's telling ghost stories again, scaring all the young ones," I reply.

She puts her hands on her hips. "Jack? I thought we went over this!"

He scrambles to his feet. "But it's the chiming hour! We had to see if we could wake her."

"Not this again," I mutter. Clara and I exchange a look. "You happy to take this round?" I ask. "I'll make sure the rest of these clowns get to bed."

"Miss?"

I spin around, still not used to the formality from these ten-year-olds. But to them, I am "miss", just like a teacher.

"What is it, Jack?"

His pale blue eyes have gone wide as he looks around the room. "Someone's missing."

"Who?"

"Bridget. She was just here with us. Right next to me."

"She's probably gone back to her room. I'll go check."

Clara comes with me, to my annoyance – I wish she'd stay and give Jack a good talking-to. But there is something creepy about wandering the hallways so late at night, and her presence is reassuring. A bump comes from above us. The Long Gallery.

"Not up there," Clara moans.

"Do you seriously think she would? She should know better." My voice drops to a whisper.

Beside me, Clara lets out a long, shuddering sigh. I know exactly how she feels. It's too late to be dealing with this. But the last thing we want to do is wake Ms Pendell.

I'm trying to picture Bridget in my head. I know she's not in my photography class, or else I would definitely know her. There are so many kids in the camp, and I know I need to try harder to get to know them. With camp being only a week long, it feels like they come and go in a flash. Some – like Jack, like me when I was a kid – come back every year. The regulars. But this is Bridget's first time.

But her name does ring a bell. And then I remember why.

Earlier that day, I'd been sitting in on the pottery class, filling in for Tyler, who was late, as per usual. Why they keep hiring that guy is a mystery. I was discreetly watching videos on my phone, keeping half an eye on the kids – but they were engrossed in their work. They weren't using the wheels so didn't need much supervision. Besides, Clara was doing a good job of leading the class. I just let her get on with it.

But even through my ear pods, I could feel the atmosphere change in the room. Like all the oxygen had been sucked from it for a moment, or everyone was holding their collective breath. Goosebumps rose along my arms. I looked up, hurriedly slipping my phone into the pocket of my jeans. Ms Pendell. I hadn't seen her up close in what felt like an age. She didn't often look in on the camp apart from her traditional speech at the start of the week. She looked older than last year – more lines around her eyes, the hair around her temples frizzy and grey. When I was younger, she seemed to tower over us all, her posture straight as the Romanesque pillars that framed the front door of the building. Now, she looked bent over, like she'd aged a few decades over the course of a year.

She stalked the room, not catching anyone's eye but carefully examining each child's work. Clara was stammering, trying to explain what they'd been working on.

Ms Pendell didn't appear to be listening, and soon even Clara fell quiet.

Then she stopped.

"Intricately done." Ms Pendell looked over the shoulder of one of the younger students, her hair tied back in braids. Bridget. She'd been making a rabbit, sculpting it out of thick red clay. "I love the way you've captured that twinkle in the rabbit's eye. So lifelike. So much personality. If you keep this up, I think you might make it to the Long Gallery."

Bridget beamed in the light of her praise. That's what it's like when Ms Pendell turns her attention on you. Like a spotlight. A feeling that you've been recognized.

I've heard the rumours circulating. That Genevieve Pendell is *past it*. Gone to seed. Hasn't produced any remarkable works of art in years. Fifteen years, to be precise. That was the year of her last big show. That's why she has to run this art camp, presumably, rather than swanning off into the glamorous life of an artist in the big city.

But there are also rumours that she's coming back. That this year is going to be her year. She's started talking about it herself – how her productivity has increased, inspiration flowing, how her muse has finally found her. I wonder if her muse came from within, or if she needed to take inspiration from elsewhere. In her speech, she'd told us about the idea of genius living external to us, like conduits we can contact. The ancient Romans believed that genius came from spirits who granted inspiration, who lived within the walls and came out to help from time to time. I'm sure Ms Pendell thought that her genius had abandoned her.

So now she attempts to cultivate it in us. If she spots our talent, you can see our confidence blossom, just as it does in Bridget right now.

"Really?" Bridget's eyes are wide.

"If you work very hard, and pour all your talent and creativity into this piece, then I believe you will be chosen. But don't slack for a moment. Talent like yours needs to be nurtured. Find that muse. And don't forget that sometimes the muse is within."

The muse is within.

Those words are so familiar.

She said that to me once. Right before she chose one of my photographs for the gallery. It's one of the reasons I keep coming back to the camp, because ever since I've been out with my camera, just taking pictures; I can't seem to find that spark of brilliance again. Knowing that my work is hung in the Long Gallery, along with so many of the grand masters – and Ms Pendell's work itself – is an honour I can't escape from. I want to recapture that. I keep hoping that maybe she'll mentor me further, help me take my art to the next level. It's all I've ever wanted to do with my life. My way of showing the world my perspective. Everything else I find hard – speaking, interacting, making friends. But when I show people my photographs, even I can tell that something changes. They look at me differently. For a moment, they see the world through my eyes, and it helps them understand.

Ms Pendell brought that out in me. I used to hate taking photos of myself. But she pushed me to dig deeper. That it was one thing to keep my audience at arm's length, taking portraits from afar using film, the subject always slightly distorted, sometimes blending into the background or just out of focus. But she asked me to do a series where I turned the camera on myself.

I hated every minute of it. It felt awkward, exposing. But when I developed the results, I surprised myself by how much I liked them. I somehow managed to tap into something that felt real.

Honest.

I felt the glow of pride in my work when Ms Pendell had recognized it too. She'd let out a gasp of surprise, her eyes shining with delight. I hadn't realized how much I craved that praise. It fed something in me, like satiating a hunger I hadn't even known was there. I wanted more.

There was a hunger in Ms Pendell's eyes as well. I can recognize that now. And I had fed it. Each day she searched through our work, looking for that morsel of talent.

That she'd found something in me, in my work … that had meant something. "Yes," she'd said. "This is one for our gallery. Well done. Very well done indeed."

I couldn't believe it. I'd made it to the wall. My work was going to hang alongside people I admire. Maybe it would lead to more. A recommendation to a gallery in Bath, maybe? Or a reference to help me get into art college? The possibilities seemed endless.

But hearing her say it now, to Bridget, I grow uncomfortable. *The muse is within*. Or maybe it's the way she's looking at Bridget. No, not at Bridget. At the sculpture. There is something lifelike about it – a spark, a personality that shines through that elevates it above the other work.

Ms Pendell rarely takes an interest in what the students are doing – unless they are candidates for the gallery, of course. So all the counsellors are intrigued, wondering who's next in the spotlight. Clearly Bridget is the chosen one. I wonder where she is now.

I'm secretly glad Clara is with me as we climb the stairs to the Long Gallery. It's creepy enough during the day, let alone at night.

I move closer to Clara as we walk down the wall. She shivers and so do I – it feels like the temperature has dropped several degrees, even though in theory it should be warmer up here.

"Bridget?" I call out. But why would she have come up here?

That's when I see it. It's the little pottery statue of a rabbit. It grabs my attention straight away, with its beady glass eyes that seem to make contact with mine and hold it.

I recognize it immediately.

"This is new, isn't it?" I ask Clara.

She stares at it wide-eyed. "That's Bridget's."

A gust of wind shoots down the corridor as she says her name, the rabbit sculpture rocking on the plinth. Clara and I both hold our breath, and I dive forward to catch it, but I'm too late.

It slips through my fingers and shatters on the floor into a million pieces.

Clara and I turn to each other.

Then we run.

My eyes snap open. My heart feels like it's racing inside my chest, like all my nerve endings are on fire.

The room is shrouded in darkness, and I realize it's three a.m. again. I catch the end of the clock bells, the chiming resonating in my chest.

I wonder if it's the kids telling stories that have disturbed me once more. I'm going to murder Jack if that's the case.

I debate whether I should get out of bed. There doesn't seem to be a window open this time, and it's cosy under the covers. But something woke me up, and I should go investigate.

What if it's another kid roaming the halls? We're going to have to start tethering them to their beds.

Like last night. We found Bridget, eventually.

Her eyes had been ringed red with tears. She was a bit shell-shocked – I wondered if she had been sleep-walking – but she seemed grateful to be directed back to her room and tucked back up in bed.

At least we don't have another one missing. I don't think the camp would survive the scandal. Can you imagine? One of Mummy and Daddy's precious art prodigies disappeared.

I swing my legs out of bed and pad out into the hallway. All is quiet. I stay still for a moment, listening to the ticking of the grandfather clock.

There is another noise, layered beneath the silence and the steady clock. A whirring sound, so faint I almost think I'm imagining it. But in the dark it seems like the rest of my senses are heightened. Someone is up at this time, and that can't be good news.

At least the sound isn't coming from the Long Gallery. Instead, it's coming from downstairs. As soon as I reach the next floor, I can see the shaft of light coming from one of the rooms. Someone else *is* awake, like me, suffering from blasted insomnia.

I lightly knock on the door of the room before opening it. There's only one light on, illuminating a girl with a long black ponytail sitting at one of the work stations. Her gaze is intent on the lump of clay in front of her. Bridget.

She doesn't appear to have noticed me come in. It's like she's in a daze, a trance. I recognize that focus as well. It's the intensity that comes from wanting to produce your best work, knowing that you're moments away from something truly great. *The muse is within.* This is what I think Ms Pendell meant the whole time. When creativity lights a fire that seems to burn from within.

For the first time in a while, I wish I'd brought my camera with me. In her, I recognize something of myself. Her brown eyes seem to almost glow, and I wonder if I could capture it on film, bring it out in my darkroom with the right chemicals and pure, distilled water. I haven't been inspired like this in a long time. But after I had my picture hung in the gallery, it was like that light extinguished. I couldn't get it back. I'd burned out that fire inside me and I've been searching, searching, searching for a way to get it relit ever since. I don't want that to happen to this girl too.

I let out a cough so as not to make her jump. "OK, I think we need to get back to bed."

"Please, just a few more minutes." She barely even looks up at me.

I almost want to watch her finish. Then I snap back to reality. Her hands grab my attention. She's been working at the clay, moulding it, shaping it, but she must have been doing it for hours – there are cuts on the pads of her fingers, weeping blood. She must be feeling the pain of it, but the obsession – the need, the drive, the desire – to get the sculpture right is too much.

"That's enough, seriously," I say again.

"What are you still doing up?" comes a voice from behind me.

I jump, spinning around. It's Ms Pendell. She looks better tonight – although maybe that's the dim lighting of the pottery room, mostly shrouded in darkness.

"I'm so sorry, Ms Pendell," I say. "I've only just found her. I'll take her up to bed."

Ms Pendell nods.

"Just a few more minutes?" Bridget pleads. "I've almost finished. Then I can fire it tomorrow. Maybe you will display it again?"

"It's far too late to be up. Please, return to your room," says Ms Pendell.

Bridget hangs her head, dejected. But she gets up and makes her way towards me.

I don't know what comes over me, but I have this urge, sudden and sharp, to stamp down on the sculpture. To destroy it somehow.

It's like Ms Pendell reads my mind. She shoots me a look, more like a snarl really, and I swipe my hand away. Bridget is oblivious.

I look at my hand like it belongs to someone else. It's a foreign object. Was I really in control? It makes me think of the broken sculpture last night. Had I tried to save it? Or had I broken it?

I avoid Ms Pendell's eye and follow Bridget back upstairs, making sure she's actually in bed, safe and tucked up, before I return to my room.

Jealousy. That's what I felt. Because I haven't had that feeling in so long. Tomorrow I'll get my camera out. I'll find that muse. The muse within.

When I wake up the next night at the same time, the joke has well and truly worn off.

Whatever the universe is playing at, I want it to stop. All I want is a full night's sleep. I look over at Clara, deep in her slumber, and envy her. But at least I know what must have caused me to wake.

I don't waste any time, going straight for Bridget's room. There are three other girls in there, and at first glance it seems like everything is in order – four campers sleeping soundly. I can see their bodies underneath the duvets, slowly rising and falling in rhythm with their breaths.

Only one doesn't move like the others. The bed is enshrouded with shadow. No Bridget.

She's tricked me. She's not in bed.

I almost let out an audible groan, but I don't want to wake the others.

Instead, I bet she's listening to Jack tell those ridiculous ghost stories again. I'll get Ms Pendell or one of the other teachers to have a proper word with him. He's keeping the kids up, scaring them until they don't want to stay in their own beds any longer. He should know better by now. And three a.m.? There's absolutely no reason for anyone to be awake at such a time.

But when I walk past Jack's room, it's quiet. There are no lights on, no whirring sound; and nothing from the gallery above. Just endless, eerie silence. I must have imagined things this time. But you know what? It's someone else's problem. I go back to bed.

That's when I see Jack. Staring at me from the bottom of my mattress. "It's happened again," he says. "You have to stop it."

I wake up groggy, barely recalling the sequence of events from the night before. This time, it's right as the clock strikes three, and I hear every gong resound in my chest. Then it hits me: Bridget is missing. I expect there to be swarms of people descending on the manor: police, detectives, her family. Search parties organized. Candlelight vigils held. But there's nothing like that.

It's quiet. Too quiet.

I go straight to find Jack. He's asleep in his bed, but I can't let him stay that way. I shake him awake.

His eyes fly open, wide with fear.

"Hush, it's only me," I say. "What happened to Bridget? She's still not in her bed."

"Bridget? Who's that? I don't know any Bridget, I swear." He rolls over, facing away from me. He's shaking; he's so scared. In my frustration I flail my arms, knocking over a glass of water on the side table.

He's mumbling something. Telling me to go away. To leave him alone. He doesn't know anything. He doesn't know Bridget.

I have an idea. I head straight up to the Long Gallery. I look for the rabbit, but it's not there as far as I can see.

Every portrait on the wall seems to stare at me as I walk down, following me. I know logically that it's just a trick of perspective, that when you paint pictures of eyes staring straight out, they will seem to follow you around the room. But these eyes really are watching, I can tell. Each one staring at me with extreme intensity. Like there's a fire burning behind the eyes.

The same fire I saw in Bridget.

The same fire I know I had, once upon a time.

Genius trapped in the walls.

That's when I see it: not Bridget's sculpture, but my own piece. The photograph. My self-portrait, the eyes staring straight at the camera, at the viewer. But unlike the other pictures in the room, my eyes don't have that fire behind them. It's like looking at an empty shell of myself. I'm sure that in the real photograph, I captured something more.

I can't help it. I think I look dead behind the eyes.

Then I look at the plaque on the wall next to my photograph. The one that describes the artist, their inspiration.

It reads: "Ms Genevieve Pendell".

But I know that's not the case. That's my photograph. I took it.

Now there's a noise. I turn to see Bridget being led down the hallway, hand-in-hand with Ms Pendell. "I'm so proud of your beautiful sculpture. You truly found the muse within," she's saying.

"Thank you, Ms Pendell," replies Bridget.

"Now we'll put this on display here, shall we? So we can be forever reminded that your talent began here. That it belongs here."

I want to rage. To storm over and break the statue. Because I know what is about to happen. And how little time I have.

But the clock ticks over to four a.m., the gong ringing. How has an hour disappeared already? Was I staring at my photograph in a daze this entire time?

"You'll be my muse, won't you?" Ms Pendell asks. "Just like all the others." They place the rabbit statue on the plinth, and as she does, I can see Bridget fade away.

"Stop! Don't let her take you!" I scream, pointing at Ms Pendell.

No one seems to hear me. Not Ms Pendell. Not Bridget. Because at the first chime of four a.m., I'm silenced. Like I never existed. I take one last look at the photograph, and that's when I see it: the fire is back behind my eyes.

She looks up at my photograph as she passes by. There's something like love in her eyes. But it's not love. It's pride. The chiming hour is over, and I've returned to where she positioned me. I'm one of her masterpieces.

*

278

The next morning is the final day of the camp. There's a big unveiling of the newest piece in the gallery. There's a parade of journalists, photographers, parents, students and counsellors from the camp. I spot Clara in the front and try to grab her attention, but of course, trapped in the photo I cannot even wave or gesture to her. She looks right through me.

"Welcome, one and all." Ms Pendell appears from the far end of the hallway. She looks different now. Rejuvenated. Her hair full-flowing, cascading down her back, healthy and rich in colour. Her posture back so she can stand at her full statuesque height. Her complexion smooth, like she's bathed in milk. "It has been a long time since I have exhibited new artwork, but I have been waiting, toiling for the right moment to make my debut again. I have been searching for my muse. But I am proud that this time, I am certain I have found it."

In a dramatic moment, the piece is unveiled, a velvet curtain falling. On the plinth is the fully finished sculpture of the rabbit. And it is beautiful. Remarkable. Because of the fire behind its eyes that burns with an intensity only she can capture.

No, that's not right. Only Bridget could capture. It's Bridget's work. I know it is. But now Bridget is caught in Ms Pendell's trap too.

I scream the truth, but no one can hear me. My screams die out, disintegrate into cries, then I'm forced into laughter – a bitter, hollow sound – as I watch Ms Pendell soak in the praise. This is how she does it. *The muse is within*. Whatever. Now I know the truth.

She owes it all to us.

Her geniuses locked within the walls.

Only Jack winces at my wailing.

He's one of the rare few. A chime child who can summon us in that special hour. That's what she's done to us: reduced us to ghost stories. Even if he suspected the truth, who would believe him? But he tells the story anyway. Maybe that's the only way she can be stopped.

I'll have to wait for the next chiming hour to find out.

SOMETHING WICKED

KAT DUNN

1

Twelve icy paw prints at my window, what glee! They are small as rosebuds and as dear to my heart as my own eye teeth. My little visitors. How perfect.

This is how I know magic is real. I call to what I want, and it comes to me.

I worked a spell last night. I do very often, of course, asking for little things, a trinket here or there, signs that my will is heeded. A frost-sharp cobweb in the garden hedge, a robin as bright and round as a human heart. These are the gifts the universe bestows upon me.

I am special.

From beneath my pillow I pull the small muslin bag of angelica, nettle, lavender and bay leaf, a pinch of salt, black sealing wax and a piece of stone from the flowerbed where all three cats are buried. It has done its job so into the fire it goes. There is a pop, the stink of burning cloth and herb; the flame goes yellow as the salt meets it, then it slips through the coals and is lost.

Morning bells toll in the village church beyond our estate, cart wheels clatter over cobblestones beyond the boundary wall. That is as far as my world extends. I am hemmed in by locks and keys, stone and mortar. Papa likes locks.

I carry my delicious secret down to breakfast, nestled in my heart right under my ribs. There is the usual spread on the sideboard of kedgeree, cold cuts, butter and jam, urns of tea and coffee, rolls that left the kitchen hot but are now small, cold rocks that break my teeth. Papa likes this because it means he can complain. I have studied him for many years now and I can assure you it is his chief occupation. If something else is wrong, then it must mean that he is in the right, which I suppose is a very logical way of ordering things. I do not much enjoy it, though.

Miss Milton, my governess, is at the breakfast table already; from the folded newspaper at one end I can tell that my father has already eaten his meal and gone to the train station in his carriage, for London and the bank. The old governess, I saw her making the beast with two backs with Father. She cried after. She was so weak and silly.

This new one doesn't cry. When she thinks no one is

looking, she likes to run her sharp little fingers over his bald pate like he is a cat to be petted.

I lift the spoon of the kedgeree, but I can feel Miss Milton's eyes following me like fish hooks. They catch at my chest and I am breathing too shallow, feeling light and slippery and unreal. Miss Milton cares very deeply about what she considers to be polite and proper but makes very sure not to tell you what that may be. The trick she wants you to perform is to pay absolute attention to her at all times, and from the shifting tide of her mood, divine what path is acceptable.

I am not to have the kedgeree, I decide. She will not like that. It will be polite for me to take a bit of tea and perhaps unbuttered toast of one or two slices.

Of course it *is* a trick. There is always some secret sign I miss, some ungoverned part of my body that betrays subconscious thought and feeling. I fail, and Miss Milton slices into me.

I am bad. It shines through.

I take my tea and toast to the opposite side of the round breakfast table.

"You are late." Miss Milton sniffs at a nasal drip that is her companion all winter. "I will have to adjust my lesson plan for today."

There is no time to apologize before she leaves, and I have only this dead little scrap of dough for company. How hateful.

I am not late, or I did not believe myself to be. It is quite the same hour as I always descend to breakfast, but this must be another silent instruction I've failed to understand. People have so very many rules, and they like to never say them because it makes them feel better than others if they can consider themselves treated callously or carelessly.

Everyone loves to be a victim.

I know better than to take my time over my tea and toast, and my stomach is quite turned anyway, all joy at my night-time guests lost.

Magic never lasts. I must do more.

On my way, I pause to pinch off a handful of lavender nubs from the dried flowers in the hallway and collect the misty cloud of a spider web from the seldom used linen closet up near the old nursery, which was turned into a schoolroom the year I turned seven and Mother was taken away. Lavender and cobweb is a very good and potent mixture for calmness and peace of mind. Lavender for soothing, good sleep and sweet thoughts; cobweb for softness, for strength in the lightest of things. A spell to carry me through.

Standing outside the schoolroom, I empty my hand into my mouth and the tea I have held there since leaving the breakfast room. Without it, I could not swallow down the lavender. The web melts on my tongue like dew. It is done.

I hear Miss Milton scratching around inside, but when I enter she is still, arms folded by the blackboard. There is a single desk in the centre of the room with a chair and a pot of ink and a pen and an exercise book. On one wall is a large map of the world coloured in pink across the Empire. Mother filled the room with a rocking horse with real horse hair, paints and pencils, porcelain dolls, a china tea set, a teddy bear, dominos and draughts, skipping ropes and a whole dolls' house that was supposed to look like our house. But all the dolls were smiling so that wasn't right, and Mother shut me in my room when I told her this.

On a fresh page I write today's date and our location in a careful hand: *28 January 1899, Gable End, Warwickshire*. It is my birthday in exactly six months. Mirror days like this make the magic stronger. I work a little spit to swallow the last lavender seeds.

Miss Milton has the title of her lesson written on the board, and I dutifully copy it down.

WITCHES

"Thou shalt not suffer a witch to live." Miss Milton's voice is high and reedy, an affectation she adopts whenever she is giving an oration. I think she might have quite liked to be a vicar if women were allowed to do such things. "Exodus, twelve, eighteen." She pauses. "Write it down, girl."

I do. It is an interesting lesson today, though I do not allow her to know it. There is still a piece of lavender wedged in one molar, and I try to subtly work my tongue to dislodge it.

"Why are you gurning?" she snaps, fingers pinched around the chalk.

"Sorry, Miss Milton."

Mouth in a flat line, she begins to scratch up her notes, reading them as she goes.

"For three hundred years, witches were hunted in this country, most notably by the great Witchfinder General Matthew Hopkins, who cleared our fenland counties of many wicked and capricious women in the years of our lord sixteen forty-four to sixteen forty-seven."

Miss Milton turns her head over one shoulder to ascertain that I am taking dictation. I keep my head down, the lavender tucked beneath my tongue. It tastes bitter.

She continues. "The signs of a witch were this: one, to have a familiar, an animal servant; two, to have a witch mark, a blemish that shows the woman to be devil-touched and that does not bleed or feel pain when pricked; and three, to float when bound and thrown into water."

I take down the last words, nib scratching through the paper. I do not like this lesson after all. Miss Milton is a hateful nasty creature, suited to bootlicking and punishing those she cannot control. I think about all her skin peeling from her in a single sheet and the noise she would make. I imagine her eyes boiling in their sockets and her teeth being yanked out with the pliers the groomsmen keep for dealing with the horses.

That is better. I am calm.

"Of course we know now that many of those women were not witches, only mad or strange or unliked, but in those primitive times, such people were dealt with in crude ways. We deal with our hysterical and dangerous women very differently in this modern era." She sets down her notes on her desk and dusts the chalk from her fingers. "A composition piece: compare and contrast the manner of containing and solving the problem of dangerous women in the seventeenth and nineteenth centuries, four pages, and I will receive it tomorrow."

Miss Milton watches me, a cold pleasure in her eyes, for she digs so very precisely into me with her words.

Dangerous women.

She means my mother.

It is very boring that Miss Milton thinks she can manipulate or control me with such transparent methods. I pity her small, grasping mind. She has made it very clear that she thinks children should be controlled, and it does not matter in the slightest that I am nearly sixteen and could very well go and marry someone in one or two years' time and be the mistress of my own house. While I still wear my hair long and my skirts short, I am not a person to her mind. I do not think I will ever be a person to someone like her.

I am an obstacle to be eliminated.

I looked on from the window of this room when they carried my mother away. A burly man held her at each corner like a large mammalian fish they had caught and could add to their collection. She flopped and wriggled, gasping at air her lungs could not breathe. It was a day as cold as this, frost across the grass and a mist around the

287

wheels of the carriage that had come from the asylum. Before they put the gag on her, she wrenched one arm free to point at the window where I watched, at me, and shrieked something with her hoarse, ragged voice. It was muffled by the men's hands, but I knew what she said.

Witch.

2

What a putrid day. It is as though the air is thick and rotten in my mouth, all crawling maggots in my nose and pus clogging my lungs. If I coughed up a fistful of rancid meat I would not be surprised. I could leave it on Miss Milton's lunch plate. Wouldn't she screech.

No, that is not a good spell.

There is a break in the winter sleet, and I am sent outside for half an hour to walk around the garden for my health. The grass is flattened from snow the week before and the flowerbeds are boiling mud. Mother used to employ a team of gardeners to attend to the scrunched ribbons of dahlias and pansies, restrain the sprawl of rhododendron and box. After they took her away, there were very few of us left. Father, Miss Milton. The groomsman who looks after Father's horse and sleeps above the stable. The cook, and a maid who walks up from the village every day to push a feather duster over the banisters and picture frames sulkily. Sulky Suky, my father calls her with a curl of his lip because he has been clever. He is so very clever and we must all know this. I did a spell once to undo his cleverness, but it didn't work. Magic doesn't work on my father. It is better to work it around him, I have learned.

I am hooking stones out of the dirt around the rosebushes when Father startles me. I drop my handful of treasures and straighten, hiding my muddy gloves behind my back. Father is like the night, black trousers, frock coat and waistcoat, white shirt and collar, bloodless face and smooth dome of his head, white beard neatly clipped to create a falsely square jaw.

"There you are."

I am very small when Father is here. When the doctor measured me I am but four inches short of his stature, but I know I am a worm beside him. I look at the grass and the rainwater on the shining toes of his black shoes. A worm wriggling in the earth on to which he can bring his great weight to bear.

"Come."

He leads us back to the house and into his study. I am never allowed in here with its great fitted bookcases and leather sets of *Punch* and Gibbon's *History of the Decline and Fall of the Roman Empire*. There is a series of animal heads mounted on the wall behind Father's desk and an umbrella stand made from a real elephant's foot. It is always dark, another piece of night.

Miss Milton is waiting for us.

I am hot and cold at once. I have done something and I do not know it. I have been a terrible bad rotten little bitch and I will be punished. I don't want to breathe; I don't want to exist.

He does not offer me a chair and I do not sit. I want to be able to run. My muscles are steel-taut beneath my cotton dress, the worm stretched into a snake, ready to dart.

"It is time you moved on from the schoolroom. You are too isolated here, and I believe it is contributing to your problems," he says from behind the desk. "Your … peculiar habits." His hands are steepled and the sharp edge of his collar digs into the flesh of his neck. Miss Milton stands at his side, radiating vindication so strongly it is a noise in the air around her, a jagged buzzing like a thousand wasps rattling the teeth from my skull.

I am too shocked to speak, but my heart beats a rapid drum: what is to happen, what is to happen, what is to happen?

"You cannot live alongside people, and you must understand your failings to be able to rectify them," he continues. "Miss Milton has given enough reports on your behaviour that corroborate my own suspicions. I have coddled you here and colluded with your whims too long. It is enough."

The words fall like fists. My father has never been a kind man, but his path has always been silence. Silence when my mother scratched blood from her own arms: silence in the face of tears; a dense, blanketing silence, weighty and final.

"I have made enquiries to place you at a finishing school on the continent." I see now the information brochure before him, but he does not offer it to me. There is an illustration of a mountain, a house. It looks strict.

"I see." They are the only words I can muster, and they sting like nettles in my mouth.

I do not know what it is I should feel at this announcement. I am a snowstorm of confusion, clear as fog, a rattling jar of stones and grit and too many thoughts needling me all over.

She did this to him. I want to think that. I must believe that.

It is easier than to accept that these are his heart-thoughts, the raw stuff his mind is made of.

"You will be here alone," I say. "Mother is not returning, is she?"

He gives no reaction to the mention of my mother. It is as though I am as neatly dealt with as she was.

"I will not be alone. It is not necessary for you to concern yourself with that. I have asked Miss Milton to stay on as my personal secretary, and I am pleased to say she has accepted the offer."

"Oh. I see."

How very glad she must be. She has turned him full against me.

The word *personal* smacks in my mind like flesh on flesh, and there are spots of pink high on her cheeks.

Wretched, craven harpy, why did she choose to nest in my home?

I have no allies here. I never have.

*

I am not aware of the next few hours. They must pass, because when I come back to myself I am in the drawing room before the pianoforte with a Chopin étude before me. My fingers ache. I have been playing.

Shaking out my hands, I leave. There is a scrap of light left and I want to be out in it, amid the damp air and purple haze of sunset. I cannot be in this house with *them*.

I walk the garden in my cloak, returning to the rosebush where my father found me, and think of what he said.

He is right, of course. He has raised me quite alone from people and so they are alien to me. The times I have come into contact with others, it has been unpleasant and frightening.

I do not like people. I do not think we are made from the same stuff. I am a visitor from elsewhere, stranded here amongst these cruel, capricious, angry things. They hate me; they can smell that there is something wrong with me. I stink of pain and grief and rejection and all the things they are most frightened of invoking into their own lives. I am their sin eater. I take on all their pain so they may safely close the door on me and call sadness banished.

I reach into the winter roses, a skinny tangle of dormant, leafless stems, for the last bloom left. A thorn grazes along my exposed wrist, a line of blood that stops at the birthmark on the inside of my forearm. The skin there does not break. I snag the flower by the petals and draw it to me, cradling it close to my heart.

My father and Miss Milton hate me, but oh how I loathe

them in return. They dictate the terms of my life, own its rooms and walls, set its rules and restrictions. They think themselves gods, and me their frightened acolyte.

There is much they do not understand.

I cannot bespell my father. My magic is not strong enough to touch him.

But Miss Milton is another matter.

There is a thicket of monkshood growing nearby, and I am careful to cover my fingers as I pluck a handful and fold them into my handkerchief. Dusk has stretched out its shadows across the lawn, the house reaching over me as I prepare my craft.

It is quick work to slip back inside and up to her bedroom. At this time she will be with the servants eating an early meal; I will be served my dinner in the nursery once they are done so I must be fast.

In the top drawer of her dresser are her linen smalls, white and plain and thin with the lye and boiling water of washing. My nose wrinkles. I would never wish to touch something so close to her, but needs must. Shaking the monkshood from its wrapping, I rub the broken stems into the cloth, careful to only touch it with my gloved hands. Sometimes a spell has no ritual, it is simply intention and action interwoven. I hold my intention in my heart, and let my action become magic.

There, a tiny flame in my heart again. A little warmth in the cold, hostile glacier of this house.

I stash the remainder of the monkshood in the bottom of

my wardrobe, carefully wrapped up alongside the rest of my supplies, the sprigs of dried rosemary, sage, thyme, mint, rose petals and crisp brown leaves, hagstones strung on a ribbon, candle nubs, salt, peppermint oil, sealing wax, matches – everything I have gathered. I touch my hand to each, pushing a little magic into them, a little of my will, and feel the soothing press of their energy back against my flesh.

The next morning, I am woken by the screaming.

3

"She did this! I know it!"

Miss Milton is on the landing in her nightdress, red welts rising along her hands, arms, legs, face, neck as I watch. Quite extraordinary. I had not thought it so powerful a spell, but I am delighted. From the pace and severity of the lesions, I deduce that she has put her stockings on first, quickly, then taken her time with a chemise. She must have thought there was a burr in the stockings, or some small, biting creature. She stripped it all off in a hurry – the remains are shed behind her trailing back to her room.

Father comes up the corridor from his room, collarless, in his shirtsleeves.

"What is this racket? What is going on?"

I take this cue to slide back into my room and quickly dress, hopping from foot to foot in glee. I can still hear her shouting, voice hitching with tears, and it makes me spin in front of the mirror, letting my hair fan out around me. The world, bent beneath my hand, if just in this one place.

No spell has ever worked this well. It is a reward, I know it, for being bold.

Miss Milton and Father do not come down to breakfast, which at first is tremendous fun. I eat two plates of toast and eggs, spoonfuls of jam, fistfuls of hothouse grapes and even half a kipper before I decide it is too full of little bones, it is like a graveyard on my tongue and that is quite the wrong mood for such a potent day.

I drink three cups of tea and crunch sugar cubes between my teeth, but still no one comes.

The shine dulls and I am cold and uncertain. I do not like this sea-ship life, the floor forever moving beneath my feet. I want solid ground.

In my bare feet I mouse up the stairs, snuffling and small. No one can hear me; no one can see me. I summon up all the rodentness in the floorboards, the traces of urine and miniature follicles of fur in the carpet tread, and the scurrying behind the lathe and plaster walls.

There are soft voices murmuring from behind my father's door. My back arches; I bare my teeth in a noiseless hiss. She is in there. He has taken her in. They conspire against me.

If I press myself up to the edge of the door, I can hear her crying still. There is a keyhole and I move my eye to it, but make out little, only the swag of curtains, perhaps the movement of an arm. I picture them together, my father becoming a different man, a man who can offer love and comfort if it suits his wants. Perhaps he has a jar of cold cream and is applying it to the welts on her skin with his thick, blunt fingers.

They both deserve more than my magic can ever bring down upon their heads.

There, voices again.

"... nasty. When are you going to stand up to her?"

"It is not that simple."

"Patrick, you're a weak fool. There is an abomination in your house and you suffer her to control us all. We are prisoners to her whims."

"Her mother—"

"—had the right idea."

"*Julia.*"

"I'm sorry." A pause, long and wet. "But something must be done. She is a spoiled brat, and you need to be honest about it for once and set boundaries. You may think you owe her because of her mother, but you cannot let yourself be dominated by a narcissist."

I don't like this. I don't like this at all.

I am a mouse no longer; I am a woodlouse scrambling in the dirt, I am a slick of oil, I am cat sick, a smashed plate, an overused midden. I want all these feelings out of me, I want them out. If I knew a spell to dig emotion from me I would; with a knife or blunt claws I would rip it out like a canker.

Today I do not want to go into the prim gardens with their tamed lawns and orderly paths. I need the darkness. I need to retreat.

In the basement of the house are the countless connected rooms of the servants' quarters. Like a badger set with only a few small entrances, they infest the underworld, cold and damp and dark. These days, there is only the cook and the occasional maid; most of the rooms lie empty. Shut up rooms of china, disused sculleries, bootrooms, game rooms, gun rooms. A room for everything and needed for nothing. There is one that calls to me, at the far end from the kitchens, a windowless, low-ceilinged space that once stored root vegetables. It still smells earthy and sour on the tongue. I like to shut myself up in it and burrow into the dirt floor and imagine myself a mandrake root, an inhuman living thing.

I press my lips to the floor so it is difficult to breathe, compressing my nose flat and sucking in air from the corners of my mouth.

One day, when blossom drifted from the trees like smoke and I first found blood between my legs, I woke up and my mother had placed a pillow over my face. She pressed it down so firmly I could not move my head or see anything; I only knew it was her because I could hear her talking. *Little witch, little witch, little witch. Devil sent to torment me.*

They took her away quite soon after that.

I am so sad, I am a sad knot of hurt, a blunt pain like a fist beneath my breastbone, pressing down on my stomach and into my lungs so I cannot breathe and I am as heavy as a rock, all these dead, cold, unloved things. I am granite and limestone. I am buried deep into the earth.

Miss Milton thinks she had the right idea. Sometimes I agree with her. No one wants me here. Maybe, if my mother had succeeded, she would still be at home and happy, and Father would be too. Maybe I was always a mistake.

I hear them searching for me for a while, the cook calling my name and banging doors in a desultory manner. Perhaps they think I ran away. I'm sure they would all be quite happy with such an ending.

I will not give them the satisfaction.

I peel myself from the ground and crawl out of my hole. I am dirty and it pleases me.

My spell was not enough. I need some sort of stronger magic, something more potent. I do not know yet what that may be, but it will come to me, I know it. Oh, rat seething maggotty hell fire, I must do something, but I cannot see a future. My mind is a hallway of closing doors. Mother has been taken. Father knows how to send me away now. It is not only that Miss Milton has won this match, but that I am losing, terribly losing, the long war I have fought since my birth.

Perhaps I can—

Every thought stops there as I reach the top of the stairs.

My bedroom door is open.

Before the wardrobe, the wolfsbane is strewn around the floor, all the precious pieces of my spell work, every witch-thing and treasure, every magic comfort. All my power, discovered. Laid bare.

And my father kneeling in horror among it.

4

Father is a storm cloud. Father is a raven come to pick out my eyes. Father is a night wail, a flat hammer head bearing down, slathering dog teeth, an axe blade.

He is so very, very angry.

I flatten myself against the door frame as he advances.

"What have you done? Little harpy, tell me the truth." He is snarling, lips pulled so far back I can see his mottled gums. I do not know how Miss Milton stands him breathing on her.

I think, then, to run, but he is on me, his hand clamped around my arm. He throws me into the room, and I smack the corner of my bedframe, spin on to the floor. My head is a swarm of bees, pain as shocking as ice-cold water. A spell, a spell, there must be something.

He stands over me, brandishing the wolfsbane, and I flinch, pulling my arms over my face. He is so furious I feel as though I am held flat to the floor, blasted out of existence.

"You are a wicked creature. You torture a poor, generous woman who is kind enough to spend her days attempting to educate your ungrateful, intolerant mind. These fantasies are those of a sick mind."

He throws the wolfsbane across the floor, then goes back to the wardrobe. My room has been pulled apart in his search, dresser drawers hanging open, my clothes strewn about, books pulled from their shelves. My magic has been refuge, dragged out into the open light of day.

"No, no, no." It is a whisper only to myself, but it shakes me into action and I begin to crawl towards him. He must not take this from me. He must not.

I cannot say what darkness will fall then.

But I am too late. I grasp at him but he shakes me off and lifts his foot.

"Magic. Isn't. Real."

With each word he delivers a blow to the wooden box that held my supplies and shaped my altar, stamping it into splinters. Crystals are smashed, dried herbs reduced to dust, candles snapped. He wrenches a window open and with the last of his rage, scoops up the detritus and flings it out.

"You are no witch," he barks.

The window slams, glass rattling in its frame.

And with that, he straightens his waistcoat, features cold but placid, and steps over me to leave. The key turns in the lock. I am alone.

5

It is all destroyed.

Nothing is left of my precious, precious things. I lie across the floorboards, tracing my fingers over their death-place, the outline where once there was power. My poor little children, gone and buried in the garden just like my little cats.

Gone like Mother.

Oh, poor, poor Mother.

I never meant any great harm, only she would frustrate me so. Telling me not to do things, or brushing my hair so roughly it pulled at my skull. She would dress me up like a doll and carry me around to play at tea and picnics, and pinch my thighs when I scowled or grew tired.

I only wanted her to stop.

After they took her, I regretted it. I did not think she would break so violently. It is not my fault she took to it so badly.

I learned all my first magic on her. The little spells that gave me back power. Perhaps I did torment her, but it was her doing. She had it coming. Just like Miss Milton.

But Miss Milton is far more robust. That is why she will win.

I lie on the cold floor for a long time. Night falls, the dark star map crossing the sky, until pink and yellow grace the horizon.

There is a deep, familiar shame settling over me. Magic?

What a pathetic, deluded worm I am. So foolish. A crack is opening beneath me. The centre cannot hold. I have lived on lies like a beggar on scraps. Father has broken it all open.

I am so sad.

What a squalid feeling. I hate it. I want to pick it off me like scabs. Better to bleed than suffer this pathetic indignity. All my lack is exposed, like a knife has been dug into my gut and the layers of skin and muscle peeled back to display the soft, rank organ within. I hate it, I hate it, I hate all of it.

If I suffer, I would that they all suffer with me.

When I open my eyes it is not yet true morning. My gaze catches on something beneath my bed, small and square: an escapee from my father's rampage.

I fish it out, fingertips grazing across the rough strip.

A book of matches.

Oh. Oh, how indecent.

I risk a smile.

Here it is, the truth: my father is right.

I know magic is not real.

I know I did this all by my own human hand. Mother, Miss Milton.

But, oh, they should have let me play my games.

6

I cut a dashing figure as I climb from my window and down the wisteria that clings to the side of the house. Quite the schoolgirl heroine. I have tucked my skirts into the waistband and have on my most delicate slippers for the best grip. As I climb I think of myself as a pretty illustration in the *Girl's Own Paper*, with plaits in my hair and roses in my cheeks. I would skip as I skirt the wall to the broken shutter that will allow me access into the kitchens – but it would not be appropriate. This is a solemn moment.

I am a heroine, but a wronged one, on a mission of retribution.

My plan is quite simple to execute. In the kitchens I root through an old storeroom until I find a bottle of turpentine. No one is up yet, but there is a light below the cook's door. I must act quickly.

I pad softly up to the schoolroom, but as I thought, Miss Milton's room is empty.

I know where she is.

On the first floor landing, the door to my father's room opens without a whisper. They are in bed together.

Good.

I take the key and lock the door from the outside.

A generous slug of turpentine soaks the hall rug, the curtains, the occasional chairs.

It takes so very much to admit my father is right.

The crack below me has widened into a chasm. The lies cannot nourish me any longer.

I am no witch.

It was never more than a silly game I played when it seemed all others were ranged against me.

He should have let me believe it. It would have been better for them to leave the lie alone. I did it for us all.

The first match catches in a bright spark of flame and it is almost an anti-climax. I toss it on to the rug, and there is a warm lick of fire in an instant, spreading out like spilled milk.

Smoke rolls across the ceiling. Then, voices.

Coughing, from beyond the door. The whole door is on fire now; of course, there is no opening it, even if they had the key.

I do not stay to watch it burn. It has taken well enough by the time I get downstairs, eating up the curtains and the wall hangings, the oil paintings and black lacquer.

When the heat is too much for me, I go outside.

It is all such a shame. It is a beautiful house, and I am sure another family could have been quite happy in it. *We* could have been happy in it, if only my mother and father did not insist on their petty, selfish ways. I tolerated them both so long, but even a heroine has her limits. No one has suffered as much as I have.

There is screaming. Smoke billows from the windows.

I never meant to hurt anyone.

Poor Father.

He could have had all he wanted, if only he'd offered me the good grace to tolerate me in return. I had found my way to cope, my way to live in this bitter, cold world.

He was too much a coward to let me keep it.

Oh, Papa. Now look what you made me do.

THE MIDNIGHT KISS

MARY WATSON

The light from the TV cast the old woman's face in an orange-yellow glow as she sat in the faded floral armchair. On the screen, a game-show host greeted the audience with a jovial cry. *Hello, hello, hello!*

The old woman shifted in her seat. Behind, in the near-dark room, three figures stole out of the kitchen. They moved quietly, carefully, knowing they weren't supposed to be there. Holly was in front with Lana close on her heels, and Ameera at the back. This was their usual order.

"It's three days before Halloween and tonight we'll be testing your knowledge of all things ghostly and ghoulish," the TV game-show host announced with relish. The audience cheered, a rote, maniacal sound. The old woman let out a wet cough.

Holly placed a finger on her lips, then inched across the

room to a door on the far side. For a moment, she was cast in the same orange-yellow glow and Lana held her breath, sure that the old woman would turn and see Holly there. But she moved quickly, with admirable stealth, and the old woman did not turn. Holly disappeared through the far door.

Now it was Lana's turn. She glanced at the woman in the chair. Her name was Dawn Connelly and she lived alone in this huge house. Dawn kept to herself, was never seen out walking, and the house was hidden down a long drive and forty acres of green fields. You could almost forget she lived there at all. No one visited any more, but occasionally people still talked about the Connelly family. They still talked about the Connelly house.

Haunted. That's what everyone said.

"For five hundred euros," the game-show host said with exaggerated enthusiasm, "what is the common term for a young female spectre who died in tragic circumstances?"

"Go." Ameera poked her from behind. Lana took a step forward, mindful of the creaking floorboards. She was halfway across the room when Dawn turned slightly, her face almost in profile. She was still, as if listening for something. Lana froze, caught in the orange-yellow light of the TV.

She stood still, not daring to move. It felt as if Dawn was waiting for Lana to take another step. Lana suddenly wanted to laugh at herself. *What am I doing here?* she thought. *Why am I creeping about in this musty old house?*

His face appeared in her mind. Miles. That was why she was here.

That was why she had to hold her nerve. For Miles.

"The white lady," Dawn said, her voice rough, and Lana's heart jumped. Was Dawn talking to her? What did she mean?

Dawn reached forward and picked up the mug on the table beside her armchair. She took a deep gulp. "The ghost of a woman who died tragically is a white lady." Her voice was clearer now and she replaced the mug, turning back to the screen.

"Is it the lady in white?" the contestant on the screen said tentatively. Dawn let out a humphing noise, and Lana nearly ran across the room, falling through the door.

Miles. Lana had to keep thinking about Miles. When he'd broken up with Lana a few days ago, it had come as a complete surprise. They'd been perfect together. Everyone said so.

"What took you so long?" Holly whispered crossly when Lana reached the hall where she was waiting.

"Lana nearly bottled it," Ameera said unhelpfully as she joined them.

"Look at this place," Lana whispered, feeling the dark wood panelling on the wall. It was intricately carved.

"I wouldn't want to live here alone." Ameera shivered. "There are ghosts here. For sure."

"That's why we're here," Holly said cheerfully. "For the ghosts. Come on. Upstairs."

The girls made for the stairs. Lana couldn't stop looking around her. The detailed wallpaper of leaves and flowers, the unlit chandelier above. Even in the dim lamplight, it seemed both grand and faded.

The girls went up the stairs. First Holly, now followed by Ameera, who'd used Lana's distraction to nip in behind Holly. Lana didn't mind. While the other two spoke quietly to each other, she thought about Miles. About her plan to get him back. Miles loved her, Lana knew he did. He was just stressed out about exams and his parents getting divorced. That was why he wanted to take a break. But Lana knew she could help him. They could be perfect again. She just needed to talk to him.

And make a deal with a dead girl.

"Your mother saw the hidden room?" Ameera was asking Holly. They were near the landing now.

"So my granddad was a plumber. When Mam was around eleven or twelve, she came with him on an emergency callout one night." Holly spoke in a low, hushed voice. Above the girls, at the top of the stairs, it was pitch-dark. "In those days all the old people in the village knew the story about the secret room. While my granddad was dealing with the burst pipe, Mam went looking for it."

Holly took the small bicycle torch from her pocket, lighting up the long, wood-panelled hallway. The painted domed ceiling above. All the doors were shut, and Lana suddenly felt the presence of unknown people behind each door, listening. Waiting. She knew that they weren't alone up there. That they weren't welcome.

"Did she find it?" Ameera sounded sceptical as she started down the dark corridor behind Holly. She seemed unaffected by the darkness that surrounded them. Unbothered that they were intruders breaking the silence of this grand old house.

"Mam was right here, in this upstairs hall, when she heard someone behind her. She nearly died, thinking it was the ghost coming for her. But it was Dawn's gran, very much alive even if she was pretty old. She showed my mam the room."

"So it's real? She saw it?" Lana said.

"She said it felt sinister. Like bad things had happened there." Holly came to an abrupt stop.

"What did Dawn's gran say about the room?" Lana looked down the hall, into the disappearing darkness.

"She told Mam the story of the stone girl."

"The stone girl?" Ameera laughed.

"That's what Mam called her. The stone girl." Holly held her flashlight under her chin, turning her features unfamiliar. "She was seventeen when she fell in love with her older sister's fiancé. She'd sneak out to see him, climbing in through his upstairs window."

"He cheated with her sister?" Ameera was indignant.

"He later claimed he didn't know it was the younger sister, that she'd tricked him. That she would let down her long hair when she was with him, and used her sister's perfume." Holly shrugged. "The younger sister claimed he knew."

"Creepy." Ameera shuddered.

"Then," Holly said, relishing the telling, "the stone girl fell pregnant. The young man offered to marry her instead, because he'd fallen in love with the stone girl. They'd grown close during their midnight meet-ups; he loved the sound of her laughter in the dark room. The older sister was furious. But she knew a secret about her younger sister. She'd been watching her and discovered that the younger sister disappeared into a room hidden along this corridor every day. Inside the room was an altar with markings they could not understand. With animal bones and dried blood. The younger sister" – Holly paused dramatically – "was a witch."

This was so like Holly, to tell this story now. Here in the dark hall of the dead witch's house. Lana felt a flicker of irritation. It was affecting her. It made her feel unsettled, which was what Holly wanted. Holly always had to have the upper hand.

"The parents were frightened by the discovery of the shrine and they locked the younger sister in the hidden room. They left her there for three days and three nights to think about what she'd done. They told her she would be confined to the house for the duration of her pregnancy. The baby would be sent to a relative."

"Brutal," Ameera said.

"When the fiancé, or anyone else visited, the family

would again lock her in the hidden room. They believed he would forget about her. They said it was to keep her pregnancy a secret, but the stone girl knew the truth. They wanted to punish her."

The girls looked down the torchlit hall, at the many closed doors. They thought about a girl locked behind one of these doors. Thumping against it, crying, "Let me out, please let me out."

"Did he forget about her?" Lana could feel Ameera looking at her with exasperated eyes. Ameera had little patience for broken hearts.

"I don't know." Holly became quiet, gazing into the darkness like she could see shapes in the shadows. "She died before the baby was born. He married the sister as planned. So maybe he did forget about her. She died in the secret room."

"Which room is it?" Lana ran her eye down all the shut doors.

"It's between the second and third doors on the left." The girls moved quietly down the hall. On the left side, the wall was panelled from floor to ceiling. "Somewhere here."

Lana turned on her torch, studying the wood. The panels were evenly spaced. It didn't look like they were hiding anything. She couldn't see a handle but the room had to open somehow.

"The grandmother told my mam that there used to be a village tradition of seeking out the stone girl. If she appears to you, then she will help you gain the affection of the one you love," Holly said. "Because she died of a broken heart, she would help women in love be with their beloved."

"A broken heart is not a medical condition." Lana sounded terse. *Chill*, she thought to herself. She'd been so tightly wound lately. "How could she help others?" It wasn't like she'd been so good at the whole love thing herself.

"I don't know. But she told my mam to come back when she was eighteen and in love, that the stone girl would help her too."

"Did she?" Lana couldn't imagine Holly's very sensible schoolteacher mam asking a ghost for help with love.

"No." Holly laughed. "Of course not."

All three girls were now pressing the panels, feeling for the catch.

"But I wonder," Holly said, "does it make the stone girl lonely that no one comes to find her any more? Maybe Mam should have come back. Maybe ghosts need people."

Lana felt a sudden chill. Like someone was behind them, watching. Something had changed. The air felt different. Altered, somehow. Then she realized: she could no longer hear the tinny cheers from the TV downstairs. Dawn Connelly must have turned it off.

"I've got it," Holly breathed as the wood slid back, revealing a small room. The torchlight showed a boarded-up window. A mattress pushed to the side.

Lana moved to go inside, but Holly flung out a hand and blocked her.

"No."

"C'mon, Holly," Lana said. "I want to see inside."

"We have to go in one at a time."

"Alone?" Lana peered around her to see into the dark room. "Is that what your mam said?"

"We each go alone into the room and call the girl."

"How do you call her?" Ameera asked.

"Talk to her. If she likes you, she'll help you. She'll let you know that she's here."

Lana needed all the help she could get. Even if it was from a ghost. Even if she didn't really believe this far-fetched story. But she would shut herself in a dark room with a dead witch if it meant getting back with Miles.

She missed him so much that she felt the absence of him as an ache in her throat, a dullness in her heart.

"I'll do it." Lana leaned forward.

"I'll go first." Holly was faster. Before Lana could move, Holly was inside, pulling the door behind her. It was open just a sliver, enough to hear Holly moving inside. The silence of the hall was complete and terrifying.

"You're going to ask for Miles, aren't you?" Ameera asked, slouching against the wall.

"What do you think?" Lana sounded defensive.

"Do you really believe a dead witch can help you?" Ameera said dryly.

"Probably not," she admitted. "But I have to do something, you know? I can't sit in my room waiting for him to message me. I have to act." She shrugged. "This is what I can do."

Even in the dim light of her phone torch, Lana could see the pity in Ameera's eyes.

Holly came out. Her face was flushed.

"And?" Lana said. "What happened? Did you see anything?"

"I felt something." Her eyes were shining. "Like a breeze."

Maybe it was just a breeze, Lana thought doubtfully.

"I left a gift for her," Holly added. "A red velvet ribbon. I think she liked it. I think she looked on me with favour."

"I don't have a gift," Ameera said. "You didn't say to bring one."

"I'll go next." Lana was also peeved. It was so like Holly not to tell them about the gift. Lana had nothing with her that she could leave behind.

Lana stepped into the hidden room. It smelled musty, like no one had been inside in years. Without warning, the door shut tightly behind her and she heard giggling. She tried opening the door, but it was locked.

She wasn't going to react. That was why they did it. Lana was sure that Holly had made everything up. That there was no girl who'd died in this room. It was all an elaborate prank to shut Lana in the room so they could have a laugh. They'd take pictures of Lana when she emerged, afraid and cross, from the room. Holly would show it to Miles and say, "Isn't it just hilarious?"

Lana could stand a bit of darkness. They'd open the door soon.

315

It was pitch-black inside. Lana pushed deeper into the room. It felt narrow, small. More like a cupboard than a room. If Holly's story was true, it was terrible. Imagine being locked in this small space day after day. Carrying a baby, while the man you loved moved on to someone else. Imagine that life ending, short and unresolved. Lana suddenly felt agitated. The more she thought about it, the more unsettled she felt.

If that had been her life, she'd be a ghost too. She'd haunt everyone who'd hurt her until they died.

Lana's eyes were smarting. Her throat felt tight. She had to get out of there. She took a step towards the door. Something brushed the small of her back. Lana leaped forward, a strangled sound escaping her.

It's my mind playing tricks on me, she repeated to herself.

She put a hand to the door. She wanted out. "OK, you've had your fun." Lana pressed her ear to the door, trying to listen for her friends. They weren't giggling any more. Or maybe she couldn't hear them through the heavy wood. Lana felt around the door. Her hands searched for the hard metal of a handle. She touched the blank wall, her search growing fevered. There was nothing. No handle. Her heart racing, Lana ran her hands over the cold wall until she found the line where door met wall. She dug her fingernails in, trying to prise the door open. But it was too thin. She couldn't get them in.

She couldn't get out.

Then, from downstairs, the sound of thumping, like a stick on metal.

"Who's there?" Dawn's voice was loud and deep. "Who is it?" The thumping noise sounded again. And then silence.

Lana pulled her phone from her pocket. Her battery life glowed orange – it was about a third full. She dialled Holly's number and waited for the call to connect. But there was only an empty noise before the phone beeped and gave up. She tried Ameera's number and the same thing happened. The bar in the corner of the screen showed that there was low signal. She texted them both but the messages failed to send.

Giving up, she leaned her head against the wall. She couldn't call her dad because he was at work. And he would be so disappointed with her. She looked again at the infuriating exclamation marks indicating that her messages remained unsent. Her battery indicator had shrunk.

Lana turned on her phone torch, holding it up to survey the space. Just looking at it made her feel a kind of despair. It seemed nothing more than a storage area and she felt an intense fury with herself for falling for the trick. Of course there was no dead witch. And now they'd run off because Dawn had heard them in the house.

Dawn never left the house. It was almost like she was trapped inside. Like she couldn't leave.

Stop, Lana told herself. *Stop thinking silly things.*

She swept the torch to the wall beside her and she saw a table. Lana turned to examine it. Animal bones. Feathers. Candles. The wall was marked with symbols. There was a reddish-brown smear beneath them.

It was an altar. A witch's altar.

Lana took several deep breaths.

The walls felt like they were inching closer. She suddenly, urgently, had to get out of the room. She moved to the door, not caring if Dawn Connelly heard her.

"Let me out," she shrieked, thumping her hand against the door. "Please let me out."

No one let her out.

Lana turned back to the room. She pointed her phone light at the shrine. Drawing closer, she studied the symbols on the stone wall, tracing a pattern. It was funny how it bothered her less now. Like she'd grown accustomed to it. What was strange was slowly becoming normal. She stared at the marks on the wall, thinking it looked almost like a face: there were the eyes and there was the mouth. She could make out long dark hair shadowing the face. The smear of blood was a dress.

The room seemed to sigh.

Lana was tired. Her eyes felt thick and itchy. She heard shuffling footsteps pass the room. Dawn Connelly must be going to bed. Lana thumped on the door again but no one came. She sat heavily on the mattress, resting her head against the wall.

Lana jerked, feeling the light brush of something touching her cheek. She placed a hand up to her cheek; it felt cold. She'd fallen asleep, stretched out on the old, musty mattress. Dreaming … she'd dreamed the cold touch.

Lana looked at her phone, seeing that the battery was a

mere sliver now. Four hours had passed. Holly and Ameera hadn't come back. She sat up slowly, her mind filled with dead girls.

Holding up her torch again, she cast the light around the room. The shape of the face carved in stone caught her attention. Only this time, it seemed more distinct. As if someone had drawn the image of a girl, whereas earlier it was formed by the markings in the stone. It was unmistakable now. The girl in the stone winked.

Lana cursed and dropped her phone.

She felt the mattress for her phone but it wasn't there. She placed her hands on the ground before her, and then suddenly stopped. She was not alone. She'd never been more certain of anything.

Something brushed her cheek. A gentle hand. And with that touch, Lana felt a mix of sorrow and comfort.

Lana trembled. Then she remembered that the stone girl would help those in love.

"There's a boy," she said very softly. "I want him to love me again."

The same light brush on her cheek.

"Can you help me?" Lana whispered, and this time something stroked her hair. Soothing, the strokes comforted Lana and she lay down on the mattress, her eyes closing. She was bone-achingly tired. Her face touched something cold. Her phone. Lana turned on the torch.

In the light, she saw the grey face of a young woman with dark hair and a crimson dress. A red velvet ribbon in her hair. Then her phone died and the room was plunged into darkness again.

Lana didn't remember where she was the next morning. The room was still dark, but she felt that the texture of the darkness had changed. It was no longer quite so impenetrable, so complete. She got to her feet, then made for the door. The wood that had been sealed so tightly shut was ever so slightly ajar now.

It was a dream, Lana told herself as she crept down the stairs. She stole out of the house, not seeing Dawn Connelly anywhere. Leaving by the back door, she ran across the field and to the road.

At home, Lana let herself in. Her dad had been on the late shift so she was quiet, trying to shake the strangeness of the night. When she'd plugged in her phone and it finally came back to life, Lana deleted her unsent messages. She was surprised to see that Holly and Ameera hadn't been in touch. That was odd. She was sure they'd have said something after leaving her behind.

Lana waited, feeling a ball of fury form in her stomach while she shampooed the smell of must and damp out of her hair. The anger grew while she dressed and did her make-up with care. At noon, she left a note for her dad, saying she'd be back later. She stuffed Miles's hoodie into her tote bag. She wanted, badly, to keep the hoodie, but it gave her a reason to go to his house. She'd tell Miles she was there to return the hoodie. Then he would tell her to keep it. He'd tell her that he'd made a terrible mistake. He'd throw his arms around her and whisper into her hair that he missed her and wanted them to be together again.

Lana had seen the stone girl. She'd survived a whole night in that room.

And in return, Miles would love her again.

It was a fifteen-minute walk, and Lana was almost sick with anticipation. She pushed Holly and Ameera from her mind, still hurt that they'd left her. Angry that they hadn't called.

Miles's car was parked outside. Lana steadied herself and moved closer. There was no need to be afraid. It had worked. She had a dead witch on her side.

She realized as she drew closer that Miles was in his car. But he wasn't alone. He was turned towards someone sitting beside him. Smiling at her. The way his eyes crinkled when he smiled made her heart skip.

A girl in the car beside him and the way he was looking at her made Lana pause. She felt like a feral dog, hackles rising.

Miles placed a hand on the girl's cheek and leaned in. He kissed her.

Lana watched, hot lava running through her as Miles kissed Holly.

Lana was distracted all afternoon while her dad cooked something elaborate. He was talking to her, but she couldn't follow what he was saying. He might as well be speaking another language entirely.

After dinner she excused herself. There was still no message from Holly, but Ameera had texted.

Wtf Lana?

Lana struggled to compose a reply and eventually, hurt and confused, she rang Ameera.

"Why did you leave me there?" Lana had meant to sound smooth, but it came out plaintive. "Why did you lock the door?"

"What do you mean?" Ameera sounded outraged. "What prank were you trying to pull last night, Lana? That was seriously weird."

"You locked me in and left me there."

"No," Ameera said. "You shut the door and locked yourself in. You were laughing. It was freaky."

"*You* were giggling," Lana said, her mind searching through the moments after the door closed, unable to latch on to anything.

"That's not what happened. You can ask Holly. You went inside, slammed the door shut. We knocked quietly, called to you. You laughed a little but otherwise said nothing. We waited a while and you didn't come out. We were pretty pissed off with you then so we left."

"Do you seriously think I wanted to be shut in that horrible room all night?"

Ameera paused. "I know you'd do anything for Miles."

When Ameera said it like that, it didn't sound like a good thing. It didn't sound like the strength Lana knew it was. She'd said it to Miles too. "I'll do anything for you, Miles." She'd breathed those words in the darkness of his room. They'd felt intense, important. And the next day, he'd dumped her.

"I wanted to talk to you about that." Ameera sounded serious.

Did Ameera know about Holly and Miles? The humiliation, the gut-wrenching hurt of it gripped her like a fist.

"I know you're hurting," Ameera said gently. "Breaking up sucks but it happens, you know? You have to respect that Miles wants it to be over. It's time to move on. Focus on you for a bit."

Lana bristled. She knew Ameera was speaking sense, but it was the last thing she wanted right now.

"Otherwise, well, it's all too much. Maybe even a little unhinged," Ameera continued. "And after last night, I'm a little worried about you, Lana."

"I have to go." Lana hung up. She lay back on her bed and began to think.

The old woman was asleep in the armchair. The TV was on mute, the changing light dancing over her still form. She was so completely unmoving that for a moment Lana wondered if Dawn was still alive. From the kitchen door

Lana watched uneasily: the TV light animating the small, craggy face and the stick-thin arms.

Lana crossed the room, snuck up the stairs. It was strange to be doing this alone. She missed her friends but she hadn't spoken to either of them. Not to Ameera after that awkward conversation, and not to Holly.

It made her stomach lurch to think about Holly. She could see them in the car. How Holly's arms had twined around Miles's neck, drawing him to her. How Miles had kissed her with such enthusiasm. Like he hadn't broken up with Lana a week ago.

Lana found the catch and the giant wood-panelled door eased back. She was better prepared today. She'd brought a giant flashlight and charged her phone battery to full. She'd even brought a gift – a leather bracelet that Miles had given her for her birthday last year.

The room was exactly as it had been before. The shrine to one side, the small, thin mattress against the wall. Lana placed the flashlight on the floor, angling it up to the shrine. She stared at the wall, softening her gaze. She stared until the marks on the wall took on a shape. First the eyes, wide and bright. Impressions in stone, but more. Then the small mouth, the tangle of hair. Finally, the blood smear that was her dress.

When the figure was complete, when they weren't simply random markings but the clear image of a girl, Lana spoke.

"I brought a gift in the hope that you will help me find the way back to my beloved."

324

Nothing happened. The girl in the stone did not wink.

Lana wasn't deterred. She sat on the mattress, prepared to stay a second night if she had to. She thought back to the previous night, wondering where Holly went while she'd been stuck in the room, and the sour churning was so painful, she doubled over. Had Holly gone straight to Miles that night? Had he kissed her while Lana had been stuck in this room?

"Please," Lana whispered. "Please help me get Miles back."

Lana comforted herself that it only hurt this much because her love was so deep. So strong. She shut her eyes and leaned her head against the cool wall.

She would do anything for him.

She felt the mattress shift. Someone had sat down beside her. She smelled the lavender perfume that had permeated the living room downstairs and her heart fluttered. Please let this not be Dawn Connelly sitting beside her.

Lana opened her eyes.

The girl beside her was young. She wore a crimson dress and had a head full of dark black hair. There was a grey cast to her skin, as if she'd lived in stone for a hundred years. When she spoke, it sounded like the rustle of feathers. "Two girls asking for the same boy." The stone girl was looking at her curiously. "You both love him?"

Lana felt the echoes of the story that Holly had told in the dark hall. Two sisters who loved one man.

"I love him," Lana said firmly. "He should be with me."

The girl watched her.

"Did you help her?" Lana couldn't help asking. "Is that why he is with her?"

A red velvet ribbon hung in her thick black hair. "I helped her."

Lana turned away. Her voice shook slightly. "Can you help me get him back?"

"She gave me a ribbon."

"I will give you this." Lana held out the leather bracelet.

The stone girl shook her head. "That's not what I want."

"What do you want?"

"More."

"I'll give you whatever you want," Lana said eagerly. The stone girl could have her jewellery and pretty things. "Whatever is mine to give."

The girl nodded. "It will not be easy" – that low, rasping voice. It sounded unused – "to undo the magic."

"But it can be done?" Lana turned back to her, not hiding her desperation.

"It can be done." A cold grey hand reached for hers. "Here's what you must do."

On Halloween night, Lana sat on Holly's bed, waiting.

It had taken everything in her to call Holly the previous day. To be the first to cave. Like Ameera, Holly swore that she hadn't closed the door to the secret room. They'd seen it swing shut, and they'd been sure that Lana had shut

326

herself in the room. That she was pranking them. Then Dawn heard them and they'd fled.

Neither of them spoke about Miles.

"Wow," Holly said, entering the room. "You look amazing. What are you supposed to be?"

Lana was confused. She'd styled her hair exactly, including the red ribbon. She'd dyed an old lace wedding dress crimson. She had painted her skin with that same sickly grey cast. Catching her reflection in the mirror, she was almost unsettled by how eerily like her she looked. How could Holly not see that she was dressed as the stone girl?

Because Holly hadn't seen the stone girl, Lana realized. It made her sit taller. Only she had seen the girl. Her bond was stronger. Holly might have got there first. Holly might have given her the red ribbon, but only Lana had seen her.

Lana would give her more.

"You need to bring him here," the stone girl had said. "Bring him to me and I will undo the magic that binds him to Holly."

The stone girl had given her clear instructions. It had to happen on Halloween. She had to bring Miles to the secret room. Lana had to wear a costume, and the stone girl told her what she needed to do.

"Bring him to this room and then you must kiss him. This must happen before midnight. Otherwise it will be too late."

"Why the costume?"

"It will make sense on the night. But you have my word.

If you kiss Miles before midnight on Halloween, he will no longer be with Holly."

"Thank you," Lana had breathed.

"But there is a caveat," the stone girl said. "If you don't kiss him before midnight, then I'll take the gift you offered. I will only take it if you fail."

"Sure. Is there something specific that you want?"

"Yes."

And before Lana could ask what it was, the stone girl had disappeared. She'd heard the shuffling footsteps of Dawn Connelly on the stairs. She had to get out of there. But she would return, and she would get Miles back too.

"Lana," Holly said, interrupting her thoughts. Lana snapped her head up. It looked like Holly had something on her mind. Something she wanted to share. Her forehead was creased slightly and Lana knew it was something serious.

Oh no, she thought. She wasn't going to let Holly confess to kissing Miles. Not before her chance to have the midnight kiss. Holly could spill all she liked after that, but it would be too late.

"What is it?" Lana asked brightly. "Are you ready to go? Ameera's on her way already. Do you think Miles will be there?"

"I don't think so." Holly sounded dull.

"I hope he is. I can't wait to see him. Wait, was there something you wanted to say?"

Holly paused, then shook her head. "Have you seen my phone?"

"You put it in your bag," Lana lied. "We should go. It's getting late."

Lana knew that Holly's phone wasn't in her bag, it was in Lana's. Along with the message inviting Miles to meet her at the Connelly house.

It had been easy to shake off Ameera and Holly at the party. Lana had gone in with them, and, after a while, she'd disappeared in the crowd of dancing skeletons and witches and devils. While Ameera and Holly danced, Lana left the party. She went outside and retrieved her bike from the nearby park. She'd left it there before going to Holly's to change.

Lana cycled to the Connelly house. She had to push the bike from where the road narrowed because it was too rocky to cycle. She turned the corner and there was Miles. At the gate, waiting for her.

Not for her, for Holly.

Miles was surprised when he saw her emerging from the dark lane. "Lana. Hi. What are you doing here?"

"Holly asked me to come. She said to tell you that she's not coming. That she's sorry but she can't do it."

Miles was quiet. He'd never been able to hide his feelings. His face was open, and it showed when he was happy or worried. Or perplexed, as he was now.

"And she asked *you* to tell me?"

"She did." Lana took a deep breath. "Look, Miles, I know it's been awkward the last week. But it doesn't have to be. We're cool, right?"

Miles seemed relieved. "Yeah. OK." He smiled, taking in her costume. "You're going to the party?"

"I've come from the party," Lana said playfully. "And now I want to find a ghost. A real ghost. Want to come ghost hunting with me? The moon is nearly full and we have a haunted house. It would be a shame to pass up the chance."

Miles laughed. "You're fun when you're like this. When you're not so…"

"So what?" Lana smiled brightly.

"I shouldn't have said that." The tips of his ears went pink.

"It's fine. Tell me."

He exhaled. "Uptight. Lately, before we broke up, you'd become so tense. Especially about us, and it was making me feel like the walls were closing in. We weren't having fun any more. Everything was serious and intense and it was too much."

"Miles, you should have talked to me." But then she smiled, even though it hurt, and said, "Let's go and find a ghost." She could be fun, dammit. She would be fun if it was the hardest thing she'd ever done.

She tugged his hand, pulling him inside the gate.

"Here?" he said. The house, dark and neglected, loomed above them.

Lana nodded and put a finger on her lips. Miles was smiling at her now in that way he had. The crinkling eyes. The hint of a dimple. The same way he'd smiled at

Holly. He twined his fingers around hers and it felt like electricity.

Holly's gift of a red ribbon was no match for this. There was more than magic drawing Lana and Miles together. They were meant to be. They were perfect.

Miles followed Lana inside the kitchen. Lana listened at the door to the living room. She pushed it open, expecting to see Dawn Connelly in front of the TV again. But tonight the room was brightly lit. There were fresh flowers on the side table and the room felt awake. It was almost like stepping back in time. Music played, a wild, passionate violin piping through the speakers.

"Come," Lana said cautiously. If Dawn wasn't in the chair, they had to be extra careful. They went into the hall and the huge chandelier was a bouquet of light. Up the stairs, Lana still holding on to Miles's hand.

"Where are we going?" He placed his lips on her neck. Lana shivered with pleasure.

"I told you. To find a ghost." Lana almost turned back. Miles seemed into her again. Maybe she didn't need to do this. Maybe they could just go back to the party and have fun.

But she had to be sure. She didn't want him to turn away from her when he saw Holly again. Lana knew that the kiss she'd witnessed was because Holly had gifted the ribbon to the stone girl. In exchange, the girl had helped her. Lana had to undo Holly's wish and the stone girl had said that Miles had to be there for the undoing.

Lana pressed at the panel and the secret door released. Miles's face lit up when he saw the hidden room. Lana flicked on the large flashlight she'd left inside the door.

"What is this place?" Miles asked, examining the shrine. He picked up the small animal skull.

"It's where a girl died of a broken heart."

Sudden movement drew Lana's eye. She turned to the door. Miles did too.

"What the hell?" He dropped the animal skull.

Dawn Connelly stood in the doorway. She was tiny, her hair short and silver. Her eyes were almost swallowed by the lines in her face. She watched them both intently.

The torch flickered and died.

Lana flicked the switch and a dull light flared, then died. She flicked it again and again, but the room remained dark.

"Battery must have died," she said.

"Who was that?" Miles said. He was holding up his phone torch now and no one stood in the doorway. He turned to Lana and his face went ashen.

"Miles," Lana said. "What's wrong?"

"Miles," said a voice beside her. "What's wrong?"

Lana turned slowly and saw her mirror image beside her. The tangle of black hair. The red velvet ribbon. The crimson lace dress. The details of their dresses were slightly different, but in the light of the phone torch, Lana and the stone girl were identical.

"Lana?" Miles said. "Which one is you?"

"I am," Lana said.

"I am," said the voice beside her.

Lana turned to the stone girl. "Stop it."

The stone girl echoed her movement. Her intonation. "Stop it."

Lana stepped forward. "Miles, it's me. Lana. In costume." She held his hand. "That" – she pointed to the stone girl – "is a ghost."

"Miles?" the stone girl said, breathing quickly. "I'm scared. I'm Lana. That's the stone girl. She's the ghost of a witch."

Miles looked between the two girls. He released his hand from Lana's. He held up both hands. "I'm sorry. I don't know what's going on."

"Miles," the stone girl urged, sounding more frantic now. "She's really dangerous. You have to make her go away."

"How do I do that?" Miles said.

"Kiss me. If you kiss me, you'll see that I am real and she is only an apparition. Then we need to get out of here."

Miles stepped towards her.

"Miles," Lana said, desperate. "I'm Lana. You need to kiss me."

"Miles," the stone girl said, "don't listen to her. I'm Lana; I'll prove it." She was beside him now. She whispered something in his ear. Miles pulled back and stared at her. Then, to Lana's horror, he drew closer to the stone girl.

"No, Miles," Lana screamed. "Don't do it."

If he didn't kiss her by midnight, the stone girl would take something that belonged to her.

I'll give you whatever you want. Whatever is mine to give. Lana had been so sure the stone girl would help her. She'd believed too hard that she and Miles were right together. Perfect. So of course it would work out. Lana hadn't expected this.

Miles drew closer, placing his hands on her shoulders. He leaned down and slowly, deliberately, kissed the stone girl.

Lana drew her hands to her mouth, stifling a scream. From downstairs, she could hear the clock begin to strike midnight. They broke apart.

"Lana." Miles gazed into the stone girl's eyes. Lana felt the wall against her back. Her phone fell from her hand. The room was plunged into darkness.

"I'll have that gift now," said a delicate rustling in her ears.

And Lana knew. "You tricked me."

"You agreed, remember?"

She'd told Miles that she would do anything for him. She'd told the stone girl she would give anything that was hers to give. And it was true, nothing she owned was worth more than Miles. But the stone girl didn't want her things. The stone girl wanted *her*.

A low wailing sound filled the room.

"What is that?" Miles said, his voice further away than Lana realized.

Turn on your torch. But nothing came out. Then she realized that she was making the wailing sound. She wanted to stop it, to clap her hand over her mouth. But she couldn't. It was too dark. A darkness so complete, so isolating, that she couldn't see or even feel her hand. She felt light. Insubstantial.

"We need to get out of here." Miles spoke into the darkness. But he wasn't speaking to Lana.

"Guess we found our ghost." The stone girl's voice was light. Playful.

"I'd rather we hadn't," Miles said. "Clever move to reference our earlier conversation about you being uptight. That's when I knew you were Lana."

But I'm Lana, she wanted to say. But she had no words, only that cold unhuman wailing.

She had no body.

She was a ghost.

Miles and the stone girl, now in Lana's body, held hands as they left. The stone girl had been right: she didn't need to worry about Holly.

Lana felt a pull. Something grounding her. She left the secret room, drawn to something like iron to a magnet. She moved through the dark into the next room, and there on the floor lay Dawn Connelly. Lana moved towards Dawn and the darkness lifted.

Lana never went to the secret room any more. She could go into the garden but no further, and sometimes that was what she did, watching out to see who might wander this way. What conversations she might overhear. But she was most comfortable here, on this faded floral armchair. She was always thirsty, though.

The TV played though she didn't remember putting it on. A talk show host was chatting to his celebrity guests. Had she fallen asleep? She was thirsty again.

She coughed, reaching for the mug on the table beside her. She muted the TV while she grabbed it. Then she turned to look at her hand. Her thin veiny arms. She lifted the blanket and saw her legs in the corduroy trousers, her sensible shoes. Old. She still couldn't get used to it.

She heard a sound behind her. The light tread of footsteps on the wooden floor. The low voices of girls.

She turned slightly, catching their reflection in the glass cabinet. She didn't recognize them at all. They must be from another village.

Lana knew more than she remembered. Perhaps it was residual memory, stored in Dawn Connelly's body. Her body now.

She had until Halloween to figure it all out. To set her trap, the way she'd fallen into one herself. And if she failed, then the Halloween after that.

She lifted the cup and drank deeply. A girl crossed the back of the room. She moved furtively, like a clever little thief.

Lana rather liked the look of that one. She hoped she would come back.

THE BEAST AND THE BEAST

RACHEL FATUROTI

> *"In the midst of her greatest splendour, although distinguished by her merit, she was so handsome that she was called 'The Beauty'. Known by this name only, what more was required to increase the jealousy and hatred of her sisters?"*

> —MADAME DE VILLENEUVE

I live by my own moral code.

My siblings laugh at me because how can an assassin – who moonlights as a mercenary – live by a "code" or standards at all?

    † I won't kill innocent bystanders or children
    † I only kill creeps & dangers to society

† I always follow through on a contract

† If an employer betrays me, the contract is revoked

AZALEA, aka Martha Banner, aka the target, falls messily between the final two items of my code. My employer won't be happy, but the code comes first. I don't care what they think.

Silently assessing her from the adjacent table in the heaving airport coffee shop, I sip my rooibos with honey, and cringe as the godawful polystyrene cup hits my lips. The tea soothes my growing migraine though, warding off the gruesome reveries that are sure to follow.

Martha Banner exudes confidence – with her neatly coiffed dyed blonde hair and manicured nails caressing her oat-milk latte. She sits poised, with a strong posture like she's permanently balancing books on her head and, to everyone else navigating this grimy airport cafe, Martha is self-assured and unassuming. But I'm not just anyone. I know Martha is a devious, backstabbing, cunning woman, whose employers want her dead for exposing their secrets. However, Martha's employers – now my employer – have shady links to human trafficking, which nullifies my contract with them.

"This is an announcement for passengers on flight 232 to Daland. The flight has been delayed due to a shortage of staff. Our new departure time is 10:50 a.m."

Martha fidgets with her rose-gold Cartier watch as tiny

fractures in her composure surface at the unwelcome delay. Even though the airline ticket beside her implies that she's travelling to Crowle for a business trip, her *real* airline ticket to Daland is hidden at the bottom of her deep-green leather Birkin bag. A young child and his father pass by my table. I stick my leg out sharply, tripping the child, who careens into Martha's table, spilling her frothy oat-milk latte down her white silk camisole.

The father apologizes profusely as he grabs handfuls of napkins and hands them to her. "I'm so sorry. He didn't mean to do that."

A woman blocks my view, signalling to the *borrowed* air hostess uniform that I'm wearing. "Shouldn't you be at the gate? They're already short on staff—"

I drive my fist into her stomach, quickly and quietly; she doubles over in pain and lands on the floor. "Help!" I shout. "Someone help her!"

While a concerned crowd surrounds the woman on the floor, I slip away, tailing Martha to the women's bathroom. Just because I won't kill her, doesn't mean I can't send her a message. Inside the bathroom, Martha scrubs vigorously at the latte stain on her top. Another woman washes her hands in the basin beside her.

I offer the stranger a soft smile in the mirror, but she flinches slightly as her eyes roam over my brown skin, neck tattoos and angel-bite piercings, among others. She scurries off out of the bathroom, leaving Martha and me alone. I lock the door.

I snatch Martha's Birkin from her, swinging it and hitting her in the face; the white basin becomes tainted and stained with her blood as the heavy bag buckle slams into her nose. Martha screams, scampering back as I advance towards her. I grip strands of her blonde hair, tugging her body towards me so we're facing the mirror again.

"You need to change your ticket to Daland."

"I'm travelling to Crowle—"

"Change your ticket to Daland. They know you told. More people will come after you and they won't leave you alive."

A sharp pain cuts through my head and I know the dream-like hallucinations will follow. I should have put more honey in my tea.

In the mirror, *he* stands behind us – the man who plagues my dreams. The stabbing pain ricochets through my body, rendering me incapacitated, and Martha just hangs in my arms, quietly sobbing and bleeding. His husky voice serenades me in a language both foreign and familiar, singing of a past life. He says my name. Whispers it. Only I can hear him. With his words comes an icy chill, and I feel it immediately in my bones. Dew forms and grows in the corners of the mirror. His tawny-beige skin, dark eyes, and slicked-back locks are all I can see as he plunges my hand inside Martha's chest cavity to retrieve her heart. Then he offers me her pumping, blood-dripping organ to eat.

Retrieving the special antidote the Merchants created for me from inside my boot, I stab the needle violently into

340

my flesh and close my eyes. After the sting, he disappears. I grip Martha tighter and speak with a voice that's not my own. "Leave. Now."

She scampers out of the bathroom, leaving me behind.

Later on that day, when I make it home – a decommissioned, abandoned restaurant, which floats by the pier – I settle down on one of the torn leather benches and bask in the privacy it offers. It reminds me of the river community deep in the Tolibeli rainforest and their floating houses: a place where I feel at one with myself.

My phone rings and I almost let it ring out, but I decide not to in the final moments. I don't tend to ignore my employer – the Merchants – or my siblings when they call; our world is unstable enough, and anything can happen. You never know when a conversation could be your last. I recognize the area code and assume that it's most likely my sister, Carmen. She's not my biological sister. I don't have any blood-related siblings. We met doing what we do.

"Carmen."

"You dropped the ball. You know they aren't happy with you, but I did what you were too frightened to do. See you tomorrow for lunch."

She hangs up the phone and an untraceable link is sent to me seconds later. I open it. It's a picture of Martha in a horrific car accident with a snapped neck.

I swallow the anger festering like an oozing wound. The Merchants appear to look after us, but only if you serve them. Everyone is dispensable – including me. I remember waking up shivering and vulnerable at the roadside almost five years ago with no memories. The Merchants concealed me from the government, who knew I was different. They never stop searching for me. I know my employers are hiding information from me.

I toss the phone across the room; it collides with the counter, splintering to pieces. Leaning over on a wooden stool, I pull down one of the brass beer tap levers to reveal poorly drawn sketches of my hallucinations. Blood. Gore. Flesh. The man. Who is he? Why do I feel like I know him?

The next day, I'm lunching with my brother Zane and sisters Sakura and Carmen at our favourite Japanese restaurant, tucked in the corner of Pennsylvania Avenue. We were recruited at the same time several years ago. They're the only real family I've ever known.

The overwhelming, heady aroma of the incense exacerbates the faint throbbing in my skull. Zane taps his choko of sake against mine.

"We're celebrating. Why aren't you drinking, sister?" he asks, knocking back the cup as if it's water. He tousles his ash-brown hair as he signals to the hostess; he's been flirting with her for the last hour. "We need more!"

I stave off the building nausea, tilting the sake into my mouth and savouring the mildly sweet, clean taste. My siblings of all shapes and creeds commemorate the occasion. A hundred kills isn't an easy feat and Zane is proud of himself, glad that he's an asset to the Merchants. Carmen and Zane don't live by a code, not like Sakura and I. She doesn't kill women – something to do with her upbringing that she doesn't like to talk about. Zane, on the other hand, is on the wrong side of unhinged, but he's still my brother.

Sakura fiddles with her chopsticks. Her demure countenance frequently lulls others into a false sense of security, but given the chance, she could decapitate a mark with the chopsticks she's holding. She toasts Zane before slowly coaxing the sweet liquid into her mouth without missing a single drop. "Kampai." Her touch is feather light. "Have you heard about any issues with our employer?" she asks in the same breath, as she spreads the red napkin on to her lap. She raises a tuna roll to her pink lips.

They're all waiting for information, which they think I have. The Merchants call me their "secret weapon" or 2-5-1-21-20-25, which stands for—

"Beauty!" Carmen barks. "You know something. We can tell there is something going on. Why are you hiding it from us?"

"I'm just a soldier following orders; I don't know *anything*," I reply.

But doubt sets in Carmen's hazel eyes, judging and finding me guilty.

"Drop it, Carmen," Zane says.

Sakura remains silent.

"I'm going to the bathroom." The migraines and dreams are becoming more and more regular. I can't help but think my brain is trying to tell me something.

When I'm out of sight, I stumble towards the toilets, my vision blurring at the edges as my head throbs and pulses. Not again. I'm strong-armed against the wall. Carmen's butterfly knife nicks my throat, drawing blood.

"You're hiding, Beauty. What are you hiding? Don't you know what's happening to us?"

I *do* know. An agent was killed in Budapest and another in Cyprus. Something is hunting us.

My dagger jabs Carmen in the thigh, and she winces.

"Someone is killing us off," Carmen growls, baring her teeth. "Organs torn out and a single red rose left on their dead bodies."

Flashes of the gruesome mirror vision with Martha penetrate my mind.

"You know something!" She slams her palm on the wall beside my head.

"I don't know anything." I fume. "Now, go back into the restaurant and eat your sushi and leave me the fuck alone, *sister.*"

Shoving her off me, I slip inside the toilet, splashing cold water on my face to erase my congested mind.

The burner phone in my trouser pocket buzzes, startling me. If I don't answer *them*, there'll be hell to pay. I kick open all the doors to check that I'm alone and lock the main door before answering the call. The voice is automated.

"2-5-1-21-20-25."

"Yes."

"34.09114882596382, -118.39301088217717."

I memorize the coordinates and immediately remove the sim card from the vintage flip phone. I snap the sim card in two and try to toss one half in the overflowing bin beside me.

But my legs crumple as I step towards it; black spots blur my vision. I hold the edge of the porcelain sink to steady myself. The sake burns the back of my throat as it travels back up, splattering the mirror in front of me. I'm not alone. The dream man is behind me again. His scent of driftwood and power fogs my mind.

I look up, but it's not the same dark eyes staring back at me as the last time; instead he has one black and one white eye socket with tentacles squirming out. Black tentacles burst out of his mouth too, dripping red. I know it's blood because I smell the iron. His skin is the colour of rotting meat, and the tentacled creatures writhe around his skin, alive.

Through the mirror, Carmen lies on the floor, lifeless. Her exposed torso is splayed open, missing vital organs. The man holds up a pair of lungs to my lips, urging me to take a bite. I stab the antidote into my wrist without hesitating.

The door rattles and everything is back to normal.

"Beauty!" Carmen shouts, further rattling the door. "What are you doing in there? Hiding more secrets?"

I pat the perspiration on my forehead with a damp tissue as I unlock the bathroom door. "I need to go."

I speed through the smog-congested city on my silver Tomahawk, swerving through the multi-lane traffic and the reckless jaywalkers. My mind zones out, isolating the sounds around me: the horns honking, chatter on cell phones, construction noise and the blue Honda Civic with a dodgy exhaust, which has been tailing me ever since I left the restaurant.

Once the traffic lights change, I accelerate from nought to sixty in seconds, leaving the Honda behind. Once I am safely out of sight, I tuck my motorbike between two houses, throwing a green tarp over it to conceal it.

The dead drop is on a side street. I take out the fawn folder from the letter box. It is filled with details of my next target. I tuck it into the back of my denim jeans and then walk casually in the direction of the motel to wait for nightfall.

I draw back the cheap curtain that has seen better days. The cloudy windows give the outside a deceptive, ethereal hue, but it's as dreary there as it is in here. The neon vacancy sign is partially lit, providing a small fraction of light to the low-level occupants of this sordid motel.

18:50

A hiss transmits from the grey and charcoal radio standing idle on the rickety table.

18:55

The air-con unit rattles to life like a Ford Mustang clinging on to its prime. In the darkness, I fight the nausea and migraines – the main prelude to the gruesome dreams, but I concentrate, indulging in the must, mildew and faint smell of stale cigarettes to keep me in the present. Leaning back on the hard, lumpy mattress, I focus on the sounds and conversations through the thin walls.

The erratic juddering of a squeaky bed.

Doors slammed and abuse hurled by a drunk man unsatisfied with services rendered.

The ring of a telephone delivering devastating news.

19:00

The melody from "the wheels on the bus" transmits from the radio, and then stops just as suddenly. Scooting my ass to the edge of the bed, I wait for my target's location.

"2-5-1-21-20-25. 40.722827208808724, -74.35657034499643."

The coordinates bring me to the "Inkaholics" tattoo parlour, which is as obnoxious as its name. My black leather thigh-highs are pasted on, accentuating my sleek silhouette, drawing the attention of the smoker at the parlour's back door.

"Are you new?" he asks, a trail of nicotine wafting by as he watches me – my body bound in a black sleeveless leather bodysuit and lengthy box braids. I pluck the cigarette from his tattooed fingers and take a drag.

Tossing the cigarette into the gutter, I kick the container used to prop the door open and leave the man stranded outside as it slams behind me.

"Hey! Let me in!" His fists hammer the door.

I'm on the clock.

My target, BELLADONA, is better known as Brandon Trent, a middle-aged white man who resembles an aged

GQ model. Brandon Trent had been hard to track down, but it seems he has a weakness for whisky and beautiful red-haired companions who like to be paid.

Using a single braid, I tighten it around the rest of my braids into a bun.

"You. Out." I point to his flame-haired mate, who bristles at my biting tone.

Defiance crosses her striking face and distrust melts in her eyes — the perfect actress. "Fine, but I'm waiting right outside."

The door slams and I'm left with Brandon and his problematic fetish for young boys and girls.

"Alexa, play music. Turn up the volume." A metal anthem belts out through the speakers. *Fitting.*

"I w-ant her n-aame tat-tat-ooed on my h-eart," Brandon slurs through the song.

"How about through your eye?"

"Wh-at?"

I fire up the tattoo gun and stab it into his eye socket, penetrating like butter as I bear down, stunning him. He squeals like a rodent.

I fight the building migraine and spots in my vision. The tattoo gun jerks as I spot *his* shape in the mirror.

The hallucinations always come fragmented, but three constants remain: the man, the gore, and the excruciating, earth-shattering pain.

The man stands by an exposed torso, consuming organs – raw, fresh, the red evidence leaking down his face, tangling in his fingers. He offers me the heart. I scream, stabbing the antidote into my neck, and I'm back in the tattoo parlour, narrowly missing a weak punch from my mark.

"You're their puppet!" he bellows, his voice clashing with the loud music. "When they go down, you'll go down with them."

My leg snaps out and I kick him hard in the abdomen, sending him sprawling over the tattoo chair and crashing into the mirror, shattering it. I hop over the chair, swiping a shard of glass from the ground, and slice his jugular in a swift motion. Blood sprays like a burst pipe.

Contorting my joints, I squeeze out of the small window and escape out on to the street.

I grab a bottle of cold beer from the bar at home, draining it and tossing the folder I picked up on to the table. The papers inside scatter with information on the next target: ROSE.

This has to be the person hunting us.

The surveillance photographs only offer views of his back or a blurry side profile, nothing clear of his face. I pick up one photograph in particular and trace the edges of his black vintage coat.

My phone vibrates and I answer, dropping the photograph back down.

"2-5-1-21-20-25."

"Yes."

"*Your next target, ROSE, is a Level 5. If you succeed, you will become a Team Leader. Failure is unacceptable."*

The phone disconnects.

I have never encountered a Level 5 threat before, which means that other agents have tried and failed. Level 5 is deadly, dangerous and diabolic.

I hear the faint click of Jimmy Choos.

Withdrawing the gun from the hole inside the torn bench, I aim it at the door of the boat, but as the person comes closer, I recognize them – Sakura.

"Put your gun away, Beauty," Sakura says through the closed wooden door. I open it for her.

She glances around, unsatisfied.

"I can't right now, Sakura," I say, piling all the papers back inside the folder.

Sakura's eyes fixate on them.

"Carmen is missing," she replies simply.

I stifle a laugh. "Carmen goes 'missing' every other week. She's off taking on extra contracts, and since when did I become Carmen's keep—?"

"Beauty." Sakura's tone is soft, but there is an edge that is almost fatal. "I am telling you there is an issue. There was a single red rose, but no Carmen. We know that you argued with her at the restaurant."

A single red rose.

"You know something, Beauty. What is it?"

"I will handle it."

Sakura doesn't utter another word as she leaves the boat.

I open the folder on ROSE again, bristling at his last

sighted location. *Tolibeli*. What are the chances that this Level 5 target is in a place I know?

I've travelled there many times before: scorching heat and untamed rainforests. The ideal location to stay hidden. But also ideal to take a target out.

With an eight-hour flight ahead, I pack the essentials, contacting an asset about borrowing his private plane. How else can I transport knives, guns and bludgeons across the world?

I signal to the owner behind the rustic beach bar in Tolibeli; his knife hammers down, chopping up fresh tropical fruit to garnish the alcoholic concoctions.

"Outra, por favor," I say, slamming down the glass as I wait for my contact, who is running very late.

"Outra bebida a sair," the owner replies, picking up my glass.

I tilt the cheap straw hat down, concealing my face from the sun. A few minutes later, my contact arrives: a local man called Gabriel who sports a faded orange T-shirt, mid-length shorts and well-used flip-flops. He adjusts the expensive sunglasses on top of his head and clicks his fingers.

Gabriel spots me at the corner of the outdoor bar, balancing on the unsteady wooden stool. Judging from the glasses and the suspicious bulge in his shorts pocket, he's been paid off. Our conversation will be riddled with more holes than my hat.

"What do you know about him?" I ask as he perches on

a stool beside me.

Gabriel's knee bounces up and down like a yo-yo. "He lives in big mansion deep in forest. But I've never had sight of him myself … only heard whispers."

It is too easy.

I pull out a printed map of the area. "Point to where he lives."

Gabriel cracks his knuckles again before circling the map with his index finger. "It's … ermm … here."

I point to the spot myself. "It's here. Are you sure?"

He clears his throat, pointing to a different spot close to the other one. "Maybe … here … not sure. It's around here."

I snatch the map, folding it up and leave money on the counter. "Obrigada."

Hours later, I settle down beside an old ally, Mariana, and the rest of her river community, fish roasting on an open fire.

Young girls screech, diving from the floating river houses. I've never asked why there are no men in their community, only women and girls, and she doesn't ask what I do for a living.

"Está de passagem?" Mariana asks, rotating the catfish so it cooks properly on both sides.

"Are you passing through?"

"Sim, estou. Partirei de manhã, mas ficarei para o festival."

"Yes, I am. I'll be gone by the morning, but I'll stay for the festival."

It's the spirit festival. Mariana nods as she works through the steps of making her famous fish stew. My mouth salivates as I watch. She calls out to the others, signalling that the food is ready to be eaten. I'm first in line with a bowl made from a hollowed coconut.

I slurp up the fish stew, making the girls fall into fits of laughter. "Isso é muito bom."

"This is great."

Soon, it's nightfall, and time for the spirit festival. It's not a real festival, but a time once a month where the river community connects with nature. They believe that everything in nature has a spirit and it's important to reconnect with it, especially to recalibrate against those who come to disturb the forest like the miners or the oil companies.

Mariana takes some red dust from the earth and blows it on to our faces, one by one. It heightens the senses and clears the mind, mine even more so, as we commune with nature. Wind rushes through my nose and I feel every single cell in my body.

I slip away from the group, moving through the wet, dense canopied rainforest, air thick with growth and vegetation. Hunting. Damp leaves slide across my skin and sweat beads leave trails down my neck. The red dust still fires through my system as flashes of sunlight through the trees guide me.

I plunge my hand into the ice-cold pool of water that I find, wetting my head and hydrating myself. I zone in to the forest around me, isolating the sounds. The fluttering and bird call from the white-throated toucan, paws of a jaguar scraping at the undergrowth and the scuttering from the forest insects. A dead branch snaps. Breathing.

I wait.

A hundred metres. Fifty metres. Ten metres.

"Tem a certeza de que ela veio nesta direção? A recompensa pela sua captura triplicou," a man asks with a flat tone, punctuated by the cock of his gun.

"Are you sure she came this way? The bounty for her head has tripled."

The ROSE must know I am here and has sent them.

"Tenho a certeza. Eu não mentiria."

"I'm certain. I wouldn't lie."

I almost snigger, but I don't want to give my position away. The others with them are close behind. Whipping my knives out, I silently move towards them and slice the gunman's hamstring muscles in a clean swipe, crippling him.

"Merda!!" he bellows, turning his gun and shooting my contact, Gabriel, in the stomach.

Fear. Piss. Blood.

Name a better threesome.

The commotion attracts the attention of the rest of the group. I dive out from my hiding spot with both of my guns cocked, firing so I hit foreheads, torsos and anywhere else fleshy. Red splatters around me along with pieces of human tissue as I duck. The slash of a rusted machete whips past me. I kick the man in the leg, sending him to the ground.

The machete wielder recovers, advancing towards me, swinging his knife haphazardly. I dive under his armpit and grip his neck in a chokehold from behind until he passes out. Another comes at me shooting his gun; I grip the weapon, slotting my hand in his arm crease, and flip him over on to the ground. I swipe the machete from the ground and slam his head with it. I don't see the other assailant. The wind is knocked out of me as our bodies collide with the soil. He punches me and we wrestle on the ground for a few seconds. We roll over in the dirt, but I gain the upper hand, climbing on his back and putting him into another chokehold. He struggles. With his face inches from the machete, I grip his hair and slam his head into the blade, impaling him.

I can't go back to Mariana and the rest until I find and kill the ROSE. This has gone on far too long already.

My bare feet move against the grey stone tiles as I scrub the blood away under the falling shower water. When I visit Tolibeli, I keep this apartment as back-up if I need it.

A draught comes in from the adjoining room. "Hello?" I call out. "Who's there?"

I switch off the rainfall shower, tugging a cotton towel from the rack with one hand and grabbing the gun secured beneath the bathroom cabinet with the other. I creep out into the apartment with the gun ready. Stealthily, I search every crevice of the apartment, but I'm alone except for my now open balcony doors. I left them closed.

My phone rings, startling me.

"2-5-1-21-20-25."

"Yes."

"Is the mission complete? Has the ROSE been terminated?"

The curtains by the balcony rustle and that's when I notice the bleeding black box wrapped in a black bow by the window. I end the call and walk towards it, checking for any traps on the side, but it's clear.

I open the box, flinching at the sight. Inside is Carmen's skin, so complete that I can make out her features, and her organs are piled on top. I pluck the vintage invitation and see that it's addressed to me and signed ROSE. It's him. I tear the invitation to pieces, leaving the box to get ready.

I'm back in the forest again, not far from where I left those bodies burning. I find an abandoned castle where only ruins remain. I picture it in its prime with the Renaissance architecture: turrets, pinnacles and pointed towers. A home fit for royalty; fit for a prince. The enclosed courtyard houses a lifeless flower garden – the brittle petals crunch under my boots.

The further I move into the castle, the faster my heart beats, a bolting stampede. I follow it, marching through old asymmetrical drawing rooms overgrown with trees until

I reach the great hall. The ROSE stands with his back to me, the black vintage coat stretched tightly over his broad shoulders.

The long oak banqueting table has been consumed by vines and the table has been set.

I withdraw a blade, the knife digging into my hand, drawing blood. "You won't leave here alive."

"You're late," the ROSE says. His voice is hoarse, like sandpaper layers his throat. I don't realize at the time, but he isn't speaking in English, instead in the foreign dialect which only resides in my dreams.

"Who are you?" I ask, right as he turns around to show his face.

He saunters closer to me; my iron resolve keeps my feet rooted to the spot. At six foot five, the ROSE towers over me, and he's close enough for me to see the whites of his eyes.

Why does he feel so familiar to me?

I get this feeling. I would imagine it's the feeling a mother would get having seen her child again after a long absence. It's not simply the familiarity, but my senses are overwhelmed by his scent and presence.

He grips the back of my neck, forcing me on to my tiptoes, joining our foreheads together, and a pulse runs through my skin like an electrical current. I fight the pull, bashing my forehead against his in anger.

The ROSE's smile grows wide until it looks like it hurts. "You forgot the mission. Not to worry, na ta-keyan. I'll

357

help you remember." He pulls his forehead back to mine, and in an instant, we're transported into the forest.

Bracing my hands on my knees, I find myself gasping for breath, the same migraine throbbing at my temple. Someone screams.

I breathe deeply, facing the ROSE, who has transformed into the creature I saw in my dreams, but he's even more grotesque in the flesh. The black tentacles are alive, squirming over different areas of his translucent skin; they appear to be tasting the air.

I search in my pockets for the antidote, but I can't find it.

"Are you looking for this?" the ROSE asks in his strange language. He holds up the antidote. "They're poisoning you. It's stopping you from seeing."

He snaps it in half, tossing it away.

"Wait," I slur.

Mariana stands beside him with Zane and Sakura bound to the trees. My head hammers, pushing all coherent thoughts out. He doesn't stop me as I clumsily cut off my siblings' binds. I turn and we're alone in the forest; the ROSE and Mariana have disappeared.

"Let's move," I say, groaning, another sharp pain forcing unwanted memories inside my head. I can feel him inside my head. How is this possible?

"Beauty, who the hell is that?!" Zane yells as we run in the dark, damp forest. "Do you know him? Carmen was right."

I gulp, my feet faltering as the migraine grows. They don't know about Carmen.

"Carmen is dead," I say.

We're taught never to show weakness, but I feel Sakura's mourning and Zane's bloodthirsty anger like it's my own.

He's hunting us.

I can feel his heart.

The ROSE materializes in front of us with Mariana. What does she have to do with this? Gathering the red dust in her palm, Mariana blows it in my face and my senses are heightened once again. "The spirit festival isn't over yet. You must see." She speaks in the same foreign tongue as the ROSE.

The ground shakes and my vision grows hazy as the migraine worsens. Sakura lunges towards the ROSE, battling the tentacles that branch out. They struggle for a second before one of the tentacles penetrates her mouth, immobilizing her.

"She's not dead," the ROSE says, turning his sights on to Zane. "I can't say the same for him."

One of his tentacles reaches out to touch me; I slice it off, causing the ROSE to screech out in pain. His blood isn't red but magenta.

I punch him, but he grabs my fist, twisting my wrist until I am immobilized too. I use the momentum to swing my body upwards, locking my thighs around his neck, suffocating him. But the power of the migraine and the dust take over, until I'm a puddle on the forest floor.

"You must see, na ta-keyan."

I feel as if I'm choking, my airway slowly restricting until a weak pulse remains. I crawl across the forest floor with the last of my energy, seeking water. At the pool, I'm staring at a face unlike my own and much like the ROSE's. I scream, the migraine fully rendering me catatonic. When my eyes eventually close, I'm flooded with dreams and the ROSE is there, but we're not on earth and we're younger.

The images come in flashes. We're on a planet with red earth not unlike the one used in the spirit festival; the planet is full of creatures who look like the ROSE ... and me. Each image unlocks a memory. We were sent here. Our mission was to test the humans to see if they are redeemable and worth saving or exterminating. We live by a code.

I no longer fight the migraine but embrace it, feeling the physical changes take over that the Merchants and I had suppressed. Tentacles spool out of different parts of my body, caressing my flesh in a strange embrace after many years apart. I stroke one; it purrs under my hand. The ROSE waits tentatively to the side of the pool. A scent that English can't describe, so I try it in another tongue that I'd long forgotten.

"Na ta-keyan," I say. *My home.*

I teleport in front of him. His black and white eyes bore into mine. I grip his head so our foreheads touch and it all makes sense again. My tentacles spark in excitement as they seek out the tentacles on his body, joining us together. As we lock lips, the thick black tentacle from my mouth joins with his, awakening all my senses.

"There's work to do," I say.

Sakura stands immobilized, but still very much alive, while Zane has been bound once more to the tree. One of my tentacles elongates and tears Zane from the tree; piss stains his trousers.

"You're unredeemable, Zane, and so was Carmen."

Using my tentacles, I tear Zane's body apart, leaving his insides in a messy puddle on the forest floor. My mouth salivates. I select his brain, consuming it for the information I need.

"The Merchants," I whisper.

"You know what we must do, ta-keyan," the ROSE whispers back. "We hunt."

'TIL DEATH DO US PART

CYNTHIA MURPHY

The bridal shop smelled … musty.

Like something ancient was hiding between the yellowing wedding dresses that hung from their racks.

Or dying.

"Smile," Mum said through gritted teeth as a prim older woman walked over to us. I bared my teeth at her in what I hoped was a vaguely presentable way.

"Welcome to Carrington's. Can I help you, ladies?" the woman asked. Up close she was even older than I had thought. There were lines around her eyes, and her lips had that kind of pursed-up cat's bum quality to them. Not a smiler, then. The skin of her neck gathered and folded gently into the high lace collar of the white shirt she wore beneath a black cardigan.

Mum nudged me.

"Oh, er, yeah. Yes, I mean." I stuck my hand out, like Mum had shown me. "My name is Laurie Tranter. I'd like to enquire about the weekend job you're advertising in the window?" My hand hung in the air, unacknowledged. I let it drift back to my side.

"The window?" The owner's rheumy eyes drifted over to a set of long black curtains at the front of the shop. "The new display isn't ready yet."

I threw a hard side-eye at Mum. Was this woman for real?

"Is that why the window is whitewashed?" Mum asked brightly. I recognized that voice. It's the one she uses when Gran is confused about something.

"Yes, yes. I like to refresh it every month or so. Keep up with the latest styles."

A quick glance around confirmed that the latest style in the shop was from the nineteen eighties.

"Laurie would love the chance to work in retail," Mum warbled on. "She's at college just down the road. A weekend job would be ideal."

"Weekend job," the woman echoed.

"The sign?" I prompted her. "In the window?"

"The window's not finished."

Yikes.

"Is it an old sign?" Mum tried. "Perhaps you don't need the help any more?"

"Help? Oh, I would love some more help!" The old woman laughed and clapped her hands together, her eyes clearing suddenly. "I'm sorry, I haven't introduced myself. I'm Mrs Carrington. And you are?" She stared at me.

"Um, Laurie."

"Well, Laurie. Yes, I suppose I could use a weekend girl these days; I think my current one is abandoning me again soon. You would be tidying, doing stock inventory, greeting customers, making tea, those kinds of things. How does that sound?"

"Good," I said, though I had no idea what inventory meant. I'd figure it out.

"Excellent. Now, how much does one pay a weekend girl these days? Ten pounds or so?"

"Laurie would be more than happy with minimum wage, isn't that right, Laurie?" I nodded reluctantly. "I think that's around five pounds an hour now."

"Good gracious, is it really? My word." She glanced at the curtains again. "But I do need the help..."

"I would love to help with the window display." I tried to sound enthusiastic. "Is there a mannequin or is it just—"

"No," Mrs Carrington snapped, twisting her head back at us. "Only I may touch the display. Do you understand?"

"Yes," I whispered, my voice hoarse. Mum wrapped her hand around my wrist and gently pulled me in the direction of the exit.

"Well, thank you for your time, Mrs Carrington; it was lovely to meet you." Mum pushed me towards the door. "Have a lovely afternoon."

"Shall I see you on Saturday then, Laurie?" Mrs Carrington said, her voice and eyes soft again. "Nine a.m. sharp?"

"Oh … er…" I looked at Mum. She shrugged. *Up to you,* she mouthed. "Maybe we could have a trial day?" I suggested.

"Excellent. The window will be revealed by then too. I am sure you will like it."

"Great." I forced a smile as I backed out of the door, Mum behind me. "Can't wait," I muttered.

I stepped off the bus and walked slowly down to the shop. I was early so I took my time, idly scrolling through my phone as I approached. The first thing I noticed was that the whitewash had been cleaned off the window. Now, instead of chalky swirls that obscured the view, there stood one lone mannequin against the backdrop of those heavy black curtains.

I stepped closer and peered in the window. So much for a display that "kept up with the trends". This looked like it had been dressed a hundred years ago. Slightly yellowed lace covered its upper half, a high, scalloped collar enclosing the throat with costume jewellery layered over the top. The mannequin's chin tilted up, its gaze peering somewhere off into the distance. Lacy sleeves came all the way down to the knuckles, one of which rested on a waist that transitioned from lace to a full tulle skirt. I squinted at the hands – since when did mannequins have such lifelike creases on their fingers?

"You're keen," a voice piped up from behind me and I swear I almost blacked out. I had been so engrossed in the display I'd almost forgotten where I was. "Oops, sorry! Didn't mean to sneak up on you." I turned to see a tall girl with red hair jangle a set of keys before selecting one and slotting it into the lock of the front door. "I'm Jo. You must be Lauren?"

"Laurie," I corrected her automatically. No one ever got my name right first time.

"Sorry! Laurie." She smiled, pushing open the door. "Welcome to the Twilight Zone."

"What do you mean?" I followed her in, across the shop floor and through another door at the back where there was a coatrack, sink and kettle. She shrugged off her black trench coat and hung it up, placing her bag on top.

"You know, that old TV programme where all the spooky stuff happened. I always feel like I've gone back in time when I do a shift here." She held a hand out for my jacket. "Coats and bags stay in here. Don't let Mrs Carrington catch you on your phone; she'll lose her tiny mind."

"Thanks for the warning." I pulled off my backpack and denim jacket and handed them over to her.

"Oh, I have plenty of those, don't you worry." She laughed, hanging my stuff up next to hers. "There's a fridge down there if you bring a packed lunch, and it's a bring your own tea bag situation, unless you like ten-year-old Tetley's."

"I'll be fine," I said, simultaneously wondering what I had got myself into. "Sorry, what do you do here again?"

"I'm you – the weekend girl. Or at least I was. It's my last shift today; I'm going back to uni tomorrow. Looks like you'll be taking over the funsies for now."

"It's just a trial," I explained, following her back into the shop. "Mrs Carrington didn't seem too certain she needed me, even though there was a sign in the window."

"Yeah, I snuck that in there." Jo walked behind the till and started pressing buttons while I hovered awkwardly. "She can be forgetful. I'd told her I was leaving, but things tend to … slip her mind." She flipped through her keys and selected a small one. "You'd better come and watch me set up; you'll be doing it on your own tomorrow. Mrs Carrington doesn't usually come in until after ten and she likes everything to be ready."

"OK." I joined her behind the scarred wooden counter and looked at the till. It was tarnished silver, almost black, something straight out of a Victorian grocery shop. "Oh my God, this thing is ancient."

"I know, right? This place only deals in cash. She won't even have a credit card machine, never mind contactless. People don't seem to mind, but it means you need to do a float each morning and evening. The profits from the day go in this safe" – she gestured to the small silver door beneath the till – "and Mrs Carrington takes them to the bank on Mondays. I've tried to convince her to do it all digitally, but she's adamant that she does things her own way." Jo chattered on, first showing me how to count out the float and then a big black notebook she called a ledger, where I had to write down the details of each sale. My head swam with it all. She finished counting out that day's float and pushed the silver till drawer shut with a little clang. "I'll show you how to put a sale through when … if … we have one."

"You don't get many sales?"

"A few. Mainly accessories and jewellery, to be honest, maybe the odd veil. I've shifted a couple of wedding dresses in the past, but everything is so old-fashioned it makes it a tough sell." She shrugged. "Most people only really come to see Elsie, anyway."

"Elsie? Is that Mrs Carrington's first name?"

"Noooo. You mean you don't know the story?" I shook my head and Jo's eyes sparkled with undisguised glee. "Amazing. Let's make a brew and I will tell you *all* about it."

Jo bustled back into the staffroom, leaving me alone and more than a little confused. I took the opportunity to take in my new workspace. The room was a basic square. From my place near the till, the front door and window display were to my right. The till itself stood beneath large photographs of happy couples that were at least forty years old if those *Stranger Things* perms and mullets were anything to go by. I wandered out, passing the staffroom door and a row of dusty veils. Several shelves laden with dainty white gloves and tiaras studded the wall to the left of me, and further along there was an open archway that led to some red-carpeted stairs. I stuck my head in, wondering if that was where the dressing room was. That just left the racks of dresses that filled the wall opposite. I trailed my hand lightly along the satin and lace until I reached the end of the row. Here, the thick black curtains that covered the window display hung ominously. My hand itched to reach out and drag the heavy fabric back so I could peep in.

"Go on." Jo placed two steaming mugs on the till counter and joined me at the front of the shop. She glanced at her watch. "We have time before she gets here. Open them."

I found the edge of the fold and pulled the curtain. It dragged across the floor and sunlight streamed in, illuminating a flurry of dust motes that rose from the fabric. I blinked once, twice, and then threw my elbow up to catch a loud sneeze. "Sorry," I muttered, but Jo didn't seem fazed at all. I tugged on the drape a little more until the semi-circular area where the mannequin was housed opened up. From here I could only see the back of her thick brown hair, which was set in curls all over the head, a long veil pinned in at the nape of its neck.

"This," Jo whispered, "is Elsie."

"The mannequin? Why would people come to see a plastic window prop?" But even as I said it, my skin crawled. Tiny hairs curled at the nape of Elsie's neck, a detail I didn't think would be on a dress model. Her skin

369

was pale and waxy and fine blue veins spidered up her towards her face.

"Check out the hands," Jo whispered.

I had to drag the curtain open even further and lean in slightly to get a proper look at them. One was propped at her waist but the other hung by her side, her fingers loosely curled. The fine lines I'd noticed before were on this hand too, decorating each finger.

"Those fingernails," I said, my skin shrinking a little. "Why do they look so real?"

"I don't know," Jo whispered.

They were long and delicate, the kind of nails I wished I could grow. Each tip was slightly yellowed and the flesh of the nail beds was pale and rimmed with a blueish tint. I looked at my own nails and without even thinking about it, I reached out to touch the hands, my fingers grazing the cool surface of Elsie's skin.

"No!" Jo snapped, and grabbed my arm, dragging me away from the display. "Only Mrs Carrington touches Elsie." I rubbed my arm as she closed the curtains. "Sorry, I didn't mean to hurt you. Just … don't touch her, OK?"

"Yeah, OK." My eyes threatened to overspill so I took a deep breath. I was not going to cry on my first day at work.

Jo tipped her head at me and sighed. "God, I'm sorry. I shouldn't have done that; I just didn't want you getting in trouble. Mrs Carrington can be very … *particular*. Here, take this." She held out a mug of tea that smelled of mint and liquorice. "It's all I've got. You can bring your own stuff tomorrow." She steered me over to one of the rickety wooden chairs behind the till. "Now sit and I'll tell you a story before Mrs Carrington gets here."

I did as she said and sipped the tea. It was weird, not something I'd had before. Kind of minty and sweet at the same time. "So why does the mannequin look so realistic?" I asked, and took a second sip. Better this time.

"Well, that's the big attraction with Elsie," she said, leaning both elbows on the counter. She was dressed like me, in a plain black T-shirt and trousers, which made me grateful that Mum had some idea what I should put on this morning. "There are a couple of different stories about her. One is that she's this super old mannequin, one that was made back in the nineteen thirties or forties when they used to take wax casts of people's bodies and then build a mannequin based off them. Weird, right? There's something way creepier about a mannequin that looks so human!" Jo took a sip of her tea and gave an exaggerated shudder.

"That doesn't explain the veins and stuff though, does it?"

"Not really. Unless the guy who made it was some kind of artist and added all those bits on to make it look super real, but I doubt it. No, I like the other story better."

The buzzer on the front door went off. Jo sighed loudly and put her mug down. "One sec." She walked over to the intercom and spoke into it. "Good morning," she chirped.

"Oh, hi. We have an appointment?" a tinny voice said through the little speaker. "To try on some dresses?"

"Of course! Come on in." Jo pressed the button to unlock the door and rolled her eyes at me. "They're early." The door pushed open and two women entered. "Good morning, ladies, welcome to Carrington's. Would you like to have a browse before we head to the fitting room? Just pull out anything you like the look of from the rack and I will take them up for you." The mother and daughter began to flip through the dresses and Jo joined me back at the till. "Are you all right down here if I take them upstairs? All you have to do is answer the door or take a message if someone rings the shop. Just shout if you're not sure of anything!"

"Um, yeah, I think I'll be fine. Should I be doing something?"

"No, you're fine for now. Just grab a duster and look busy if Mrs Carrington comes in. And remember – no phone."

"No phone," I echoed. "Sure. Where's the duster?"

I kept myself busy until Mrs Carrington arrived, pulling headdresses from the display and carefully dusting each glass shelf. I must have banged my hand on something as I did it because the ring finger on my right hand swelled up, not only painful but all tight and purple looking.

"Hey." Jo appeared at the bottom of the stairs. "Keeping busy?"

"Yeah." I lowered my voice. "Mrs Carrington barely spoke to me; she just went upstairs to you."

"That's totally normal, don't worry. You've done a good job! Want a brew?"

"If that's OK?" I held up my hand. "Do you have any paracetamol or anything? I've, erm, hurt myself. I don't know what I did but it's really sore."

"I might have some in my bag." Jo took hold of my fingers and winced. "Ouch. Did you trap it in something?"

"I don't think so. I don't actually remember doing anything to it."

"Come and put it under the cold tap," she suggested. "See if that helps." I followed her into the tiny staffroom where she filled the kettle and then directed me to the sink. "There. We get a twenty-minute break now and an hour for lunch at one p.m. I usually bring my own salad or something, but I thought we might go to the chippy today – what do you think?"

"That sounds good," I said as the cold water numbed my fingers. I had a couple of pounds left from my bus ticket and the sandwiches in my bag were probably warm by now. I looked over my shoulder to check the room beyond was still empty. "Do you have time to finish your story from before?"

"My story?" I moved so Jo could rinse our mugs from earlier and watched her drop a tea bag in each one. "Oh! I was telling you about Elsie!"

"Yeah." I'd done my best to avoid looking at the window display while I was cleaning, but I hadn't stopped thinking about the strange mannequin. I let silence hang in the air as she filled the cups with steaming water, and I dabbed my hand on a threadbare tea towel. My finger was still purple but numb, at least for now.

"Where was I up to?" Jo closed the door and invited me to squeeze on to the tiny sofa that was hidden beneath the coatrack. I dodged the bottom of her trench coat and sat down.

"You were about to tell me the other story about the … about Elsie."

"Ooh, yes." Jo's hazel eyes lit up. "So Mrs Carrington is pretty ancient, right? I think she's eighty-something, which means she was born in…"

"The forties?" I supplied.

Jo waved her free hand. "Yeah, that sounds about right. So the story is Mrs Carrington grew up, got married, had a baby, you know, all that heteronormative shit they made people do in the olden days. Mr Carrington opened this shop for her to work in after they got married and eventually their daughter, Elsie, came to work for them too."

"Elsie? She named the mannequin after her daughter?"

"Oh *God* no. And don't let her hear you calling it that, either."

My hand was starting to hurt again. "Wait, I'm lost."

"Elsie is just what the locals call her. It was in nineteen eighty-four, I think, when the real Elsie went missing. My gran told me the story when I started working here. She had been engaged to be married, but the week before the wedding … poof. She disappeared. Some people say it was a tragic death covered up by the family, others say that she found out her fiancé was cheating on her and she ran away." Jo paused to take a sip of tea. "Personally, I like to think she had a secret lottery win and went to live her best life somewhere warm, found a new life selling crystals or being a lesbian or something. Anyway, not long after her disappearance, Mrs Carrington got a new shop mannequin. Only this one was eerily realistic and, some say, looked uncannily similar to her daughter, Elsie."

"What?" I reached for my own tea, more to hide my unease than anything. Goosebumps had exploded down my bare arms. "You think she got it to keep her company or something?" My eyes widened in realization. "Oh, you don't think Elsie died and Mrs Carrington had a wax cast of her made? To keep as some kind of weird souvenir?"

"Worse." Jo grinned maliciously. "My favourite rumour" – she leaned closer and lowered her voice – "is that Elsie died and Mrs Carrington preserved her somehow, keeping her and dressing her up to look like the bride she should have been. Sick yet tragic, right?"

"Wait." The hairs on my arms stood up so violently that the skin there hurt. "Are you saying that people think that's the real Elsie?"

"Yep." Jo sat back, pleased with herself. "People only really come here because they think that's a dead girl in the window."

*

375

I spent the next hour and a half talking myself out of ringing Mum to come and get me. There was no way that story could be true. No possible way.

"Jo, dear, I'm off for lunch." Mrs Carrington appeared at the bottom of the stairs, a soft measuring tape draped around her neck. She barely acknowledged me as she collected her coat and bag. "I shall be back within the hour."

"Of course," Jo said, looking up from the ledger where she was copying over product numbers from some jewellery tags she had managed to sell the mother and daughter from earlier. The door clicked as Mrs Carrington left the premises without so much as glancing back. "Finally!" Jo sighed, handing me the pen. "Here, you finish writing up these and I'll go to the chippy. I need to be quick; she doesn't allow it normally because of the smell, you know? But I've found if I eat fast and Febreze she's none the wiser."

"Great." I said, even though the thought of being in here alone filled me with dread. "Let me get you some money."

"No need, I just got my student loan. My treat to say good luck here." Jo laughed.

I didn't join in.

"Are you sure?" I asked. "I can always go if you like?"

"Nah, it's fine. I kind of fancy the girl who works in the shop next door, so any excuse to pop in there too." She wiggled her eyebrows. "See you in ten."

"Bye." I watched her leave, and I couldn't help my eyes

drifting straight over to the window display. "Don't do it, girl," I told myself. "Don't do it."

Just one more peek. I walked over to the curtain. And pulled the drape over a tiny bit, just so I could see the back of the head. The veil was loose now, hanging slightly on one side. I must have dislodged it when Jo pulled me out of the display before. It would be obviously askew to Mrs Carrington – if she noticed she would know we'd been messing around in here. A sharp glint caught my eye as I scoured the red carpeted floor beneath the mannequin. A pearl-headed pin lay there, obviously the one that had kept the veil in place. I picked it up, ignoring Jo's warning about touching Elsie, and replaced the veil, my fingers brushing hair that felt very human. I let out my breath as it stayed put and took a tentative step into the window.

I wanted to see her face.

Elsie's skin was smooth and waxy, but there was a faint tracing of veins around her temples and beneath her eyes. I was fairly sure she was wearing make-up too. Her cheeks and lips were unnaturally red, and mascara clumped along her long lashes. Her brown eyes were glassy beneath them.

It was like she was holding her breath.

I crept out of the display, not wanting to be caught in there again. I checked the veil one last time and pulled the curtain across, retreating to my spot behind the till, where I patiently waited for my chips.

*

"Hey, Mum. I'm back." I pressed my face against the glass of the front door and sighed with relief. Cool. Nice.

"Hey, Laurie." She stuck her head out of the kitchen. "How was your first … what's wrong?"

"Nothing. Just hot."

Mum gently pulled me upright and pressed the back of her hand against my forehead. "You are hot. Come on, in." She took the bag from my shoulder and ushered me into the hall. "Too much excitement. Let's get you some paracetamol."

"Mmmkay." Everything was too bright. I squeezed my eyes shut as far as I could without blocking off my vision completely and I followed her into the kitchen. I peeled my denim jacket off and dropped it to the floor, fanning the back of my neck. Goosebumps exploded there and my teeth began to chatter.

"Oh, sweetie, you have a real fever! Here." She popped two little white tablets out of a packet and dropped them into my hand, placing a glass of water into the other. "What's that?" She pointed at my hand. My finger was still purple and swollen, magnified by the water in the glass it was now wrapped around.

"Oh, I hit it or something." I swallowed the pills and finished the cold water in three long gulps.

"It looks like you've damaged the nail." Mum took the glass and held my hand lightly. "It seems to be lifting. Oh, you poor thing, I hope it's not infected. Let's put some cream on it and I'll keep an eye on you." I didn't want to think about what lifting meant, but I could feel it now she'd said it. Like the nail was pulling away from the skin beneath it. I shuddered.

"Right, bed for a couple of hours." Mum steered me towards the stairs and followed me up, her hand resting lightly on my back. My feet thumped on each step. Why were they so heavy? I stumbled into my room and collapsed on to the bed as Mum pulled my trainers off. "In you get." She tucked the duvet around me as I clenched every muscle in my body in an effort to stop the shakes. Everything felt spiky and my face was burning, but the rest of me was so cold. I burrowed down into the sheets and curled into a ball. My head was spinning as darkness started to creep across my vision.

"Laurie?"

I looked up. It wasn't Mum, but a dark-haired lady. Her face looked strangely familiar, but I couldn't place her until my vision cleared and I realized she was wearing a wedding dress.

Elsie!

"What the...? What are you doing here?" The words scraped the back of my throat, a searing ache that seemed to suggest I'd been eating broken glass.

"You invited me." The lights flickered and we weren't in my bedroom any more, we were back in the shop window, but the sky outside was a dark, inky blue. "You invited me," she repeated.

"I didn't."

"You touched me," she said. At least, I think she did. Her face was still waxy, her lips and cheeks stained red but immobile. She stood in the same position she had been in all day, one hand on her waist and the other hanging by her side. I stared at her clumped eyelashes, the veins in her brown eyes. "You aren't supposed to touch me."

This time her mouth did move. Fine lines cracked at the corners as her lips parted, flakes of wax forming as it began to split. Bruised, purple skin lay below the death mask, angry and grotesque against the stark whiteness. Elsie's eyes darted around, faster and faster until they began to blur. As though she was trapped.

My stomach lurched.

The wax started to soften now, long, slow drips distorting her face, dragging down her eyebrows and collecting in creases below her eyes. What were once red lips smeared across her face and beyond it, an angry, black mouth stretched open, strings of wax and decaying flesh hanging like entrails. My throat burned.

What was left of Elsie leaned forward, wrapping inhumanly strong hands around my upper arms in a vice-like grip.

And it screamed.

"Laurie! Honey, wake up!"

"Let go. LET GO OF ME!" I peeled my eyes open as I shoved my mum off the bed. The duvet was knotted around my legs and my heart was racing. A dream.

It had been a dream.

"Jesus, Laurie." Mum climbed to her feet, rubbing the bottom of her back. "The doctor is here. You've been asleep for hours and you wouldn't come round." She touched my forehead again as our familiar family doctor approached with his black bag. He propped it on the floor and opened it, pulling out a thermometer.

"Still feverish?" he asked, his kindly face creased in concern. Mum nodded. He placed the thermometer in my mouth and I closed my eyes, sinking back into the pillows. I was drenched with sweat. "Can I see your finger?" Dr Ralph asked. I had forgotten about my hand, but now it started to throb again.

"Here." My arm was like lead, but I managed to drag it out from under the covers.

"Oh God," Mum said, her face draining of colour.

I glanced down at my pale sheets. A trail of almost violently red blood had followed my hand out, my ring finger covered in a mixture of crusted brown and bright red. I lifted the duvet carefully only to see a large patch of blood clotted on the cotton.

There was a human fingernail in the middle of it.

"Thanks, Dr Ralph. Take care." I heard Mum show him out as I curled under the blanket on the sofa where she had moved me. My bed sheets needed changing after the massacre. The doctor had dressed my finger – the nailbed had been pretty mangled from where I had ripped the nail off in my sleep. "How you doing?" Mum came back in.

"OK. I need a quick shower, though." I felt a bit more with it but tired, achy. Like I'd been in a car accident or something.

"Are you sure you're able?" She sat next to me and stroked my hair. "You were pretty out of it. You scared me!"

"I know." I shuddered, the fever dream still fresh in my mind. "I'm sorry. And yeah, I'm OK, I think."

"Just sit down if you get lightheaded and don't get that finger wet." She nodded at the huge bandage as she helped me up. "We don't need to see that again tonight."

"Agreed." She followed me upstairs and collected clean sheets as I wobbled to the bathroom. I closed the door behind me, turned on the shower to let it warm up and leaned my weight on the sink. I stared into the rapidly fogging mirror. My brown hair was wild and loose, blue eyes ringed with day-old mascara, and I had flecks of dried blood on my face from the nail incident. I started to tie my hair out of the way, but my finger was useless so it took way longer than normal. The bathroom started to fill with steam as I stuck my head under the tap for a drink of cold water.

God my throat was sore.

I started to peel my sweaty top off when I felt the water reverse direction, like it had hit my stomach and been rejected. I raced back to the sink, retching as water flooded out of my mouth, the back of my throat burning with pain like I'd never felt. My stomach emptied itself, but the pain in the back of my throat intensified.

Something was *stuck*.

I cleared my throat, trying to force out whatever was in the back of my windpipe. A fit of coughing racked my body and my knees buckled slightly as something dislodged and hit the porcelain. I straightened up, the steam in the room thick now, and peered into the sink.

Lying next to the plug hole was a long, thin dress pin, the kind with a small, white pearl at the head.

It was wrapped in a knot of thick black hair.

"You think you'll sleep?" Mum placed a glass of water on my bedside table and perched on the end of my bed.

"Yeah," I lied. I didn't tell her about the pin. It was too weird. I must have … swallowed it by accident?

"Well, just ring my phone if you need me. And don't worry about getting up for work. I'll call Mrs Carrington first thing. I'm sure she'll understand."

I breathed a sigh of relief as she left the room, plunging me into darkness as she flicked off the light switch. There was no way I was ever going back to Carrington's, but I'd worry about telling them that once I was better. I burrowed down into the clean sheets, plugging headphones into my ears. Anything to drive away the intrusive thoughts.

My throat was burning.

I scrolled my phone for something soothing. I found a podcast that would help me sleep and started following the silk-voiced man's instructions. Close your eyes. Clear your mind. Breathe in. Breathe out.

Breathe in.

Breathe out.

Sunlight tugged at my eyelids. Morning already? I didn't feel rested at all, and my body was so stiff it refused to stretch itself out. My eyes seemed to peel open of their own accord, and it took me a few seconds to realize that I wasn't looking at my bedroom. Instead I was looking at a busy road.

I was standing in the window at Carrington's.

"Wh—" My mouth refused to open. What the hell? I tried to glance around but my body was frozen solid, my eyes the only thing that would move. I forced my gaze down and could just about make out the white lace that covered my chest and arms – one arm propped on my waist, the other hanging loose. I tried to reach up and touch my face.

Nothing.

I couldn't move.

"Good morning, Laurie!" Mrs Carrington's voice tinkled in my ears, and I forced my eyes towards the door. A petite brown-haired figure entered.

Me. I was looking at me.

"Good morning, Mrs Carrington."

I wanted to scream but nothing came out. I was looking at *me*. That was my hair, my voice, my outfit. Yet it … wasn't quite me. This me held herself differently. It was a more *confident* version of me.

I tried to cry out but the wax on my face swallowed the noise.

"I am popping out for some milk for the staffroom." Mrs Carrington patted the other me on the arm. "Will you be OK alone for a few minutes? I know it's your first day without lovely Jo."

"Of course," the other me said, disappearing into the shop and out of my view. I strained my neck as hard as I could, but it was no good. I was trapped. I watched as Mrs Carrington left the shop and walked past the window, desperately trying to signal her with my eyes.

Then I heard the curtains behind me whisper along the ground.

"Thank you, Laurie," a voice said. It was my voice but *not* my voice at the same time. "I've been waiting a long time for this." My body walked around to face me, smiling a familiar smile. My smile. "Don't worry, you'll get used to it. Kind of. And who knows? Maybe one day someone will set you free." She chuckled. "It won't be me, though." My body looked at her hands, one finger tightly bandaged, and tugged at a lock of hair. "No. In fact, I think I've been here for long enough." My body leaned forward and giggled conspiratorially. "I quit! Do you think I should leave a note for my captor before I go?"

I tried to plead with my eyes, harder than I'd ever tried to do anything.

"Oh, don't give me that look," my body snapped, frowning. "My mother kept me trapped in that infernal contraption for almost forty years. All I wanted to do was run away. You can't imagine how that felt." She cocked her head, eyes crinkling at the corners, amused again. "Well, maybe you can." She winked at me before walking away and closing the curtains. Brown eyes, I noticed. Not my blue eyes.

Elsie's eyes.

CONTRIBUTORS

AMY McCAW

Amy McCaw is a huge fan of *Buffy*, 90s horror and all things macabre, and her books combine elements of these. She is a BookTuber, BookToker and the author of the award-winning and bestselling *Mina and the Undead* series.

The title of THE HOUSE WITH TEETH popped into Amy's head with absolutely no context but she had great fun fleshing it out into a bloodthirsty house with a mind of its own.

Amy's not afraid of many things, unless you happen to have a needle – then she'll probably cry and need immediate chocolate.

MARIA KUZNIAR

Maria Kuzniar spent six years living in Spain and travelling the world, which inspired her children's books, *The Ship of Shadows* series. She is also the author of the bestselling *Midnight in Everwood* for adults and can be found in her cosy loft in Nottingham, drinking hot chocolates surrounded by books.

She was inspired to write THE WOLF AND THE WITCH by her Polish heritage and fearless babcia, who makes the world's best pierogi. Her love of all things spooky and witchy probably stems from a childhood spent watching *Buffy the*

Vampire Slayer on repeat.

Maria is scared of a long list of things, which makes her a terrible person to watch a horror movie or walk through a graveyard with, but excellent at imagining all kinds of creepy goings-on in the shadows.

KAT DUNN

© Jamie Drew

Kat Dunn grew up in London, but has spent time in Japan, Australia and France. She's written about mental health for Mind and *The Guardian*, and worked as a translator for Japanese television. She's the author of *Bitterthorn*, and the *Battalion of the Dead* trilogy.

Kat was inspired to write SOMETHING WICKED because of her love of deliciously creepy unreliable narrators like Merricat in Shirley Jackson's *We Have Always Lived in the Castle* – she loves a twist and characters we never know if we can trust.

Kat is not scared of anything like spiders or clowns (though they are horrible), but she is scared of her mind playing tricks on her. When you're alone or in the dark, your imagination can conjure up so many more monsters than really exist in the world – but that doesn't make it any less terrifying.

KAT ELLIS

Kat Ellis is the author of YA horror-thrillers including *Harrow Lake* and *Wicked Little Deeds*. When she's not writing, Kat can usually be found exploring ancient ruins and cemeteries near her home in North Wales.

THE VISITING GREY was inspired by the Welsh legend of Mari Lwyd, a veiled spirit who goes door to door on wintry nights, singing for food and hospitality. Kat grew up hearing variations of this story and decided to put her own horrifying spin on it!

She is terrified of pretty much anything that lives in the sea, but especially sharks.

© *Dujonna Gift*

RACHEL FATUROTI

Rachel Faturoti is a British-Nigerian screenwriter, poet, editor and author of middle-grade novel *Sadé and Her Shadow Beasts* and the young adult novel *Finding Folkshore*.

Beauty and the Beast is probably Rachel's least favourite fairy tale, so she decided to do a retelling and make it into a story she loves with all the best bits.

Rachel fears spiders.

KATHRYN FOXFIELD

Kathryn Foxfield writes dark stories about strange things. Her fascination with the creepy and weird can be blamed on a childhood diet of Point Horror, Agatha Christie and *Dr Who*. When she's not writing, she likes to lurk in haunted caves, seedy tourist attractions and overgrown cemeteries.

Kathryn wanted to write a story about a creepy doll, but ended up writing one about how the scariest monsters can be hidden in plain sight.

Kathryn is afraid of her own imagination.

DAWN KURTAGICH

Dawn Kurtagich is the author of *The Dead House*, *The Creeper Man*, *Teeth in the Mist* and *Blood on the Wind*. Dawn leaves her North Wales crypt after midnight during blood moons. The rest of the time she exists somewhere between mushrooms, maggots and mould.

AND THE WATERS CREPT IN was inspired by the ghost of Gwydir Castle. Legend has it that the 5th Baronet, Sir John Wynn, murdered a chambermaid with whom he'd had an affair, walling her up behind a wall of the North Wing. The story only truly came alive when Arawn, King of the Underworld Annwvn, who appears in the first branch of the Mabinogi, made his appearance in her imagination, bringing with him the Afanc, a lake monster from Welsh mythology.

Dawn is terrified of herself.

AMY McCULLOCH

Amy McCulloch is a Chinese–White author, raised in Canada and living in London, UK. Her writing credits include the #1 YA bestselling series *The Magpie Society* with co-author Zoe Sugg. When she's not writing, she loves climbing mountains, travelling and drinking really great coffee.

THE CHIMING HOUR was inspired by a bout of insomnia when she kept waking up at three a.m. to stare at the same painting on the wall opposite her bed. There's something so sinister and creepy about being awake at that hour – and she wanted to explore that in a story.

This might be a strange one, but Amy is afraid of the bottom of escalators! She's heard too many warnings about getting her shoelaces sucked into the machinery and always has to take an extra big step at the end. Woe betide anyone who might be blocking the exit – they're getting barged out of the way.

CYNTHIA MURPHY

Cynthia Murphy is a YA writer from the North-West of England. She has a long-standing love affair with all things scary from Point Horror books to 90s slasher movies. Cynthia is married to her best friend and they are ruled by a Romanian rescue dog called Loli.

Cynthia's story was inspired by a mannequin in Mexico known as *La Pascualita*, who some locals believe to be an embalmed human being. Look her up – we dare you!

Cynthia is afraid of heights!

© *Elizabeth Evans*

MELINDA SALISBURY

Melinda Salisbury is the four-time Carnegie-nominated author of seven books for young adults, including *Hold Back the Tide* and *Her Dark Wings*.

Melinda doesn't know precisely where the idea for SAINT CLOVER came from, somewhere at the junction of religious mania, consumption and flowers, it solidified into the horrible little story it is.

For a long time, she thought she was scared of heights, but it's actually the edges that frighten her.

LOUIE STOWELL

Louie Stowell is the author of the bestselling *Loki: A Bad God's Guide* series. She previously worked in publishing for 15 years. This is her first YA story. She's excited to be able to swear in it.

Louie is a huge fan of *Buffy* and all vampire stories, especially funny ones. Writing this, she asked herself: what would happen if vampires turned up at an exclusive girls' school in London? (Definitely not based at all on her own school, whatsoever.)

Louie is afraid of her old head teacher reading this story.

ROSIE TALBOT

Rosie Talbot (she/her) belongs to the leafy wilds of Sussex, England where she works as a bookseller. A lover of the spooky and macabre, Rosie writes stories that are like her hair: dark, twisted and certainly not straight.

HOW TO DISAPPEAR is inspired by the woods near her house and a preference for terrifying fairies that will rip your face off.

She has submechanophobia, meaning she is scared of man-made objects submerged in deep water. Don't google it. Just don't.

© *Nazreen Essack*

MARY WATSON

Mary Watson is the author of *The Wren Hunt* duology and *Blood to Poison*. Originally from South Africa, she now lives on the west coast of Ireland.

Mary had an image of a deceptive kiss at midnight, and of the final lines of the story, and knew that they somehow fit together.

Mary probably watched too many horror movies too young because she is terrified of possession, of being taken over by something or other.